I Was a Willow
Memoirs of a Frolicking He-Goat

I0599648

Yaga M. Staretz

Chalk & Wonder Press
Philadelphia U.S.A.

LCCN (Library of Congress Control Number): 2025908928

ISBN: 979-8-9925040-4-0 (Paperback)

ISBN: 979-8-9925040-8-8 (Hardback)

Edited by Sandra Desorgher and Mary Ann Domanska

Cover Art (AI generated) designed by Mary Ann Domanska

Cover Layout by Shelly Rabuse

Printed by Chalk & Wonder Press in the United States of America

chalkandwonderpress.com

First printing edition 2025

To
my grandmother, Michalina Figura,
and
my husband, Steve Brady.

The title of this book is a line from Balladyna, *the Polish romantic drama, by Juliusz Słowacki (1834). In the play, a character is transformed into a willow tree by a vengeful nymph. Upon returning to human form, he tries to describe what he witnessed as a willow but he is not believed.*

PROLOGUE

My name is Adam Czulartian. I am a resident of *The Home of Divine Providence*, a retreat on the outskirts of our capital city. I have lived here for almost twenty-five years, supported by allotments from state subsidies to the Home and by private donations from my niece Nusia. As I do not earn my keep and have never really done so, I am often referred to, with a sneer, as a charity case; which should by no means be understood that I have ever felt particularly bothered by my condition, been idle, unhappy or indifferent to the world around me.

The Home, a gabled wooden structure comprising a residence and a chapel, lies just outside the official limits of the Capital, within walking distance of a railroad station and a village; but despite its location, the Home is almost totally concealed from the world at large. It is surrounded first by a high heavy-gauge meshed fence and then by a forest of pine trees (planted here by governmental decree – all in neat rows – some thirty years ago as a monument to the dead of the War). It is only from the windows of the uppermost turret that one can survey all of the surrounding scenery: the pine woods, the station, the village and, if the day is clear, the skyline of the city. And so, those who live here see little of the outside and venture there very seldom, and likewise, those residing outside the bounds of the Home visit it infrequently and know little about it.

My room, though not at the very top, is high enough to let me see the shimmering lines of the railroad tracks as well as a portion of the railroad station itself. It is larger and brighter than most private spaces allotted to those who live here, and it is designated to be for my use only, not to be shared with anybody; a state of affairs making me the object of some envy here. Of course, it is only because of my status as a protege of my niece, whom the Home regards as its generous benefactress, that I have been allowed such quarters.

The Home of Divine Providence is run by a group of monastics, brothers of a holy order, whose main occupation is planning and overseeing the activities of their wards, that is, us, a group of lay men of diverse backgrounds and inclinations. The work of the holy brothers, our guardians, is in turn monitored by higher over-seers, called the governors, individuals of power, who live on the outside. And though they are not a physical part of the place, the governors' influence on the wards' lives has been quite perspicu-ous.

The Home has also a few benefactors, individuals of means and generous instincts, who live on the outside, have no official authority over us whatsoever, but from whose munificence the

Home benefits quite a bit. Nusia, my niece, is considered to be one of them. She has not visited our place in the flesh for at least a decade now, and her communications to me, once frequent and lengthy, have dwindled to two short notes within the last year; still, her financial offerings to the brothers on my behalf have been regular and most liberal.

In addition to comfortable private quarters, I have also been allowed to have a workshop of my own, where I can pursue undertakings of my own choosing and do so at any time I please. It is in this workshop of mine set up in a back room of the basement of the Home where, from a multitude of materials, I construct items of various forms and uses; predominantly masks. And it is here, while working, that I often reflect on life, people and my own condition.

I also write, but only in the privacy of my room, keeping my writing activities as discreet as possible. And though I have never been forbidden to write, out of caution, to avoid by chance arousing the ire of the Home's guardians and governors, I take pains to hide almost every page I produce (priding myself on having been able to construct an ingenious secret stash below the window sill in my room). From time to time, though, I give some of the completed pages to a friend from the outside who takes them out of the Home tucked inside his double-bottomed briefcase. The man I so entrust with my efforts, Stationmaster Jaworski, is an occasional liaison-person between the Home and the world; and the briefcase in question is the one he uses for carrying newspapers, magazines and sweets into the Home on occasions when he comes here to pay a visit to the brothers.

If what I write ever indeed reaches the public at large, in all likelihood many will question the validity of my words. The world has always tended to consider me unstable, unpredictable and unreliable. And besides, I, a denizen of a protective asylum, am presumed to be out of proper contact with the actualities of life. Be that as it may.

In recent weeks it has been Nusia who has most frequently occupied my thoughts and my writing endeavors; her growing up and acquiring the knowledge of the ways of the world, that is.

My niece was born in the city of Wielow, the capital of our erstwhile Eastern Provinces, on a date which, for reasons having nothing to do with her existence, has entered most history textbooks and encyclopedias. But since she claims that one's life starts only with the beginning of one's memories, hers started a few days before she left Wielow for good, when she was about four and a half years of age.

PART 1

FIELDS OF OUTCRIES AND BLOSSOMS

1.

For Nusia it began with big lights in the sky. She was carried onto the balcony and told to look up and... there they were; a skyful of blazing bulbs, bursting stars, beams and flashes of rocketing lightness; space filled with dizzying glares and wondrous reflections; magic that turned the night into the brightest of days and the dark city into an illuminated stage. It was Adam who carried her and who told her that the lights she saw were fireworks.

It is the evening of Easter Sunday, and in Wielow there have always been fireworks on Easter, so Adam tells her. They stand there on the balcony, he holds Nusia above his head with both his arms and tries to show her the great spectacle that is unfolding around them. He shouts: "Happy Easter!", "Let us praise Jesus Christ!", "Hallelujah!", and he urges her to do the same. As the city becomes brighter and clearer to see, he shouts louder, "'Hallelujah! Hallelujah!" And because of the sounds, resounding and thunderous, which are coming at them from all directions, he has to strain his voice to the utmost to make sure that it will carry over the din. He tells Nusia that the noise is coming from cannons saluting Christ's resurrection, as it is customary to fire cannons on Easter Sunday. He feels elated.

He does not tell Nusia the whole truth. Fireworks and festal cannonades, commonplace as they once had been, have not been expected this particular year by anybody. They have not been seen or heard in Wielow at all for four and a half years, the period considered to be one of the saddest and most trying times ever. (As is well known, in times of hardship, the Lord, often implored, is only rarely hailed, and never with anything as extravagant as blazing lights and cannons.) Neither does Adam tell his niece that he, a life-long non-believer, is calling His name not out of reverence, but merely out of joy which on this night has made him forget everything for a while.

So here they are, the two of them, suspended on the balcony, watching the world agleam, screaming their hearts out, when all of a sudden – just when a giant starry ball explodes over their heads – they are seized from behind and with force pulled from the balcony into the interior of the building. Shortly afterwards Adam finds out that what they have just seen and heard and enjoyed so greatly has not at all been part of an Easter celebration. What they have witnessed Adam hears later described as the prelude to a massive air raid; not an everyday bombing, mind you. Actually, for years he will hear that it was by all counts one of the most spectacular and most cleverly executed aerial strikes of the War.

Amidst lights, blasts and screams they are dragged away from their place of pleasure and they are separated; Nusia is thrown on the floor, covered with a blanket, wrapped into a bundle and pushed out of the door onto the stairway. The stairs are full; people pour out of every door, heading downward, all looking horribly ungainly and confused; all trying to find a shelter from bombs in the cellars of the building. Some push their way through and try to run, some yell at others to hurry, and quite a few weep. Nusia, carried in the arms of her father, cries harder than anybody else; she wants to be back with Adam on the balcony to watch the starry balls. And as he too descends the crowded stairs, he can hear his sister, Nusia's mother, scolding her little daughter and calling somebody "damned blasted idiot", quite possibly him, but he does not bother to find out. Adam dislikes his sister's voice, so he tries not to listen.

A few days after Easter a motor truck appears in front of the building in which they live. It is a mammoth-size vehicle with a bulky roofless trailer attached to its tail end. For hours it stands right beneath their windows while it is being loaded by Boleslaw, Nusia's father, and two hired men. Konstancya, Nusia's mother, tells Adam to stay inside and help with packing. As usual, she seems to have everything well in hand and to know exactly what she wants done. She talks a lot, frequently reminding everybody that there is not much time. The truth is, of course, that nobody has the slightest notion how or when, if at all, they might be interrupted or forbidden to leave. And the people who live on their street, just as one might expect, watch them carefully, whisper to one another, snicker and shake their heads knowingly. Probably most of them would want to flee the city too, but lack the ways and means to do so.

In those days in the spring of the fifth year of the War, when what was still to come seemed more and more unfathomable and the way of escaping from oncoming terrors is usually seen in flight, even a horse-drawn wagon or a motorcycle with a sidecar fetch exorbitant premiums, that is, if they can be gotten at all. Yet, they have at their disposal a large motor truck, a trailer and two hired drivers. It is Adam's brother-in-law, Boleslaw, Nusia's father, a man who knows people that count, who has procured the motor truck. He is a figure of great importance in the underworld of the black-market, a fact widely recognized; and so, dealing in the unobtainable is simply what he does as a matter of routine. But even for him, known as the Grand Sharp, a person of unusual talents and extensive connections, getting that huge motor truck was not easy at all. Sums larger than usual had to pass through more hands, higher ranking individuals to be brought into the proceedings, and larger quantities of clandestinely slaughtered pork and clandestinely distilled liquor to be transferred from his secret cache to a locale adjoining the headquarters of the Special Occupying Police.

Nusia is allowed to stay on the balcony and watch the loading. She is thinking of how big the truck is, whether it is big enough to take all the things that are inside the building. She is not thinking of how the truck has been secured; and since she believes that her father is an exceptionally insignificant person, she is not thinking of him either.

The truck and the trailer cannot hold everything that the family would want. When all that is considered to be absolutely necessary is loaded and no free space is left, save one corner inside the trailer, Adam's mother, Nusia's grandmother, asks if she can use this very last free space for the contents of her special linen chest and a basket with samplers she made in her young days. "You certainly cannot, mother. I am really surprised that you even ask!" Konstancya sounds indignant.

She does not allow Adam to use this space for his personal trunk either. "What will you think of next!?" she exclaims in anger. It is in this trunk where he keeps his masks.

Let it be explained here that Adam – by conviction and life-long practice – is a maker and a wearer of masks. He has always thought of masks as a part of human garb at least as important as, say, hats, shirts, shoes, belts or necklaces, and has firmly believed that the general human habit of concealing or altering the appearances of various parts of the body by covering it with appropriate attire should be extended to the face. And so masks, in his view, are like all other wearable objects – playing parts at times of utilitarian items, at times of pure adornment and enjoyment for the senses, and occasionally of symbols. Not everybody shares Adam's views on masks, naturally; yet of all those who have ever expressed displeasure with his creations, or even plain disdain towards them, it has always been his sister who showed her feelings the strongest. He remembers well that when she heard him for the first time say in public that masks should not be treated differently from any other apparel, she emitted a blood-curdling scream that startled everybody in sight, and then apologized for his behavior, mumbled something about his illness and violently dragged him away from the gathering. Her total lack of appreciation for masks stems of course from her general ignorance and also her natural predilection towards biased judgements.

When Adam watches her fill the last of the free space on the trailer with a hamper stuffed with things she calls her personal mementos, he becomes really piqued. From his abandoned trunk he takes out the mask she hates most, a wooden animal head with horns, beard and a movable lower jaw; and he puts on this mask determined not to take it off for a long time.

So garbed, he joins Nusia on the balcony so that together they can watch the two men hired by Nusia's father. Nusia is fascinated. The two are professionals, of course; they know all about roads and how to avoid unpleasantness on the way. That Boleslaw managed to get not just one such man, but two, is no mean accomplishment; but, as Adam knows, his brother-in-law is something of a genius. As he intends that they spend the shortest possible time on the road with no unnecessary stops for sleep and rest, he has hired two drivers who are to take turns.

Adam's pre-War history textbooks used to tell us that Wielow (the city which Nusia's family was about to flee) achieved greatness after it had fallen under the rule of his country some long centuries ago. It became the fairest and most enlightened place of the Eastern Provinces and a stronghold of the nation's religion and traditions. The pre-War books would stress, though, that Wielow's passage through history has often been marked by upheavals, strife, tribulations or outright disasters, but that no matter what calamity would befall it, the city would rise again, in glory greater than before. This capacity for recovering from even the most severe blows (displayed both by the city and the whole nation) was ascribed to the people's virtuousness and righteousness and to the intervention of God on their behalf (though, as Adam always knew, it was not so much God Himself as the Virgin Mary and selected patron-saints interested in the affairs of the nation that were truly responsible for his country's cyclical resurrections). But during the War, just like in the times of past disasters, the people would often forget their appointed lot and raise voices in blasphemous outcries against the Almighty, doubting the willingness of Heavenly powers to act on their behalf.

As some may still remember, the War erupted after the two powers of the Continent: the Great Eastern United People's Power and the Invincible Western Superior Realm makes a pact in secret about the division of the Continent between them and thereupon strikes the free states of the Continent, taking them one by one as their slaves or vassals. As Adam's country happens to lie between the two powers (GEU People's Power to its east and IWS Realm to its west), at the outset of the War it is split between the two.

Adam learns of the War from radio announcers; in a waiting room of the maternity ward as he is awaiting Nusia's coming into this world. The following day the city is struck from land and air; barricades are mounted, trenches dug out, sirens blown and voices on the radio advise the citizens on defense and urge them to hold out; and Nusia and her mother come home from the hospital which is being evacuated. The forces of the GEU People's Power enter Wielow a week or so later; and those who watch them march through the city's streets find them to be a crude and shabby looking army.

The victors clear the city of the barricades and trenches, adorn the walls of buildings with cheerful placards and declare – through their own radio announcers and street loudspeakers – that they are bringing with them peace, justice and the rule of the people by the people. Two days after their coming they send the first dispatch to a labor camp of trains full of those citizens that could turn out to be dangerous to the people's rule. And a few days later they order the first series of executions of those who are a threat to the well-being of the people themselves. Shortly thereafter they also form the New Economic Commission which issues a decree denying the legitimacy of the age-old laws of supply and demand; and so factories start producing things of no use, fields stop yielding, and long lines appear in front of stores and empty shelves inside.

As permanency should never be expected from any of men's schemes, not even two years pass since the two powers signed their pact, when the IWS Realm betrays the GEU People's Power; it attacks its partner in war and seizes its lands. And so the GEU People's Army is pushed east, and all of the Continent falls under the rule of the Realm. The citizens of Wielow are in agreement that, compared to the People's forces, the Realm's Army looks more commanding, better fed and tailored, more self-confident all around.

The new victors get rid of People's placards and paste on the buildings' walls their own announcements concerning the future of the city; and then they provide everybody with rationing coupons, classificatory descriptions of self, identification documents and badges to be worn at all times. The inhabitants of Wielow thus are assigned to appropriate jobs and quarters; and those who are not fit to work or live with others, or to live at all, are so informed. And shortly Wielow is cleared of those who are least fit to live: Hebrites and Gypsies, deemed impure. Day after day these least fit are loaded in large batches on swift trains and taken to some far-off places of no name. It is rumored, as only some knew for sure, that they are transported to specially designed facilities to be disposed of there, all of them, a batch at a time, in chambers sanitized and precisely equipped for the task. And those who are not themselves designated to die, carry on even if they sometimes cringe and shudder, as if disregardant that thousands around them are rapidly vanishing. After the city becomes cleansed of Hebrites and Gypsies, the occupying authorities proceed, with greater deliberateness, to rid society of all those others who might prove undependable: idlers, thinkers, jesters, artists, and the like.

But in the third year of its rule over the Continent, the Realm suffers an unexpected reverse of fortune. Its all-powerful armies are suddenly attacked; from the east by the recovering forces of the People's Power which are making their way west again, and from the west by the eastbound armies of the Great Far Western Allied Sovranties, a power distant from Adam's country, known to the local people only through books and word-of-mouth.

It is the GEU People's forces which on that Easter night brings off that spectacular air attack on the city. The city survives and remains under the Realm's rule, but everyone knows that the second coming of the People's Army is just a matter of time. As the inhabitants of Wielow are never sure whether it is the People's Army or the Realm's Army that they fear more, they are of divided opinion on what might happen to them in the near future. Adam's family chooses to flee, as you might remember; on the big motor truck procured by Nusia's father.

Many are ready to seek safety some distance away from the city, but few are equipped to journey as speedily and comfortably as Adam's family, as only very few possess his brother-in-law's talents and contacts. But it is by no means he who decides on getting the family out of Wielow. It is Adam's sister, Nusia's mother, who sets her mind on leaving. And one of the reasons behind her resolve, Adam is certain, is the Povolians.

The Povolians are the direct descendants of the original founders of Wielow and as such claim all the rights to the city and the lands around it; even though at the time of their rule Wielow was merely an insignificant encampment surrounded for miles by the wildest of forests, as Adam's old history textbooks would always point out. Anyway, when the War brakes out and the country falls, the Povolians (intermittently a docile and an unruly crowd in the past) suddenly see their chance. For the promise of independence they sell their souls to the Devil; that is, some of them do. They are ready to pay any price asked of them, no matter how high, and to do any jobs assigned to them, no matter how hard or even debasing; as long as the image of a free Povolia is looming in front of their eyes. Adam's sister believes that the Povolians are the foulest fiends ever created by the powers of darkness.

It is on the night of the Easter bombing during that long vigil in the basement that she makes up her mind about leaving the city and going West. The local Resistance is weak and indolent, she says the following day, the People's forces are at the gate and the treacherous Povolians are ready to strike on their own any moment, and so the only hope for the nation is in the fight waged by the forces of the Resistance in the West; so she is telling her family. Her husband, Boleslaw, feels confused, particularly about the Povolian nationalists. He asks her why they have to be fought by the patriotic forces from the West, from hundreds of kilometers away, while they, the Povolians, are not in the West, but right here in the Eastern Provinces; and she replies that he lacks intelligence and love for his country.

Adam has often marveled at his sister's uncommon gift of speeching, an ability to produce with no effort a flow of words expressing the most convoluted thoughts and yet appearing to listeners as straightforward and even inspiring, and to sound particularly convincing when she would meander the farthest from logic and truthfulness. Yet, she is not an outright liar, he believes, since her gift extends to being also able to convince herself of the truthfulness of her own words. When she was talking to her husband about heroism and patriotic duty, she hardly hinted that it was plain fear that made her want to flee.

Adam cannot remember seeing much of her during that night in the basement, if for no other reason than because of the lack of proper light in the place. But he knows that she was sitting atop a pile of dilapidated furniture, a little distance from everybody else, probably with her hands around her knees and eyes closed, imagining herself in the rank of some gallant partisan battalion awaiting the enemy in the thick of a fragrant fir forest, a man's military khaki shirt on her, a rifle and a bayonet ready in hand. He does remember, though, that sometime toward dawn when some of the crowd gathered in the basement started dozing off, she burst out singing:

Oh my rosemary open your blossoms,
Oh my rosemary open your blossoms,
I will go to my beloved,
I will go to my only one
And I will ask her...

This is, of course, an old sentimental ditty, commonly considered to be patriotic. Adam has no idea what the basement crowd thought of Konstancya's singing, that is, those who were kept awake by her voice, but he personally felt most bothered; the underlying meaning of the song always eluded him, and he definitely disliked the tune, and he absolutely loathed the piece in her rendition.

So, early on Easter Monday, as soon as they are back in their quarters upstairs, after that long night in the basement, Konstancya tells her husband that they have to leave the city immediately and go west where all true patriots were fighting. Since she never wanted to have anything to do with fighting, he wants an explanation; and she has nothing but contempt for him. She is ashamed of him, she says, ashamed of his smugness, his low desires, his associations with all those rats that profiteer from the War and human suffering. She is ashamed of his black-market eggs, his black-market butter and his black-market sausage; ashamed of black-market yarn for Nusia's sweaters and black-market flannel for Nusia's underwear, particularly of all these things for Nusia, since there is no greater sin a man can commit than to expose a young child to corruption. Nusia listens to all this with mouth agape. She knows that what her mother is saying is very important; her mother is an extremely important person, and so her words have to carry great weight.

Boleslaw heard before about the shame he was bringing upon his wife. He is reminded of it frequently and regularly, always at the mention of the death of his younger brother who – in the early part of the War – as punishment for printing anti-People's leaflets, was publicly executed by a People's firing squad in front of the Bernardine Church in Wielow. What Konstancya says is that in view of that heroic young death the life of her husband is particularly disgraceful. And what he always replies is that he well knows how worthless a life he is leading and how gladly he would give his life for the Cause, like his brother did, if he was only capable of it. "I am such a weak man, my darling," he often tells her. Then sometimes he asks her whether she herself has ever tried to do something truly big. And she then answers that nobody should expect sacrifices from a mother, whose primary duty in life is to protect her child. But it all seems to be changed now; Konstancya, Nusia's mother, says that she wants to join the forces fighting for liberation and to make her own mark upon history.

Boleslaw tries to dissuade her from the notion of going West. He talks about uncertainties and the unreliability of his contacts, and about greater difficulties with provisions and people further away from the city. He even says that once he is away from his home base of Wielow, he may not be able to support his family at all; but she cannot be swayed. Later that day she packs a small suitcase and announces her leaving alone, on foot if necessary. So, obviously he has to do something. A few days later he procures a small car which can take five people.

But, when they are ready to begin their journey, Adam's mother, Nusia's grandmother, who is just about to get into the car, stops dead next to the car's door. She cannot bear leaving everything behind, she says through tears. With but the slightest inducement mother was able to weep profusely like no one else Adam knew, or moan painfully, or just sob quietly. And she has shed especially prodigious quantities of tears on many an occasion since the War started. Yet rarely before has anything come close to the amount of tears she produces on this occasion; the rivers of tears flowing down her cheeks and breasts, all the way onto the pavement, forming a puddle next to the little car which is supposed to take them away.

She cries over her beautiful Bechstein concert piano to be left behind for savages to ravage, over her pictures, her books, her leather sofa, the tea set with pink rosebuds... "They are our lives, memories, civilization..." She cannot stop crying and remembering all those other things, precious and irreplaceable, that they have already lost since the War began. And then she says, a little speck of a smile moving around her mouth, that if they could get something a little larger than the car that Boleslaw brought, they could take at least a few things; things that Nusia will inherit from them one day when everything is peaceful and normal again and Nusia is a big girl ready to get married. She kisses Nusia and calls her a poor, little bird who will never inherit anything from her family.

Konstancya starts then contemplating Nusia's future too. She asks her husband whether he really loves his little girl and wants to leave everything the family has to a horde of Eastern Kalmyks or some other vile creatures who will in a few days pillage and desecrate every home in the city. (Nusia is not sure who exactly the Kalmyks are, but since she has heard of them before, she knows that they have something to do with destroying people's finest and most beloved things.) As it turned out Boleslaw does not think much of the Kalmyks either. So that's how he comes to get the big motor truck, the big trailer, and the two professional drivers.

The Home of the Divine Providence

This morning in the dining hall right after breakfast I asked Jan, who sits next to me, if he still had any vivid recollections of the air raids he experienced during the War. I was not interested in Jan's personal stories, but was merely hoping that my question would start one of our dining-table discourses we, the wards of The Home of Divine Providence, enjoy sometimes quite a bit; the half-an-hour period after a meal being the only time we are allowed to indulge in more or less unrestrained conversation on any topic we choose. But today after I asked him the question about air raids, Jan got up from his chair in a fury, called me "brainsick" and rushed out of the dining hall slamming the door behind him. Immediately after that, as anyone would have predicted, Brother Hyacinth, guardian of table manners, announced that our fellow-ward Jan would be swiftly and appropriately reprimanded for breaking the rules of the dining table. Still, a minute or so later an interesting discussion ensued. The participants divided themselves into two camps: one, those who felt that certain deeply personal and painful remembrances of the past should be left alone, unexplored by strangers; two, those who maintained that no person's experience or feelings are ever so unique and personal as to be granted immunity from being known and investigated by others.

Just when they are ready to climb onto the motor truck, cousin Radomir appear on the scene. He carries a suitcase and a small bundle and says that Kocia told him that he could tag along.

"Kocia" is what Adam's sister is called by some members of the family, which is a hideous diminutive of "Konstancya", which, by the way, is not her real name at all. In her infancy at the official baptismal ceremony she was given the name "Mieczyslawa", a rather attractive name of local origin, which she in her later life rejected as not suitable, renaming herself with something that she considered more appropriate. Adam, however, continues on occasion calling her by her original name, which never fails to incense her, to a degree equal only to her fury over his wearing masks.

Radomir was Adam's second cousin, one of the great number of the relatives on his mother's side; tall, self-assured, around twenty, considered by Nusia to be the most exciting man on earth. He is thought of quite highly by Nusia's mother as well, being often described by her as exceptional and talented. He is the only person outside the immediate family to whom she has offered a space on their motor truck.

When she sees him coming, she welcomes him with a cheerful, "How wonderful that you are here, Radomir!" Mother, on the other hand, greets him with a kiss full of tears, probably to let him know that she is aware of how precarious his existence has become of late. Radomir, a member of the local cadre of the Resistance, has been just designated by the Special Occupying Police of the IWS Realm as a wanted man, charged with assaulting an officer in the Realm Army. He has also been hounded for some time by the Povolian Freedom Fighters for reasons of their own.

Nusia, overjoyed at the prospect of having Radomir with them, wants him to sit next to her on her grandmother's leather sofa, between the piles of blankets and pillows, a perfect place to play house. However, Nusia's father steps between Radomir and the truck and says that the young man will not be journeying with them. "He is not coming, he is not! I am telling you all!" bellows Boleslaw. He may have a number of diverse reasons for not wanting Radomir around, but it is probable that his disliking the prospect so strongly is related to his knowledge of the hazardous circumstances under which cousin Radomir now lives.

Adam does not recollect what it finally takes for his brother-in-law to change his mind about Radomir, but since Konstancya is unshaken in her decision to have him with them, her husband has to eventually give in. Radomir climbs on the truck, makes himself comfortable on the sofa next to Nusia and happily consents to become the father of Marianna and Zuzanna, the two dolls that are traveling with them.

Not even five minutes pass since they started their journey and Nusia sets up house on the sofa, when she notices that her dolls' companion, Trabal, the stuffed elephant, is missing. It is a large and handsome-looking animal with movable ears and a velvet trunk, and Nusia is quite attached to him. Good toys are not easy to come by, and Boleslaw acquired this one from a certain Realm dignitary in exchange for a fine antique Meissen teapot. Of course, Nusia's mother now tells her daughter to forget about Trabal and occupy herself with all the other beautiful toys of which she – a very lucky girl – has so many; but when Nusia bursts into tears and recalls that Trabal has been left on the balcony, her father yells to the driver to stop. He then jumps off the truck and runs back to their place to fetch the toy.

They stop on a quiet, side thoroughfare, not far from their old building; and they wait there for Boleslaw to come back. But he does not return to them. Konstancya sends first one of the drivers and then Radomir to find out what is keeping him, and when those two return she is told by them that her husband has been taken away, from right in front of their building, flanked on both sides by men from the Special Occupying Police, Trabal the elephant in his hand. The men had the official black uniforms on, and they looked as if they meant business, the driver and Radomir report to her.

Nusia does not understand their words, but she crawls over to the trunk where her grandmother sits and presses her face against her grandmother's hand and kisses the rosary that her grandmother is holding. She is scared; she believes that one can perform magic with a rosary, though she is not sure how it should be done, except that kissing the beads has something to do with it. She begins feeling safer only when she understands when her mother is saying that they should start immediately.

Konstancya says that under the circumstances there is absolutely nothing they can do for her husband, except to pray, of course. She also tells them that they are very lucky indeed that the black-uniformed men did not spot them or their motor truck; and she insists that they go at a faster speed than before. And she promises the drivers an extra reward if they manage to get them to their destination safely and in a time shorter than planned.

Mother is terribly distraught. She asks why they cannot try to do something for her son-in-law, the father of their poor little bird, at least wait for him for a little bit longer. But Kocia chooses not to answer her. Adam suggests then that mother, either on her own or together with him and his sister, could go to the headquarters of the Special Occupying Police and inquire there about Boleslaw, and, if necessary, plead on his behalf. But Radomir calls him a moron and Kocia gives him a disdainful look. Adam tries to tell them then that it is unlikely that the occupying authorities would try to liquidate them, three bystanders who (unlike Boleslaw or Radomir) have hardly ever partaken of any proscribed activities; but Mieczyslawa Konstancya glares at him with anger and in a threatening manner tells him to stay put and keep quiet.

After further reflection Adam too is not sure about the correctness of his reasoning. But he hopes that Boleslaw, who has gone so far through so many perils of the War with such remarkably good fortune, will find a way out of this unpleasantness on his own and will rejoin them shortly.

Nusia is not afraid of anything anymore. She quickly forgets about Trabal the elephant and about her father. She is back on the leather sofa with Radomir, Marianna and Zuzanna, two dolls traveling with them, and she laughs every time the truck bounces from one side to the other. She asks Adam to join them on the sofa as she would love to play with his mask with horns and a beard (the only mask he managed to take with him, as you might remember). He hands her the mask and allows her to put it on, which is the very first time that he lets her do such a thing. The mask is big and heavy, and so she has difficulty in handling it, but she is perseverant and careful. When she eventually puts it on, she cannot see anything, since the slits in the mask do not fit her eyes, yet she is obviously delighted. She gives out a loud, happy yell and jumps up and down on the sofa. Shortly she becomes quite giddy both from the motion of the motortruck and the excitement of the new experience. It is the first sensation of happiness that she will recollect.

Their destination is a town just south of the provincial capital city of Kramow, some three hundred kilometers west of Wielow, the home of a man named Pawlik who owes Boleslaw money and favors, and who has pledged to him eternal gratitude. Pawlik, a trader in art, on many an occasion of his business visits to the Eastern Provinces, after having profitably exchanged quantities of artware and cash with Boleslaw, always reminds them all that if in need, and in the vicinity of his home, they could count on his, Pawlik's, assistance.

Mieczyslawa Konstancya has never seemed to care much for the man, a vulgarian he is; yet now – on her way to his home – she tells them that at the end of their journey, at Mister Pawlik's, they will find not just safety and hospitality, but also a spirit of true patriotism. She also decides that it will be ill-advised to tell Pawlik about that disconcerting incident with Trabal, the stuffed elephant, and what happened to her husband. They will simply say that Boleslaw is well, busy and sending his regards. And when asked about the situation in the Eastern Provinces, they will state that it is somewhat difficult, but far from really serious. And above all, when asked about her husband's plans for the future, they will make a point that his prospects are quite bright indeed, even in the eventuality that Wielow is taken over again by the GEU People's forces. And of course immediately after they arrive, they will present to Pawlik the gift crate that Boleslaw has prepared for him.

Let it be understood here that Boleslaw sent Pawlik a dispatch announcing their intended visit, but – the times being so tumultuous and uncertain – he knows his message may not reach Pawlik in time, and so Adam's brother-in-law, wise man that he is, decides to have some gifts ready for their prospective host. In order to lessen the impact of their possibly unannounced visitation, he assembles an impressive collection of hard-to-find items, well, items practically impossible to obtain anywhere in those days, such as smoked ham, silk stockings (dozens of pairs), extra-keen razor blades and fountain pens of foreign make; all to be given to Pawlik as a sign of their appreciation.

Adam tries to inquire of Konstancya a number of times how, once in Pawlik's home, she sees her own future role in the Resistance. He asks how she is going to enlist in the first place, and then whether she really intends to fight, and if not, what other assignments she might be given, but she does not answer. She just mumbles something about things taking their due course and gets horribly annoyed.

As a point of some interest it should be mentioned here that at the outset of the War, when the family still all lived in Wielow, Adam was in the possession of a scalpful of hair, his own hair, that is. It was thick, curly, crow-black; and he kept it long, changing trends in fashion notwithstanding. Nobody in his mother's family had such hair. Adam inherited it from his father, a dealer in felt for gentlemen's hats by profession and a poet by avocation; a man whose ancestors had come to Wielow from Asia Minor. Adam also has his father's black eyes and a large beak-shaped nose, and he often wonders by what trick of Nature his sister Mieczyslawa Konstancya was born with green eyes, light-brown hair and a small, shapely nose. It is his hair that got him twice in trouble during the War.

In the first year of the War, when the Eastern Provinces is still occupied by the People's Power, he is assaulted by a People's officer who is trying to keep order among those waiting in line in front of a grocery store. The man grabs Adam by his hair and yanks him out of the line, spitting at him and screaming something which sounds obscene. Later, when some of those in line smuggle Adam back, he is told by a man behind him, obviously knowledgeable in the language, that the officer disliked his hair and called him degenerate and unworthy of the privilege of buying food meant for normal-looking working-class individuals.

Two years later Adam is set upon by a soldier of the IWS Realm, right in the center of the Square of the Virgin Mary as he is taking a walk with the little Nusia. The soldier grabs him by his hair and starts dragging him all around the Square and, disregarding his and Nusia's protests, continues doing so for quite a while, laughing and expelling words of which Adam understands only two: "Heb" and "dirty". Then he pulls him to a stone fountain, and still firmly holding his hair, repeatedly dips his head in the water. He is pressing Adam's head to the very bottom, and while talking about washing his dirty hair clean, he does not stop laughing. When he is through at last, Adam drops limp on the ground next to the fountain, but the soldier quickly props him up, pushing his slumped body against the fountain's stone as hard as he can, making sure that he is set up properly for display.

Then Konstancya, who is to join him and Nusia in a stroll, appears at the Square. She helps him to his feet and leads him home holding his arm, but also, in a most uncharitable way, she hisses into his ear that she has had it with him and that something will have to be done about his hair. And she indeed take care of things.

Only a few hours after the incident at the fountain, Adam sees himself in the mirror transformed: short-cropped pile on his head and yellow-blond all over, even his eyebrows; the new coloration being a result of the use of the chemical known as peroxide, which, by the way, Konstancya obtained through one of her husband's black-market connections. From that moment on, until the day when the big motor truck took them West, she regularly performs the ritual of peroxidizing him, as she considers it her personal mission to make sure that Adam stays a changed man.

She trims his hair, wets it thoroughly with the peroxide and then keeps it pressed for hours to straighten it out. After a few months his hair becomes straighter, of platinum-blond hue and somewhat scantier. She is pleased, but still insists that her brother not show himself in public places since she can not do anything about either his eyes or his nose. As a point of clarification, let it be stated here that neither Adam nor the rest of the family were classified by the occupying Realm authorities as impure and hence intended for elimination, yet Konstancya feared that Adam's exotic looks could lead to him being identified as such.

At any rate, in order to further protect his person, Adam one day came up with the idea of Hebrite masks, a facial garb which could successfully hide his Hebritic features considered objectionable.

His creations were not elaborate at all - just cheerful cardboard faces with golden locks, blue eyes, dainty noses, dimples, etc. - yet they turned out to be practical; that is, when Adam wore them in public, he was never stopped or assaulted by anybody. Of course, the family would rarely allow him to go outside, and so he did not have much chance to fully evaluate the usefulness of those masks; and he left them, together with all his other masks, in Wielow, in the trunk which Konstancya did not allow him to take.

About two hours after they leave Wielow, when there is no chance that they will turn back, mother plunges into spasms of heartrending wailing. She suddenly remembers that she has left the peroxide behind; she forgot to pack it, she says, leaving it, in her inexcusable absent-mindedness, on the shelf in the bathroom; and she will never forgive herself for what will happen now to Adam, her ill-fated son. Konstancya then becomes quite upset too, but not for long. After a short reflection she decides that it is inconceivable that somebody like Pawlik (their future host and savior), with all his connections, will not be able to obtain some peroxide for them, one of the simplest chemical compounds on earth.

The Home of the Divine Providence
Today is Sunday, the day I am not permitted to spend time in my workshop. Sundays in the Home are for worship, meditation and reading. On Sunday mornings everybody with the exception of me and the ward called Szymon, attends religious services in our chapel. Other wards skip the services occasionally, but only the two of us have

consistently refused to participate in them. We do so, however, not out of true philosophical conviction, but because we love to have all the papers and magazines to ourselves, even for one little hour of the duration of a Sunday service. The fact is that the Home gets only one set of reading material once a week, and even though Brother Boniface, guardian of indoor recreation, makes sure that there are no fights or squabbles among the wards about who is going to read what and when, there is still never enough reading material for everyone. Today I read in one of the papers that it is demanded of certain Hebrite individuals that they cleanse themselves of certain unpatriotic deeds of the past, though no names or specific deeds were mentioned. I asked then Szymon, a Hebrite, whether he felt threatened in any way, but his answer was that he had no idea if he should feel threatened, but that if he was in danger, he might ask me to make him a Hebrite mask, the kind I once told him about.

2.

Adam's mother, Karolina Milewska, was the daughter of Alfons Milewski, a master hatter from Wielow. She was born into the clan which for some two hundred years was producing not only hatters of outstanding skills and gentlemen's hats of superior quality, but also a great number of women of uncommon loveliness and devotion to their spouses. So they were always told. The Milewskis were prudent, hard-working, devoutly religious and respectable all around. They considered themselves to be co-founders of the Bernardine Church (one of the finest places of worship in the city); and it was there that for generations they occupied the same seats in a masterly carved pew with a full view of the main altar.

When mother was eight, and just orphaned by her mother, she was sent by her father to the school run by the Sisters of the Ursuline Order, which was regarded as the place best suited for the cultivating of young gentlewomen. One of only a handful of artisans' daughters at the Ursuline establishment, she nevertheless flourished there. She graduated with honors in music, and then, by becoming bethrothed to an attorney-at-law, was to assume a social position to which none of the Milewski women had ever aspired. But her destiny changed the moment she laid her eyes on a dark-haired Levantine with the unordinary name of Czulartian, whom she saw for the first time through a half-open door leading to her father's office. He stood in front of Alfons Milewski and gestured profusely, expounding on the quality of the felt he was trying to sell; mother was spellbound. Two weeks after that encounter she and the young felt dealer eloped. They were married in a ceremony unattended by anybody they knew. Adam's sister was born in the first year of their marriage, and he came a year later.

The married life of Adam's parents was blessed with never ceasing joy; mother told them on many occasions. Father's success in selling felt was modest, but his accomplishments in producing poetry quite notable. His works, printed in local magazines, were also published as a book; a beautifully bound volume of lyrics dedicated to mother.She played the piano a great deal. And together they attended poetry readings, plays and even risque cabaret performances. They lived without financial worries, happily spending both the capital father had inherited and mother's dowry (which she received from her family at the birth of Konstancya).

Father died in the fifth year of their marriage; killed in a duel, in which he served as a second to a couple of distant acquaintances. He disliked violence deeply and through the whole time of preparations for the event thought of ways of not letting it happen. Unfortunately, he was a split second too late, when at the moment the shooting was to start – in an attempt to prevent bloodshed – he rushed towards the duelists and placed himself between them, right on the route of the two crossing bullets.

Shortly after his death mother discovered that all her funds had been exhausted; and since she felt lost amidst the intricacies of the practical matters of life, she turned to her family for help. They then took her and the children under their wing; gave them home and upkeep; and kept them as their dependents for some fifteen years that followed.

Mother would say that she failed her children miserably. She would also urge the two of them to work on their characters and feel grateful to the family; two recommendations she was repeating verbatim after her father, her brothers and her brothers' wives, who, in all truthfulness, did try their best to bring up Konstancya and Adam properly. Of course, Konstancya (a.k.a. Kocia), in her typical arrogant manner, always claimed they never did more than their second best. But the Milewskis did put a lot of effort into making Kocia and Adam educated and respectable; and when despite all their endeavors on their behalf the two ended up on the stage, the family felt hurt and disheartened, naturally. They also felt terribly disappointed with mother, whose harmful influence on her children they failed to countervail.

While Konstancya, part of the befrilled chorus, danced and sang on the stage of the Wielow Operetta, Adam, a few streets away, at the National Theatre of Dramatic Arts, assumed in front of the public character-roles of varied size and unusual variety. The two of them were often complimented on their natural gifts and on their efforts; and it was foretold many a time that both of them would one day reach the very heights of theatrical success. But it happened that they both left the theater quite early in their lives, to the considerable sadness of mother, mind you.

Adam abandoned the theatrical profession at the age of twenty-two during the run of a drama in which he played a young Medieval prince, betrayed and imprisoned; his first leading role. One evening during a dungeon scene, in the middle of soliloquizing on life, death and betrayal, he, the wretched prince, suddenly remembered a joke which he, Adam C., had heard a day earlier; precisely at the moment when he was to deliver some of the most tragic and profound words of the drama. As he began experiencing an attack of uncontrollable laughter, he turned his back to the audience and clanged the chains around his body so that his outburst of hilarity would not be heard; and the audience indeed never knew what transpired. At the following night's performance he laughed again, this time at a different joke that suddenly turned up in his memory. The curse of joke-remembering went on, night after night; at each performance he laughed harder and clanged his chains more vigorously, and received louder and longer-lasting applause from the audience. And each day he felt more befuddled, angry at himself and miserable. After a few weeks of such misery he left the theater for good, with the resolve to devote the whole rest of his life to reflective and speculative study of the human psyche and mankind's irrationalities.

Kocia's renouncing of her career a few months earlier coincided with her announcement of her marriage to Boleslaw Jastrzab-Rytwianski, son of one of the richest wheat growers and pork producers of the entire Eastern Provinces. The news of the marriage was received with bewilderment; not only was Boleslaw of noble lineage and possible heir to great wealth, but she, prior to her engagement, was known to be passionately entangled with Kazimierz Rytwianski, the younger brother of her fiance. Besides, Boleslaw was not nearly as handsome and morally upstanding as his younger brother; so would everybody say. Actually, he was thought to be highly uncultured and strongly prone to association with those of questionable morals and inferior roots. It was common knowledge, for instance, that he was a regular patron of gambling houses, that he was often interrogated by the police in relation to matters of a scandalous nature, and that some of his closest associates were lowly Povolians. Also, no one was certain who his mother was, since he was the issue of the first, and short-lived, marriage of the old Rytwianski (which made him, by the way, only a half-brother to Kocia's former lover Kazimierz). Some rumors had it that his mother was a Tatar princess, some others that she was a daughter of a Hebrite innkeeper from Lublin, and a few that she was a Povolian of peasant blood who before she married the master of the house, had served as a maid in the Jastrzab -Rytwianski household.

Some speculated that Kocia was marrying Boleslaw, rather than Kazimierz, simply because he was the one who proposed the marriage. Others held that both the brothers proposed, but she chose the one who had the better chance of inheriting his father's money; as, indeed, in spite of all his shortcomings, Boleslaw was the favorite of his father, an ailing, twice-widowed gentleman. However, public conjecture concerning her was not accurate; the world did not really know her, Adam always felt. If she had only wanted to, she would not have had difficulty in making any man propose marriage to her; and her love of money and luxuries was never the driving force of her life. What really propelled her into anything she ever did was her total and unashamed love of self, Adam never doubted. So, when she met Boleslaw, whose self-sacrificial devotion to her and eagerness to suffer any humiliation for her went beyond anything she had ever known, she simply could not resist the temptation of trying to experience marriage to that kind of man.

Shortly after Kocia and Boleslaw were married, mother and Adam moved in with them; on the urging of Kocia, obviously, as she felt that it was her duty to take charge of them. She began showering them with attention. In order to revive mother's musical skills, she bought her a Bechstein concert grand piano of great cost and made her take music lessons from a pedagogue of the Conservatory; and then she presented her with a life-size bust of Paderewski on a marble column and insisted that mother keep it next to her piano for inspiration. And as for Adam, she made him undertake exhausting studies in breathing, elocution, fencing and foreign literature, all to help him nurture and refine his acting skills. And when he forsook the theater, she decided that he was ill, and began a search for ways of curing him. On her orders he had to undergo many lengthy medical examinations involving testings of his brain; at home he was taken care of by a succession of live-in nurses; and he was regularly sent to spas and sanatoriums, accompanied by a strong-bodied male (Kocia's choice), to whom she referred as his dresser, but whose sole function was to make sure that Adam would not appear in public with a mask on his face.

In his love for her, Boleslaw gave up his wicked ways; and shortly he and Konstancya became one of the most socially important couples of Wielow. And when Boleslaw's father died and left him most of his huge fortune, Kocia's estimation of her own importance started reaching dizzying heights. That she, an ex-chorus singer, the daughter of the penniless widow of a Levantine felt dealer and the granddaughter of a hatter, became accepted in the high society of Wielow happened only because it never even occurred to her, egomaniacal person that she was, that things could have been any other way.

She took now singing lessons from the voice coach of the Opera; and gave singing recitals before a crowd of personal guests in a rented concert hall, in the light of silver candelabras especially brought in for the occasion. She became an accumulator of some of the most extravagant and bizarre of contemporary art, even had her Christmas tree every year decorated by avant-garde artists. She had all her undergarments and hosiery shipped in from Paris. She took flying lessons. She smoked a pipe and wore men's clothes on many an occasion. And she made sure that she was elected the vice-chairman of the Wielow chapter of the Society for Promoting Closer Cultural Contacts with Other Continents. Adam called her a gaudy mummer who turned her life into a garish pageant of immodest dramatics with herself as the principal star.

Mother, who seemed a little bewildered by Konstancya's new life, would often express her doubts about the rightness of the course that her daughter was following. Not that she herself was unwilling to partake in enjoyments that Kocia was now able to offer her. She had her morning tea and confitures in bed, and during the day spent hours shopping for fineries. And as her daughter was not interested in domestic affairs, mother most gladly supervised the household staff, personally planning elaborate menus or arranging freshly cut bouquets in beautiful translucent vases. She listened to records and played her Bechstein for hours on end. And of course she attended charity affairs. She regularly reproached herself for her immoderations and her fondness of material comforts, though usually not for long. On the days when her sense of guilt struck her particularly hard, she would break into tears, grope for her rosary and pray for absolution. She thought of Boleslaw, her son-in-law, as the kindest and most generous of men, but at the same time she suspected the presence of some demonic forces within him.

Grandfather Milewski and the rest of mother's family never felt quite at ease with the idea of becoming related to people of the status of the Rytwianskis. Not that Kocia made it easy for them. She limited her contacts with them to a single set of presents sent to them on St. Nicolas' Day and to a single set of invitations to one of her singing recitals.

The War took them all by surprise. It rapidly brought an end to all the pageantry and abundance. Charity balls, fancy menus, travel, servants, avant-garde art and rooms filled with silver candelabras were all gone without a trace, in an instant, as if they were only a part of some past distant dream. On the order of the occupying authorities of the GEU People's Power, Boleslaw's money and properties were taken away from him, including the sumptuous house and a considerable portion of the house's contents. And the family was moved to small quarters in a part of the city mother called most inelegant. Shortly thereafter Boleslaw was informed by the occupying authorities of the scheduled execution of his younger brother and ordered to witness the event. And then he himself was called in front of the People's High Tribunal and charged with the crime of being an enemy of the people.

In those days in Wielow many were pronounced the people's enemies, but while most of them stayed imprisoned or were sent to their death, Boleslaw, as if by a miracle, was set free after a while and then allowed to live undisturbed. No one was certain how his release came about; neither did anybody have a clue as to the route of his subsequent ascent in the underworld of wartime swindlers and desperados. Nobody knew for certain how he conducted his affairs, but almost everybody agreed that he was able to perform feats that very few could. He dealt in whatever commodity might be in demand - food, information, art, work permits, routes for escape, guns, ammunition; and he dealt with anybody from any side; so at least it was said. And his luck seemed to hold out undiminished, for years, under both the People's Power and the Realm. There were, of course, those who thought of him to be a traitor and a criminal, and would impute to him the blackest of deeds. But there were also those who saw in him a savior of lives and ideals and, hence, a fighter for freedom. Extraordinary as it might seem that anybody would associate his fraternizing with the enemy and peddling of deadly weapons with saving anybody, Adam somehow always thought that stories of him being a savior had to be true. Well, whatever else he might have been doing in those days, he kept the family well, safe and comfortable, that is, well, safe and comfortable by wartime standards.

As concerns the wartime fate of the Milewskis, let it be mentioned that under the GEU People's Power their hatting business (premises, tools, ribbon, felt and all) was nationalized and they themselves were turned into employees of the State. And with the coming of the Realm their business was again designated as a state enterprise, which was charged with supplying headgear for the Army, felt insoles for soldiers' boots, and crepe ribbon for military medals.

They left Wielow in the spring of the fifth year of the War; mother, Konstancya, Adam, Nusia and cousin Radomir.

Placed among Konstancya's miscellaneous effects, they flee the city atop a large motor truck driven by skilled men hired by Boleslaw, Nusia's father; except that Boleslaw, as you probably remember, is not with them. They look at the city for the last time already from a distance and see it all spread out on its many hills; the roofs, domes and towers clearly exposed in the brilliant light of that afternoon. The city of unexpected vibrant colors has the glow of a freshly painted canvas, clean, unmarred; no lesions or wastages of the War visible.

In later years Adam often wondered whether he would have tried to take a really good look at certain places in the city just before he left, had he known that he was not to return; like a side altar in the Bernardine church, of which in his youth he thought as the only ecclesiastical structure worth noting, but of which now he cannot even say whether its central image was a statue or a painting.

Their journey is by and large uneventful, that is, after Boleslaw was taken away and they took off in so great a hurry. They would run into a road patrol or a roadblock once in a while, hear a warning siren or an explosion, or even see a bomb dropped from the sky; but these were all things to be expected.

As they travel, they meet on the road those who, like they, have left their homes behind; on trucks, on wagons, on foot, always with bundles; but there is never time enough but for the briefest exchange between them. They usually just trade the news of the day or general predictions about the course of the War. The further west they go the more often they are asked about the GEU People's Army whom residents of the Central Provinces have yet to see. People wonder whether that Army is really as barbaric and uncouth as stories have it, and whether it has a chance to defeat the Realm forces completely.

Their truck does not always follow the main road. Most of the time it trudges along narrow and bumpy paths, which seem not substantial enough for its bulk and weight. They travel mostly by night, and by day they wait a great deal. They doze a lot; and when they watch the world go by, they usually say nothing. When it is cold, they get covered by the heavy and ill-smelling tarpaulin which their drivers draw over their heads like a shroud. The two men take care of most of the business with the outside world; they do most of the talking, and bribing, when necessary; they decide where and when one is to eat, to get off the truck or to duck into a road ditch. The two also sing a lot, and mother finds their songs highly obscene; and so she tells Nusia to cover her ears; which Nusia cannot be persuaded to do as she wants to learn every one of the beautiful songs that the gentlemen sing, the words in particular. Mother does not scold the men, though, since she has been instructed by Kociathat that under no circumstances should she antagonize their absolutely indispensible friends. Konstancya sings too, but, at least when the truck moves, the wind created by the motion, mutes the sounds of her voice. Mother says the rosary many a time; she also plays cards with Radomir; and she tells Nusia stories of princesses and dragons. Adam reflects on the various events of the past few days and finds that Easter Sunday, when he and Nusia watched the illuminated sky over the city, to have already receded into the distant past. He also thinks of designs for new masks he may make in the future. And he notices that nobody mentions his brother-in-law Boleslaw.

It took them four days and nights to cover the distance between Wielow and the town where Pawlik lived; some three hundred tedious and wearing kilometers. Yet Konstancya for decades would tell her audiences that that journey was one of the most wondrous adventures of her entire life. Most probably, out of the total experience she has decided to remember one afternoon when the sky was blindingly blue and the air was full of dizzying smells of freshly budding nature and she thought that she had the whole world at her feet. They all sit under a row of fine sorb trees, waiting for one of the drivers to get back from a nearby village where he has gone for supplies. The man returns in triumph. He brings a keg of beer and more food then they have seen in months. He has two village boys helping him carry the provisions. The boys laugh and say that the night before the partisans took two villages up in the hills, and the depot and the bridge below, and got rid of every single soldier of the Realm Army, so there was not a single Realm son-of-a-bitch left now within a radius of at least fifteen kilometers. Adam remarks then that one should not be too confident about such matters and that the Realm soldiers might still be hiding somewhere. But no sooner did he say this than Radomir jumps at him with clenched fists, ready to strike, shouting that the partisans will be back too, stronger than ever; to which Konstancya says, predictably, that Adam is incapable of either feeling or thinking.

It is then that she all of a sudden musters tears in her eyes and says in ecstasy that what happened in the hills was just wonderful and she wishes they could celebrate this great event.

"And why not?" responds one of the drivers. "The lady wants to celebrate, so let's celebrate!"

Within minutes they are indeed celebrating; with beer, head-cheese and sausages, beets and horseradish relish, bread and bimber, that home-distilled wartime wonder and horror of a brew; all spread out on one of mother's blankets beneath a large willow tree. They go through several rounds of toasts and hand-shaking, then hand-kissing of the ladies and cheek-kissing of the rest. At the peak of these festivities one of the drivers bows before Konstancya.

"Could we request of the lady, our great artist, to sing something for us," he says.

Then both the men insist on her doing something classy, like in the good old pre-War days. They obviously have heard of her singing career; and there is no doubt that she is thrilled with their asking her to perform. The two then rush to the truck and clear the Bechstein concert grand piano of anything that has been covering or blocking it. Then three pairs of male arms (including those of Radomir) lift Kocia off the ground, carry her high up in the air and place her right next to the piano. Immediately afterwards the same arms hoist mother and seat her in front of the open keyboard. Nusia is enthralled. Adam, who has not participated in the earlier festivities, decides now to engage himself in eating and definitely not listening.

Not hearing them, however, turns out to be impossible; from the heights of the motor truck, mother's piano and Konstancya's voice carry very powerfully and can be heard clearly throughout the newly liberated fields and woodlands. So, Adam puts on his horned mask and begins to dance, making sure that he moves his feet and arms and the jaw of his mask in a rhythm always different from the one which is coming from the truck. Nusia joins him, and the two of them are having not a bad time after all.

By and by a crowd gathers in front of the truck; villagers and partisans, male and female, young and old, incredulous; and Mieczyslawa Konstancya, self-indulgent and unrestrained, sings for all of them. She carries on for several hours; going through all the female arias from all the operettas known in this part of the world, it seems; she sings in her native language as well as in foreign tongues, and she sings some of the better known tunes more than once. And she does not just vocalize her csardases and polkas, but dances them as well. She finishes at dusk with a venture into opera, with what Adam knows is considered one of the most demanding arias in the world's operatic repertory. And the crowd just stays there through all the hours, till the very end; no words spoken and no commotion or any signs of excitement among those gathered; and no applause either. They just stand and watch her and nod their heads in amazement at a spectacle the likes of which they have not beheld before.

Well, in all truthfulness, Kocia is applauded, and even begged for encores; but only by the gentlemen of her own party and a handful of young partisans who have taken positions right next to the motor truck. All these young men ogle her intently and greedily, but none of them, Adam notices suddenly, as much as cousin Radomir. In the course of this afternoon he has acquired a singularly ravenous and yearning look, also the most idolizing one that Adam has ever chanced to see on the face of any young man. He looks only at her, and she is of course completely aware of it; and he wants to believe that she sings only for him, and she obviously loves every moment of making him believe that it is indeed true. When she finishes and several pairs of outstretched male arms are ready to help her off the truck, he is the one who lifts her off, places her on the ground and then voraciously kisses her hands.

Before they resume their journey that evening, the drivers, Radomir, Kocia and mother, accompanied by some young partisans, go through a few more rounds of beer and bimber. And before she falls asleep, Nusia confides in Adam that she has the most beautiful mother in the whole world.

And the following day, when they are on the road a good distance further on, they hear that around midnight of the night before soldiers of the IWS Realm recaptured the hills and at dawn executed two partisans in the market square of the village from which their keg of beer came from.

The Home of the Divine Providence

It was late when Brother Hyacinth, guardian of table manners, came to my room last night. He brought me a cup of cocoa (by all counts my favorite beverage), my daily treat, which – let me emphasize – I have been able to enjoy primarily thanks to Nusia's generosity to the Home. To my horror, Hyacinth said that cocoa has become so scarce and expensive that I would have to be satisfied from now on with not more than two cups a month. He then expressed his regret about the situation, assured me that he understood that my craving for cocoa could be most powerful, but advised me to learn to fight carnalities of any kind. While I was drinking, slowly, heavy-heartedly, savoring every drop, Hyacinth was leafing through papers that I had in my room, making me nervous. I became alarmed at what might happen if he stumbled upon my secret stash. I was infuriated

with his behavior and ready to tell him to stop poking his nose into
my business, but somehow I did not find enough courage to say what
I intended. At least, as far as I can tell he did not find anything of
interest to him.

They arrive at the house of the man called Pawlik in the afternoon. The place where he lived was on the outskirts of town right
between potato fields and the town dumping ground. The house
was made of red brick, was partially surrounded by barbed wire
and was guarded by a bunch of Alsatian dogs. The drivers said that
in pre-War days it probably served as a warehouse of some kind.
At the time of their visit it was used, as they found out, both as a
storage facility for goods of all sorts and as a private residence for
Pawlik and his female companion. Whether it was Pawlik himself
who actually owned all the goods or whether he was only handling
them or looking after them for somebody else they never learned.

They were not expected, but were let in politely nevertheless.
They were greeted cordially, but informed very quickly that not
much could be done for them.

"Times are terrible, worse then ever," says Pawlik ominously.
"You cannot trust anybody; nowadays you just pray, for your own
survival. This hell of a war has made us all horribly callous and
egoistic."

But after the special gift crate (the one Boleslaw so thoughtfully
provided them with) is opened and its contents carefully examined, Pawlik and his woman begin to sound somewhat encour-
aging. Still, they are not sure whether they can have anybody stay

with them for any length of time. And Pawlik cannot say whether he can take upon himself the responsibility of storing in his house the contents of the motor truck and the trailer.

He looks over the vehicle that has brought them to his doorstep. From all sides he carefully examines the truck and the trailer; he touches some of the furniture, squeezes the sofa, tries the piano, opens drawers in the bureau, taps a few crates, and then bursts into laughter.

"My beautiful lady, your husband is absolutely incredible...what a brain!" He takes Konstancya's hand in his and pats it affectionately. He smiles to her. He tells her, his speech flowing with warmth and good will, that he cannot find words strong enough to express his admiration for somebody who, in times like these, has managed to obtain such a splendid motortruck, and a trailer, and two of the finest drivers, and who not only got his family out of the hell of Wielow, but also saved from destruction so much of his property.

Konstancya smiles back at him, ready to reciprocate with some pleasantry of her own, when he all of a sudden changes again. He moves away from her a few steps and directs his eyes back onto the truck.

"Let's look now at my gorgeous red-head with the yellow flower! Which crate is she in?" His manner is all business.

Mieczyslawa Konstancya turns into a piece of indignant marble, and, appropriately, announces to him that if he is talking about The Red-haired Lady with a Yellow Rose which he once saw in their place in Wielow and admired so much, the painting in question is not anywhere on the truck and he will not be able to admire it this time. "And besides, it is my private piece, sir, never to be sold," she says with dignity.

"Oh, my beautiful, you are entirely mistaken. The Red-haired Lady is mine," Pawlik laughs and explains to her in some detail how already a long time ago he made an arrangement with her husband about the painting. "I have already paid for it, my dear, I assure you. And I know that a man of your husband's honesty would have never forgotten any business agreement."

"But there was never any deal made involving The Red-haired!"She chokes with fury, beginning to understand that Pawlik is making any future hospitality to them contingent upon that particular painting.

It was a piece by somebody of only moderate acclaim; a hazy pastel of a plumpish nymph or such, which Adam always disliked. It had been given to Konstancya as a present by her then-lover Kazimierz still some time before she married Boleslaw. She seemed to be quite attached to the picture, and, despite her contempt for "the traditional", always referred to it as a work of great artistic merit. Pawlik never thought of it as exceptional, Adam has no doubt, yet he wanted to buy it from her and had offered her a good deal of money for it more than once simply because that picture of a languid nymph became somehow an undetachable part of his post-War existence he could not stop envisioning.

You see, during the War dreams tended to be extravagant and protracted; and as the War dragged on with no end in sight, visions of a war -free universe would sometimes become obsessive. What Pawlik saw was a grand, end-of-the-last-century mansion in Kramow, with tall stained-glass windows, swirling staircases, walls ornamented with pearl-and-honey shaded forms of exotic leaves; and in it, encased like precious jewels, were his paintings, all his own, one of the finest collections of this type in the world. His great exhibition, open to a selected public, was going to be called La Belle Epoque, a feast for the eyes; painting upon painting exquisitely displayed against the lavish interiors. The moment he had laid eyes on The Red-haired, he knew that it belonged there.

He can see it now, he says, clearly, at the head of the stairs leading to the second floor; not a great painting perhaps, but one perfectly setting the mood for whatever is coming after it. And so, Kocia has to give in. The painting is dug out from one of the crates and presented to him. And his feelings of benevolence towards everybody thereupon become boundless. They are invited to stay overnight and are promised that all their affairs will be taken care of.

When they sit down to supper, prepared and served by Pawlik's woman, the general mood is quite hopeful, if not to say cheerful. It seems now that there will not be any particular difficulties with placing their lives under Pawlik's patronage and even finding storage for Kocia's belongings somewhere in his home. But no details of their lives with Pawlik are discussed this evening as their host's mind is far too preoccupied with plans for his own, more distant, future. He cannot stop admiring the portrait of The Red-haired Lady with a Yellow Rose and talking about the beautiful fin-de-siecle gallery he is going to open as soon as "the whole bloody mess" is over.

They all sit at the table in Pawlik's best room. The food is not festive, but it is served on a fresh tablecloth and portions given them are generous; and bread and bimber are served throughout the whole meal. It is only Pawlik who drinks the liquor in any quantity; he pours it into a tall glass (the kind used for serving tea or milk) filling the glass about one third, and then drinks the contents in one long gulp. His face gets a little redder, his voice louder and his already massive belly more prominent. After he pours into himself some two carafes of the stuff, he calls for something "finer and smoother"; and his woman puts a bottle of cognac in front of him, even though she expresses some apprehension as to how so much liquor might affect his temper and powers of judgement.

Pawlik cradles the new bottle in his arms for a few seconds, and then turns to Kocia with a warm smile on his face, "Your husband, dear, what a man..."; the new bottle comes from Boleslaw's gift crate. He opens it, takes a whiff and tells the woman to bring him a proper glass. He is just ready to savor the new liquor when the sudden barking of the dogs outside makes him stop. Pawlik and the woman freeze for a moment, and then jump to their feet and rush to the window. After a few seconds of staring into the night they decide that it must be Weber, a colonel in the army of the Realm. Pawlik curses and hits his fist against the window sill.

"Must have gotten lonely again, that God-damned Realm bastard," he says forgetting his civil tongue, "and that God-damned fucking motortruck of yours sitting outside! What if that swine Weber noticed it?!"

Pawlik and the woman have to think very quickly now. After all, Weber represents the occupying authorities and Adam and the rest, including their hosts, are the occupied enemy; so, naturally, Pawlik may be asked by somebody like Weber to explain what they are all doing in his house. Upon the briefest reflection Pawlik decides that it is the presence of Radomir and the two drivers (strong and regular looking males, all three of them), more than the presence of the others, that may arouse Weber's curiosity; and so, he orders the three of them to run to the attic, find a good hiding place there and remain there until recalled. And before he opens the door to let his guest in, he manages to wrap The Red-haired iin a bath towel and to push it under the divan in the room where they are gathered.

Weber, a colonel of the Elite Armed Forces of the IWS Realm, is not alone; there is another officer with him, a younger man of lower rank. Pawlik greets them with some kind of "I am delighted and honored..." -phrases in the Realm language, with deference referring to Weber as "a great art connoisseur", the phrase he then carefully translates for Kocia and the others; all of which probably means, Adam believes, that Pawlik and Weber are involved together in some under-the-table dealings in art. Then Pawlik introduces Kocia and her family to the two officers as his distant relatives, all famed artists-performers. However, he probably does not describe their occupations in correct language, since through the whole rest of the night Adam gets the impression that the two men think of them as being connected with a circus; which is just as well, since nobody asks Kocia to sing.

It is a squeaky gramophone playing hits from before the War that provides the musical background to the little gathering. The woman serves food and drinks to everybody, and changes records many a time; and they all drink (with the exception of Nusia, of course). Adam decides that everything around has suddenly acquired a softer and pleasanter quality: the air in the room, the furnishings, the light, the voices and the music. The two Realm officers are extremely well-mannered and charming, also totally taken to Nusia, a little girl who does not feel like going to sleep. Pawlik, flushed and contented, plunks himself onto the divan and hums. Bimber and cognac flow in an uninterrupted stream, and they dance; mother in the arms of Colonel Weber, Konstancya embraced by the younger officer and Pawlik with both his hands on the buttocks of his woman. Nusia and Adam, when not on the dancing floor themselves sit on the divan and observe the scene with interest: the figures floating lazily in a manner disregardant of the tune coming out of the gramophone, half-closed eyes full of expectations for pleasures yet to come.

Then suddenly Nusia stops watching; she crawls under the divan and pulls out the portrait of the Red-haired from under it. She is unraveling the towel very carefully and slowly when Pawlik catches sight of her. He gasps, blurts out some obscenity, drops his woman and rushes to Nusia to retrieve the painting from her. But she looks him straight in the eye and says that the pretty picture belongs to her mother and she, Nusia, wants to look at it. Pawlik expels another obscenity, seizes the painting and pushes her away.

It is then that the two officers decide to get involved. They scold Pawlik with what seems to be genuine anger at somebody abusing a little child. They also express what seems to be genuine interest in the painting. Weber takes the picture in his hands, unwraps it completely and stares at it with admiration, muttering something which, Adam is sure, means '"beautiful, beautiful". Pawlik demands his picture back. "It is mine! It is mine!" he roars, first in the Realm language and then in his own. His face swells and darkens. His two guests continue looking at the Red-haired, nodding and uttering things which clearly infuriate him more and more. And then the two of them, two officers of the Elite Forces of the IWS Realm, laugh. Their laughter, loud and derisive, aims straight at him, a small-time art trader with a grand vision for the future.

Already enraged, Pawlik turns then into a revenge-thirsty ogre. He unbuttons his shirt, letting his giant belly - a mound of rising bread-dough - pour out; he breathes hard, retches, squats and leaps towards Weber. And then he hits him on the face with all his might. "Swine...dirty Realm swine...this is going to be my show, not yours, and you...all of you swine will never live to see it," he sputters and cries, and punches, and punches again, as hard as he can.

Suddenly he stops, looks blindly in Weber's face, steps back a little and embraces his enormous dough-like belly with both his arms, as if trying to push the mounds of flesh somewhere into the inner cavities of his body. They can all see his belly becoming smudged with red; the red color coming from inside, seeping through his tightly pressed fingers. Then they notice the younger officer put a gun in the leather holster attached to his belt, snap the side of the holster shut, straighten out the belt of his uniform and then spit at Pawlik.

The two officers exit and drive away. The Red-haired, left behind, lies next to the divan. Pawlik lies nearby, groaning, in a puddle of blood. He still holds his hands on the bulge of his belly.

No one approaches him, each riveted to one spot, a few good steps from where the puddle is forming. Radomir and the drivers are called down from the attic; they make motions as if intending to lift him off the floor, but in fact they do nothing. They all stay terrified and impotent, capable of only staring at the horror, from which actually they would want to flee. When the woman at last puts some rags on Pawlik's abdomen and tries to pour water in his mouth, she does so most awkwardly, shaking and crying; and cursing his drinking as well as the Red-haired and the whole lot of them who have brought on the disaster. And Pawlik remains on the floor, bleeding, groaning and slowly losing consciousness.

Mother talks about evil and tries to place Nusia on the divan with her face towards the wall, so that the little bird should not see the sight on the floor. But Nusia asks why Mister Pawlik is not getting up and she refuses to lie down with her face to the wall. Radomir is telling Kocia that he is ready to do anything to help, but she just stares at Pawlik and does not listen. And Adam's experienced ears can clearly hear his sister mumbling to herself that Boleslaw, the man she married, has failed her again, and that if it had not been for his spoiling Nusia with toys like Trabal, the stuffed elephant, Pawlik would have never been shot.

After a while the woman decides to go to town to find a doctor and a priest and asks that mother, Kocia and the rest keep an eye on her poor Mister Pawlik. But shortly after she is gone Konstancya says that they should all leave immediately. Actually it is only after one of the drivers says that they are not in the safest spot now that she regains her power of speech and energy and explains to them that indeed Pawlik's house can be raided at almost any moment now by Realm soldiers or Realm police, and that they will all be questioned, arrested or, most probably, executed on the spot. Then she personally, in the face of mother's disapproval, puts The Red-haired back in the crate from which she took it some twelve hours earlier. And she says that it is time for her to decide where they should go next.

Deciding on their next move does not take her long at all, for she has in her possession a list her husband gave her to be used in case of unforeseen difficulties: the names and addresses of Boleslaw's western contacts arranged in order of presumed reliability. Since at the top of the list happens to be an address in the town of Dobce on the Raba river, Kocia decides that Dobce is where they should go. She also suddenly remembers of having heard of the place before, an exceptionally quaint spot in a mountainous region.

The drivers, however, point out that in order to get to the place they will have to travel upwards of forty kilometers on bad roads, exceptionally poor and dangerous roads, they emphasize; a proposition they did not originally discuss with Konstancya's husband. And since even getting the truck and trailer out of Pawlik's premises and back on the road in a hurry is going to be no picnic, they suggest that some new financial arrangements be discussed. Konstancya becomes terribly angry at the men and answers them that the matter will be discussed only after they reach Dobce and that they should not worry about any financial rewards due them for as long as she is in charge. But since the men seem still not to be satisfied, mother digs out from among Kocia's personal things a pouch containing Boleslaw's miscellaneous valuables. "They are real gold," she says shyly to the men, handing them two pairs of cufflinks, "quite nice and not cheap in fact...", and then to her shocked daughter, "Boleslaw would not use them now anyway, would he?"

Just as their motor truck starts moving slowly out of the enclosure of Pawlik's property, the woman returns. She is alone, out of breath, and sobbing. The doctor she knows was not at home. And another one refused to come. The only priest in town is busy preparing for two funerals that are to take place in the morning. And God knows what will happen to Mister Pawlik now, unless they could take him to some hospital on their truck. When she hears that they are going to Dobce, she brightens, because it is in this very place that Mister Pawlik knows a doctor who runs the local hospital, a really fine gentleman, a true Christian always ready to help another human being. And so, could they consider taking dear Mister Pawlik with them?

Konstancya obviously says "no" to this bold request, but the woman is quite persistant and persuasive. She is sure that the good doctor from Dobce will do his best for Mister Pawlik and that he could also do a good deal for them all, generous that he is, and so influential in the area there. And so Kocia agrees to take him, and mother praises her, saying that she will be rewarded one day in Heaven for this magnanimous deed.

Things on the truck and trailer are moved, crammed further, piled higher. The unconscious Pawlik is at last lifted off the floor and then carried to the motor truck by the drivers and Radomir, all heaving under his weight. He is laid on the truck's floor; and they have now no space to move freely or sit comfortably. Nusia asks whether they are taking Pawlik's dogs with them too; the creatures, which have not stopped barking since the shooting, have made a great impression upon her; she would want to have a dog of her own very much indeed.

Pawlik's woman stays behind. She says she will follow them to Dobce as soon as possible, but for the time being – though she anticipates the worst for herself – she will have to stay, just to gather her thoughts and take care of Mister Pawlik's property for which she is now responsible. She expresses her thanks to them, particularly to Konstancya; yet, some time later when they are already on their way, the drivers divulge the opinion that the woman has been unappreciative, cheap, with no manners whatsoever. They cannot get over the fact that for all the trouble they may encounter in transporting a dying man (with a Realm bullet in him) she did not offer them any material compensation, money or whatsoever; did not even mention it. They are particularly incensed when they remember the piles of valuable goods stored in the house, a very large stock which they had a chance to notice while hiding in the attic. Konstancya shares the drivers' feelings completely and calls the woman a low and vulgar creature.

They found themselves on the road an hour or two after daybreak. Just as they got underway, the first drops of a heavy spring rain fell on them and their possessions on the truck. What they at first thought was but a short-lived spring shower turned into a torrential downpour which accompanied them through the whole journey - from Pawlik's red-brick warehouse all the way south to the foothills of the mountains. The tarpaulin is drawn over their heads and they are enveloped in darkness. They can feel the motor truck move slowly upward; and from the way it reels and sways heavily, they gather that the slippery roads on which they are proceeding are turning to mud. And then the canvas gives way, letting the rain from outside reach them on the truck. They try to maneuver their bodies away from the inpouring water, but to no avail.

And Konstancya is singing! And not just her standard repertory. Here she is treating them to some of those operatic arias delivered by the accursed (usually tuberculous) heroines right before their deaths; Adam cannot believe his ears. And when she stops, letting her dirges only very slowly die out in the air, it is to demand that something be done immediately about the ventilation in the truck as she cannot possibly go on singing in "this unbearable stench of blood". And since nothing can be done, she faints, or at least Radomir says so. It is much too dark for Adam to see what is really happening, but he can hear their cousin crying, " Oh darling Kocia, don't...don't faint, wake up! I am with you..." Soon Nusia cries too. Then mother also says that indeed the odor of Pawlik's blood is terribly strong and she herself feels nauseated, whereupon she faints, or nearly faints. Then comes the worst: to the rhythm of the pounding sway of the moving truck and the throb of the gushing water, Konstancya, suddenly revived, starts telling them the story of her life. Adam has heard her reveal to an audience details of her life before (as she is proud of her knack for telling stories and knows well how to turn a single plot-line into a variety of tales); yet, he does not remember her ever before attempting to bare the events of her entire life and to produce anything of a mood so somber and of particulars so sordid.

It is probably then that Nusia hears for the first time how horribly untimely was her coming into this world. She can hear her mother say that young and innocent creatures should not be allowed to be born in times as horrible as these; and also, that her mother, in her great wisdom, tried not to allow little Nusia to see the light of this world. Choking on her tears, Nusia's mother tells them that she did not succed in having Nusia's prenatal existence terminated only because of some sudden and unexplainable weakness that took hold of her on the day of the appointed visit to the doctor who was to perform the necessary deed. But she still remembers the name and the exact address of the man, she informs them.

Their motor truck labors harder and moves slower by the minute. And then it stops altogether. The drivers say that they cannot go any further, not for a while. The roadway ahead is flooded, they say, and it is only through luck and their know-how that their truck did not get stuck anywhere in the valley, but is atop a hill, safe.

Adam feels cold and numb. Nusia, her body hunched and cramped at his side, shivers and cries for a dry blanket. Konstancya carries on still for a while, but then stops, as if touched by magical force; and so, except for the monotone of the rain, not a sound is heard. Adam then dozes off into a state of no recall and no awareness, and stays so for a good few hours.

When he comes to, it is raining no longer; the canvas is drawn away from above their heads, the sun shines brilliantly, there is motion among the crates, and the drivers' cheerful voices give them instructions how to get off the truck. Then Kocia emits an unearthly shriek. She has discovered that Pawlik is dead.

His body is heavier than before; and even Adam is called upon to help move him off the truck. Konstancya shows them the exact spot where she wants the body deposited, but once they place it there, she does not know what should be done next. She is considering simply pushing the dead man into the drainage ditch at the side of the road, but because of the overflooding of the terrain, she cannot tell where exactly the ditch is; and then she is not sure whether such an action would be viewed by any chance as sacrilegious.

Water surrounds them from all sides, a brown-green sea with thousands of floating branches and stalks, so there is not much that they can do. They spend the rest of that day and the following night on the truck or right near it; Pawlik's body, wrapped in a blanket, on the ground next to the trailer.

The following morning some of the water is gone, but they are told by wailing and lamenting passers-by with bundles on their backs that they will not be able to get anywhere. These people tell them that the Raba river has overflowed and the bridge got damaged and villages flooded, and people and cattle perished. They also say that God must have again turned His face away from them, the occupied nation, even though only three days earlier He was still on their side. It was only three days past, they say, that He let the partisans take one of the Realm's outposts on the Raba and abduct the local chief of the Occupying Police, and hang him from the highest pear-tree in Dobce, just as the son of Satan deserved.

After they walk to the river through a rain-soaked meadow to see the flooding with their own eyes, they know that they will have to wait for the water to subside and the bridge to be repaired. And Kocia tells them that she will be the one to take care of the rationing of their provisions. And while they walk back from the river, she, a woman of a myriad of ideas, says that the sight of the rushing water has inspired her, that is, made her realize that there is a way of disposing of poor Pawlik's body. It is quite a simple way, she explains, actually, a most dignified way, well, in fact a beautiful way.

Before dusk she orders them to wrap Pawlik in several blankets, from top to bottom, tight, and then tie his mummy securely with ropes. And then she tells them to kneel around him and pray for a few minutes in silence; then she orders Nusia to say the *Our Father* loudly and clearly, "for the soul of poor Mister Pawlik, as a good girl should", and afterwards she herself sings one stanza of her favorite,

"Oh, my rosemary open your blossoms." Mother disapproves of the song, since any words with strong patriotic connotations, she says, should be reserved for soldiers, and even then only those struck down by the enemy on a true battlefield. But Konstancya tells her with indignation that Pawlik, once a racketeer and a drunkard, died like a hero; he redeemed himself completely when he so bravely attacked that despicable Realm officer, she says. And she intones her song again.

When all the praying and singing is done, she orders all her four men to lift him and carry him to the river and depose him on the water. And while they struggle with his ever so heavy body, she keeps on telling them that when letting him go, they must aim at the main current, as she hopes that Providence will see to it that the now so powerful Raba river will carry the body north, all the way to the shimmering crystalline blue sea.

"Burying heroes at sea has been practiced for millennia all over the world," she declares.

"Oh, dearest Kocia," whispers to her the somewhat concerned Radomir, "we are quite a long way from the sea, a good five hundred kilometers, I would say."

Still, as she wished, Pawlik was deposed on the debris-filled, khaki-colored Raba and taken by the current. And if it were not for the strength of a willow tree whose branches they managed to clutch, the four of them, his four pallbearers, would have slid down the muddy walls of the river together with the dead man.

A few seconds after its trip to eternity begins, the blanket-wrapped mummy, pushed by some inexplicable force, suddenly stops, turns around and moves sideways towards a dark and muddy inlet; a spot totally inaccessible to them. They stare at the motionless corpse, not saying a word to one another, and Adam regrets that he has not made a mask for the lifeless face now partially visible from under the unravelling blankets. But then a sudden onrush of brown water carrying a huge piece of roofing (with red shingles and a section of a chimney attached to it) hits the blanket-wrapped body, pushes it back towards the center of the river and drives it forward with unusual strength; the unlighted eyes and the awry mouth disappearing from sight.

"What a relief," says Radomir.

"How wonderful," says Kocia when she sees them returning from the mission, "I knew it was the right thing to do."

The Home of the Divine Providence

Saturday evenings are for watching the weekly mystery plays put out by our national TV as The Golden Cobra Mystery Hour, definitely the most popular TV program at the Home. Watching the cobras is strictly voluntary, but I do not think that anybody ever misses them. Tonight we watched a comedy-thriller, received with exceptionally great enthusiasm. The viewers found especially funny those parts of the play in which the two protagonists were suddenly faced with the problem of finding a way to dispose of a dead body; they were forced to hide their corpse in the most unlikely places and then carry it around town, running into all sorts of obstacles. When the two men with the corpse walked into an elevator in an office building and then got stuck between floors, all of the room in which we were gathered started bouncing with ear-splitting laughter, which could not be stopped for the longest time. After the show was over, Brother Boniface told us that if we, the wards, cannot behave with a higher degree of emotional control, we would not be allowed to watch the cobras again.

3.

It was several days before the Raba River subsided and the bridge was repaired; days of magnificent weather and rationed provisions. They lived on what food there was on the truck, except for one loaf of fresh bread and a slab of bacon fat which mother got from a local woman in trade for Nusia's Sunday dress.

During those days mother also gave away things from their stock on the truck with no trading involved: pillows, rags, pots, pans, tools, aspirin tablets, and even her personal down quilt, wonderfully warm; all to alleviate the lot of various flood victims passing their motortruck. She, of course, immediately reproached herself for having deprived Nusia of parts of her rightful inheritance. She also became a little fearful of what her daughter might say to this extravagant generosity.

But it turned out that mother had nothing to worry about; Konstancya was not going to find out about anything. Since her mind was absorbed now in matters far from the mundane, she could not possibly notice disappearing pots, quilts or aspirin tablets. You see, after Pawlik's funeral, she started spending most of her time away from their motor truck; taking the air and meditating. A warm breeze was rapidly drying the whole of sprouting nature, so she could easily venture now afield on ambles and hikes; along the road, along the river, into nearby woods and villages. But she did so despite the warnings of the drivers, despite the Realm military vehicles appearing on the roads again; despite anything that anybody could say against such ventures. Adam wondered about her new boldness, since he knew that she never went anywhere alone. It was Radomir who followed her at all times.

They could all see him come closer to her and take her hand in his; and they all heard them talk and laugh. Then they watched the two of them disappear slowly beneath the horizon, or somewhere behind the trees or in the reeds at the river, as their voices little by little ceased coming to them. And mother and Adam try to calm and restrain crying Nusia who wanted to run after the two of them.

They enter Dobce at midday. The red-roofed town, painted in saffron-yellow and washed in sunlight, is at rest. Or so it appeared. They are neither interrogated nor greeted by anybody; and save some local children who observe their procession with a certain curiosity, nobody seem to be noticing them at all, not even a Realm patrolman on a motorcycle who passes them on the principle thoroughfare.

They ride through the central market square with a bell tower in its middle, and then through cobble-stoned streets with two and three storied balconied houses; and they notice that the houses are not of great height and that some of their roofs are slumping in disrepair. Then they go through the unpaved portion of the town, passing vegetable patches, a pump well, a blacksmith shop and a walled cemetery; and they notice how quiet it was all around. They eventually stop in a small blind street next to the rear gate of the cemetery.

"The spot is good, real quiet," the drivers say. "And they will all think we are a hearse." They grin, and pull the tarpaulin low and tighten it fast, making the objects on the truck and trailer invisible.

But within minutes after they stop, they are approached by a man who most politely inquires if by any chance they would not want to refresh themselves after what he presumes has been a long journey. He introduces himself as the warden of the sacred burial grounds of the town, also in charge of the funereal pavilion, and expresses his hope that they will not mind using the facilities of a mortuary.

"I keep everything sanitary, believe me, even in times like this," he assures them. And I always disinfect the bathing tubs myself after every usage. An herbal bath could be really beneficial to you, madam," he turns to mother, who, he notices, looks greatly fatigued. 'The herbs are my own blend. Wonderful for the laxating of muscles." Mother agrees on a bath without a moment's hesitation.

The warden turns out to be helpful all around; he tells the drivers where to get fresh provisions and he gives them directions to the address on the special list of reliable contacts which Konstancya got from her husband. The Dobce contact is a woman to whom the warden refers as "the doctor's widow", a somewhat haughty lady and quite well-off, he says. And he describes her house as fine, fine indeed.

And so, on this very afternoon, the four of them (mother, Kocia, Nusia and Adam) go calling on the doctor's widow, Boleslaw's business associate, the person at the very top of his list of reliable contacts. She opens the door for them personally, but stands there right in front of them without a motion, a towering figure of a woman, blocking any possible entry into her home. She listens to Konstancya for a while and then interrupts her by saying most arrogantly that she has never in her life met Boleslaw Rytwianski; the name alone sounding completely unfamiliar. She refuses to give them any information whatsoever and remains unmoved by hints of money or other compensation for possible kindness to them. Kocia is speechless. They turn back. But some distance away from her house, the woman calls them back in order to give them "something for the little girl". She hands Nusia half a bar of milk chocolate wrapped in silver foil, and then shuts her door on them for good. The sight and the smell of this unexpected gift overpower Nusia; despite the protests of her mother and grandmother, she devours the whole piece within seconds after she manages to peel off the foil. It was on that day that she became addicted to milk chocolate.

Later the same afternoon Konstancya decides that - poor Mr. Pawlik's absence notwithstanding - they should look for his friend, the kind-hearted doctor from the local hospital, the man praised so highly by Pawlik's woman. But, to their disconcertion, when asked about him, local people tell them that they had never heard of the man. The local folks are certain that no individual of the name and description they give them has ever as much as set foot in town, their town being small and everybody knowing well of what is going on and who is who. Besides, there is no hospital in Dobce or anywhere within a radius of many kilometers, they say, the only hospital in the area having burned to the ground right after the War started.

Konstancya then says that the deceitful woman will one day pay dearly for her lies, as the good Lord will not leave such a crime unpunished; and then she adds that considering the woman's character, no one should be too surprised. The drivers agree with her.

"This is exactly what one should have expected from such a stingy big-buttocked cow, dear lady," they say.

Towards evening of this long day they are invited by the warden of the cemetery to take tea with him. He apologizes for not hosting them in his proper house, but only in what he calls his wartime lair, which turns out to be a not badly refurbished deep, vaulted crypt. Inside the crypt there are a hot coal stove, a big brightly-lit carbide lamp and several rugs spread on the floor. It was an inviting place, Adam recalls, and their host, a slight, bald man, remarkably agile for his apparent age, was most gracious. The food was delectable too; first herring with cream, and then tea and biscuits with cherry confiture on the side. And nobody was anxious to return to the motor truck for the night. Nusia spent most of her time with a stone figure of a weeping angel, kneeling and praying together with him, wiping off his tears, brushing his hair, covering his bare arms with her sweater. She wanted to stay in the crypt forever. She was carried out, after she fell asleep.

The following morning Konstancya, full of fresh energy and resolve, tears up the list of the names given to her by Boleslaw. They are not going to deal anymore with any of his business acquaintances, she says, as there are plenty of other kind of people around, a more respectable sort. They will stay in Dobce, she announces, since this small, pretty and out-of-the-way town is the only type of place where there is still some chance of finding decent people.

But two days later, a good many things of theirs gone (given to various people in exchange for food or advice), they are still on the motor truck; even though they have walked from street to street and house to house for hours on end, within the town and beyond, knocked on doors, asked questions, smiled, begged and often lied. Konstancya even bought from a village woman a triangular black kerchief (the kind that local women would wear to church or on some other special occasion), which she draped around her arms, ready to show herself to the world as a widow; and she tied a little black ribbon to Nusia's hair as well. People will look upon them with greater compassion and greater willingness to help, she says. As her intensions are pure, she is sure that understanding God will forgive her this little deception. But then since she feels that her husband may indeed be dead, is it really a deception, she wonders.

"Oh, Kocia, you look so enchantingly beautiful in black," gasps cousin Radomir.

After two and a half days, their motor truck still in the same spot next to the rear gate of the cemetery, the warden of the cemetery advises them to leave. The local Occupying Police is planning for the pre-dawn hours a series of raids in town, a retaliatory action for the hanging of their chief by the partisans earlier last week, he says. He suggests that they go further south into the mountains to a place he calls the Hidden Vale, a locality taken by the partisans earlier that spring and still held by them. He has a friend there, known in the area as the Apricot Man, a fruit grower and the owner of a spacious house and the largest property in the Vale, a man who is known not to turn down those in need.

The warden also offers to keep in storage for them while they are gone some of their effects. Though all the large crypts are already filled to the brim with household items belonging to various local owners, he says, there is still space available in a few smaller vaulted tombs. He will not charge them anything for the storage, he assures them, but would certainly appreciate a small remuneration, which he would apply towards upkeep of the grounds.

It is then that their drivers say that they may as well leave all their things in the cemetery, since they will not have the motor truck for much longer. The two of them as well as the truck and the trailer have to go back to Wielow, they explain. And since they are already long overdue, they are planning to take off this very night. Of course, the family can go back with them, they say, provided that they leave behind Radomir, the wanted man, and all their things, which have been definitely drawing much too much attention. In general, they also say, they have had more trouble with the whole lot of them than with anybody they have driven before. "We've had more than we bargained for, dear lady, they say to Konstancya, "and frankly, enough is enough!"

"Go then, go! Go right away, you shameless men! The sooner the better! But without my motor truck and my trailer!" Konstancya shouts at them, claiming thus that the vehicle in question is hers. "Have you forgotten that it was my husband who purchased this motor truck and this trailer?!"

In answer to her words, the men produce a bunch of officially stamped papers which claim a different ownership; to which she replies that these documents are fakes which were procured by her husband only for the purpose of getting them all safely out of Wielow. Well, what she says might be true or it might be not, but she obviously has no knowledge whatsoever of the nature of the transaction that Boleslaw made back in Wielow. Not that it matters now one little bit. As long as the men are set on leaving, it is of little consequence knowing who really owns the motor truck or whether it has to go back east right away. And there is absolutely nothing Konstancya can do about this matter, except, of course, try to entice the men with more money.

Money, however, they do not want. "It's just paper, dear lady, paper, and nothing more," says one of them.

"And that paper, lady, is becoming more and more worthless with every minute," says the other.

So, as she brings forth a profusion of tears, mother once again reaches for the magic pouch with things that once belonged to her son-in-law. She says to Konstancya that there is not much left, and her daughter tells her to take out one thing at a time, very deliberately, and give the possible choices a lot of thought. At the end they decide to part with the two most precious things that the pouch contains: a gold chained pocket watch for one of the men and a solid gold cigarette lighter for the other. The men are impressed. They kiss mother's hand and call her the finest lady that has ever lived; and they bow before Konstancya and promise her an additional full twenty-four hours of their time and of their motortruck's services.

Before they start that evening for the Realm-free hidden Vale, Konstancya entrusts the warden with a couple of her trunks and a few pieces of furniture. And the old man accepts her property in an astonishingly professional way. He marks each item with pink chalk and then writes out (in duplicate) a detailed claim ticket, struggling to make every letter legible. And when Konstancya gives him, as a token of her gratitude, Boleslaw's signet ring, the warden immediately writes out a receipt for it (again in duplicate) deeming it payment in full for the storage of her belongings.

They reached the Vale in the dark of the night, and so they were able to see it for the first time only in the morning: clusters of wooden houses and checkered fields girthed with silver cliffs and green ribbons of forests. A pretty sight. And then they found the house of the Apricot Man, indeed finer and statelier than anything around, made of flatly-hewn logs, but large, well -contrived and unsparingly adorned with an intricately carved lace of wooden trim running along the railing of the porches, around the roof line and at the heads of wooden pillars. And the Apricot Man himself appeared tall, sturdy, handsome-looking. He greeted them like a friend and said that they could stay with him; not the slightest sign of surprise or annoyance at their visit.

He leads them to his orchard, stops at the edge of an expanse of land on a small incline with a multitude of trees in neat rows, and makes a broad movement with his arm. They do not understand at first, but he is patient with them; this can be their space, he repeats, all of it, provided that they do no damage to his trees. In rain they can stay on his porch, which is large and has a solid roof. They can also have all to themselves a small outhouse on the edge of the property, but on condition that they take upon themselves the task of proper scrubbing and disinfecting of the place. He also promises them some goat's milk for Nusia at every evening milking. They are dumbfounded and Kocia tells him that his proposition is unacceptable.

She eventually takes his offer, a few hours later, after they find out that all the houses, barns and sheds in the Vale are full, those belonging to the Apricot Man included. The fame of the freed Hidden Vale must have spread far and wide, since everybody they encountered that day appeared to have come from a different part of the Realm-occupied world. But there was no room left for them, not indoors. And the Apricot Man turned out to be the only person willing to give them sufficient outdoor space. Mother calls him a decent man, who, for all he gave them –the orchard, the outhouse and the goat's milk – asks nothing in return. But Kocia says that the man did not give them anything that he had to take from himself. "My, my, he has positively put himself in danger for our sake!" she sneers.

The drivers were as good as their word; they left, just as they had promised, exactly twenty-four hours after they were given the watch and the lighter that once belonged to Adam's brother-in-law. But before the designated hour of their leave-taking, the two helped the family set up their new household among the blossoming trees of the orchard of the Apricot Man, their new benefactor.

The two are willing and efficient. First they take all the things off the truck and trailer; then they remove from the bottom of the truck a few loose planks which they place on the orchard's ground for the heavier items to rest upon and not be in danger of sinking into the soft orchard soil; and then they carry everything, one item at a time, into the orchard, a distance of several hundred steps. They also buy for the family from a local farmer a one-burner iron stove for cooking. And they sell Konstancya one of their old military-style rain capes for covering an item or two of her belongings.

Yet, they did not part on friendly terms. The men refused, and firmly at that, to sell Kocia the tarpaulin they used for covering the truck and trailer. She was willing to pay them almost anything for it; which, in her present position was not much, she admitted; but she appealed to their finer feelings as well, to the graciousness and kindheartedness that they had already displayed. Mother also implored them most urgently to be magnanimous, explaining what their kindness would mean to everyone, especially to little Nusia. But the men remained unyielding. Kocia then, straight to their faces, called them contemptible, and stated that she did not want to have anything to do with them for as long as she lived.

But after the men were gone and she carefully surveyed their new living quarters, Mieczyslawa Konstancya announced, not without satisfaction in her voice, that a good deal of what was taken from Wielow was still with them, and all in good condition: the Bechstein, mother's leather sofa, her own dressing table, the main wardrobe, most of the chairs, crates, boxes, and Nusia's toy chest; certainly more handsome looking now than on the truck, and, obviously more accessible. Nusia too felt that their new home was not without advantages; she discovered on that very first day that the orchard – trees, furniture, crates and all – was an exceptionally suitable place for playing hide-and-seek. She also right away set up her own household with Zuzanna and Marianna.

Unlike Konstancya and Nusia, mother did not feel light-hearted at all. The sight of their household items sprawled so directly upon the lap of Wild Nature made her feel personally insecure and vulnerable. Yet, it was only after her visit to their private outhouse that she plunged into true despair.

It should be explained here that the little privy, which during their stay in the Vale Konstancya would call a stinking latrine and to which mother would always refer as "that place", was, as far as Adam was concerned, an esthetic wonder. It was wrought out of the same type of flatly hewn logs as the house of the Apricot Man, with the same type of intricately carved trim all around, outside and inside, even around the opening leading to the receptacle. It had a carved-out heart in the upper portion of the door, serving as a miniscule window to the outside; and it had a perfectly fitting heart-shaped shutter for closing this little window. It was a smaller version of the main outhouse which was situated right behind the Apricot Man's house. Their little privy differed from the principal one in one respect, though: it did not have a back wall; instead, in the rear it was open to the wide view of distant mountains and forests. And this was by no means an oversight. The Apricot Man explained to them that it was unnecessary to waste good lumber on putting up a fourth wall, since the back of the little house sat on the edge of a steep hill covered with prickly hawthorns and stinging nettles, and so there was really no chance that anyone would want to come up from that direction and disturb the person using the outhouse.

The point is that the quaintness of this little place was quite lost on mother, for she was a person afflicted with the crippling condition of fears directed towards the absence of indoor plumbing, in the same way, Adam believes, that some other people might suffer from the fear of spiders, mice, thunder, lightning or deformed dwarfs. And so, the moment the Apricot Man mentioned the scrubbing of the privy, she trembled; and when she actually saw the place with her own eyes and realized that it did not even possess proper walling, she collapsed.

She is lying now flat on her leather sofa, staring blankly at the sky above, looking withered and drained of all energies. She does not say anything at all, lacking strength enough to even cry. Only from time to time her body lapses into faint spasmodic shivers accompanied by soft whining sounds coming from its innermost part.

It is quite far into the night when she gets up at last. She kisses sleeping Nusia, calling her a poor little homeless bird; and she kisses Adam (something she has not done for a long while), calling him her poor boy who will never find any peroxide for his hair.

"Sleep well, my dearest," she whispers to them all, "and do not worry about me staying up. I know I could not possibly fall asleep tonight... not in a place like this. Maybe tomorrow... though I am not sure that I'll ever, ever again be able to sleep at all."

Radomir is not going to sleep that night either; he has decided to watch over them, as he wants to be absolutely sure that they are safe and undisturbed. He spreads out his bedroll right next to Kocia's couch; he crawls under the covers and turns on his side, facing his beloved.

In the middle of the night mother wakes up Adam; she wants him and Radomir to help her cover the piano with a heavy Persian rug she has unrolled and spread on the ground. She cannot bear the thought that any damage could occur to her magnificent instrument. She also mentions again the tarpaulin which the heartless drivers refused to sell them, and she insists that Radomir and Adam right away start looking for some other protective coverings for Kocia's beautiful furniture. They try to do what she asks of them, but in the darkness they falter, stumble and make very little headway.

When Adam lies down again it is nearly four in the morning; but before the dawn comes he is once more aroused, this time by the singing of a bird, a nightingale, according to mother. The bird carries on in a rather euphonious way; and as Adam has never heard a performance like that one before, he finds himself listening attentively. Nusia, mother and Radomir are listening as well. It is only Kocia who manages to sleep through this whole night till late morning uninterrupted by anything or anybody, not even by Radomir who gets half-way out of his bedding, puts his arms around her and whispers: "Listen, Kocia, a nightingale is singing for us."

The following afternoon mother decides to cook them a meal. She does not recollect having ever seen a stove like the one they have been provided with by their drivers; she is worried about having only one burner; she has no idea what she should use for fuel; and she is not very good at cooking. At Radomir's suggestion they make a foray into the nearby forest for some dry branches and cones, and on Konstancya's insistence thay load two large suitcases and a bag with the wood they manage to gather. No sooner do they emerge from among the trees into the open than they are stopped by a local man with a rifle who informs them that pilfering is a crime, particularly in wartime. He threatens to shoot, ignoring Konstancya's comment that dead wood should be considered public domain. In the end he lets them go unharmed, though with one suitcase full only. As their stove proves to be not easy to handle, mother runs out of wood before the potatoes are quite done and water for tea boiled.

It is during this meal that mother and Kocia once again get into a discourse on altruism and aiding others. While Kocia reduces her feelings to one word: "pigs", which is supposed to describe the humanity around her, mother claims that altruism means doing good to others despite oneself, in which case it is so difficult, nay, impossible, that it should never be expected of anybody. To this Kocia says "bunk", but agrees with mother that no one should count on anybody's good heart; and she swears that, as for her, from now on she is going to steal if she has to, wood or whatever.

Then suddenly mother falls again into a state of collapse. She lies sprawled out on her sofa, eyes upward, lifeless, for the longest time, without a word or motion. And then she tells them that she has just remembered that time shortly before Christmas this past year, when a Hebrite man with a little boy came to their door, and she refused to help him, refused to take his little boy and hide him. She was alone with Nusia and Adam when he came, and maybe that's why she was afraid. The man said that he had no strength to run any further, but that the child should live; he said that if he and his little boy were caught, they would be sent to one of those places where people are disposed of, where it is said that they sometimes make soap out of humans. He did not care anymore if they used him, he said, but what kind of soap could they make out of a thin little boy. Why would they want a little nothing like that, he asked mother and showed her the boy's little arms. She hugged the boy and asked Nusia to hug him too; and Nusia did and gave him one of her dolls to play with; and mother gave him milk and a bag of raisins that were meant for a Christmas cake, and she collected all her Christmas eggs and was going to fry them for the boy's father, and then she heard the door to the quarters next to theirs slam and the woman who lived there talk to someone on the stairs; and then she also heard shouting on the street. Or maybe only thought that she did. All of a sudden she became paralyzed and dumb; dropped the eggs on the floor and with horror waited for the worst. But nothing happened; the sounds from the outside, whatever it was that she heard, were gone. Yet, when she was able to talk again, she said to the boy's father that she could not take his boy, that is, not then, not when all the people in the building were up and about. She told him to come back later, only much later, well after dark, when nobody could see them. But the man and the boy did not show up; and she told Kocia and Boleslaw about them, and they said that the man must have found a safe place somewhere else. But she knew it was not true.

Now in the Vale, Mother lies sprawled on her sofa, flat on her back, sobbing. "What is the punishment for letting another human being perish, Adam?" she asks.

On the morning of their third day mother tells them about the terrifying dreams that tormented her during the night. In one of them Adam was apprehended by some black-clothed men in front of the rear gate to the Dobce cemetery; he was tied up, gagged and draggd across the town all the way down to the Raba river and thrown into the middle of the lethal current. She is suddenly so concerned about his growing hair (with more and more black showing) – even though they are now in a Realm-free locale – that the same morning she makes him a protective hat. She cuts up her own woolen jacket into appropriate pieces and sews them together into an outsize head-covering, with a visor, ear flaps and straps to be tied under the chin; and she asks of him to keep that hat on at all times. He agrees, to please her and because he cannot obtain proper materials for mask-making (everything being so terribly scarce), and thus cannot make for himself a Hebrite mask, or any other face-covering which could protect him from those who might dislike his natural appearance.

In another one of her dreams mother sees little Nusia crying for a piece of milk chocolate, all alone, in a torn dress, pale, emaciated, stranded behind their privy in the jumble of ugly nettles and prickly hawthorns. The dream signifies, she says, that shortly food will be even more scarce and their homeless little bird will be the primary victim of the coming hard times. She suggests that they quickly learn from local peasants all they can about edible grasses, leaves and roots, since these are things, she predicts, on which they will depend for their livelihood.

Konstancya does not place much stock in dreams, that is, not her own dreams; she sneers at mother's gloomy forecasts and calls her "petty" for being concerned about such trivia as food, money or depletion of their possessions. She tells mother to give up immediately her preoccupation with dreams and her anxiety about material things, and instead use her leisure time, of which she now has so much, in pursuit of more worthwhile matters, such as schooling Nusia in music or giving piano recitals for the inhabitants of the Vale. "You should feel privileged, mother," she says, "to be given this opportunity. Just think, your music can actually inspire some of those rather pitiful peasants by whom we are surrounded!"

Mother tells Kocia that she will not play for anybody, and that she likes to be shallow and materialistic, but to this her daughter says that she will personally decide on the offerings of mother's concerts and feels that Romantic masters will be best, with their emotional ballads, nocturnes, exuberant peasant marches and the like. As for so-called every-day material concerns, she will take care of them personally, she assures mother.

And so, as soon as she finishes her preliminary planning of performances she and mother are going to present for the uplifting of the local populace, Mieczyslawa Konstancya is ready to address the practical realities of their new life. She borrows a bicycle from the Apricot Man, wraps her black peasant kerchief around her shoulders, and is ready to take off. She is going to resume her search for a home for them all and to find a paying job for herself, she informs them. Radomir wants to go with her, but she orders him to stay. She tells him to take care of things during her absence, that is, to make sure that Adam, Nusia and mother will not get into trouble.

She is back before sunset, joyful, proud of her accomplishments. First, she was treated to a sumptuous meal by their friend, the warden of the cemetery (in his crypt, of course), and also received from this gentleman a jar of marinated herring as a gift for mother. Then, she bought an old pre-War reading primer for Nusia, as it is time they start thinking of her daughter's formal education. She purchased the book, she explains, at a Dobce apothecary where she went looking again for peroxide for Adam's hair and Valerian drops for mother's nerves; items which, by the way, she was not able to obtain. The only thought on the prospect of finding a new home and employment that she conveys to the family is that she is most optimistic.

Adam does not recollect exactly how long they stayed in the Hidden Vale; five weeks maybe, six, possibly more. All the blossoms fell off the trees in their orchard during that time; and all the trees got covered with green foliage and fruit, but the fruit stayed hard and bitter, not ready to be picked yet. And they did not have the orchard all to themselves for very long. One morning they started sharing it with three sizeable families, whom mother and Kocia found untidy and crude. Within minutes after their arrival these newcomers took over the better part of the slope, their effects and numerous children spilling into what Kocia considered her family's personal domain. We eventually were forced to move our things closer together and then negotiate boundaries; but we never succeeded in keeping these newcomers' children, subsequently called "The Orchard Pack", away from us. Besides the presence of the young Pack, it was also the sight of a large tent that one of the new arrivals brought with them which became a source of great anxiety for mother and Kocia. The two of them ogled the tent continually and speculated in chafed whispers, particularly during nights and cold spells, on the life of those endomed by it; on the warmth and comfort which these strangers were able so selfishly enjoy.

Food was of course the biggest concern, even though Kocia was telling them that it was not. The Vale simply had more people than it could provide for. Nature in this season was not yet able to bring forth the new crop. And there was no place on the outside to go for assistance, for the law of the occupied land ruled that every scrap that man or Nature could produce had to go for the occupying Realm Army, which struck now on two fronts, had to be fed better than ever. The family did not fare well, obviously. Yet, they were not nearly so badly off as one might have surmised from the stories that mother and Kocia would tell in the post-War years. The truth is that they were in possession of so many tradeable goods that their survival for at least a few weeks was assured. (Let it be mentioned, for instance, that a set of Kocia's silver forks and knives brought them a heavy sack of potatoes, and her Empire-style bureau got swapped for nothing less than a large crock of fresh lard!)

The most notable presences in the Vale were the uniformed and rifled men of the forests, the partisans, known as "the boys", sworn-in members of the National Underground Army, who would regularly descend upon the Vale, to contact their liaisons, replenish their supplies, find merriment among the local folks, deposit their wounded and dead in places more befitting than the beds of mountain ravines or forest creeks. They were held in great esteem by the people; they were considered to be mighty, brave, steadfast; worthy of trust and loyalty, and all the food that the Vale could produce, as well as burials in coffins made of the best of the local larch and birch trees.

Already during his first week in the Vale, Radomir approached some of the local partisans; and in another week or so, just as he always wanted, he himself joined the ranks of these forest warriors. Kocia would love to go with him, she says, but can't because of her family she has to take care of when her husband is gone. He feels guilty, asks for forgiveness and mumbles something about one's first duty being towards one's homeland. But, Adam notices, he really sounds like a little boy who is asking to be praised.

As his new duties in the Underground Army do not require that he stay in the forest all the time, for a few days after he said his goodbye, he still spends a good deal of his time in the Vale. To be precise, he-the newly-sworn partisan, uniformed, gallant-looking-while away from his unit, is spending all his time with Kocia, the woman he adores and lusts for. And she too chooses to be only with him during that leisure time that he is given, even forgoing her trips to the outside of the Vale and her daily singing. When she sees him coming out from behind the hills, she rushes to him, her lover - no longer an awkward youth but a man of will and power; and so, in his presence, she renders herself weak and dependent.

They drift together through the Vale, in disregard of the weather or the time of day; and they yield to their desires with no restraint whatsoever. They lie amidst trees, at roadside bushes, behinds barns or in open fields; without hiding or caring whether or not their union, their fevered looks or disarranged garb might be observed by anybody. Adam finds Kocia's behavior pitiful, but he lets her be. Actually, most of the onlookers from the Vale look at her and Radomir with unseeing eyes. The truth is that during wartime and states of temporariness, rules that concern lust and decorum often differ from those in time of peace and stability. The Vale folks have decided that a pretty widow and a boy-hero ready to lay down his life for his country can be allowed to revel in lustfulness for a few days, if that is what they wish to do.

It is only mother who watches them with distress and tries to save them from the power of sin. But Kocia is beyond salvation; neither harsh reproaches nor gentle appeals to her conscience affect her in the least. Her only reply to mother is that Radomir needs all possible encouragement and affection. It is also Nusia who occasionally suffers because of the two. She cannot understand why they, the two people she cares most about, leave her behind, so cruelly disappear from her sight, and not let her be part of the world that they share.

Then one day, just as the local people predict, Radomir gets orders to move on to some more distant places and does not return to them anymore. Mother sheds tears and begs Saint Anthony (her favorite saint) to save Radomir's immortal soul together with his young body exposed to new mortal perils. "He is such a nice boy, but so foolish...," she says to Adam. Kocia looks gloomy for a day or two, but then cheerfully announces that it is time for her to resume her trips to the outside world.

Mother is worried about her now more than ever. She does not look well, she says. And indeed she seems to be growing more slender and worn by each trip, Adam has to admit; but he feels envious of her. Envious of the amount of energy that her body continues to possess.

And then comes still another grief for mother: Nusia becomes a member of the Orchard Pack. There were children everywhere in the Vale, hordes of them, creatures of varied histories of parentage and orphanhood, in all states of health and degrees of lice infestation, and Nusia, who had never known many children in her life, found them irresistible. And those who were not afflicted with illnesses severe enough to be quarantined, were let move unrestrained. Nusia was the smallest in the Pack, and so she usually occupied the rearmost position in this rambling and prowling group, and often had to endure insults and blows from all those bigger than she. Yet, she never let herself fall far behind the others and could never be persuaded to quit. Following the Pack, she would often disappear from sight, sometimes for hours, returning only when the others did so or when the pangs of hunger overcame her; breathless, bruised, soiled beyond recognition. And she never fell prey to any illnesses that most children of the Vale sooner or later would contract; her only complaint was occasional distress caused by extravagant consumption of roots and greens purloined by her during the Pack's forays into the neighborhood gardens.

The Home of the Divine Providence
The food at the Home, which has never been outstanding fare, has terribly worsened as of late, and Brother Klementior, the recently nominated guardian of food and cooking, is without doubt one of the worst culinarians I have known; and yet, today the wards were told by Brother Hyacinth to thank Brother Klementior and congratulate him on his latest achievement, some ghastly pudding consisting of water, potato starch and an artificial sweetener. It was during our after-meal half-an-hour discussion period, when the wards were in the midst of the most involving verbal intercourse, that Hyacinth

interrupted us in mid-sentence by asking all of us to rise, leave the table in an orderly fashion and march to the kitchen. Obviously, the participants of the table discussion were most displeased; yet, we did go to the kitchen, as ordered, and in the words we were told to use, we praised Brother Klementior on his accomplishment.

It should be mentioned here that it was in the Vale that Adam painted his face for the first time. He was always interested in ancient rituals of body painting, as obviously related to those of mask wearing, but it was for the amusement of Nusia and the rest of the Pack that he put on the paint for the first time. He had practically nothing to make masks from those days (except for perishable leaves and brittle cones), nobody willing to spare a scrap of any material; being forbidden, under threat of severe punishment, to appropriate even the smallest quantity of metal or lumber. But paint was not in short supply at all! With nobody objecting, he could either dig it from the local streams and thus obtain the beautiful earth colors of yellow, brown and white; or he could just reach for Nusia's toy chest and retrieve from it a box of watercolors in all hues of the rainbow, hardly touched (a present to Nusia from her father before they left Wielow).

He became quite expert in the art of applying paint; and every time he put on a fresh design on his face, neck or chest, the young crowd would roar in delight. Predictably, mother and Kocia responded to these new endeavors of his negatively. But, knowing how impenetrable their minds could be, Adam did not bother to explain to them the reasons behind his actions.

Mother fell into the dark deep of melancholy on their first day in the Vale, as you might remember, on that first afternoon when they set up their housekeeping amongst the trees of the Apricot Man's orchard and she visited the wall-less outhouse for the first time. During the weeks that followed, as she was not re-inspired by anything to make her see life in brightness again, she only sank further into this frightful state of depression.

As their bodies grow thinner and scraggier and Kocia's remaining belongings – ravaged by birds, insects, the elements and the local children – undergo their own retrogradation, so did mother's mind deteriorates ever so swiftly. She is not able to rest at all, to play her piano or even pray; she only talks of Kocia's shameful conduct, of young partisans going into the world to be brought back dead and of Nusia's body, grime-ridden and scarred. She turns into a fiend for ablutions. She scrubs Nusia with pumice stone and pours steaming water on her; she orders Adam and Konstancya to the stream to bathe and launder their garments there, even on rainy days; and she herself pilgrimages daily to the dreaded fulsome outhouse – a bucket and dirty rags in her hand - to perform there alone her special cleansing rites. It is there inside the little house that one morning the Pack discovers her weeping. They rush to tell Adam that she looks sick and very odd; and when he arrives at the spot he finds her kneeling in front of the opening to the receptacle, with one arm and her head inside the hole, as if intentionally inhaling the fetor rising from the foul pit beneath. Only slowly does he start understanding that she is trying to reach to the very bottom of the pit, to the very inside of the masses of human excrement, to retrieve from it her rosary which, she explains, she tossed away a day earlier in a blasphemous outburst of anger. It takes a solid struggle for Adam and the Pack to remove her from the outhouse and convey her onto the sofa under the fruit trees.

In the days that follow, her rosary irrevocably gone, mother recalls sins of her life, one by one. They are numerous, of the gravest sort, and she remembers them all, from her earliest days. Her greed, that evil aspiration to possess, unnatural love of things of no worth; her idleness and vanity, every hour of her existence wasted on self-gratifying frivolities and vapid thoughts; her disregard for the feelings of others; the horrible neglect of her children's needs; her cowardice, dishonesty, duplicity. She posed in front of the world as one having religion while in fat she had none. She sent her husband to his death by telling him before that fateful duel that his duty as a second was to reconcile the two parties. She killed the little Hebrite boy whom she first gave raisins and then sent off to the streets. She has done only wrong in this world, horrible wrong, which can never be atoned for, no matter how hard she will try, she says. And so, she cannot go on living.

Then Konstancya falls ill too. Adam does not recollect her ever having suffered from any serious bodily affliction, and so he is a little disquieted. She has a high fever and intense aching; and a doctor from a nearby barn tells him that it is due to overexhaustion; and another man (who, according to the locals, only claims to be a physician) says that it looks like a bad case of mumps which she has probably contracted from one of the children from the Orchard Pack. But neither of the men is able to instruct Adam as to how she might be helped. After two days she is still feverish and in pain, lying on mother's sofa, too weak to walk. And mother just stares at her for hours on end, without a word, with only feeble motions of her arms letting the Pack and buzzing orchard insects know that they are a terrible nuisance.

Suddenly Adam knows that it is up to him to save them.

4.

It was after he understood that there was nobody in the Hidden Vale who could come to the rescue of his so gravely ill mother and sister, that Adam decided to seek help on the outside, in the open world which he had not visited in many weeks.

The thought of venturing out on a quest, all on his own, surprisingly, makes him feel energetic and confident in his abilities. Not that he has any idea how he is going to handle the specific tasks ahead of him. The night before his trip he borrows a bicycle from the Apricot Man, who only reluctantly agrees to give it to him, and then for a period not longer than one day. That night he also prepares for himself two packages: a small one containing boiled potatoes and pieces of bread rind to sustain him during his travels, and a larger one holding a pair of his old house slippers and a pair of his old winter boots, as he has heard that any footgear is really sought after and can command a high price at places like, for example, the Dobce market square.

As soon as the sun's first rays start seeping through the orchard leaves, Adam is in front of Konstancya's mirror working on his appearance. First he cuts off his hair and shaves his head clean. Then he paints his face. He uses mostly blue, yellow and black; on his cheeks he draws two triangles converging at the base of his nose; he encircles his mouth and eyes with broad curved lines, and on his forehead he places a pattern of small arrows and circles. His face finished, he places a garland on his head, a rather elaborate creation of leaves and feathers, which he wove together the night before. It is only when he is ready for his journey that he realizes – at the last look in the mirror – that he has just recreated from memory, quite unconsciously, a face from a picture he used to have in his collection in Wielow: the image of a young tribesman dressed for a courting party. He is angry at himself, embarrassed even, about the inappropriateness of his makeup, but since he is pressed for time, he decides not to change anything.

At this moment he notices Nusia staring at him. She is not saying anything, but her eyes sparkle and her nostrils twirl and her hands clap silently, which means that she loves Adam's new face. That very second he decides that he is taking her with him. He paints a quick design on her face too and makes her a small garland out of a few twigs from a nearby apple tree. At the time when the two of them leave, mother, Konstancya and the rest of the orchard are asleep.

In order to find their way out of the Vale they have to stop several times as Adam has to ask for directions; and more than once they have to turn back and retrace their steps. Several times they are held up by partisans patrolling the routes to the Vale, as they want to know who the two of them are and what they are up to. Also, Adam has to push the bicycle uphill, help Nusia climb and also carry his two packages and Nusia's two dolls. So, when they eventually reach the other side of the mountains and are able to see the road leading straight down to the town of Dobce, they cheer loudly.

It is an unpaved road which looks wide and straight, sloping gently downward towards the yellow-hued town in the valley. It has the dark border of a spruce forest running along its one side and a view of open fields along the other. It also has a small path running along the side of the fields on which Adam can see walking figures of kerchiefed peasant women with bundles on their backs. He decides then to take the very center of the main thoroughfare, which, judging from the presence of a variety of wheel tracks on it, is meant for vehicles. He attaches the two packages and Nusia's two dolls to the metal rack behind the bicycle's seat, and then he wraps his coat around the crossbar to make it ready for Nusia to sit on it. Only after she is comfortably positioned on the bar, he himself mounts the seat. Once astride the saddle, he takes in the whole view with delight and inhales the lovely pungent aromas arising from among the spruce trees.

He tries to start slowly, but it is quite beyond his powers to resist a whirlwind that within seconds pulls him and his bicycle upward and onward, with the speed of a swallow carrying them to their destination. They dash forward, and Adam does not pedal, steer or feel the ground; he ceases seeing the fields, trees and the peasant women; he can only feel the wind enfolding his body and smell the air intoxicating his brain. Their velocity increases, they become lighter, Adam and Nusia raise their arms and they sing; for a few moments they are most gloriously airborne.

Their trip in the clouds comes to an end, however; most suddenly, with an abrupt thump and smart, amidst terrifying shrieks and the stamping of a thousand feet. They find themselves lying in the middle of the road, all covered with dust, among a scared and hurried herd of goats, with their bicycle and their garlands sadly cast off a few steps away from them. A fat peasant woman, waving her fist and a stick over their heads, is yelling into their ears that she is going to find a way of dealing with Satan's seed like them, and that if a single goat of hers wanders into the woods and gets lost, she will skin them alive.

Before the two of them have time to rise and offer to help her in retrieving the herd, they are hit again; this time by a Realm military jeep which unexpectedly bolts out of the woods. It turns into the road with fury, roaring wildly and raising clouds of dust; and after it runs them over, does not stop for even a split second. It leaves them dismayed and badly bruised, their bicycle damaged beyond repair, one of the goats dead and the peasant woman seated on the ground in a state of deep shock. When after a while the goat owner rises to her feet, she is still in a trance. Without a word, and without a glance at the dead animal or the live ones dispersing in all directions, she starts slowly walking ahead; and her face seems to be completely vacuous. And Adam wonders whether the blow of a military jeep has deprived the woman of her wits for good.

As Nusia and Adam cautiously get up and straighten themselves, there appears on the road a motorcycle with a black sidecar
attached to it. The motorcycle passes them slowly and the man on
it looks with some interest at them, at their battered bicycle and
at the corpse of the goat. He rides on. Then a little further down
the road he stops, hesitates, and then turns around and approaches
them again. "I am on my way to town. Want to climb in and come
along?" he says to them. And Adam accepts his offer without the
slightest wavering.

The man does not talk much to them, except to ask unaffectedly
if they are itinerant artists going to perform at the Dobce fair which
is taking place this very day. Adam tells him that they are not, but
that under the circumstances, giving a performance may not be a
bad idea at all; and he explains that in his youth, before he joined
the National Theatre in Wielow, he often acted in skits at country
fairs. And he starts thinking what he could do now in front of the
Dobce audience after all these years of not having performed in
public. The man remarks then that before he tries to perform, he
should obtain a permit from the occupying authorities of Dobce
allowing him to do same. 'They seem to be pretty damn strict
about such things,'" he says. "And keep also in mind that now in
wartime, fairs, country or any other kind, are quite different from
those you might remember from pre-War days." These are his very
last words he says to either of them.

They stop in the middle of the market square, where already
hundreds of people have gathered. Adam and Nusia climb out
of the sidecar and look around; and the man and his motorcycle

just disappear from their sight, leaving them no time to thank him or say goodbye to him. It happens to be the day of the yearly spring fair at the Dolce market square and they are immediately swallowed by the dense crowd of humans and animals, and Adam starts thinking of how he could possibly exchange his boots and slippers either for cash or some other negotiable item. He is also considering the possibility of trading Nusia's dolls (both, like his shoes, luckily retrieved from the accident on the road). He can tell that the scene is dominated by kerchiefed huckstresses crouching over their goods heaped upon carts, wheelbarrows or directly on the ground; and so he tries to decide which of the haggling women he should approach and how exactly he should initiate the transaction. They move in the throng slowly and with effort, pressed upon from different directions, shoved, pushed about. Several times Adam tries to get closer to a stand with goods and a huckstress behind them ready to explain his business, but each time somebody moves in front of him, blocking his vision and squelching the sounds of his voice.

They are both aching and horribly tired; and Nusia asks to go to a place where she could sit. Adam wants to rest too, finding the thoughts of his business plans, jambed by the noisiness and stench of the market, more and more difficult to handle in an orderly fashion. Then, as if some good fairy came to their rescue, they notice in a far-off corner of the market square a pink caravan and a merry-go-round right next to it. They push through the crowd and within short minutes find themselves at a site almost completely mob-free, where they can see right in front of their eyes flying swans and winged horses hopping and whirling around to the tune of an old waltz. Nusia claps her hands, says that she is not tired anymore and would like to ride a pink swan. Adam tells her that they will have to postpone any carouselling till later, and suggest that they rest first, sit on a bench near the pink caravan's door and watch the merry-go-round from there. Nusia agrees.

But their plans go awry, before they even have a chance to reach the bench. They are intercepted on their way to the caravan by some strong – muscled individuals, who rapidly and violently immobilize them and then remove them from the fair. Adam has not the slightest notion who their assailants are and what they might possibly want of them.

We are asked again and again who we are and what we have been doing at the fair; and since his brain feels muddled and his senses blunted, he stays silent. Then a vision of the trembling Nusia and the black silhouette of a man next to her comes into focus in front of his eyes, and suddenly he knows where he is. The room they are in looks exactly like what Adam has been told the interrogating rooms of the Special Occupying Police always look - windowless, with bright electric lights and walls adorned only with the familiar portrait of the Supreme Leader of the Realm and the large-size black emblem of the Realm painted on a stretched-out canvas. Nusia is sitting on a stool with her hands tied behind her back and her feet tied to the legs of the stool; and the man next to her, dressed in the black uniform of a functionary of the Realm Occupying Police, is busy watching her. Adam's hands are also tied behind him, and he is being questioned by another man in black who is sitting behind a desk. There are also in the room a female stenographer in a uniform and a civilian interpreter with a mouthful of gold teeth.

The moment he realizes where he is, Adam quickly explains that though he is an actor, he was not performing at the fair, and that under no circumstances would he have done so without an official permit from the occupying authorities, and also that at the time he was detained he was actually on his way to the caravan to inquire about possibility of obtaining such a permit. But, he notices, his interrogator shows little interest in the matter of a permit. Instead, he keeps asking him about his relationship with an individual called the Whip.

"The Whip ...your friend the Whip... What can you tell us about your friend the Whip?!" The gold-toothed interpreter shouts in Adam's ear.

When he just shakes his head in confusion, not being able to answer any of the questions, he is told that it is known to the occupying authorities that the individual commonly known as the Whip, a notorious criminal, has been in the area recently, and moreover, was actually spotted and identified as a man on a motorcycle with a black sidecar riding into the market square not more than an hour ago.

"And he was not alone, was he?" grins the interpreter. "He had two people in his side car, the two pretending to be clowns, a big clown and a very small clown," the interpreter bursts into laughter.

Adam has heard of the Whip before, and so has, he presumes, everybody else in his part of the world; but when he thinks now of the man on the motorcycle who gave them a ride into the town, ordinary-looking, matter-of-fact, he cannot imagine him and the Whip - Whip the Bold, Whip the Valiant, Whip the Martyr - being one and the same. Nobody knew what the Whip looked like or what his real name was, but they all knew that it was he who had more luck than anybody else at blowing up bridges that carried Realm tanks or at sabotaging factories that made Realm ammunition or at planting bombs at cafes attended by Realm officers. It was also he who, after being caught and tortured beyond human endurance, was capable of escaping from the most impenetrable prisons, through chimneys, sewers or cracks in a wall. The Whip was one of the most revered leaders of the Underground Army, for whose continual success the people of the country prayed and on whose behalf the churches performed secret masses devoted to Saint Kunegunda, the patroness of fires, explosives and desperate escapes. How Adam's life could have so suddenly become linked to that of the Whip seems incomprehensible. But, strangely, all of a sudden he feels almost pleased, nay, exhilarated; even though in the past he always thought of the Whip's actions with horror.

His examiner informs him from behind his desk (through the gold-toothed interpreter) that the Special Occupying Police, firmly set on apprehending the criminal, had their men follow him today and learned all about his moves. "But just as they are ready to seize him, he gets away by disappearing - you could say by dissolving into thin air - after entering the door to the pink caravan!" the interpreter honks in Adam's ear. "Curious finding you in front of the same door a few minutes later, very curious!"

Then Adam is told that the Whip will be apprehended and brought to justice, no cheap tricks of his being of use to him; yet, even though this dangerous criminal is already as good as dead, prisoners like Adam are obligated to cooperate with the occupying authorities. "For your sake and the sake of your little girl!" The examiner and the interpreter shout together.

When Adam says that he cannot possibly cooperate, the man rises from behind his desk and walks straight to him, stopping about one-step distance away from him. Then he asks him again how much he knows about the Whip, the local Resistance and the pink-painted caravan. And when Adam repeats that he knows nothing, he hits him on his face with the open palm of his hand. He hits four times, each blow stronger than the one before; and then he steps back and looks at his palm, to which now adheres some paint from Adam's face. He looks at his palm with disgust, takes out a handkerchief from his pocket and furiously wipes both his hands. And while he is doing so, he talks to the others, but of that the interpreter conveys to Adam only that there is a lot of stinking dirt on him. And when Adam hears that last remark, he cannot help retorting immediately (and with a considerable amount of anger too) that the substance on his face is not dirt but paint; and that what they all can see on his face happens to be an excellent copy of what is worn by young sexually ripe men of the islands of Oceania, where said males, in accordance with ancient rites, try to woo their chosen females by making their masculine bodies more enticing through elaborate application of paint to their skin.

His interrogator demands a detailed translation of this statement, and as it is presented to him, he again takes a position behind the desk and commences asking questions, this time, however, only referring directly to what Adam is saying. So encouraged, Adam continues talking. And when he realizes how profoundly ignorant his interrogator is and also how curious and bewildered all the others in the room are, he cannot withstand the temptation to really show his knowledge to this ignorant and coarse group. So, right there, in an interrogating room of the Realm Occupying Police, he, Adam Czulartian, a prisoner, his hands tied behind him, delivers a lecture addressed to them, his captors, for the sake of their enlightenment.

He talks to them at length; on the customs of the so-called savages, on tribal art of body painting and on sexual observances of places they have never heard of. And they all listen. When he finishes, his black-clad examiner gets up from behind his desk, moves in his direction again, and, like before, stops just a few centimeters shy of his person. This time he does not strike, only glares wrathfully at him and says that he deeply dislikes people who try to make a fool out of him. Then he announces that the prisoners will be given twenty-four hours to think and to remember; hours which will definitely be their final on this earth if Adam decides by any chance not to cooperate.

They are then removed from the interrogation room and placed in a house of detention. As the town jail has been recently blown up by the partisans, they are deposited in quarters temporarily set up in the basement of the building once belonging to the Dobce grammar school; the school insignia still in place over the arched entrance. The place is overcrowded, and so they are put in a narrow corridor among remnants of some gymnastic equipment. They are ordered to sit on the floor with their backs against the old soil pipes; then, after a chain is fastened around their waists and feet, they are chained to the pipes and finally they are chained together.

After their jailers leave them, Adam tells Nusia that as soon as they are free, he will make her a set of swan wings, just like the ones she saw on the merry-go-round, and also that he will look for her dolls that were taken from her by the men in black. She is very quiet; only after a while she asks whether she could have her dolls back right away and have something to eat and drink; and when he tells her that there is nothing to be had, she asks for just one small piece of milk chocolate wrapped in silver foil. And when he says that chocolate is not available either, she sobs a little bit. Otherwise, she seems to accept her lot with not much protest.

The Home of the Divine Providence

Last night when we were watching the evening TV news broadcast, all of a sudden Lech, one of the wards, stood up and announced in the most defiant manner that he was fed up with listening to the drivel that passes for news on our national TV; and then he said that he was also sick of the ways things are run at the Home; and do we know, for instance, that Brother Simplicius, the head guardian, gives parties in his office at which the brothers and invited governors gorge themselves on succulent pork tenderloin, hare pate, poppy seed cake and the finest wine. Then Lech climbed on a chair and shouted, "And you, wards of The Home of Divine Providence, when did you last taste poppy seed cake or some decent pork? And you!" He turned specifically to me. "When did you have your last cup of cocoa?" Those were the very last words that Lech spoke, since he was carried out of the room. He was resisting, but the brothers presented a force too formidable. As far as we know, he was carried up to the attic, which is the usual place where one is carried after some exceptionally drastic incident of rule-breaking. However, considering that Lech's outburst went beyond any rule-breaking that we have known to date, it is possible that he was taken to some place we have not yet heard of.

Here they are, chained, on a wet, littered floor, immersed in darkness, hungry, with a death sentence hanging over their heads, but Adam feels little discomfort, confusion or even fear. He is wondering whether the man who gave them a ride to the fair indeed was the Whip, and if so, will he be ever able to recognize him and will one ever find out who he was before the War started, and also how he ever got to be called The Whip. He also realizes that this is his very first time in prison and he is not a bit frightened, while on so many occasions in the past, when at large and with no imminent danger nearby, he was scared out of his wits. Amazingly, this night he is capable of perceiving things clearly and is even trying to devise scenarios for their escape.

Suddenly, he sees two figures with flashlights emerging from the dark of the interior of the prison, both walking in their direction.

One of the men, who carries a machine pistol in his hand, takes a position a couple of meters away from them, while the other comes very close. He kneels on the floor right next to Adam and intently stares in his face; and Adam recognizes him as the gold-toothed man who served as the interpreter at the interrogation earlier that day.

He tells Adam that his extraordinary poetic gift and so much knowledge of the world that he showed in his lecture made a deep impression upon him, a humble servant of the Realm. Adam must be a Povolian, he says, judging both from his Eastern accent and the fact that only someone of Povolian blood could be a true poet and a sage at the same time. "You are my brother...Povolian...like me," he confesses in a harsh whisper, his face directly next to Adam's, his eyes glowing, his mouth reeking of alcohol and partly digested food. Adam feels faint, but as his mind is clear and full of deceit that night, he says that he indeed is the son of a Povolian mother; and as proof of his roots recites an ancient prayer in Povolian (which he learned during his theater days for a part he played). He also tells the man that Nusia, his temporary ward, is the child of a leader of the Povolian Freedom Fighters, and he whispers into his ear the name of one of the most dreaded Povolian chieftains known in wartime Wielow.

Adam feels proud of himself, particularly when the man pats him appreciatively on his shoulder and orders his subordinate, the man with a pistol, to unchain them. Then he tells them to rise and follow him in silence. He leads them out of the prison into the old school courtyard, and from there through a sloping cobblestone passageway into a narrow and winding street where he stops in front of a wooden house.

Inside the house he lights a carbide lamp and motions them to follow him to his place upstairs; then he invites them in and orders the man with the machine pistol to stay outside at the head of the stairs. Once inside his quarters he takes a few gulps of a drink directly from a bottle which he takes out from his pocket. Then he places the bottle and the lamp on a table and quickly dives under it. From underneath he pulls out what looks like an assembly of tin canisters and cans of various sizes; and Adam cannot in the least fathom what he is up to.

He talks for a while with the purpose of impressing his guest. He actually has quite a bit of power in the Occupying Police, he says, has everybody's confidence; but no matter how important he may become, he will never forget his life's mission of bringing about free Povolia. Then he asks for Adam's assistance. Yet, when Adam asks what he might do for their motherland of the future, he says that there is no time for gabbing. And when Adam asks if he and Nusia could by any chance consider themselves free, the man gets angry and tells him to make sure that the child does not interfere with their work.

Briskly he leads Adam from the first room, some kind of a kitchen, into another room, which looks more like a parlor, and says that this is where there is going to be a party if Adam does his job right; and then points to a bolted door at the other end of the room. He anxiously rubs his hands, and orders Adam to look through a shutter in the bolted door. Adam peers inside, struggles to discern things in the dimly-lit space and realizes after a while that he is viewing three naked female figures, huddled together on a mattress on the floor.

The gold-toothed man says gasping with anxiety and hunger that these are wonderful women, some of the best in the district, as he - an important official of the Special Occupying Police - always has his pick. His eyes glare, his voice pierces the depth of Adam's ears, and Adam begins to understand that he wants to be painted. Not just on his face, but all over. He wants his body to become firm and alluring, capable of exciting love; his arms and his thighs to achieve the power of mighty steel and his member to become so swollen with lust and so unyielding in its hardness that it could drive any woman out of her mind. He bursts into tears; he has not been able to have a woman in months because his body is no longer vital, and women cannot take into themselves bodies which are not vital, even though he always tries his luck with the best of females.

He drinks again, this time from a bigger bottle which he takes from a cupboard. After he heard Adam talk about body painting and those naked men of the islands, he knew that Adam was the one who could help him. They are back in the kitchen and he points to the cans and canisters arrayed on the table, "The best of oil paint from our local warehouses," he says proudly. "And now look at those brushes!" From under the table he retrieves several large flatly shaped brushes, probably intended for wall painting. Then he starts undressing.

At this moment another deceitful stratagem comes into Adam's head. He tells the love-starved man that the courtship dance is not performed singly, but in groups, since it is the movement of a group that will inevitably produce might in men and the sexual thirst in women watching them; and so he suggests that he call his man from the stairway to participate in the rite. The Povolian not only agrees, but also insists that Adam joins in; and he offers him a drink from his bottle. When his underling, the man with the machine pistol, hesitates about taking his clothes off, the Povolian strikes him on the face and orders him to strip and to drink the contents of the bottle to the very bottom.

They are all three stark naked; also pallid and lusterless; and Adam starts creating on their bodies brightly-colored patterns of stars, waves, circles and triangles. And as he does so, he tells the Povolian that they are acquiring the most powerful bodily adornments known to men. But when his job is finished, the man barks in dissatisfaction, asking why there is no green on his member; bright, shiny green. Since Adam does not have the required shade in any canisters, he rapidly makes a new concoction of blue and yellow; and while he is preparing the mixture, the man goes into a rage with impatience. Violently he presses the base of his penis and screams in a feverishly wild cadence, "Make the cock green! Make it green! Make it green!" When at last Adam is ready, the man yanks the canister and the brush out of his hands, and himself does the job of applying the new color to his member. And Adam sees the green flesh under the brush expand and stiffen, and hears the Povolian give out a triumphant yell and he drops the canister and the brush, rushes from the kitchen to the parlor straight for the bolted door, unbolts it and runs into the little room behind it, greeted by the terrified screams of the women inside.

When his underling, who once carried the pistol, realizes what has happened, he too puts a generous quantity of green on himself and he too rushes into the room behind the door with a bolt; and the cries coming from that little chamber become louder. As the door is now open, Adam is able to look right into this place of gleefulness and howling; the two men chase the women around, trying to pour the remnants of the green paint on their breasts and legs.

It is only after some minutes that Adam becomes aware of Nusia's presence in the parlor. He had told her to make herself comfortable under the kitchen table, but he does not know whether she was there all the time or not. Anyway, here she is, next to him, together with him staring at the mattress on the floor and the five naked figures on it, all gasping and screaming, in motion, oddly and fancifully entangled with one another. The group on the mattress is oblivious to their presence, and so Adam decides that this is his and Nusia's chance to flee. The gold-toothed Povolian will never give them their freedom, will just dispose of them when sobered, Adam is certain. So, just as he is, without putting his clothes back on, fearing that he has already lost some precious time, he lifts Nusia off the floor, and holding her tight, rushes out of the place. He runs down the wooden stairs and on to the dark and completely quiet street.

He runs, on and on, blindly, breathlessly, fearing the moment when his heart and lungs will stop supporting his legs. Through the maze of the town's streets and yards which he cannot recognize, he races for safety, even though he does not know either his route or his destination. And when he remembers that it is already hours past the time the curfew bell rang, he accelerates his speed. Then he hears a loud popping noise, shots maybe, and he notices two Realm military motorcycles coming out from the dark at the other end of a square he has just entered. He is sure that the military patrol saw him, and so he turns back and tries to run faster. He races now through a narrow alley, then through some wider open space, and then suddenly he sees a tall, shadow-covered bulwark rising from the ground blocking his further flight. He stares in despair at the forbidding shadow, and then, with relief, recognizes it as the wall of the Dobce cemetery. But as he starts running along its side hoping to reach the well-familiar rear gate and knows that he is not far from it, the sound of the military motorcycles, closer than before, stops him again. He freezes, and then with all the strength he can muster throws Nusia over the wall; and then he himself climbs to the other side.

They lie on the ground motionless and silent, and Adam becomes unfeeling for a while. He wakes up and tries to stir Nusia too, but she does not respond; and he is caught in the grip of a terror, as he believes that the fall from the height of the wall has killed her. He hits his body against the ground, over and over again, with all the strength and violence in him; he tries to tear and bruise his skin and to deform his limbs; and he howls in wrath and despair.

It was their old friend, the warden of the cemetery, the man in charge of the funereal pavillion, who brought them back to life. He went to a great deal of trouble for them, scrubbing and bathing them, rubbing their bodies with spirits of turpentine and oils, dressing their wounds, feeding them and clothing them. He was compassionate, patient and wise beyond the usual measure of human virtues.

Adam watches him move around the tiled room he calls his laboratory and asks him whether by any chance they are not callously purloining what duly belong to the dead , and not the living; the usage of the deep stone tub in which their bodies have been bathed, and all the oils, scents and clothing which they are now wearing. And the warden simply answers that they should not trouble their consciences about the matter, since within the confines of this hallowed place entrusted to his care there is an abundance of things of all sorts: fine garments, fresh linen, soaps, oils, perfumes; baskets, boxes, coffers, shelves, drawers, all full to bursting. Regardless of circumstances, even at times of the great personal deprivation, the warden clearly explains, people always give most lavishly to God, and to the dead, probably in the hope of ridding themselves of the burden of the multitude of sins they constantly commit. And when Adam is contemplating this amazing phenomenon, the old man hands him a small crystal bottle, almost full, and asks him to take it as a present for his mother. He says that the perfume in it, exceptionally fine, belonged to a lady who recently had her sister buried in the Dobce cemetery. The lady had had the flask for years, but never opened it as she considered it so precious as to be used only on the most special occasions. Yet, after her sister died, she gave the perfume to the warden asking him to use it on her dead sibling, as - she apparently admitted this without blush - she had always treated the deceased in a rude and unfair way, and felt that her sister wanted to possess such a perfume but was too poor to afford anything that extravagant.

The Home of the Divine Providence

A few days ago after breakfast I casually remarked that there exists an extraordinary number and variety of sexual stimuli never even hinted at in literature. At first my words were received with silence and embarrassed looks, but after a few minutes various wards started, haltingly at first, recalling incidents from their lives as illustrations of my point. Well, the dining-table discussion on sex has been going on for several days now, with no end in sight; purely personal descriptions giving way to more general, abstract argumentations. And tonight Brother Hyacinth when bringing me my cocoa (my first cup in more than two weeks) said that he was delighted that I had managed so successfully to divert the wards' unhealthy, nay, destructive, thoughts with which they had been preoccupied recently, towards some infinitely more relaxing area of mental exercise. When I asked him what he meant by unhealthy thoughts, he mentioned the obsession about food or paranoid views on the brothers' lifestyle, and added that Lech was particularly delusional.

They stayed in the cemetery for a few days, got back their strength, felt sated, rested and thoroughly content. And as soon as they were able to move about without much difficulty, the warden allowed them to assist him in the cleaning of his laboratory, in trimming coffins before burial ceremonies and in planting of begonias and red sage, chores that they enjoyed a great deal. And before they left, he gave them a large bagful of victuals and medicinal preparations to take back with them to the Vale.

It is a hay wagon (belonging to one of the warden's friends) that drops them on the road leading from Dobce to the Hidden Vale, the same road on which they started their quest a few days earlier. This time they are going in the other direction, of course, on foot, following the small beaten path along the side of the road rather than taking the center of the thoroughfare. Adam finds the walking a bit strenuous, especially because of the heavy bag he is carrying, but he is telling himself to proceed carefully and prudently and feels relieved that now he is in possession of a map and a set of instructions of what to do and what not to do while walking along country roadways.

They have been on the road for just a few minutes when a large wagon appears within their sight. It is pulled by two horses, and it has two people on the front seat: a man holding the reins and a kerchiefed woman. According to the instructions given to Adam by the warden, when passing a peasant's wain one is supposed to nod one's head politely in the direction of the wain and say: "God let you prosper" (without trying to make eye contact or to start a conversation). So, at the sight of the wagon Adam does exactly what is deemed appropriate, and then hears, "And He will see to it,", which is the expected reply to his greeting. But then, surprisingly, the wagon, rather than simply passing them, stops; the woman jumps off her seat and, approaching them quickly, motions to them to stay in place. They do so, and she stares at Adam, scrutinizing him from top to bottom for a minute or two, and then she exclaims, "Why! That's Adam!"

It is only when he looks straight in her face for the first time that he realizes that she is somebody he knows: wide toothy grin, wide-spaced eyes, disc-like cheekbones: mother's first cousin Adela, in her day one of the most notorious women in Wielow. He is bewildered, does not know what to say, except, "Adela?! Here in the mountains?!"

The woman bursts out laughing and with no explanation introduces her companion to the stunned Adam, "Adam, this is Farmer Burak," and then him to Farmer Burak, "Burak, this is Adam," and then she adds, "Mister Burak, you would never believe it, but Adam here is the most eccentric creature that ever lived."

Burak, who does not seem to be the least bit surprised by anything that is going on, asks matter-of-factly what the word "eccentric" means, but she tells him that she will explain it later. For the time being she is only interested in hearing what Adam has to say.

"Whatever happened to your priceless hair? You are not recognizable, except for your nose, of course! Burak, have you ever seen such a nose?" She roars with laughter. "And who on earth is this?!" she asks sighting Nusia for a few seconds. The way she poses the question implies that she does not believe that Adam could be the father of Nusia, or any other children for that matter. "Has the War been kind to you all?"

An hour or so passes, and Adela, whom Adam has not seen in some seven or eight years, asks him every possible question, interrupts a number of times, demands explanations, chuckles and laughs out loud, particularly when hearing about mother's travails with the wall-less outhouse and orchard's insects. Anyway, after she hears all she wants to hear, she turns to Burak, "Well, Mister Burak, as you see, they will have to move in with us."

"As you say, Miss Adela," he nods.

5.

Adela, whom they so unexpectedly encountered when walking back to the Hidden Vale, was a daughter of Waclaw Milewski, Adam's great-uncle, the brother of Alfons Milewski and his partner in the hatting business in the pre-War days. She was the only person mother ever considered a friend, Adam felt, and definitely the only one of whom she was genuinely envious.

Adela had a man-sized stature, exceptionally good brains, a sharp tongue and a gift for generating trouble, and so, since her earliest years, she was the object of great worry for her family, Adam was always told. No wonder then that when upon finishing her schooling she got engaged to be married, everyone concerned about her became relieved; particularly that her husband-to-be, a silversmith named Gruber many years her senior, was a man of quality who owned a mind-numbing silver shop and two buildings on the Square of the Blessed Virgin. Destiny had it, however, that Adela was not to marry; just after her trousseau was ready to be sent to her fiance's home, she told the family that she was giving up Gruber in order to enter a university and the world of scholarly endeavors. With that announcement she made history; she became the first woman in the family who had ever expressed the wish to enter an institution of higher learning That Adela's parents eventually gave her their blessing, was probably because Gruber behaved in the most gentlemanly manner about the whole unfortunate affair; he even married Adela's sister Anna a few months later and remained close to them all for the rest of his life.

After a few years at the University, Adela lost interest in academia. She moved to the grimiest and gloomiest section of the city, called the Puddles, a place reputed for sin, crime and an astonishing number of undernourished children; she took a job there as a schoolteacher, settled in a room above an iron shop, and then took a lover. This new man in her life, a Povolian and an ex-wrestling champion, was often described by mother as a romantic and a rebel, Adam remembers well. It was he who inspired Adela to acts of which she had never dreamed before. And mother, in those days terribly down-hearted in her newly-acquired widowhood, would venture to the dreaded Puddles regularly just to be able to talk to her cousin, for in mother's eyes Adela was a fortress of spiritual stoutness and the most daring creature on earth.

It was on the day that the world saw Adela's picture in the paper that the Milewskis forbade mother to visit the Puddles again. Apparently the picture showed Adela, and her Povolian lover, on some kind of a rostrum, addressing a cheering and unruly-looking crowd. A neighbor who showed the picture to the Milewskis described it as a city scum rallying against decent citizens.

Adam does not remember the details now, but knows that even after that famed picture had appeared, Adela continued showing herself with her lover in public places, rallying, laughing into megaphones and getting into rows with public officials. And when mother would say that Adela usually rallies for just causes, she would be told by the family that no matter how worthy a cause, making a vulgar public display of oneself was inexcusable. Adam also knows that a few years later Adela's lover died (having succumbed to the pulmonary illness so many of the Puddles' poor would contract), that mother started visiting the Puddles again and that Waclaw Milewski was ready to forgive his daughter her transgressions, but never did so, as Adela embarked upon another horrible caper.

Taking everybody by surprise, she expressed her intention to run for a seat in the National Diet, declaring herself to be an Independent, intent on bringing to the attention of the Capital the plight of all underdogs, the Povolians in particular. And her picture started appearing all over the place, and more than one caption called her a menace to national stability. The family felt martyrized and humiliated, finding it particularly painful to show themselves in front of the congregation of the Bernardine Church and to look the venerable Canon Banasz, their confessor, straight in the face.

The worst came very early one Sunday morning when Adela and her adherents set up a rostrum right in front of her father's house. Adam watched the whole event. With a megaphone at her mouth and the voice of God, Adela thundered through the quiet streets of Wielow, proclaiming to the awakening city the deeds of certain individuals—window-breaking and mud-throwing at the Povolian Youth Center, the beating of a Radical Party member, and the boycotting of Hebrite bakeries. She swore she would personally drag the criminals to court and see them rot in prison for the rest of their lives. And then one of the neighbors from across the street stood in his open window, in a nightgown and a nightcap, and roared back at the rostrum, telling her that one day he and the other patriotic citizens of the city would publicly whip her, wring her neck and then hang her body head down, in a manner befitting a traitor and a whore. It took a crowd of policemen to terminate that particular rally. The Milewskis thought that the world had come to its end and wondered why God had chosen to try them so grievously. And when Adela's mother died some weeks later, everybody said that it was Adela's doing, even though the woman had been known to suffer from serious stomach trouble for years.

Adela lost the election; and for some ten years afterwards, amazingly, she lived a respectable life, supporting herself by a quiet clerical job, making everybody believe that she had reformed. But, just when it looked that the days of her bawdy exhibitions were long gone, she struck again.

Taking everyone unawares, one day she committed herself to writing. Her short narratives suddenly began appearing in *The Spirit*, a weekly of nation-wide circulation; not that they were ordinary stories, mind you. They were, according to most people that Adam knew, shocking and often vicious tales of Wielow and its residents. She called her tales *The Memoirs of the Maiden from the*

East; she signed them simply 'The Maiden' and she never referred to Wielow or her characters under their real names either, and yet the whole city claimed that they knew exactly who and what she was talking about. And so they were saying that she mocked and degraded the whole city, including her own family and friends; her own father and his hatting business, the Ursuline Sisters and the University who both educated her, the venerable Canon Banasz who gave her her first communion; silversmith Gruber who forgave her the humiliation he suffered from her, Anna Gruber, her loving sister, her relatives, her neighbors. She did not spare anybody; she derided them all with no mercy or tact.

Adam rather liked her stories, though not nearly as much as critics who called them revealing or readers outside Wielow who voted them the most hilarious magazine column of the year. *The Memoirs* made it to the national radio, became a fixture on the Sunday-Night Comedy Hour (with one of the country's top comediennes doing the part of Kocia); and Adela received a high journalistic award. The Milewskis, however, renounced and disinherited her, officially and irrevocably. And Kocia told mother to break all ties with her, once and for all; which mother did.She regretted her action quickly, but when she was ready to attempt reconciliation, she found out that Adela had left Welow to become one of the editors of *The Spirit* in the Capital.

The War found Adela, as she told Adam, in the Mountains where she was spending her annual holidays.

Upon Adam's and Nusia's return to the Hidden Vale after those few days of their most unusual adventures and trials, they find mother and Konstancya in improved states of health. They look quite worn, but fully aware, in possession of their faculties, and mobile. They also seem strongly agitated; so much so that they greet the two of them with hysterical shouts and ugly reprimands. Konstancya calls Adam a dangerous criminal and her daughter a selfish and thoughtless child; and mother says that she almost died because of them. They do not want to know anything about their adventures, so they say; and they do not notice what Adam and Nusia have brought with them, so they pretend. They turn away their heads from the huge pile of foodstuffs and medicaments given to them by the warden, now proudly displayed in front of them. They even refuse to notice that both Nusia and Adam are now cleanly scrubbed and neatly and properly dressed.

Adam tries to explain to them what happened, but they refuse to listen to the story of their ordeals and accomplishments (both of which so obviously exceeding anything that has ever befallen his sister). Kocia can only talk now about Adam's "stealing Nusia from her". This accusation and her lack of appreciation of his efforts infuriate him terribly. He puts on his frolicking he–goat mask, as he calls it now (which, luckily, he finds to be where he left it), and he makes a terribly loud clapping noise by opening and closing the mouth of the mask, and makes the racket as close to her ears as he can.

Some hours later when mother and Kocia seem to have calmed down a bit, Adam tells them about his remarkable encounter with

Adela and Farmer Burak, to which revelation his sister says that he is very ill indeed, and mother implores him to stop inventing fibs. After he repeats his story, trying not to omit a single detail, mother starts whimpering and says that it could not have possibly been Adela, as the real Adela, so wronged by her, would have never forgiven her. And Mieczyslawa Konstancya blurts that she does not wish to hear another word about "that heinous person".

Two days later Farmer Burak appears in front of them,

"God let you prosper!" he says to them from atop his wain. "I am here from Miss Adela to collect you all."

"I am delighted to meet you, Mister Burak," says Konstancya.

"If you have to get your things together, you do that now," answers Burak.

Konstancya then just smiles graciously, turns around and begins packing.

It is only the hauling of mother's piano from under the plum tree to the platform on the wagon that takes time, effort and their asking for the assistance of some strong men from the Vale; the loading of all the rest of their things is done by Burak and Adam alone, and finished within a few minutes. Since mother's leather sofa, Konstancya's pier glass and all the dining things are gone from the lot - exchanged for medical care mother and Kocia required during their recent illnesses - all that they take now with them consists of a single mattress, two pillows, two torn rugs, one small crate, two suitcases, the one-burner iron stove and Nusia's toy chest.

And so, they leave the Apricot Man's orchard and the Hidden Vale to move in with Adela and her hosts, the Buraks. Their destination is Burak's farm, a lone place, further south, occupying a vast slope of an elevation popularly referred to as the Witches Barrow.

Farmer Burak had a large, rough body, which some of the locals likened to an overgrown and crooked beech tree, but he was a man of reason and even disposition. He tended to accept his fate, no matter what it was that might have been coming towards him, calmly, without dissent, in submission to God's ways; but at the same time he never let anything happen to him without pondering over the event for a while. He did not profess to have much wisdom or knowledge of any kind, but he let his will be known to those placed by the Lord under his charge: his wife and children. He was stern with them and would mete out punishment when he deemed it deserved. He used neither a whip nor a birch, as others might have done, but just his own bare hand, heavy and powerful; and he never allowed anger get the better of him. His wife (locally known as Buraczka) would listen to him quietly and respectfully and do what was required of her; and his brood, likewise, would submit to his rule in an orderly and dutiful manner.

As Burak's wagon, with Adam, his family, and their belongings on top, is making its way up the Witches Barrow, the Burak family come out from their house to form a tidy line alongside the front wall; the twenty-year old daughter at one end, then the eighteen-year old youth next to his sister, and so on, by age and size, all the way down to the wee-infant son in a basket held by

Burak's wife at the other end. There are ten of them: Buraczka and nine children; they all face the road on which the wain is coming and they all respectfully bow in that direction. Buraczka steps out towards the wagon; she holds in front of her an earthen platter with a loaf of bread and some salt which she asks them - as is the age-old custom - to share with her and her family, thus letting them know that for as long as they remain under their roof, they, the Buraks, and their guests are one.

Adela shows up. She embraces mother and tells her that the loss of weight has improved her figure considerably; she orders Nusia and Adam to make themselves useful by helping the little Buraks pick up some dry wood for fire; and she asks Kocia, most casually, "And how is your singing nowadays, dear?"

Kocia murmurs under her breath something about Adela being disgustingly insensitive. Having her singing held in low esteem is insult enough, but being treated as a too familiar and insignificant acquaintance of somebody like Adela she cannot bear. And there is another thing; Kocia finds Adela's intimacy with the Buraks disturbing. "Treating them as if they were her equals and intellectuals one moment, and then as her slaves and total morons the next one!"

But mother does not see it that way. "How did you meet these wonderful people, Adela?" she wants to know.

And Adela tells her that she was right in the middle of writing a story on soils, seeds and ploughing, with Burak as her informant, when the War started. And as she decided not to return to the Capital, as not much of the Capital was left after the bombing and her paper was no longer in existence, Burak suggested that she come to live on the Witches Barrow.

"But you have so much authority here..." Mother is full of awe and admiration.

"That's simple," answers Adela with the wickedest smile. "Burak is madly in love with me, haven't you noticed?"

"Oh!" says mother, surprised. "I would have never... but it is kind of romantic, isn't it..."

"Mother, for goodness sake, it's preposterous! It is not just inappropriate, it is so... unsavory!" Kocia is outraged.

Burak's house is low and squat, built of wooden logs held together by layers of gray daub. It is covered with a thick thatch, and inside it is divided in two by a narrow breezeway from which a number of doors lead to individual chambers. Burak's domestic animals are all kept in their own thatched dwellings attached to the back of the house. The room assigned to the new guests has a small curtained window, a table, a couple of benches and five neatly arranged beds of straw, one of them intended for Adela with whom they are to share their lodgings. Before their arrival it was her private place which doubled as a school room for the young Buraks and other children from nearby villages.

This educational enterprise run by Adela is obviously a clandestine operation, for the educating of the young of the country in their native tongue has been outlawed by the occupying authorities. She has just moved her school outdoors, to a low recess between slopes of rye and potatoes, among some birch trees, she tells them. And she expects all of them to help her run her school, she says; to which request Kocia replies that they will be glad to, but that they are qualified to provide education only in the area of music and performing arts, and mother says that at present she could not possibly teach any music, her piano so terribly out of tune; to which Adela says, "rubbish".

Mother is indeed deeply troubled by the thought of her once so exquisite an instrument having turned into a raucous noisemaker. Not that she has given up all hope for its future. As a matter of fact she hovers about Burak and the others carriers of her instrument with, "Please, gentlemen, you have to take pains not to drop it or hurt it more. You have no idea how long it has been exposed to the destructive elements!" And she begs Burak to find a spot for her piano somewhere under his roof.

And so Burak's sons and two men from the village push the instrument in the direction of the house, slowly and steadily. And they stop only when the piano reaches the entranceway and gets wedged in the door. It cannot be moved any farther, in any direction, it turns out, not an inch. Then Burak says that even if it could be pushed through into the breezeway, it could not be moved into any other part of the house, with all the other doors in the house a good deal smaller than the front entrance. And Buraczka says that they cannot leave the piano in the breezeway, should not even think of it, as such a monster thing would block the passway and make it so narrow that no man or beast could go through.

"Then why shouldn't Burak simply chop it up into sticks which we could use for the fire? It's out of tune anyway," laughs Adela.

"Why can't he chop off a part of the door?!" cries mother.

"And after we get it all outside again," Adam cannot resist saying, "what about lifting off a part of the roof, then lifting the piano up and dropping it in the middle of the kitchen where there is plenty of space, and then putting the roof back in its old place, which all should not be difficult as Burak has plenty of ropes around and the roof is just plain thatch."

"Splendid idea, Adam, splendid!" roars Adela. And Buraczka starts begging her not to let such a horrible disruption take place.

In the end, despite mother's tears, it is an axe that touches her Bechstein concert grand piano; though not all of it by any means. It is a mere few centimeters of wood on one side of it that have to be chopped off; and the job is done exceptionally neatly. It is performed by Burak's sixteen-year-old son Oles who is known to be extremely good with his hands. The following day the piano, now a small part of its flank shaved off, is taken to the stable behind the house, where, in the vicinity of the main manger, it will stay, only mildly affronted, for the remainder of the War.

Mother does not sleep much that night, but she seems to be at peace and content. "I like the smell here," she says stretching on her freshly-made pallet of straw. "And it is so quiet around here... you don't think that it is all over... I mean the War?"

Their first Sunday on the Witches Barrow is a festive one, Saints Peter's and Paul's Day as far as Adam recollects; and the Buraks try to look their all-out best. They scrub the wain clean, they air the blanket that goes on the seat and they bath and shine the horses. They also bath themselves; Burak and the boys in a trough behind the barn, and Buraczka and the girls in a smaller wooden washtub in the garden on the side of the house. Buraczka wears a bright green kerchief with a pattern of red roses on it and two strands of beads she got from Burak on their engagement. Burak - more in the fashion of some townsfolk than local farmers - wears a dark blue pinstripe suit, a blue shirt and a brimmed felt hat, all of which he purchased in a prosperous year some time before the War. All the little Buraks have their hair neatly combed back behind their ears; and all of them, with the exception of the youngest three, have shoes on.

But it is Marysia, the eldest, who looks most splendent, dressed in Kocia's evening gown of gold lamé, almost undamaged. Kocia had it made for one of her singing recitals and so she keeps it as a memento of those days of her artistic glory. She lends it to Marysia on the urging of mother who, with tears in her eyes, watched the girl struggling to mend her own well-worn Sunday dress. At first the Buraks did not let their daughter even touch the gown, the glittering, sleeveless and backless garb, evil temptation that it is. It is only after Adela advises them to let Marysia have the dress for the day, that they consent. Adela is good with words; she simply explains to them that there is no better way to honor the Lord than by wearing in his Home things that are beautiful and befitting the wearer, and also that the girl should wear some other garb under the dress so as to cover those parts of her youthful body, which, if exposed naked, could lead the minds of some of the parishioners away from holy thoughts. And so Marysia departs for church wearing a sleeveless gold lamé dress over a white long-sleeved shirt made of homespun flax. And those who see her that day say that she looks grand, like some queen, which is what Adela predicts that everybody would say.

The Buraks set themselves in the wain, bid their guests goodbye, and Burak says that on an important holiday like this one, he, with his mind at peace, leaves them and his farm in the hands of the Almighty. Mother, of course, remembers how long it has been since she herself last visited church, but she does not go with the Buraks since neither Kocia, Adela nor Adam are interested in going with her. Kocia believes that it would be unwise to show themselves anywhere in public after Adam's recent escapades in Dobce; and Adela and Adam simply do not frequent church services.

The farm remains undisturbed during the Buraks' absence, but as Adam and Nusia roam the grounds, they witness something odd and puzzling—something that makes them stop, open-mouthed. As they walk from the stable through the breezeway back to their room they see an old tattered couch which suddenly looks like a huge yawning mouth. Its bottom part is on the floor, as expected, but its upper part is raised and turned towards the wall. Suddenly, right in front of their eyes, there materializes a figure emerging from the bottom of the open couch. It is a man, pale, very thin and disheveled, who stretches, looks around for a few seconds, and then quickly leaves the room practically brushing against them. He doesn't seem to notice them and he heads towards the stable. Adam and Nusia decide to follow him. He now goes through the stable, across the paddock, and into the backyard, where he stops at the same trough Burak and his son bathed in earlier. He fills the trough with rain water from a nearby barrel, he strips, bathes with the Buraks' leftover soap, then dresses and hurries back into the house the way he came. Adam and Nusia again follow him, witnessing his disappearance back into the couch as the yawning mouth closes behind him. The old tattered couch looks like it always does.

In the evening, as they all gather in the kitchen, Burak, quite pleased with himself, is telling them about a transaction he concluded that day, right after holy mass, regarding a sale of seven unregistered piglets from the unregistered sow that they have been raising in secret; a real good deal, he calls it. Marysia, now with an apron over Kocia's lamé dress, is serving the food; she hums and every few steps lifts the edge of her dress and swirls around. Burak once or twice murmurs something to her about the sin of vanity, but only half in anger. The man from Pcim who is buying the piglets is honest and promised good money, Burak says; and the way the piglets are going to be delivered to him is so clever that the occupying authorities will never find out a thing. Then Jas, the eldest, says that it may not be for long now that one will have to hide farm animals from the authorities, as the War may be over soon, he heard some talk, and so the Realm will be no longer and so there will be no authority to sequester the beast.

That night they are also given larger than usual helpings of potatoes and sour cabbage, both heavily topped with cracklings of bacon and onioned mushrooms, and all that with double the usual quantities of thick, cool clabber to drink. And they all declare it to be the best meal they have had in ages. And just then, when Adam praises Buraczka for her superior cooking and is ready to ask questions about the mysterious man from the couch, the very man walks into the Buraks' kitchen. The man's voice sounds thin and faltering, just what Adam would have imagined it to be.

"Blessed be our Lord Jesus," he says.

"Forever and ever, amen," answers Burak, while making room for him at the table.

Buraczka piles a generous portion of food on a clean plate and nobody seems the least bit surprised. The man sits down, notices strangers at the table, and says almost apologetically, "My name is Wiktor... I could not quite resist the smell of the cabbage and the cracklings," his voice and manner telling them that he is not of the local peasantry.

"Are you by chance a neighbor of the Buraks', sir?" Adam's sister decides to use one of her more enticing tones.

"He is a magician. I know!" exclaims Nusia.

"What kind of magic do you think I perform?" the man asks her politely.

"You just get in and out of furniture," Nuia replies.

The man stiffens, drops his spoon, rises, and gives Burak a frightened look; and then he runs out of the kitchen.

"Mr. Wiktor, please return to us!" Buraczka rushes after him. "Mr. Wiktor, God has protected you so far so he will keep on protecting you. The child didn't mean any harm.... please be returned!"

Adam tries to question Adela and Burak about the man but receives no information from them; not that evening.

A few days after they meet Wiktor, Adam is awakened by bangs at the door and by Adela pulling him out of his straw nest and yelling in his ears to make himself ready and useful immediately. (During their stay with the Buraks, Adela reminds all four of them at any opportunity about the necessity of making themselves useful, which, of course, drives Kocia out of her mind.) So now, Adela pushes Adam out of their chamber into the breezeway, and there he sees some of the Buraks rushing past him and hears the news that a Realm military truck is heading towards the farm. Gasping Jas tells him to help with moving the unregistered piglets from the stable to the hollow. Adam is guessing that the unregistered animals must be the same ones which are intended for the sale to a man from Pcim and he wonders where the "hollow" might be, when a large wheelbarrow with the squealing and squirming sow appears in the breezeway. The hurried Burak pushes the load through, and two of the little Buraks try to hold the animal in place. They roll the sow into a little chamber where set against the wall sits an old tattered couch which Adam has noticed before; except that now the couch looks like a huge yawning mouth: its bottom part on the floor, as expected, but its upper part - torn cushions and all - raised and turned towards the wall; and inside it, somewhere in the interior of the mouth stands Oles with only his head, shoulders and arms visible. The sow is rapidly unloaded from the wheelbarrow and handed to the youth inside the couch who, with no small effort, pushes it underneath in order to render it invisible.

When Adam gets to the stable, he hears Jas ordering everyone to form a row stretching from the piglets' hideout in the stable to the hollow under the couch. Jas positions himself at the stable's end and Oles at the hollow's end, and all the rest of them are to space themselves evenly in-between. And thus the human chainwork springs to action. They are all parts of a racing conveyor belt; the unregistered little piglets snort and squeal in misery while they are being whisked, one by one, through the air – live rockets of little bulk and heft – until they find haven in the secret hollow under the couch. Well, the very last one does not make it; to Adam's greatest embarrassment, it slips through his hands and rolls down the breezeway. Of course, he tries to amend his clumsiness and runs after the yelping animal; but before he has a chance to retrieve it, Nusia picks up the piglet, and pressing it tight to herself, runs outside. And there is not much anybody can do, since at that moment Buraczka at the doorway gives them a signal to close the couch immediately and disperse.

When Adam gets outside, there are already in front of the house a Realm military truck, a jeep and a bunch of Realm soldiers moving about. The commander of the group asks Burak questions and Burak tries to answers them. The man's knowledge of the language is only slight and Burak does not understand him very well, but he tries to be as respectful to his interrogator as he only can. The commander's questions seem to relate to the whereabouts of the mother of the piglet in Nusia's arms and the rest of the brood.

The farmer most humbly explains that the piglet, all alone, was found just the other day in the fields by his children; probably lost in transfer by a Realm convoy passing through the area. The commander does not seem to either understand or like Burak's story, and so he keeps asking his questions over and over again. And as Burak has only just this one story to give, the commander shouts at him angrily, threatens him with prison and a noose and then kicks him in the stomach. Then he orders his soldiers to search the whole place; and he himself turns to Nusia and asks her where the pigs are. He smiles to her, and so she smiles back and, without a word, leads him straight to the magic couch.

The man gives the old cushions a few stabs with a knife. He rips them wide open and plunges both his hands into the couch's inside. He searches violently, throwing pieces of dirty, wooly innards all around the room. When he finds nothing, he shouts at Nusia, kicks the couch's side and tells his men to continue their job. And so they do, with a vengeance. They open chests, cupboards and trapdoors. They kick and upend tables, benches and troughs. They tear sheets, rip mattresses, break dishes and strew about fodder and straw. And at the end they remove from the house all the bread, lard, cabbage, potatoes and other edibles they come across.

While they load their booty on the truck, the Buraks gather in front of the house and quickly form a tidy line, with Burak and Buraczka at either end, and all the rest of them in-between, by age and size, evenly spaced. This time they kneel, lower their heads and repeat after Burak the words of supplication addressed to the commander, "Please don't make us starve, good sir!" Adela pushes Nusia into the line and tells her to kneel and say what the others do.

Only when they are ready to depart the commander turns his eyes towards the Buraks; he then comes closer to them and all of a sudden pulls the sixteen-year-old Oles from the line. "To headquarters we take him, for some questioning," he says.

Buraczka prostrates herself in front of the man, "Please, good sir, don't, I will pray for you and your children for all my life if you let him be..." her stretched-out fingers clutch at the commander's shoe.

The truck and the jeep are ready to leave when the commander changes his mind. He tells his men to release Oles, and with a broad smile on his face accepts Burak's bows and words of thankfulness; and immediately afterwards he orders his men back to the stable. A few moments later the soldiers return, leading with them one of the two cows that the Buraks keep on the farm. The farmer is dumbstruck; bent in half, on his knees, his arms reaching to the animal, he tries to plead again, but no words come from his mouth. "Well, we are taking your cow then, rather than your boy; don't you prefer it?" The commander grins.

The military motor truck and the jeep slowly turn around and start descending the Witches Barrow, the black and white side of the Buraks' cow showing from under the tarpaulin.

"I am allowed two cows on the account of a big family. You have no right. That's all I have. We will starve! Please sir, have mercy. I can't feed them without milk. That's all we have. You have no right, sir, no right. We will all starve! Have mercy!" Burak goes on pleading even after the military convoy is gone out of his sight. But after some few minutes he lifts himself up, stretches his crooked frame a bit and says that they will have to sustain with one cow.

They do with but one cow indeed, and do not starve, not really; not with the stock of rye flour and potatoes left, hidden somewhere in the recesses of the barn, and the chicken, geese, a goat, and good earth's bounty that was coming to them together with the warm days of summer. But, Adam's and Nusia's personal lot worsens quite a bit.

The Buraks look upon the two of them with great disfavor, obviously blaming them for the loss of that beautiful black and white cow, their nourisher. Yet, let it be stressed, gentle and quiet that they seem to be by nature, they rarely express their thoughts and feelings aloud. On the other hand, Konstancya, Adam's sister and Nusia's mother, lets everybody know her sentiments concerning the matter in a distinctly vocal and provoking manner. Their transgressions are so serious, she says; that she will have to take strong punitive measures against them, to curb their freedom, that is. And so she starts demanding, constantly, that they account for their movements; she forbids them to take walks on their own; she forbids them to paint themselves (and even destroys all of Nusia's watercolors from her toy chest); she forbids Nusia to visit the room with the couch and to play with the farm animals; and without any provocation she threatens Nusia with tying her fast, and permanently, to some stable object so that she cannot move around and cause more trouble.

Let it also be mentioned that after that episode of the despoiling of the farm by the Realm searchers, mother begins experiencing bouts of terrible heavy-heartedness at the thoughts of their inability to repay the Buraks for their losses. And so one day she gives Buraczka a little embroidered handbag she used to wear before the War to soirees and such, her very last thing of any value whatsoever. Shortly afterwards Kocia does her own bit; she tells Marysia to keep her gold lamé dress for good.

The Home of the Divine Providence

Lech is not yet back with us, but Stefan, his roommate, one of the nicest men at the Home, the owner of a little aquarium, has showed up after several weeks' absence from the dining table. As I am not always "with it", as they say, and so it took me a while to realize what has been going on. Here is what I have found out. Two months ago Stefan wrote a letter to our chief guardian Simplicius in which he apparently questioned some of the basic rules of the Home and demanded general voting by all the wards on all issues vital to their welfare; and also stated that he would immediately start polling the wards on questions concerning the rules of the Home. In response to that, Brother Simplicius forbade Stefan to conduct any polling or to talk to anybody about the issues mentioned in the letter. He apparently also expressed his dismay that Stefan, a long-time ward, has so completely forgotten himself, and that he doubted the wisdom of the existing rules which had been designed with the expressed purpose of protecting the wards; the same wards who – by their own admission and the consensus of society – were quite incapable of making decisions concerning their lives. When Stefan did not obey Simplicius's order, he was disciplined by being excluded from the dining hall; and then, after he persisted in his recalcitrance, he was denied all sweets with his meals. For two weeks he consumed dessert-less meals, in his room, in the company only of one of the guardians and the fish in his aquarium. But as during that time he still continued circulating a copy of his letter among the wards, and his questionnaire on the rules of the Home, the Special Council of the Home decided to withhold from him all food and other life necessities for the fish in his aquarium. It was only after the fish in his beautiful little aquarium (which he kept on a pedestal next to his bed) started to die one by one, that Lech, Stefan's roommate, became angry.

Mother often confides to Adam her thoughts on Burak. She muses on his kindness and generosity towards them, and on how hard-working and resilient he is. Mother also gets affected strongly by the notion of Burak in love. "And why shouldn't he worship her? Why shouldn't he have given himself over to her? There is nothing unnatural about being in love!" she says. "True, he is simple, uncultured, the father of a family, and well beyond his youth, and well, she is a little peculiar, not at all what you might call attractive, no longer in the bloom of youthhood - all true; but what does it have to do with love?!" Mother also considers it to be the most natural thing in the world that Burak invited Adela to live on his farm. Of course, mother is certain that when Buraczka saw this big-bodied, loud, city woman, she was quite a bit awed and confused; and she most probably suggested to her husband, likely more than once, that Miss Adela might find herself more comfortable in some different household in the village, possibly with more room and fewer children; but Burak would not listen. Mother is also sure that he would scold the poor woman for such remarks so severely (or even strike her, God forbid), that she stopped talking about the matter. Mother sees Buraczka's predicament clearly and feels sorry for her, yet she finds Burak blameless.

Let it be mentioned here that only one more time is the farm raided that summer, and with no serious consequences at that. The Buraks receive a warning about the visit well in advance, Nusia and Adam do no harm, and nothing was taken away.

As the Realm is losing the day and the number of partisans in the mountains is increasing, visits to local farms by Realm soldiers become less frequent. People grow less fearful and more defiant of their occupiers, whose days in their lands, they believe, are numbered. Adam, for one, ceases wearing his protective hat (the one mother made him in the Hidden Vale when she had no more peroxide for him), and he even lets his hair grow: long, black and curly, just like in the old days of safety.

They see now the partisans of the Underground Army daily; armed, belts of ammunition crossed on their chests; sure of themselves, despite their out-moded rifles and ill-fitting uniforms. They greet people on the farm with their military salutes and quietly ask about the affairs of the place. Sometimes they carefully look over the entire premises, every corner; and at other times they just wander about leisurely; and they always talk to them with politeness as to equals. Burak treats them with respect, but never tells them that they are welcome in his home; practical, non-violent and cautious man that he is. And he never calls them "our boys", the way others do.

But when they do stay for the evening, uninvited, they ask of the farmer only some bread to go with the drink that they have have brought with them, mostly beer seized at raids on Realm-run breweries. And when they stay longer and Kocia sings for them and Marysia puts on her white shirt and the gold lame gown to please them, Burak gets annoyed. Not that he shows his displeasure while the men are in his house. Only once, when a young corporal, a liaison man for the area, kisses Marysia in front of everybody and calls her his sweetheart, Burak's angriness breaks out into the open. He pulls Marysia away from the man, hits her on the mouth and orders her to change her garment.

The Buraks work the whole summer doggedly hard, seizing greedily the smallest dole they feel is due them from Nature's riches. On the Day of Our Lady of the Fields, their festive garb donned once again, they receive holy communion and march in the church procession celebrating the beginning of the yearly crop gathering. And when their first harvest of the season turns out to be plentiful, they are thankful. With an offering of freshly dipped candles taken to the church, they acknowledge the Holy Virgin's benefaction to them and ask for Her continual generosity towards the farm.

Adela, mother and Kocia teach school at the birch-tree patch, or try to. Most of their pupils come irregularly or not at all, detained at their homesteads by various farm chores which are particularly heavy at harvest time. But no matter how many of them show up or when, Adela holds her classes daily, at regular hours, the way she has set out to do. And mother and Kocia have to submit to her rule, no matter how much they dislike the idea.

Nusia and Adam try hard to make themselves useful, as they are told. They pick mushrooms and wild berries for meals, they collect dry cones and sticks for the kitchen fire, they feed the chickens, and even clean the coop and sweep the yard once in a while. A lot is expected of them and they don't get praised much.

And they also learn something about Wiktor, the couch-dweller. It was at the beginning of the war when Burak found him, sick and disoriented, crouched on the ground next to a tree. He took him home and fed him and Wiktor told him that he was a fugitive. It was ruled by the occupying authorities, the man told the farmer, that he was a dangerous mind-poisoner and a Hebrite. As Wiktor terribly feared being seized by the Realm authorities, Burak let him use as a hideout, when needed, a hollow under one of the chambers, a storage place he had dug out in the times of prosperity before the war. He then covered the entrance to the hideout with an old couch which had a movable upper part. To the bottom of the couch he attached a removable panel with hinges and springs, and then nailed the sides of the couch to the floor, so that it could not be moved. He taught Wiktor how to get in and out of the hollow through the couch. And so, Wiktor had lived in the couch almost five years, spending most of his time by himself within the confines of his underground chamber; even when there was no apparent necessity to do so. He learned to communicate with the earth above by means of sound signals he devised.

Still it is not an uncheerful summer for either of them. When Kocia is not around, Adam watches Nusia and the little Buraks making merry; and he laughs. Their flower garlands and tree-bark masks on, the children float about in the green ocean of Burak's meadow; they fly and dance across the fields and listen to the echo at the woods' edge; and in the courtyard behind the barn they play hopscotch and splash about the water from the trough. And Adam manages sometimes to give mime performances for them and to teach them to think of funny names for things. And right after the last of the rye and oats are hauled away to the barn, he and the children follow Burak to the empty field and watch him perform magic with his plough. Burak, reciting his incantations, walks besides the plough pulled by one of his horses and makes sure that both the animal and the plough obey him. Big chunks and little clods of soil alike are rapidly dug out, brought to light, thrown up in the air and dropped back to the ground a second later; the earth is turned inside out, every root and stalk cut up, every littlest mouse or grub dislodged, yet, within seconds the field is all smooth and calm again, except for small rippling here and there and the thinnest of tracks, soft and even. And as they all silently goose-step right behind Burak's horse and plough on that delicately wrinkled path, they giggle from time to time and then try to hold their breath to make sure that they march in proper file and stay clear within the confines of the narrow trench freshly furrowed.

The summer lull ends on a Sunday, at dawn, on the day when Nusia turns five; not that her birthday has anything to do with the astounding events of that day or that Nusia's birthday is celebrated in any way. (Kocia believes that since her daughter's coming into this world happened at one of the most catastrophic moments in the history of mankind, the day should not be held in observance.) Anyway, by the time they get up that morning, all of hell has already broken loose: the earth tremors, the air is filled with deafening din, and the newly-rising sun is cloaked with clouds of gray smoke. For a while they think that the ground under their feet will erupt and all of the Witches Barrow, forced from its natural foundation, will topple. Later that day they are told that it is an offensive by the partisans of the Underground Army, with people all over the country together with them, rising against the occupier. What they hear is hard to imagine and account for: the whole country battling the Realm forces, for the first time out in the open, right at the moment when all signs have been saying that the War and the Realm's power over the lands they occupy will end any day regardless of the intervention of the occupied people.

6.

Indeed, it was said many a time that summer that the War was coming to an end at last. The two powers bent upon annihilating the Realm moved across the Continent with speed greater than in months past; the armies of the Great Eastern United People's Power in their victorious offensive westward, from the East; and the armies of the Great Far Western Allied Sovranties in their triumphant march eastward, from the West. The Realm-occupied territory grow smaller, the Realm's armies weaker, and the forces of the two victorious powers got closer to each other. And the two – a good few months before the Realm was defeated utterly – declared themselves, independently of each other, to be the liberators of the world and the protectors of those whom they delivered from the Realm's yoke.

By summer's end it is firmly predicted that for Adam's part of the world deliverance will come in the winter or, at the latest, by early spring. Why then can the people not just wait patiently for a few months for that day of victory which is already in the works? Why suddenly do the ill-armed partisans and ill-fed people decide to take on the Realm forces which only a few months hence were to be crushed anyway, by the mightiest powers on earth? Don't they know that, even for the so-greatly weakened Realm, they are no match? Is their thirst for personal revenge on the Realm so untamable? Or is their desire to share in the glory of the victors so overwhelming? Not many ask those questions during the Insurrection, though. It is only much later – when the Insurrection becomes known as the Folly - that it is concluded that the insurgents of that summer went onto battle believing that the Almighty Himself would perform a miracle on their behalf.

You see, it is during that summer that the people start weighing in earnest all that they know or hear about the two liberators; and, as if for the first time, with clarity unparalleled, everybody sees that what the People's Power has in store for them are harsh laws, dreariness and deprivation, with any personal wealth forbidden; while the Western Sovranties are to bestow upon them leisure, mirth and abundance: money for which anybody can reach and liberties hitherto unknown. Being rather frail, in spirit and body (like most others throughout the Continent), obviously, the people long to be liberated by the benevolent giant of the West. But, towards the end of the summer the armies of the Western Sovranties are still some thousand miles away from the borders of Adam's country, while the GEU People's armies, with all of the Eastern Provinces already taken by them, are right next door. And so it becomes obvious to all that the deliverance for their lands is to come from the gloom-bearing eastern neighbor, and not from the West, the people suddenly know. Unless God decides otherwise.

And so, with that sudden order to hit the Realm with full force and out in the open, the leaders of the Underground Army try to bring to pass what they believe He has always intended for their lands. With this unexpected strike they will reclaim from the Realm whatever is left of their lands, before the GEU People's forces have time to do the same, they think, and then they will create anew their independent state, and then they will try to uphold this independence until that time when the GF Western Allied forces enter the eastern part of the Continent and save everybody from the predatory moves of the People's Power.

The Home of the Divine Providence

And so it came to pass that the brothers, our guardians, fearful of discontent among the wards, started to encourage them to discuss (even away from the dining-hall table) the pleasurable subject of sex, a subject matter almost disallowed in the past. In turn, the wards decided, most ingeniously, to take advantage of the situation and to start communicating among themselves by means of a language code in which all direct and indirect references to matters objectionable to the brothers would be made by substitute words and phrases, those substitutes being totally derived from the area of sex and sexology. As Jan put it, when he first mentioned the code to me, "Imagine the name of a certain part of the female body as a code name, say, for pork tenderloin (a foodstuff we have not seen here in a while). Straight talk about a piece of pork would make them furious, but they will not object to us saying that we would want to have a piece of you know what." Of course Jan is crude, but I understood his point quite well. Most of the wards were able to learn the code quickly and adapt themselves to a new mode of speaking with no difficulty, deriving a good deal of enjoyment from pretending to talk about one thing while actually saying something very different, that is, making dupes out of the brothers. What it all amounts to is that the wards in their attempt at improving their existence at the Home chose a subterfuge rather than, say, a loud complaint, an open challenge or an outright rebellion.

As it comes out from hiding, the old Underground Army acquires the name of the National Army; and its fighters, erstwhile partisans or the boys, are now called soldiers, who were wearing their military uniforms, insignia, rank and guns all out in the open.

For three months the Witches Barrow quakes and reeks of smoke, and the sound of gunfire reverberates throughout the farm loudly and fearfully. Mother prays again with renewed ardor and a fresh reserve of tears, her fingers moving in small circular motions, as if unceasingly, fondling the beads of her long-lost rosary. Burak – no rebuke towards the doings of the Almighty – goes on, in the way it had always been meant for him to do. When soldiers stampeding across his field interrupt his autumn rite of sowing or when the stricken earth suddenly begins to crater in front of him, he just hunkers down, crosses himself hurriedly and then hurls himself flat on the ground; with a heavy haircloth sack over his head – made one with the soil underneath him – he waits, for as long as necessary, for the assault to pass. And Adela, her school officially moved back indoors, keeps on telling them all to go on too and keep themselves useful.

The very first wounded that they see are brought to the farm on the day that Burak and his eldest boy Jas are busy making sour cabbage for the winter food stores. When the soldiers come, Burak and Jas are inside a wooden vat, their naked feet immersed in the mounds of salted cabbage shavings, trampling on the substance within. They march and shuffle, and turn about; and while they so crush and subdue the element under their feet, squeezing out of it all the savory juices, they chant uninterruptedly, "...asking for a happy day, so that we are always blessed, our souls saved..." There are three wounded on the stretchers, and the National Army soldiers who bring them to the farm call upon Burak to give their men a keeping.

When they walk into the kitchen, mother and Kocia are vowing in whispers not to touch a single shred of sour cabbage during the remainder of their lives, and barefoot Nusia, grabbing the edge of the vat, begs to be taken inside it. When they ask him where they could place their men, Burak, no break in the rhythm of his shuffle, tells Jas to get out of the vat and make room for the wounded in the stable, but then decides that the beasts should not be disturbed and the three wounded soldiers be better put in the barn, in the very back of it, under the loft. After Jas and the soldiers are gone from the kitchen, Burak lifts Nusia off the floor, places her in the cabbage and orders her to march and chant together with him.

The very same evening, just a few hours after Burak lets the three wounded soldiers be placed in his barn, the Insurrection calls upon the farm again. They all are gathered in the kitchen, like always, when, as if out of nowhere, Jas shows himself in front of them looking so strangely changed that they barely recognize him. He stands tall and prideful-like, dressed as if for church, shoes shined and neatly laced, hair combed back, Sunday hat in hand. He does not slump when he turns to Burak, just wedges his chin in his chest and says with a voice that does not sound like his, "It's time for me to go, sir."

He is being awaited down in the valley, he says, and has to go right away, but will be back before long, for sure before winter, as he knows that the fight will be over before it gets really cold. It has been two years since he learned to use a rifle from the partisans in the forest, and he can now aim and shoot with the best of them. And Burak says nothing to all this, just shakes his head and hunches his shoulders a bit, maybe in disbelief or maybe in sadness or maybe because he does not know what to say.

But then Buraczka rushes to Jas, her arms raised and stretched out, ready to fend off any trouble coming towards him. "Miss Adela!" she cries. "Miss Adela, you know everything, so you tell them not to take him, tell him to leave him alone!" And she does not plead, as is her custom; she orders Adela. But Adela does not say anything, not a single word.

"You stop this needless yelling and be respectful to Miss Adela, woman." Burak rebukes her, but Adam thinks that he does not sound as sure of his words as he usually does when telling her what to do.

"Nobody is taking me, m'am. I am going on my own," Jas says to his mother.

Two days later Marysia takes her leave of the farm, too. She has decided to join her corporal, the man who kissed her once in front of everybody and called her his sweetheart. She leaves at night when the household is all asleep. She wakes Adela to tell her that she will be going with her man to his post outside Kramow, but that the two of them will be married that very night before they get there, by an army chaplain stationed in the village of Pcim. She asks Adela to plead to her parents for forgiveness. She also asks her to take good care of her gold lamé dress.

More wounded are brought to the farm, and Burak does not know where these men are to be laid out. He has just got the barn ready for the autumn threshing, polished two mighty flails and moved the three wounded he had there before into the stable so that he could have all the room he needs; the barn being not the right place for the sick anyway, with all the dust and chaff flying off the threshed grain. And he has no room in the stable now either, after he has crammed his animals all in one enclosure to make space for the three wounded. He asks Adela what should be done, and she tells him that the new ones can be brought into her quarters. And so, mother, Kocia and Nusia move out of Adela's room into a little chamber where Burak's three daughters sleep; Adam is allotted a space behind the kitchen stove; and Adela takes a portion of the floor across from him on the other side of the kitchen. Burak makes her a bed of fresh straw and tells Buraczka to cover it with a clean sheet; and he makes sure that the bed is placed neatly flush with the wall right beneath a row of holy pictures.

The man who is in charge of the convoy that has brought the new wounded introduces himself as Sub-Lieutenant Sila, the regimental medical officer. He is tall, strong-bodied and full of medical know-how he tries to impart to the people on the farm before leaving the invalid soldiers with them. Kocia finds him most alluring.

It is bimber vodka about which he wants them to be aware above all. He warns them, after he deposits two bottles of the stuff in the newly-created sickroom, against attempting any unwarranted consumption of that prodigy of wartime ingenuity. He explains that bimber is the most valuable analgesic and antiseptic in the possession of the National Army. Then he demonstrates how a carefully measured blend of that liquor and well-water can be used for the cleansing of wounds; and also how the same bimber, when poured in very small quantities into the throats of the sick, can restore to normalcy their heartbeat and mental balance. Sub-lieutenant Sila with gallantry kisses the hands of all the ladies present, including confused Buraczka, and states, his voice resonant and trustful, that he is leaving in those delicate hands the fate of the men of his regiment.

Kocia glows with joy. She has to do something special for their little infirmary, she says. She rushes into the woods, all the way to the other side of the Witches Barrow – reports of discharging guns notwithstanding – and brings back with her an armload of purple autumn heather; for the boys to enjoy, she announces. She then takes out from her crate The Red-haired Lady with a Yellow Rose and props it up on top of the crate for the boys to see. The glass over the picture has cracked and partially fallen out, and so the rose and some of the Lady's hand are now marred by smudges; and Kocia says that it is precisely because of the injuries that the Red-haired Lady has suffered that the picture will be now appreciated. Till late night she walks around the infirmary smiling and whispering into the ears of the laid-out soldiers. While Adela puts a fresh dressing on the arm of one of the men, Kocia smiles to him and asks "It is not hurting, is it?" and then sings for him Oh my rosemary...in the rhythm of a lullaby.

Still more wounded are brought to Burak's place the following day: contorted bodies in rags dank with blood and grime, rasping groans coming from their throats. At their sight mother swoons and Buraczka crosses herself in panic. Sila, who is carrying with him more bimber and a chest full of medical implements, tells them right at the doorstep that he will need them, every one of them; and then he demands that the kitchen table be immediately scrubbed and disinfected and the largest soup kettle filled with water for sterilizing his surgical tools.

Adam does not remember who is assigned to what job, as he is not given enough time to think or look at anybody except Sila and a soldier on the operating table, but he knows that they all toil through interminable hours. He still remembers the painful awareness of his own body during those hours – his jerking, twisted nerves and tortured muscles trying to obey the orders given to him by the voices around him. With efforts he never knew before, he helps to hold the wounded men in place and tie them with rope to the legs of the kitchen table; he struggles to strip them of their blood-impregnated uniforms; he pours bimber down their throats, holds chloroform rags over their faces, directs a flashlight onto their limbs or abdomens... And when he feels weaker and the vision of Sila wielding his knife appears more hazy in front of his eyes, he begs to be released from his duties, but is not answered. He is only ordered to tie another rope, soak another rag with chloroform or fish for fresh clamps in the depth of the boiling water in the soup kettle. And when he is at last told that it is all finished, he is unable to stop either the swimming of his head or the quaking of his limbs.

Shortly after the last man is taken off the table and placed on his pallet in the sickroom, sub-lieutenant Sila, the regimental medical officer, himself takes a gulp of bimber. He breathes deeply and generously praises all of them. They make a first-rate crew, he says, and the farm makes a fine hospital, a first-rate place. Kocia is at his side, becharmed by the man's self-command and strength; a fresh rag in her hand, she offers to wipe the sweat and blood off his face. She calls his skills unbelievable and tells him that most certainly he will enter one day the roster of the great heroes of this war. And then she asks him whether by any chance he is not a graduate of the Medical Academy of Kramow, the best. And he takes in another gulp of bimber and tells her that it was not the Academy, but his father's shop. "A barber by trade he was, and so am I, barber surgeon, that is. At your service! Got good training, though, and then really went at it during the time in the Army. Can't beat experience against schooling, madame."

The following day dies one of the soldiers in their infirmary. He is one of the three who were brought to the farm on the very first day; he had bandaged arms, a patch over one eye and no coat. He has never said as much as one word to anybody, and they have never learned either his name or his rank. Adam puts a mask on him made from pieces of dry wood and spent cartridges; Burak buries him in the lower part of the meadow; and Oles, the boy renowned for the dexterity of his fingers, carves him a cross out of a birch bough.

And so it comes to pass that Burak's farm becomes an establishment officially recognized by the National Army: a hospital at the service of the fighting men. The regiment gives Burak a handgun and a paper with the Army stamp on it, both to be carried on his person at all times. The regiment presents him also with a white banner with the sign of a red cross, to be hung on the outside of the main house. As told, he puts the gun and the paper in a hiding place, but hangs the banner above the door in full view of everyone.

With all the space needed for the Army's men, all the regular residents are moved into the kitchen, where they arrange their sleeping nests in two rows along the wall, some good two meters clear of the operating table, just as Sila instructed them. And the hollow under the couch becomes a special storage chamber for bimber and turpentine, on account of Sila being very much impressed with the clever contraption – its moving panel, solid hinges, springs, the sides all nailed to the floor.

Adam is released from his duties around the operating table after he by mistake saturates a rag with turpentine rather than with bimber, then forgets the rag on the kitchen stove and thus sets in motion a process of combustion which spreads fire from the stove top onto the floor. The fire is extinguished before it charrs the floor too heavily. Sila does not have to interrupt his work on amputating a limb in this particular case; but Adam is ordered from then on to work away from the kitchen. He is assigned to cleaning the sickroom, which means trying to keep the floor and the soldiers' sickbeds free of excrement and other soilings; a job he finds disagreeable, yet considerably less strenuous than assisting Sila.

It is Oles and Burak who eventually become Sila's chief aides; the youth on account of his nimble fingers and sharp eyes, and Burak because of his natural powerfulness, unmatched in the feat of immobilizing those whom insufferable agony would otherwise not have allowed to stay motionless on the operating table. Mother and Adela do the laundry, change the straw on the sickbeds and tear rags for bandages. Buraczka cooks and feds the sick. Konstancya spends her days dispensing among the patients stories, songs, smiles and purple heather she gathers in the woods. And Nusia, whenever her daily chores are finished, carefully bandages the new wooden doll Oles carved for her, and then smears the doll and the rags with juices from squeezed berries.

Officer Sila runs the place with determination extraordinary; and though his efforts do not always end in success, he does admit with sadness, his losses, when thought of in numbers, are not high, he adds with hope in his voice. And he never stops praising them all for their work. But it is only Oles, Burak's second son, whom Sila promises to recommend to the high command of the Army for the award of a military cross.

Oles has gifts of all sorts: he knows how to talk to rooks and daws or call a fox out of his hole; he can repair farm equipment like no one else; and he is able to carve anything out of any wood, like singing pipes out of reed or human figures from linden boughs. It is because of this great cleverness of his, Adam hears, that some of the locals suspect him of being in cahoots with the wicked one himself. Anyway, since he knows by sight, sound or touch every path, creek and tree in the neighboring mountains and in all of the Raba valley, it is he who becomes Sila's courier and the trusted dispatch-bearer for the regiment. It is his own notion to put to use his witchery in order to serve and please Sila. "I'll return by tomorrow morning with everything you want, lieutenant sir, if father lets me have the wain and the horses, sir" he says.

Burak consents and Oles takes off, with papers signed by Sila in his pocket. He is back the same day well before dusk, with wagonful of cargo, and there is not a scratch on him. This is the time of some of the heaviest fighting on the Raba, but the lad has no story of how he reached the warehouses or how he crossed the river with all the artillery fire going on. He only says that it has not been much of a tussle. He unloads the crates and barrels from the wagon, and then patiently waits for the sub-lieutenant to examine the lot: chloroform, gauze, tapes, syringes, flasks, tinned goods, bags of flour. Sila nods his head with approbation; and when he finishes his inspection, he stands to attention in front of Oles and salutes him with his hand raised to his forehead.

By the end of September all of the valley is in the hands of the National Army. The sounds of discharging guns that has been for weeks dinning into their ears gets fainter, the smoke clouding the sky recedes, and the freshest contingent of the wounded brought to them comes from further away. And the word spreads that the National Army is marching north, taking the main roadway to Kramów; and people all around rejoice. But then in mid-October they suddenly hear that the Realm forces spread out between them and Kramów are receiving fresh reinforcements and start blocking the lines of supply to the mountains.

At the end of October comes bleak days and coldness. Oleś gets only one small load of coal for the hospital, and there is not much wood left on the farm either. And so they try to stay in the kitchen as much as possible, the best heated spot in the farmhouse; and at nighttime, when the fire in the stove weakens and the chilliness on the outside increases, they feel that they are lucky that they have enough straw to burrow in and that fate has placed them during those cold days in such great nearness to one another.

On the last day of October, that time devoted to the dead, ghosts and memories, they go to the lower end of Burak's meadow where their recent dead are buried. As is ordained by the age-old custom, they light candles, place them on the freshly-raised mounds of meadow soil and say,"Let them have eternal rest, oh Lord..." They listen to the hissing of the wind and sounds of some faraway battle; and soldiers who have come with them to the graves say that there is hope for as long as their men hold on to the Raba. Burak thanks Heaven that the day's fighting is taking place a good distance from the farm. Shortly afterwards he hauls towards the barn the last of the potatoes from the fields and tells Adam to help him carry some of the heavier sacks.

In the beginning of November the Realm forces take back most of the Raba, moving again into the mountains in the south. More men are brought then to their hospital's doorstep; and the farm houses more wounded than ever before. And the operating table is rarely let rest from Sila's labors.

One night on his way back to the farm, Oles's wagon is hit by a volley of bullets; one of his horses is struck dead and Oles himself receives abundant wounds. He struggles up the hill with one animal only; and by morning he delivers his cargo to Sila, as promised; but his body is in such a wretched state that he collapses at Sila's feet. As he spends the next several weeks in the sickbed, he can no longer carry out his duties for the National Army. Not that there is anything anywhere left to be brought from the outside; previous stocks exhausted or destroyed. Buraczka says that it is the evil eye that so many have had on him that caused Oles's injuries and all the harm he came to, all on account of his cleverness that people begrudged him.

It is a day or so after Oles's misfortune that the Buraks' youngest, a little infant boy that just learned to crawl this past summer, gets ill too. Sila gives him a tincture of some kind, puts a cold compress on his forehead and rubs his convulsed neck, telling Buraczka to pour lots of liquid into him and keep on applying compresses to keep his fever down. But the boy does not get better; fever, violent spasms and vomit tear his little body with no relief for days. He dies at dusk, when Sila is attending to the other sick and the wounded. Burak digs his son a grave the following day, right next to where the others have been buried.

After the burial Buraczka ceases talking; she moves around, does her work , but no words come out of her. She also shows signs of a malady; she coughs hard, trembles and groans harshly in her sleep, but turns away from Sila when he offers her bimber and aspirin and some cupping on the chest.

They hear her voice again some days later, suddenly, in the middle of a night when the wheezing and howling of the wind and the moans of dying soldiers are keeping everybody disquieted and awake. All of a sudden Buraczka tells them that she can hear the baying of the wolves in the forest and the voice of her oldest boy Jas calling for help. She cries out with a terror-riven voice that Jas is coming towards her from the darkness of the woods; he is surrounded by wolves on all sides, strange wounds all over him, his eyes not seeing, but his wounds glowing in the dark. And at dawn when Adam looks through the window outside to catch the first sight of the day, he sees an eerie vision of two shadowy figures climbing up the path towards the house, carrying on their shoulders what looks like a body wrapped in a piece of cloth. "My Jas! My little son! My little angel torn by wolves!" Buraczka runs towards the men, wailing, reaching for the body they carry.

But when the body is placed on the ground and the shroud unfolded, it is not Jas that they all see, but Marysia, the daughter who left the house after her young man had summoned her. She has a military khaki shirt on, and she is smaller and younger than Adam remembers her. She looks fresh and untouched, except for her hair which in the back of her head appears matted and smeared. She is buried on the patch among the birch trees where Adela used to have her school.

Immediately after the ceremony Buraczka removes herself from the company of others, retiring to the barn where she lies in a dark corner, half-buried in the straw, her braids undone, her face smeared with ashes. Burak reminds her that God's will cannot be changed and that there is plenty to do on the farm. "You better do something with yourself, woman!" he upbraids her. But she does not pay attention to his words, and remains in the barn without making a sound or a movement.

When after a few days she resumes living among the others, her cough seems to have eased up, her arms shake less, and she talks again; she is like her old self, except for her eyes, Adam believes, which glower now in a way he has not seen before. Her gaze, stony yet penetrating, makes him wonder if he could ever succeed in putting a mask on her face that would dispel his uneasy feelings about her.

Towards the end of November also dies sub-lieutenant Sila, the regimental medical officer, surgeon exemplary of the National Army. They are told by soldiers who brought them more wounded that Sila had died in the line of duty, hit by shrapnel while carrying an injured man from a field near the Raba river. Then comes the first heavy snow of the season, and shortly thereafter no more wounded are brought to them; and by December there are only a handful of ill men left at the hospital. Most of those who outlast their terms of treatment and care there simply walk away, parting with those who have looked after them hurriedly and usually in silence.

When all of the Raba valley is retaken by the Realm at last, a complete silence falls upon the earth. The people on the farm wake up one morning to such stillness that they are able to hear the sounds made by hovering rooks flapping their wings and by snow falling on the earth. It is only then, when this great quietness comes, that they know that it is all finished. After three months of fighting, havoc and carnage, the National Army is no longer. This time around the Almighty has not let the hopes of His children be fulfilled or their wishes granted.

They also know that it will not be long before they will see the Realm soldiers again, this time bringing to them punishment for deeds committed during the past three months. And the people on the farm, terror-stricken, decide to rid the place of anything that might bear evidence of their crimes.

They scour off blood stains, and they burn sheets and straw from the sickbeds. And as they also throw onto the pyre uniforms, epaulets, stripes and belts, they make sure that all the invalid soldiers have nothing but peasant robes on them. They bury deep in the meadow ground Sila's needles, clamps and knives along with bottles of bimber and chloroform and the handgun that Burak got from the regiment. Konstancya, against Adam's protests, shears his head clean. Adam places his frolicking he-goat mask in the deep of the hollow. Mother recounts her past sins again. Buraczka talks about wolves coming from the forest and one of their ex-patients swears that he did not join the National Army out of his own volition.

And Burak, shovel and pickaxe in hand, is ready to raze to the ground the cemetery which he himself has erected in his meadow; a few neat rows of earth mounds, each having a birch-wood cross with a name or a mark scratched on it and a birch-bark mask attached to it. But when he is to shatter the first grave, he is stopped, he tells them later, by a Voice warning him not to touch ground which, though never consecrated by the words of a priest, has nonetheless attained sacredness.

So, they ready themselves for events to come. But as the heavy snow keeps falling on them, day and night, they get cut off from the world and thus are spared for a few days the sight of the Realm soldiers and their judgement over them.

The Home of the Divine Providence
Our secret language code has been an immense success. It has not brought about any real changes at the Home (but nobody expected that in such a short period of time), but it has freed the wards from

various frustrations that have plagued them before and it has turned the brothers (unaware of the code's existence) from rigid, humorless disciplinarians into a bunch of permissive gigglers. Last night, for instance, after supper one of the wards asked permission to read us a story, which turned out to be one of the smuttiest pieces ever written. The reading, which was interrupted several times by enthusiastic applause and commentaries, went well beyond the normal time allowed for such activities, but Hyacinth granted us the extra time willingly. The point is that the narration (written in the code) was none other than a free translation of Stefan's questionnaire on the rules of the Home; the same questionnaire that has been banned by the brothers and ordered to be consumed by the fire of our kitchen's oven. And today, as another example, it was decided, jointly by the guardians and the wards, that we would stage a play at the Home; a loose adaptation of one of our classics, in the original a poetic drama, but in our version a sex farce with music. It will be written in the code, obviously, and its characters will stand for various guardians and governors.

One bitter morning while the muffled in snow Witches Barrow is awaiting its judgement day, Nusia and Adam discover two bodies inside the barn. They look lifeless and heavy, not much different from the loaded grain sacks next to them. They lie in the middle of the threshing floor, baled up in cobwebs of icy snow; iridescent, they seem to be emitting light in all directions. At first they are not sure whether what they see is human or not, and so they decide to keep their distance. Then they call Burak, who too needs a few moments to summon his nerve, but says after a while that the two must be soldiers of the National Army, whatever is left of it. As they might turn out to be bodies of live men after all, Burak removes some of the ice and the snow off their faces and extremities and says that they should be hauled into the house.

The two men are deposited in front of the kitchen fire; and the rest stand guard over them to watch them thaw. But as they are not coming to life, the people disperse slowly and wonder how long it should take before they dispose of them. It is Nusia who is the first to notice some hours later that one of the frozen soldiers has blinked and the other has moved his knee.

When they know that the men are live indeed, they strip them, dry them and dispose of their military uniforms and others incriminating effects; the same way they got rid of all the things that were once part of the hospital. Then they perform on the two men healing rituals they learned from the late Sub-lieutenant Sila. They stare at the two denuded bodies and remark that they are not as badly damaged by wounds as some of their earlier patients, but that they look far more meager than anybody they have laid eyes on in recent months. They wonder which side of the woods the men came from and whether they were not by any chance from Sila's regiment. They also talk about clothing them and worry that they do not have many wearables left on the farm.

Before they fully come around, the two men fall into deep sleep again, right on the floor in front of the fire, with nothing on them save Buraczka's old kerchiefs. A few hours later one of the men wakes up; he yawns, looks around in confusion and pulls up the kerchief to cover his neck and scraggy shoulders. He crawls in the direction of the fire and then turns his head away from it, towards the center of the kitchen where all the people are gathered. He stares at them hard, bewildered and annoyed, and then fixes his eyes upon Nusia. He is ready to say something to her when she springs to her feet. "Radomir! Radomir! He came back!" she screams.

It is indeed he, their second cousin, boy-hero, a soldier, the man for whose affection Adam's sister and niece were once vying; only a decade or so older than when they last saw him. Mother, Kocia and Nusia are all three at his side within seconds; they shriek and ululate over him, letting him know how inexpressibly happy they are that Fate has returned him to them.

"How can you be sure it's he?" asks Adela, who has not seen him since his childhood years in Wielow.

"Please, Adela, stop saying such things!" shouts mother. "Can't you see that he looks exactly like his father, your own brother?! Same nose, hair...and the legs. Have you forgotten that you used to call him Walking-on-Stilts Piotr? One cannot possibly be wrong about those legs!"

They give Adela their word of honor that the man under the checkered kerchief is her nephew Radomir, but she refuses to believe them. The emaciated creature does not resemble anybody she has ever known, she says. Kocia calls her insensitive and tells the vague-gazed Radomir not to pay attention to her, and assures him that he is back home among those who love him.

Adela acknowledges him only some hours later while the whole household is ready to retire for the night.

"Mister Burak," she says, pointing to the sleeping Radomir, "you'll never believe it, but this thing here on the floor with the beard and these hairy legs is supposed to be the son of my brother whom I remember from centuries ago. Good God! Have you ever seen such legs, Burak?!"

Burak does not remember that he has. "And all skin and bones, Miss Adela," he says.

"Yes, one could say he is quite lean. Still, as far as his height goes, he might be just about your size, wouldn't you think? You could probably find him something among your things, trousers or such. You have got something left, haven't you, Mister Burak?"

"As you say, Miss Adela," says Burak and in short order brings to Adela his dark blue pinstripe suit, which he has probably taken from the coffer hidden under his conjugal bed.

Adela does not want to accept it. She tells him that his Sunday best should not be wasted on the skinny creature on the floor; but there is no arguing with Burak. "It is not too good if it is for your kin, Miss Adela." he says.

Well, after Burak has thus given his Sunday suit to the son of Adela's brother, mother and Kocia have to agree with Adam at last that there is something wrong with Buraczka's eyes, that they glitter unnaturally and bore into things menacingly, and particularly so when she fixes them on Adela. Mother is horror-stricken. "She is going to do something horrible!" she cries. "Is there any way we can not let it happen, Adam?"

Buraczka did not do a thing, though; except for her eyes, she remained her humble, unobtrusive, quiet self. It was Radomir and his companion that started raising hell on the farm. Mind you, except for their cough, frostbitten extremities and the general lankness, the two recovered splendidly, within only a few days after they had been placed under the care of Burak's household; and yet, instead of words of gratitude towards those who made them whole again, they raised the noisiest and ugliest hue-and-cry against everybody. They demand their uniforms back, and when same cannot be produced, they scream and holler in outrage. They call the people on the farm barbarians, skunks, desecrators, opportunistic cattle; and they make threatening gestures. Radomir reaches for Adam's shaven head with "coward" on his lips, and then with scorn and wrath tries to tear from his own body Burak's pinstripe suit.

He stops ranting only after a choking in his throat and a flow of tears prevent him from further production of articulated speech. Then Kocia gently takes him in her arms and strokes his hair. Yes, they are all barbarians and cowards, she tells him; and she, of course, would have never been part of their vile deed if it hadn't been for the sake of others, for the safety of innocent little things like Nusia, or the little Buraks who, their lice and uncouth manners notwithstanding, are still creatures of God. But he, her Radomir, is a great hero, even without his uniform.

That he and his companion acquired the status of supremely valiant demigods became clear to everyone after Kocia had coaxed out of the two (despite their coughing and stuttering) a detailed account of their adventures and then repeated that story to everyone, in her own words, more than once. It was a long tale, and Adam does not remember all of it, only the part about the two of them getting into a mountain cave from where they were shooting at the enemy in order to cover the retreat of their group, but not being able to get away themselves, as the grenade that shattered the wall of the cave, trapped them inside; and when they dug out themselves eventually, the earth was all covered with snow, impenetrable and alien. Kocia tells Radomir again that he sacrificed himself to save his comrades-in-arms, and that she is so proud of him, and that one day the whole world will hear about the Great Insurrection and his part in it; but for now, when the occupiers have still power over them, she advises him to be wise and not to talk about his military glory. And she gives him a big maternal kiss on his forehead.

The following days bring a little thaw and news from the village that fighting had broken out again, right on the other side of the river; but it is no longer the National Army battling the Realm, but the all-powerful People's Army. "The mightiest army on earth, many say it is," Burak tells them after talking to some people from the valley.

Thus the People's Army comes to the Raba valley earlier than anybody would have thought, and Burak's household does not see Realm soldiers on the farm again, as they had expected. Only Adam and Burak see them one more time for a brief moment. It happens one day when everybody is inside the house, except

Burak out in the field, that Adam suddenly spots some Realm soldiers through a crack in a boarded window; just a handful of them moving away from the farm, quickly and in disarray, some down the hill, some towards the woods, some climbing the field above the farm. Just when Adam is about to tell everybody about them, Burak walks into the kitchen. "Blessed be our Lord Jesus," he says, as if he had not seen the others in a long time, and he is very pleased with himself. Through some clever trickery he has just rid them of a whole company, maybe a full regiment, of Realm evildoers, he says. The Realm soldiers he encountered in the field wanted to know if he had seen any of the People's forces yet, and so he told them that the People's soldiers had already reached the Witches Barrow and made their quarters right here on the farm, several dozen People's fighters armed to the teeth with machine guns and grenades, having also with them a mighty cannon which they stashed in the barn. Burak chuckles and nods his head, "told them, the Satan's seeds, that the People's fighters were as fierce as angered boars, ready to kill any Realm soldier they would spot, and so gave them advice to run for their lives, 'as far and as fast as you can, good sirs,' I said. And so they did. Amen."

The Realm forces are indeed fleeing the mountains, as it turns out, but the People's soldiers have yet to fight their way through a new Realm front that has formed just north of the Raba valley. So for a few more days the people on the farm are left all to themselves, unoccupied by anybody.

Burak, after having heard stories of the harshness of the People's rule and seizures of private properties, prepares himself for the worst. He stows and buries anything that is still lying around, God forbid, ready for taking. He places all the fowl and a goat in a new enclosure in the highest spot of the loft and covers all the trap doors and new partitions with heavy bales of straw, and reinforces the hinges on the couch which leads to the hollow.

But even before the People's Army comes to call on him, his household is to go through yet another trial. This time it is the Povolians prowling now in the mountains that have turned into terror-sowing desperados; abandoned by the fleeing Realm troops and fearful to return to their homeland now all of it in the hands of the People's Power, cheated out of their rights, humiliated by fate again. On Christmas Eve they hit the valley below the Witches Barrow, pillaging the villages and setting fire to the homes.

A pillar of hellish blaze is rising from the bottom of the Witches Barrow luminating the area and strewing through the air the moans of the stricken valley. Burak and all the others come out of the house and with fear stare into the fiery abyss. And then, from among howls and wails, there comes to them a soft musical murmur; a hum, a chant, which turns into a clear melody and a song which Adam recognizes: a marching air commemorating some ancient Povolian glory. The song grows louder and stronger, until it explodes into a deafening cry summoning men to mortal battle. And then before their eyes materialize ghostly figures of singing Povolians themselves. They ascend the slope one by one, marking the rhythm with the pound of their boots on the soil and the huff of their lungs expelling the violent notes; each man carrying a lit torch in hand.

The people of Burak's household instantly form a row alongside the house, drop on their knees and prostrate themselves on the frozen ground; they wail out prayers, as instructed by Burak; and he himself, his arms stretched out towards the shadowy figures with torches, begs their would-be assailants for mercy. But, heedless of Burak's plea, the Povolians move closer, with two of them sprinting ahead of the rest. The two raise their torches and wave them in triumph; and with a quick backward sway of their bodies – to the rhythm of the song that never wavers – send flaming cudgels arcing through the air. The torches scorch off into the sky and then descend onto the section of the roof above the chamber that was once Adela's schoolroom. And before long the thatch over that part of the house becomes consigned to flames.

But farmer Burak, man of great faith, does not lose his possessions to the ravaging flames on that Christmas Eve after all. As he watches the flames devouring the roof he had built with his own hands, he does not stop calling out to the Creator for help; and he is answered. A few minutes after the torches are thrown at his house, the still of the night air is interrupted by a vehement gale of wind. The people sway, the house shakes, trees bend down; the Povolians stoop closer to the ground and lower their torches; and the flaming thatch hit by the fierce blows of the howling wind is pushed off its base. Right in front of everybody's eyes, the burning mass, divorced from the rest of the house, glides through the air – like a fiery volant sleigh – until it stops directly above the dumbfounded throng of the Povolian assailants and with wheezing and whistling plummets onto their heads. The Povolians scatter in panic; and shortly thereafter fresh gusts of wind reduce the fire on the fallen thatch to a few insignificant flickers.

Shortly after these events, which from then on will be known all around as the miracle of the burning thatch, Burak undergoes a change. His body straightens out quite a bit and his bearing grows proudful; and his voice gains in force, particularly when he recounts how, with the help of God and the Holy Virgin, he managed to scare the life out of, first, armed Realm troopers and then a Povolian mob, and how he made them all, Satan's servants, flee in terror. He also seems to have lost his fear of the People's Army, which, by the way, right after Christmas is reported to have crossed the Raba river. After he makes a journey to the village to learn the latest on the approaching forces, Burak tells everybody on the farm that the People's Army will do no harm to anybody; it will simply bring peace, and a new and just order.

"It will be called People's Democracy," he tells them. "A man said that they will take away from those who have too much and do not need it all for themselves, and then they'll give it to those who have too little, the poorer ones. That's what the man said. They will cut up large estates into smaller parcels and deed them over to the needy ones, like me and my family," Burak sounds almost inspired.

Konstancya becomes terribly huffed about all that, and calls him an ignorant man. But he will not be silenced. "It is not wrong to take something from a man who does not need it and give it to somebody who does. And Miss Adela herself said many times that it was a great shame that I did not have enough, just that wretched mountain soil, rock and clay."

"Would you, please, explain things to him properly, Adela!" cries Kocia. And she reminds Adela (who herself had not yet experienced the People's rule) about the horrors that took place in the Eastern Provinces after the People's Power had taken it at the outset of the War; about Adela's own father forced to leave his house and to move to the Puddles into a state-run tenement; about silversmith Gruber, once Adela's fiancé, dispossessed of his silver and sent to a penal colony; about Canon Banasz, once Adela's confessor, defrocked by order of the People's authorities and assigned to the labor of pavement repairs.

"Well, the quantities of silver in Gruber's shop were definitely excessive," says Adela, not moved to any further reflections, except: "Oh, my! Canon Banasz in civilian clothes digging holes in streets must have been quite a sight to behold!"

One day shortly after Burak brought them his latest news of the People's Army, Adam hears him talk to himself. They are both in the stable: Adam is feeding the sow in one corner and Burak is cleaning around the animals at the other end, and his voice comes to Adam from behind the cow the farmer is attending. He is telling the People's authorities how many hectares of land he can use, and how many milking cows and sows. "And one stout bull and one good horse to replace the one that was killed by bullets the night my son Oles was bringing supplies for the hospital, if you please, kind sirs," says Burak in his address to the new authorities.

7.

The first soldier of the victorious army of the Great Eastern United People's Power appears in front of the inhabitants of Burak's farm early at dawn, at a time when no one is yet risen from their night's rest. He pushes the door to the kitchen open, and they wake up.

They move inside their straw nests and then freeze at the sight of the gun directed at them. The soldier motions them to go to the wall with the holy pictures on it, which faces the door at which he stands. The features of his face are obscured by the morning shadows, but the people can clearly see his hands and the gun aimed at them. He does not move from his position, except to adjust the direction of his gun quickly after the back door opens and the Buraks (who have slept in the adjoining chamber) walk into the kitchen. Burak bows to him and the whole Burak family joins the rest of them, and the soldier redirects his weapon towards its previous bearing.

More People's soldiers come in and more guns' muzzles get fixed on the wall with the holy pictures. The soldiers do not insist that they all stay motionless, but make sure that none of them goes away from the wall. The soldiers talk to one another, raise their voices and laugh; they also address the group at the wall with some loud words from time to time, but are not understood by anybody. They laugh noisily, possibly at them, a row of ungainly figures shivering from cold, unclean, dredged with straw. When a new man enters the kitchen, by all signs the commander of the others, the laughter ceases at once; the bodies of the soldiers stiffen and their guns spring up, back to their proper position of readiness.

Looking straight above their heads, the commander talks to Burak's party in their own language. They have been liberated from the Realm's occupation by the People's Army, he tells them, and their nation has just joined the new brotherhood of people's republics. They are at last free, but the GEU People's Power, their friend and neighbor, will not abandon them; its Army will stay with them for as long as it is necessary for the new order to be established.

When after a short pause he talks again, he requests that they immediately relinquish all arms and ammunition in their possession. Burak tells him that there are no guns on the Witches Barrow, but the man repeats his request. Burak crosses himself and swears to his household's virtuousness, but the man insists that they surrender their arms. Burak crosses himself again and says that he is poor and "had no time ever to play with them guns and munitions, good sir, like some rich folks do."

The commander's eyes empierce the wall with the holy pictures in silence. Then he looks straight at them; his mouth opens and new and urgent sounds come out. If they have any information about either hidden weapons or any anti-People's activities, they should report it to the People's Army headquarters on the Raba. Above all, he says, they should consider it their duty to report anything they know of the activities and of the hiding places, yes, hiding places, of any ex-fighters of the treacherous and now happily extinct Underground Army, for a short while known as the National Army. At the mention of the National Army, Radomir and his companion jerk as if readying themselves to a charge forward, but the commander is no longer paying attention to any of them as his eyes are turning away from the wall towards a bench next to the stove on which stands an enameled pail with milk from the past night's milking, almost full.

Before the soldiers of the GEU People's Army leave them that day, they help themselves to the milk, which was intended for the morning meal.

The soldiers of the People's Army are gone, and Burak ruminates on the inexplicable ways of God's doings in this world; on the People's power fighting the Realm, on the National Army fighting the Realm too, on all of the people helping the National Army to fight the Realm, and on everybody later being scared of the Realm on account of them helping the National Army, and on the People's Power saying now – after the Realm and the National Army are both beaten and gone – that the National Army fought against them and not against the Realm, and the people being scared now of the People's Power.

He also muses on his luck and cleverness: making sure that after the Insurrection all proofs of their partaking in that event were razed, all the hospital things burned and destroyed, down to the smallest scrap; and the gun, the one that Sub-Lieutenant Sila, God-rest-his-soul, gave him, buried really deep. "Only you people keep your mouths closed about things. And you son," Burak turns to Oles freshly recovered from his bullet wounds. "You just don't ever tell them how you got that limp."

Oles then asks Adela whether it all means that he will never get the military cross that the Sub-Lieutenant promised him. Adela tells him that most probably he won't, and then laughs, "If you really want to have a cross, why won't you make one for yourself, you know, from some scrap metal or something. You've always been good at smithery!"

At this moment all of Radomir's pain and anger accumulated within him erupt again; Adela's doing, for sure.

He again tries to tear Burak's pinstripe suit off his body; he cries, coughs and spurts out insults; against injustice, against the People's Power, against Adela and her friend Burak, against the whole horrid world which has already forgotten about the Fight and the Cause so many died for. And he stops, like on previous occasions, only when his tears make it impossible for him to continue and Kocia takes him in her arms.

And she again tells him that she knows that there will come a day that he will be able to tell the world the whole truth. And then she adds, an almost mischievous smile on her face, that he should not tell his story after all, but write it. He has always had that gift, an extraordinary gift; and so she vows to him that as soon as things get settled a little bit, she will take command of his life and make sure that he does not waste his talents and miss his true calling.

Oh, how Adam disdains her at this moment and how he envies her! He has never been good at making plans, any plans (at least not since he left the theater), but during the past few months he has not been able to think of any future events at all, unless they were clearly destined to fall within the space of an hour or so immediately ahead of him. He remembers that through the remainder of that day while Buraczka is suddenly again calling out names of her departed children and mother keeps asking whether the War is really over and they have been granted independence, Kocia is talking of enrolling Radomir into some university as soon as possible.

Those familiar with the history of the War know that in that early January, when the People's soldiers paid Burak their first visit, the War is not over yet; the Realm, crippled and weakened, is still battling its two adversaries. It is only in mid-spring when that once-power finally falls and the Continent becomes formally divided between the two victors. Yet, in that January, for the lands where Adam lives, the War has indeed already ended, as from then on, the westward-bound front of the People's Army, like a moving rampart, will shield them from the action and cut them off from the rest of the Continent, making anything that is happening over there, on the other side, of absolutely no consequence to them.

As for independence, well, people on the farm read about it in several freshly-printed circulars which are delivered to them by a uniformed man from the People's headquarters on the Raba. They also hear it being announced through a megaphone by a village man standing at the foot of the Witches Barrow. Both the man with a megaphone and the one with the circulars say that the country is now in the possession of a free-acting government, begotten out of the people's will upon the ashes of their shameful past. It is only mother who asks what it was that the whole country, millions of people, now half-starved and homeless, did in the past to be ashamed of; and also who elected their new government?

In the weeks following their first visit, soldiers of the GEU People's Army call on Burak's farm several more times. Each time they search the premises and question all the people on the farm. On some occasions, for the purpose of special questioning, those selected are taken by a military vehicle all the way down to the People's headquarters in Dobce. However, Adam has to admit nobody is ever treated in an impolite manner – that is nobody seems to be hit, spat upon, or bodily assaulted in any other fashion.

They are always taken into the same room in which a few months earlier Adam had been quizzed about the Whip the Unbeaten. The bare electric bulbs and the desk of the chief interrogator looks exactly the way Adam remembers them from that previous occasion, but some of the decor of the room has changed. The canvas with the emblem of the Realm is gone, and so is the portrait of the Realm's Supreme Leader. In their place now hangs a portrait of the Highest Commander of the People's Power and two banners: a large one in the national colors of the People's Power and a small one in those of Adam's country. Since all of the inquisitors now seem to be fairly well acquainted with the language, no interpreter is used during the proceedings (as a matter of fact, a couple of the men are actually locals, Burak points out later). During the interrogations Adam and his family are asked about the Whip, and also about the other leaders of the National Army; but those questions are put to them in a perfunctory manner; probably because it is common knowledge by then that just about all the leaders of the National Army have either expired on the field of battle or have been captured by the People's Army. The main concern of the interrogators appear to be the personal role of the interrogated in what they now call the rebellion against new rulers and their personal knowledge of any local enemies of the new order.

It is during their first visit at Dobce's headquarters that Radomir is removed from their midst to be detained somewhere else for further questioning. His removal takes place immediately after one of the interrogators states that Radomir's pinstripe suit, obviously several sizes too big for him, still looks mighty fine on him, and Radomir in reply passionately grunts that he hates the suit, and Nusia quickly explains that he hates it is because it is not his and he should have his own because he is a great hero. (On their return to the farm, despite Adam's protests, Nusia gets slapped and whipped all over by Kocia, and then tied to the kitchen table for a period of several hours.) A few days later it is mother who is removed from the interrogating room. After some particularly long and grueling examination, she breaks down into tears and says that she feels so miserable and confused, particularly about the country's independence, that she would like just to crawl into the hollow under Burak's couch and stay in there without seeing the world for the rest of her life. The following day the farm is visited by a special squad of People's soldiers and Burak is asked to disclose to the new authorities the secrets of his underground chamber. Luckily, as Wiktor has decided to remain outside from now on, the hollow has been emptied, and so the soldiers find nothing in it; that is nothing save the frolicking he-goat mask, which, despite Adam's objections, they impound.

After that, it is only Burak, Oles and Adam that are taken down to the headquarters. The farmer is asked to confirm the rumor that during the recent events he, his son Oles and his guest Adam ran a hospital for the soldiers of forces hostile to the People's Power. Burak looks the chief interrogator straight in the eye and shakes his head with a grin. "Not us, good sir, not us. We are just poor farmers, and this one (Adam) just a farmhand, simple-minded at that; and we never had anything to do with them rich people and were not part of their fighting. The most we did was to bury some of their dead that fell near my house; didn't want them to rot on my ground or be ravaged by wolves and ravens. Buried them, that's all. But didn't even bother to given them proper funeral-like prayers, good sir."

Burak and Oles are released, but Adam is transferred to a different building for further examination. He is asked again about the hospital and about his interest in mask-making, but after two days of questioning, he is judged as difficult and is transferred to the basement of the old school building, where some months ago he and Nusia were prisoners of the Realm. But this time Adam is not chained. In point of fact, he is free to walk around as well as to talk to other prisoners. In a distant corner he notices Radomir (the pinstripe suit still on him) who smiles to him faintly, asks him whether he has noticed the foulness of the air in the place and then points to a partition behind which is the women's section where mother has been kept.

Adam manages to talk to her through a hole in a wooden board. She cries and complains about the cold, and says she knows that she is not going to last for much longer.

Their imprisonment is terminated before too long, though. After about a week since Adam's detention, they are all three released. It is their old friend, the warden of the Dobce cemetery, who meets them outside the jail's gate and informs them that they owe their freedom to a certificate presented to the newly-created Security Council of Dobce by the Medical Examiner of the also newly-created Town Council; a document stating that all three of them: Radomir, mother and Adam, are victims of fundamental unsoundness of mind called paraphrenia.

Their friend is too modest and too pressed for time to explain to them further that the man who has produced the certificate is his personal friend who wrote the said document on his urging, and also that the man is the town pharmacist, who only temporarily, in the absence of a physician in the area, is serving as the Medical

Examiner on the Town Council. The warden finds still enough time to present them with gifts (a large bar of soap and three warm sweaters) and to advise them to be cautious and humble when dealing with the new officialdom. He reminds them also that they, strangers in this region, are nevertheless known to some of the locals from their activities during the Insurrection; and so he recommends that they move on, settle some distance from Dobce and find themselves some solid occupations, both as means of support and proof to the authorities of their usefulness to the new order. Before they part that day, he also makes sure that the Security Office returns to Adam his mask.

Later, back on the farm, they all talk about the amazing phenomenon of the old warden's prestige among the locals and his official standing in the community having not diminished a bit, despite all the sweeping changes taking place everywhere.

Their friend's advise on leaving the area notwithstanding, they stay on. For one, they cannot go back to Wielow and the Eastern Provinces, as places of such names do not exist anymore, they are officially informed; that is, they are no longer part of their country. Under different names (in People's language) they are now on the other side of the country's eastern border forming an integral part of the Great Eastern United People's Power. After being officially told about the situation, Kocia starts behaving as if everything relating to her past life in the East was suddenly expunged from her inner being. She is doing exactly what is expected of her, for all of them of Eastern roots are now supposed to delete from their minds memories of their past; and the first thing which they are suppose to know is that the territory they came from has always been within the borders of the GEU, and not their own country.

Kocia would love to make their new home in the Capital. The best place for Radomir to pursue his higher education, she says; and also what a wonderful change for her, who has always felt unfulfilled in the confinements of provincial surroundings where she was forced to live through all her life. She will find them jobs in the Capital, in the theater, of course. Musical comedy is what she envisages as the future: she, in singing parts, any kind; mother, in the orchestra or coaching the music backstage; Adam, in small comic character roles. "You can be genuinely funny, Adam, if you only want to!" Yet, she cannot embark on that new adventure, not at the moment. There is no easy way of reaching the Capital; the roads encrusted with ice and snow, and the railroads not yet rebuilt after the recent devastations. Also the Capital lays in ruin, they are told, with some parts of it effaced altogether, as if they have never been in existence before. And besides, Konstancya has no money, none at all, to get her to any destination. Then the temperature drops to lows they have not yet experienced this winter and they find themselves with not enough clothes to venture anywhere, so she decides that they best stay with the Buraks for a while longer.

In the meantime Burak, their host and upholder, brings his plea to the High Commissioner of the region. Encouraged by Adela, he requests that – in consideration of the size of his family and the inferiorness of his land – he be placed on the roll of those eligible for land grants under a new act of estate parcelation. Just at the time when he submits his request, the largest local estate, that of Count Czerwinski, is being cut up; the count himself in whereabouts unknown. His wealth, now in the hands of the Office of the High Commissioner, is piece by piece apportioned to the neediest of the area, justly and swiftly; so says the Office. Burak has enough wisdom not to hope for much, but he believes that at least something should be coming his way, as to a deserving one.

But no land is granted to him. It is officially determined that citizen Burak of the Witches Barrow, a suspect in anti-People's activities during the period immediately preceding the liberation, is already the owner of more square hectares of arable land than befits one farm household.

But Burak will not let go. As he knows what is right, he swears to God that he will prove to the new authorities that his land is no good, and also that he is an honest man. He just needs to explain real properly to those new men in authority how things are, and they will change their minds about him, he is sure. With Adela's help he works on a lengthy new petition; and after a week he has a good five pages of it ready, all in his best handwriting. He means to deliver his letter in person directly to the High Commissioner. But as he lays his plans, an unexpected visitor to the farm, a man Burak once befriended, tells him otherwise.

Burak's friend pays his visit in the middle of the night. He drives up the Witches Barrow in a small motor truck covered with dark tarpaulin. He knocks on the door, calls Burak outside, talks to him for a while in a whisper and swears him to secrecy. He is a young man who until not long ago worked on Count Czerwinski's estate, but who has most recently been appointed to be a committeeman in the Office of the High Commissioner. Burak did him some good turn in the past and also helped bring back to life his brother who was laid in Burak's hospital during the Insurrection, and so this young man wants now to repay the kindness, at a time when the farmer has been disfavored by the new authorities. As he is close enough to those in power in the Office, he knows that Burak will not get any land, however hard he may try. But as he wants to do right by him, he has decided to make Burak a gift on his own, that is, without the knowledge of anybody from the Office.

"Straight from the Count's estate," he says pointing towards his motor truck. He pulls away the tarpaulin and presents to Burak: a milking cow of rare beauty, a pair of geese of the finest breed and a bagful of almost-new garments from the Count's own dressing room. Burak cannot believe his eyes; he is dumbfounded. The young man does not want thanks; he just helps unload the gifts quickly and asks Burak again not to betray him. He hopes that his visit has gone unobserved and that the disappearance of the cow, the geese and the clothing will likewise be unnoticed. The following morning Burak makes them all swear that they will never try to find out about the goings-on of that night or breathe a word to anybody.

The Home of the Divine Providence

Today is Monday, the day I usually dread. Mondays at the Home are for laundering, review of past sins and general cleaning up; and there are two guardians assigned to the supervision of the day's duties: Brother Celestus, the guardian of physical maintenance of the Home and Brother Honore, the guardian of morals and upright behavior. I dislike washing or tidying up of any kind, and particularly detest being told by Celestus to get my workbench and tools "spanking clean". Today, however, I was told by both brothers, with smiles on their faces, that I can be excused from any cleaning because of my work on the play. As you may recollect, we are putting on a play (a licentious farce with music, all written in the secret language code invented by the wards), an endeavor that all the wards and the guardians have embraced most eagerly. For the past two weeks I have indeed been very busy, designing masks and costumes, helping build the set and studying the part I am to perform. In general, the level of excitation and enthusiasm at the Home is without precedent; Brother Simplicius has been coming to our rehearsals and warmly applauding everything, Brother Hyacinth is on the set-building crew ; Brother Klementior wants to handle the props; and the handsome Brother Euzebius has agreed to play the part of the Bride and offered to sew the bridal costume personally. Also, our dissident ward, Lech, has been returned to us after his long detention in the Home's attic and asked to do the music for our play, as undoubtedly Lech is a superb musician. Lech agreed to create the necessary musical score and also to provide the accompaniment, mainly on his favorite instrument the bassoon, which, by the way, was also just returned to him. It was some two years ago when his bassoon, after one of Lech's unbecoming outbreaks of temper, was removed from his possession by the brothers and, despite his and our pleas, never returned to him, that is, until now.

As he does not want at the moment to draw attention to himself and stir up any trouble, Burak decides not to take his petition to the High Commissioner, not for a little while; all on account of his young friend, the committeeman. But shortly after his friend brings him the gifts, the farmer decides to forgo the idea of any petitioning altogether; this time on account of another young man, a People's soldier named Kiril.

While the People's Army is still fighting their final battle over the Realm somewhere in the West, most of the People's forces stationed in the Dobce area are already quite worn, fatigued of the toils of war, anxious for a taste of peace. Their orders are to curb unruliness among the locals and to keep their distance from them. Yet, to experience things they have not been able to savor in a long time, People's soldiers are ready, some of them – against orders – to make closer acquaintance with the local people.

One night a group of them walk into Burak's kitchen. They take off their overcoats, hats and boots and throw them about. They drink bimber straight from the canteens they have brought with them, and they pound the floor with their bootless cloth-wrapped feet in order to get rid of the chill-induced rigor that has set in their bodies. They laugh and talk noisily, and invite the others to get closer to them. And after they warm up, they sing, stamp their feet and slap their legs in the rhythm of their songs, and they insist that the others join them. They also make obscene gestures and let out vulgar cheers.

Mother is afraid of them and wants Burak to throw them out, but he only gives her a stern look. "If he cannot force them out of here, then we should leave and go somewhere else," she whispers to Adam, knowing that with the awful cold outside and most of the farm in ruination there is no place they can go.

So nobody leaves the kitchen, not even when the soldiers, set at ease by drink and song, take over most of the kitchen floor and the space for the rest of them shrinks to just a few feet along the wall. Not even when the air around becomes thick, foul smelling.

The soldiers are urging them to join in the revelry. But only Oles answers their call by trying to match the soldiers' song with music he is making on his singing-reed pipe (the one he carved this past fall for Sila to admire). When after a few trials he hits the right notes, the soldiers cheer and launch themselves into frenzied leaps to the tune of his pipe. Then they offer him a drink from one of their canteens; and when he declines, they just press the canteen to his lips, yank his head back, open his mouth and pour the liquor in.

Through much of the night they sing and dance while Oles plays for them. They also eat groats which Buraczka prepares at their request. And before they leave, they take from the farm's food supply a large quantity of edibles, as much as they can carry.

After they are gone, Burak asks himself and Adela whether it was right that he did nothing to oppose their rowdiness and ungodliness in his house, and whether it is wise to come down upon those who have authority over you. Before he retires that night he also beseeches the Almighty that the People's soldiers never again show up at his house.

But a few nights later they receive another visitation. This time only a solitary soldier. They recognize him from the previous visit: the most skillful dancer of the group. He is large and dark, and asks to be called Kiril. They do not understand his speech well, but they guess that he does not wish the others to know about his whereabouts, and also that he considers the people on the farm to be his special friends. He stays for several hours; he eats, drinks and tells Oles to play for him, the same tune over and over again.

After that night he becomes a regular visitor to the farm. He calls them all his friends, wants to learn their names, offers them drinks from his canteen and slaps their back and shoulders with loud, hearty swats. Still, they all dislike his presence among them a great deal and want him gone. But, for fear of inflaming him to anger, nobody upbraids him or tells him to leave. And each time he comes, Adam wonders what has made him choose Burak's place over some others. There are moments when he believes that it is Oles, pale, limping youth with the singing magic pipe in his fingers, that has beguiled him. But at other times it seems to him that it is just the smell of the place and the sight of the kitchen fire and Buraczka stirring the groats in the kettle that have drawn him to the place.

They never see Kiril sober, but one night when the Devil Bimber has laid hold of him more potently than usual, they see him changed. On that night, before he even takes off his overcoat, he begins to pound on his chest and to bawl wildly, letting them know that he is full of sorrow, his afflicted heart bleeding profusely. He has with him two canteens with bimber; he drinks the entire contents of one right away, and then gives the other one to the men in the kitchen, making sure that every drop of the liquor is consumed by them. When he warms up and his limbs get lighter, he requests that Oles play the music for the dance he did at his first visit.

He hops, shuffles and bounds about for several minutes, until - after a rapid succession of deep squats and high leaps - he drops to the floor like a dead man; only his heavy breathing marking his life. But a few minutes later he is back on his feet, ordering all the others to join him in dancing. He insists that they find partners and dance in pairs. Nusia and Adam, and a few others, do as told; they hold hands with one another and move their feet to the music coming from Oles's pipe. But Kiril bawls again, lamenting over his broken heart and his wretched lot of not having a partner for himself. Nusia then leaves the dancing group and runs to Adela who, weary of the scene, is at that moment making her way to the secluded corner behind the stove. "Adela, please dance with Kiril because he has no partner. You have no partner either, so you dance with him. He is so sad and cries, so dance with him, please!" begs Nusia.

Kiril's tearful eyes move in the direction of Adela; he did not notice her movements before, and so this sudden discovery pleases him greatly. He calls her name. As he can only see her back, he yells to her to turn around; but she does not listen. He yells some more and orders her to dance with him, but she just barely moves her head and – without as much as giving him a glance – tells him to go to hell. He howls in pain, and then, with all the fury of a spurned suitor, leaps towards her and drags her to the center of the floor.

She tries to free herself from the grasps of his arms clutched around her torso; she kicks him and hits him with her fists and calls him names; and since she is no weakling, almost as tall as he and not the least bit drunk, she will not be subdued. She struggles hard; but it is not long before Burak comes to her aid. With the Herculean power of his clenched fists he delivers such a forceful blow to Kiril's neck that this assailant of Adela loses his balance and falls down. Adela slips away from Kiril's grip, but Burak keeps on striking, his body downthrown. And the stricken man responds only by expelling loud, raucous sounds. For a few moments the people in the kitchen hear nothing but harsh breathing and see just two massive figures one on top of the other, almost motionless.

But when the man underneath at last stirs and moves his arm in what seems to be the direction of the pistol attached to his side, Radomir jumps up on him. And in a flash two other men rush to the center of the floor too: first, Radomir's old companion-in-arms (the one whose frozen body Nusia and Adam discovered in the barn some time before), and then, one of their ex-patients, the very last one that still resides with them on the farm. Burak, Radomir and these two men are all on top of Kiril; mounted upon him, they cover him with their chests, legs and arms until Kiril just disappears from the view and the four men take possession of his body completely. They bear down upon it, they pound at it from all directions, they maul it and ram it into the floor. When they stop and retreat to where they all were just a few minutes earlier, no sounds can be heard coming from Kiril's mouth any longer.

He lies in the center of the floor – encircled by the shadows of the huddled figures and the glow from the carbide lamp hanging from the ceiling beam – a still, dark body, with blotched face all awry and black bristly hair, revulsive. The body of a man who can offend no longer; of a stranger who has told them that his name was Kiril and who has called them his friends, of a fighter in the Army that has power over them.

Later that night, not a sound uttered, they carry him out of the house. Since the frozen ground does not yield even to the hardest blows of ax or shovel, they cannot lay him together with the others, in Burak's meadow among the birch crosses. Instead, they depose him in a far-off place deep in the woods on the other side of the fields, in a dried-up ravine to which they are led by Oles. They place him on the frozen ground and then cover him with hardened blocks of snow and all the rocks and branches that they have strength to gather. And then they walk home a long roundabout way, longer still as Oles, who is leading them, drags his injured leg slowly, in pain, and they try to make sure that no betraying tracks are left after them.

Back in the house, for hours Adam tries to unbend his hardened icy fingers bleeding from cracks in his skin and to bring out a congested icy mass that seems to have suffused his entire chest. He is not able to talk, and so cannot answer any of Nusia's questions about Kiril. Her mother tells her, though, that he took ill, and had to be helped by the men of the house to get down the Witches Barrow.

The following day two of the participants in the execution, Radomir's companion-in-arms and their last ex-patient, leave the farm. They go separately, with few words, in haste, never to be seen or heard from again. Konstancya calls the two departed men cowards, yet shortly after they are gone, she tells Radomir to leave too. But he just pulls on the lapel of his pinstripe suit and says that there is no place for him to go. She does not mention his leaving the farm again, that is, not until the following night after two officers of the People's Army pay them a visit.

Just before they walk in, when Oles from the window signals their arrival, Kocia manages to seize Nusia's arms and, twisting them mercilessly, breathes into Nusia's face that as much as one sound to anyone about anything, and Nusia's beloved mother will die from a terrible hurt and Nusia herself will meet her own end in a smelly dungeon full of snakes and bats. The People's officers ask them questions regarding a matter most grievous, most grievous indeed, they say. They want to know about local criminal elements who have been spreading corruption and drunkenness among the soldiers of the People's Army. They warn them that they mean business and that they will be back shortly to ask more questions and get some better answers. Early next morning Konstancya and Radomir take off together.

They are back the following day, returning, Adam presumes, from a visit to the only person Kocia knows in the area, the warden of the Dobce cemetery. She has acquired the name and address of a trustworthy person in Kramow, she tells them, somebody who could help them all in making a new beginning. Unfortunately, she says, they have no way and means of getting to that city. "Only a little over fifty kilometers, which is no distance to speak of, straight north, the road almost all cleared by now. But nobody to take us there!"

Then in a short while she experiences a revelation, "But of course! Mister Burak can help us! Mister Burak definitely does not want us on his farm anymore, with all the trouble we might cause him, some of us, I mean." There is not a quiver in her voice. "It will be in your best interest if you help us leave the area, believe me, Mister Burak!" She shifts her gaze meaningfully towards Nusia and Radomir, letting the farmer know that he cannot count either on Nusia's continued silence or on Radomir's not getting in trouble with the new authorities.

At first he insists that he has no power to help her, then he says that he will think about the matter, and then later, after Adela asks him whether he indeed could do something to get them out of his hair, he tells Konstancya that he will try.

At night he goes to his young friend, the committeeman (the one who recently brought him the gifts from the Count's estate) to ask his advice on finding transportation to Kramow. And after that visit he says to them all that he is going to do what has to be done, what those wiser than he know is necessary. Then he tells Oles to kneel together with him in front of the holy pictures and ask the blessed Virgin to forgive them their sins and to watch over the farm.

Immediately after the prayer the two of them go on to slaughter one of the two milking cows that are kept now on the farm; a somber and toilsome ritual they perform on the threshing floor of the barn. They choose the younger and fairer of the cows, the one from the Count's estate, given to Burak by his friend only a few weeks earlier. "It was never meant for me to keep this one, the fairest beast ever," Burak keeps on saying through the whole day as he and Oles do their work on the dead animal. They sever the head and the limbs from the rest of the body, they wrest out the innards and remove the hide; and they carry the cleaned carcass from the barn into the kitchen to properly quarter and section it there. Till late at night they cut the carcass up and carefully trim the pieces of the bared red flesh; and they separate the choicest cuts from the rest.

The following morning Burak puts the finest pieces inside a heavy sackcloth bag and takes them to Dobce, to offer them to the man who, according to Burak's young friend, has more power than anybody else in town. And in the afternoon he takes another bag of meat down to the Army barracks on the Raba as a gift for one of the supervising officers, the man in charge of trucks, jeeps and other such vehicles. On his return home he tells them that he hopes that those powerful men will keep their word. Burak divides the remainder of the meat, all inferior fare, into two: one half to sell at the Dobce market square and the other to keep on the farm.

The men on whose behalf Burak made an offering of his cow do keep their promise. Three days after they accept his gifts, they send to the farm a military motor truck driven by a man who says that he is on his way to Kramow and willing to take some people with him.

Kocia congratulates Burak on his feat of procuring a vehicle for them. But the farmer looks glum and downcast, does not say anything to her words of praise and admiration. Nonetheless, before they settle themselves under the oily tarpaulin, he brings them some straw to lie on, a fresh loaf of bread and a couple of banknotes from the small pile he received for the sale of some of his beef. He also summons a few local men to help load mother's piano on the truck.

While the five of them: mother, Kocia, Nusia, Radomir and Adam, assisted by Burak, are getting settled, his family, shivering from cold, are all standing against the front wall of the house, in a crooked row, gazing somewhere beyond the spot where the motor truck is. The people from the truck wave goodbye to them and shout out words of thankfulness, but Buraczka and the rest just stare straight ahead, taking no notice. Then as the driver turns on the engine and is ready to start, out of the house rushes Adela, who calls upon the driver to wait. She is holding a small suitcase and pulling by the arm Wiktor, the couch dweller, whom Burak gave shelter during the war. "Well, goodbye, Burak," she quickly extends her arm to him. "Stay healthy and take good care of those children of yours." And then she pushes Wiktor onto the truck and follows behind him and then shouts already from the top of the truck, "Have you ever calculated how much I owe you for all these years; you know, room, board, and the kerchief and things. Well, when I am rich again..." she laughs.

And he just stands there unbelieving, panic taking over his face and body. He seems to ready himself for a leap forward, towards the truck, as if with the intention of willing it to stop. But he does not move from where he is, just lowers his head and hunches his shoulders; his whole frame suddenly heaving. Then he asks her if she is going to be back, his voice coming to them already from some distance. And she leans out of the moving truck, laughs some more and shouts in his direction that she will be back in the summer, and if not this summer then some other summer, for sure.

It is a military motor truck with the red emblem of the People's Power on its front and rear that is carrying them to a new beginning. The man who drives this vehicle and takes charge of them provides them with official papers to be shown to military or civilian patrols if necessary; and he explains to them that he is traveling to Kramow to attend to an official matter assigned to him by the newly created Office of Internal Security, and also that his duties will be taking him not just to Kramow, but to a great number of other places on the way to that city as well. And so, their journey will take a little while, about two weeks, he predicts.

Their first stop is, on their request, the Dobce cemetery. Their friend, the custodian of the holy grounds, treats them to a meal, and then shows them some of the recent devastation: fragmented stones, defaced inscriptions, gutted burial chambers. The old man, saddened as he is, does not seem to be prey to any kind of cynicism or despair. Yes, he has heard rumors about the new authorities conspiring to replace the traditional burial rites with something new, unheard of and ungodly, but he does not believe a word of it.

He is confident that as far as burying the dead is concerned, things will go on more or less the way they always have. Generous that he is, he gives them for their journey, a bag of confectioneries, two silver coins, and a few items of helpful information.

They stop at villages, roadhouses, railroad depots, churches; just as the driver said; and at each stop he talks to the local citizenry, asks questions, nods and writes down some information on a pad provided by the Office of Internal Security. On occasion he emerges from his conferences with bags or bundles stashed under his arms; local folks' gifts to him for favors conferred upon them; and once in a while he shares a little of his bounty with his passengers. He rarely converses with them, except to remind them from time to time to be less conspicuous during the periods of his official interrogations and also to take good care of the padded military overcoats he has lent them for the duration of their trip.

For the first few days of their journey the air stays arctic and the ground snow-laden. Then, all of a sudden a vigorous warming comes down upon them, and the ice and snow rapidly soften. Before the end of their traveling there starts to reveal itself the dark-patched earth; pitted, blemished, marred now by all that in the past few months has been closely shrouded by freeze and snow. From inside mounds of melting ice now rise carcasses and helmets, shattered weapons and fragments of human habitats; and on the fields appear people scouring the land filled with the remains of the War. Konstancya looks up at the new, warmer sky and decides that springs is upon them.

Some days hence they find themselves in the jam-packed main room of a partly demolished postal building on the outskirts of a small town near Kramow. They buy there hot tea from a local woman while Nusia is trying to move through the crowd in the direction of a vendor displaying sweets of various kinds. It is then that she spots her father. Not that she knows who he is. He looks familiar, and so she stares at him; but as soon as he notices her and starts working his way through the mob towards her, she rushes back to Adam, startled. She pulls on Adam's sleeve and tells him to watch out, and so he glances in the direction Nusia points out and notices the approaching man's grin, but, like Nusia, does not recognize him. He knows the man only when he gets completely close to him, shakes his arm and says something to him straight into his face. At the moment Adam knows who the stranger is, he also realizes that he is missing some front teeth.

Nusia's father hoists her from the floor and mumbles something in her ear and, on her request, puts her down again. He kisses mother on both cheeks and asks her why she is bawling again. He looks with surprise at Adela and gives her a swift hug. And then he searches the nearby crowd with his eyes. When at last he sees Konstancya, clinging to Radomir with whom she shares a military padded overcoat, he does not move towards her; he just smiles awkwardly and gapes at her with joy and wonder. But as she beholds him with fright in her eyes, shriveling under her black peasant kerchief, he rushes out towards her and roars joyfully, "I bet you thought I was dead!"

PART 2:

ROOMS OF WHISPERS AND DUST

8.

By the time Nusia reached the age of ten most of her wartime deprivations have become mere memories, summoned by her mind only on occasion, usually for the sake of enlivening current doldrums. She now lives a life of affluence, comfort and self-indulgence; all of which also leads to her acquiring considerable notoriety. A good many residents of the city of Broscin, where she and her family now reside, know of her at least from talk, call her "brat" or "lump" behind her back and believe that she rollicks in the lap of luxury to sinful excess and will, accordingly, one day get her deserved comeuppance.

She lives now in nearly palatial quarters on the handsomest street in the city, called the Boulevard, where she sleeps in a canopied bed and plays hopscotch on a Bukhara carpet. She is driven around in a chauffeured limousine, even to her school if a day is cold or rainy. She never lacks for milk chocolate and other such treats. And she spends many an afternoon, right after school, at the grandest hostelry in Broscin, called the Firmament; either talking to assorted customers at the downstairs bar Rigolo or just sitting on a cushioned bench in the lobby and watching the guests come and go.

For her tenth birthday she is to go to the Firmament to dine there in the Porphyry Room, at a white-draped table; and she is to request anything she might fancy. Let it be explained that the Firmament, one of few buildings in the city that has emerged from the War almost unscathed in all its pre-War glory. It has a ballroom, two restaurants, a bar, and oversized mirrors and marble columns on every floor; and it is officially designated as the only establishment in the city fit to accommodate and entertain important government officials. Nusia has been visiting the place regularly (either alone or with Adam), and she is familiar with all its areas extremely well, even the kitchen and the ballroom; but it is its main restaurant, the Porphyry Room, that she considers to be most elegant and most suited for spending one's leisure time.

Before proceeding with Nusia's adventures in the Porphyry Room on her tenth birthday, a small digression is certainly in order. It has to be emphasized that it is not only the conditions of Nusia's life that have changed so remarkably in the course of those four and a half years since the reader saw her last; all of her family, even Radomir and Adela, enjoy now existences which are described, by all who know them or of them, as those of utmost comfort and privilege. Now, how their ascent has come about needs, obviously, a little explanation; though, thinking of it, their route from that crowded, demolished postal building near

Kramow to the most elegant street in Broscin, the Boulevard, has been quite straightforward.

As you might remember, it is in that building, while they were journeying from Burak's farm towards a new life, hungry and in rags, that Boleslaw spotted them in the crowd. After some probing he gives them an account of his life of that period of his nearly year-long absence from them. He makes his story simple and brief, and no amount of quizzing will make him, ever, augment it or fill it in with any details they might be curious about; his missing teeth, for example.

Just when they were ready to leave Wielow - so his narrative goes - he was indeed abducted by men of the Realm Occupying Police and thrown into a prison cell; from which, however, he was freed a few days later by the blast of a bomb dropped from a People's plane on the prison building. He crawled out of the debris of the crumbled walls and ran away from the city, directing himself west towards Kramow. But, greatly hampered in his movements by the rapid advances of the westward-bound battlefront, he stopped his journey for a time; and for the ensuing months, until the fighting ceased altogether, he tarried in a little out-of-the-way town, making his living there from winnings in nightly games of dice and stud poker with some local tradesmen. He picked up his family's trail shortly after leaving that town, when he met a man on the road whom he recognized to be wearing his overcoat. After the man explained how he had obtained the coat, Boleslaw had no difficulty in tracing the coat's history back, to the day when his wife, Kocia, pawned it at the Dobce haberdasher's, a place where she was quite

well remembered. It was a man at the haberdasher's who referred him to their friend, the warden of the Dobce cemetery,
who in turn told him that his family was on their way to
Kramow traveling in a military motor truck with the People's
red emblem on it. "Oh, you are clever, the whole lot of you!
Getting a fancy military truck and a security fellow to drive you
around! I will be damned! And me worrying about you all that
time!" Boleslaw roared with pleasure, and gave Konstancya a
look full of admiration.

Boleslaw goes to Kramow with them; and on the very day of
their arrival he manages to get for them lodgings, large enough
to accommodate everybody; a heated attic, quiet, not too heavily
infested by mice. And the following morning he goes out to town
to see what is up. From then on he stays out all day, joining them
in their attic only at night, never saying much about his daytime
affairs, but not ever returning to them empty-handed. And in less
than two weeks – the others still terribly disoriented in the new-
ness of their situation with little clue about how to fashion their
post-War lives – Boleslaw tells them that as for him he has decided
to set up a stand with assorted merchandise at a place called Saint
Stephen's Market; a sure way to stay afloat for a good few months,
he says. And he expects all of them, without exception, to help him
set up the stand, especially that none of them has anything better
to do. Predictably, Konstancya protests, cries even, calling him a
low huckster, a paltry peddler and a con-man who is dragging his
family, his tender-aged child, into the muck of disgrace; but the
following day she does go with the others to Saint Stephen's. But

even after she takes to the task of sorting out some of Boleslaw's merchandise, her eyes burn with ire and her lips remain clenched.

Saint Stephen's is a large place, crowded with booths, a huge assortment of buyers and sellers, mounds of merchandise rarely seen during the wartime period and a spirit of exuberance, if not plain jubilance. However, the Market is condemned by the new authorities (who call it an ulcerous vestige of the country's past) and is fairly regularly raided by the people's militiamen who make occasional arrests of those partaking in the market's activities. Boleslaw is not worried, though. Those arrested by the militiamen always return, he says, not much of the merchandise is ever confiscated, and the Market, just about the only place in the city with anything to buy or sell, will not be closed down in the foreseeable future. And so, they are all with him there almost every day helping him to man the stand and sell his goods.

When one day the whole of Saint Stephen's begins buzzing about an imminent raid, Boleslaw, who is clearly is in control of the situation, simply instructs them as to the place and manner of the prescribed getaway. They manage, quite adroitly, to collect the most valuable items from the stand, dash straight to the side door of a nearby church and then hide there in an alcove behind an altar, they all giggle. Well, not all; it is then when they make it safely to the niche beyond the altar that they notice that Konstancya is not with them.

Later, when things are safe again, they obviously query everybody at Saint Stephen's about her, but they find no one who remembers having seen her. They approach the authorities, military and civilian, but get no help from them either. The following day, they go in person to all known places of detention in the city, and the weeping mother is even allowed to look into the prisons' cells, but Kocia is nowhere to be found. Suddenly, some thirty hours after her disappearance, she walks into their attic, looking radiant, with her hair combed to one side in a fashion not seen on her before, and she greets them with a casual, though rather pleasant-sounding "Hello!"

Adam's reaction to both her disappearance and her reentry into their midst is definitely less charged than that of the others; yet he finds her rambling story, or rather the tone and the implication of what she is saying, quite curious.

"Of course I was arrested right away... and of course I would not have dreamed of resisting detention... Wasn't I in the wrong? Weren't we all? What we were doing was illicit... I felt ashamed... oh, so deeply ashamed... And they were quite wonderful. Naturally, they were doing their duty as citizens of our country – fine, brave citizens. Oh, I am so happy that it all happened to me..." she smiles a little-girl-who-is-promising-to-be-always-very-very-good smile.

And she goes on telling them about her soul-searching, two-hour long sojourn behind bars, about her encounter with some all-powerful brigadier general who, while inspecting the jail premises, suddenly cast his steely eyes on her, of all the prisoners, and asked her whether she felt repentant. And then she tells them of the light she saw all of a sudden, and her remorse, and the promise she made not to ever, ever again break another law.

"So when was it that they let you out of jail?" asks the uncomprehending Boleslaw.

"But I was telling you," she answers, "yesterday, sometime in the afternoon."

"So what were you doing for the next thirty hours? Everybody was looking all over for you!" he presses on.

"But I just told you all," she says impatiently, "I was with the general."

"Oh, Kocia... what did he... did you...?" Radomir's face stiffens.

'What did that creep want of you?" Boleslaw demands.

"Oh, nothing, absolutely nothing," she responds eagerly. "He just listened, most beautifully. I sang for him."

The following day a soldier in a well-pressed uniform comes to their attic with a box of chocolates, some sheet music for Konstancya and orders from headquarters to tune mother's piano. And a mere few days afterwards Kocia is performing in front of a large and cheering audience, mostly officers of the army of the GEU People's Power and the local people's army. And, shortly after that first singing venture - through the further support of her new friend, the brigadier general - she becomes transformed into a performer of consequence. Not that she has not been predisposed for the role to begin with. When she is now driven about in sleek, black cars, or is invited to important affairs and introduced to noteworthy people, or is furnished with gifts and bodyguards, she accepts all such turns as things naturally due her. And she, the star, never talks to her new acquaintances about her husband, a pre-War nobleman of wealth, at present the owner of a stand with assorted merchandise at Saint Stephen's Market.

Still, it has to be admitted that she works hard on her success. She exercises her voice through the day indefatigably so that she can give her all to her audience at night. She sometimes sings well into the wee hours of the dawn, even after the military band that accompanies her departs for the night, pouring out thus her soul to her officers from the rickety bandstand all alone, her voice not dampened by the sound of a single instrument. And she has to learn a great number of totally new pieces, since – on the advice of the general himself – she expunges from her repertory most of her old numbers, as "stale" or "offensive to the officers of the GEU People's Army", even her all-time favorite *Oh my rosemary open your blossoms* piece; which saddens her a bit, though not for long. And she has to take language tutorials, since many of her new songs have to be rendered in the GEU People's Power language, with which she is only faintly familiar.

It is Kocia's patron, the general, by that time promoted to the rank of major general, who opens up before her the auspicious prospect of going to Broscin, the most important city in what is now officially called the Newly Recovered Western Territories. Since the general (to whom Kocia always referrs to as Jozef M., by the way) is being sent to that western region as the chief of Security for the Broscin district, a position of power almost unlimited, and personally promises that he will look after her and guide her talent, and even have an opera house erected for her, Kocia decides to place her future in the general's potent hands.

So that's how Nusia comes to live a life of plenty, resides on the handsomest street in the city and have her tenth birthday party at the most elegant restaurant in Broscin.

It is her father who made all the appropriate arrangements for her birthday dinner at the Porphyry Room. It is also he who has introduced her to the Firmament in the first place and who meets her there during her visits. However, he usually stays with her only for a minute or so, waves to her from behind a column next to the exit, "Have a terrific time, babee!", and then disappears. He never tries to stay on, sit at the table with her, or talk to her some more, not once; and she never misses him. Once he is gone, she does not think of him again; though if she did, she most probably would not like the idea of him at her side during these periods of fun and banqueting among the gilded-frame mirrors and crystal chandeliers.

Only once, Adam remembers, she actually says that she is glad that her father is not with them. It is one evening in the Ballroom of the Firmament; three of them at a table: Nusia, Adam and cousin Radomir. There is a big crowd of people, all the chandeliers lit, the violin playing a Gypsy tune, people dancing. Nusia orders three cups of cocoa with whipped cream and three pieces of hazelnut torte, but Radomir does not touch his portion, and so Nusia divides whatever is on his plate and in his cup between herself and Adam; and Radomir does not even notice that she has done so. Konstancya, Nusia's mother, is sitting at the opposite end of the room, her face away from them; and Nusia is able to see only a little bit of her dress, the flowers on her table and the medals on the military uniform of a gentleman sitting next to her. Suddenly her mother steps out onto the stage into a bedazzling circle of colorful lights and not only becomes visible to everybody, but also makes all of the rest of the place slide into darkness and insignificance; Nusia's heart stops. She does not hear her mother sing, just watches her shining figure and enchantingly lit-up face and feels proud of the loveliness and importance that the woman in the spotlight, her own mother, is exuding. Immediately after the performance Nusia runs towards the stage, but as she reaches the edge of the illuminated circle, her mother gives a final bow, hurries back to the bemedalled military gentleman she is with, and then, smiling and glissading among the tables, makes a quick exit, followed by her companion known to Nusia as Jozef M. Nusia rushes after them, but is quickly intercepted and brought back to her own table by the head manager of the Firmament, a man called Emil, who pinches her on her cheek, calls her his sweetheart and asks whether there is anything more she desires that evening. And she, without hesitation, says that she would love some green beans with buttered crumbs for herself and more cocoa and whipped cream for all three of them. And after Emil leaves, she says that she is glad her father is not there that night as he would not have appreciated her mother's singing. "He never does, mommy says," said Nusia. But it is only on the day when she dines at the Firmament on her tenth birthday that she tells Adam that she dislikes her father, dislikes him a lot.

They are sitting in the Porphyry Room, Nusia and Adam; they are waited on by a man in a white jacket, and Nusia is addressed as "Honorable Lady". They watch the goings on in the Room as reflected in the large mirror beside them; they view their own reflections and try on their new dryad masks made especially for the occasion (which they do not keep on for longer than a few seconds at a time as, according to Emil, most guests of the Firmament are not favorably inclined towards mask-wearing at mealtime). Nusia decides on double portions of appetizers and desserts, on green beans and fizzy mineral water and against any main-course dishes. However, well before desserts, their celebration is interrupted; sadly, never to be resumed.

As luck would have it, they hear some loud and excited voices and then notice in the mirror two female figures advancing rapidly towards the foreground of their viewing area. The first one, whom they quickly recognize as Emil's lady friend, Lala, her hair and dress in terrible disarray, is very obviously being chased by the second one who is menacingly shaking a partially open umbrella in the air. They scream and race across the room, the sharp tip of the umbrella approaching the back of Lala's coiffure. But when it looks that Lala will not be able to escape, the woman behind her skids suddenly, just when she is trying to swerve around Nusia's and Adam's table. She slithers to-and-fro about one spot on the marble floor and then falls down flat, with a thump and an outcry, her umbrella crashing into the surface of the mirror; and Lala makes it safely through the door on the other side of the Room. The woman rises from the floor; and while she grimaces and rubs her hip and thigh, angry, Nusia fixes her eyes on her and then, with happy recognition, informs Adam, "This is Mister Emil's wife!" And without skipping a second, her mouth full of buttered beans, she shouts out, "Missus Emil! Missus Emil! Are you all right?!"

"What the hell do you want? And who the hell are you?" She gets closer to Nusia's face. "You are... of course I know who you are - the child of that scum, that pimp who is turning this hotel into a filthy gutter." And then with her voice rising threateningly, "Outrage! That fat greasy brat, a child of a pimp, a whore-hawker, in this place! Stuffing herself... on the house, of course. But there is order and justice! There are authorities! And something will be done! There are authorities!"

Nusia is devastated; she suffers unbearably at any mention of her weight and appearance. She ceases eating, her head droops, her voice becomes throaty, "She dislikes him and because of him she dislikes me." Nusia for the greater part of her young life would refer to her father as "he".

Emil's wife, righteous and most unpleasant as she is, will not do anything, not even try, Adam is certain. She well knows that changing the inner workings of a place like the Firmament, with all of Emil's and Boleslaw's contacts in higher places, is beyond her powers. Still, Emil does not want unpleasantness of any kind, and so shortly after his wife leaves the Room, he sends there his assistant from the office to tell Adam and Nusia that they should make themselves scarce, that is, that they should go immediately into the service closet off the Grand Lobby and stay there until the time Nusia's father is ready to collect them.

After the man leaves (without mentioning their unfinished meal), Nusia discovers that the upper panel of the door that has just been shut on them has a small glass pane through which is visible a portion of the Grand Lobby. And so, she and Adam can see guests and personnel trotting about, luggage being brought in and taken away and the gilded coop of the lift moving up and down. They hear people in the Lobby buzzing and coughing, and Emil's assistant calling out orders. And then they sight Emil himself and Nusia's father, only a few paces from their viewing glass pane. They stand close to each other: Emil, tall, slick-haired, angry, yells and demands answers; and Nusia's father, small, stooped, apologetic, smiles and explains. Emil wears gray, soft and plain, while Nusia's father wears brown, ironed stiff, shiny brass buttons, golden-edged epaulets and cuffs, and a golden badge on his breast pocket. Suddenly the two men smile to each other and their encounter seems to have reached its end; Emil gives Nusia's father a pat on the back and Nusia's father bows politely to him. Minutes later he appears within their view once again, Boleslaw, Adam's brother-in-law, as of the last four years an employee of the finest hotel in the city of Broscin, a senior bellman of said hotel, a confidante of the manager himself, an entrepreneur in his own right. This time he is in the company of a lady whose valise he is carrying. He moves gingerly and grins to the lady; and when she hands him some money, he bows respectfully. And she does not look at him, but only lets him know with a motion of her hand where she wants her case placed. It is then that Nusia stops looking through the pane, retires on the floor, hunched down, her head between her knees, and says to Adam that she dislikes her father, dislikes him so so much.

The Home of the Divine Providence

Two days before the dress rehearsal of our play (this erotic musical written in our secret language code), at the peak of excitement during the final preparations, when nothing indicated that our show would be anything but a roaring success, one of the wards, Tytus, whispered to me that something grievous was going to happen very shortly. He then explained that Nature strives for balance; and since life at the Home had been going so blissfully and smoothly for so long a time now, an abrupt turnabout of events was unavoidable. And here I am reporting with great anxiety that Tytus' prophecy has actually come to pass. I have no idea how the brothers learned about our language code, but they did; and so the season of mirth at the Home and the befooling of our guardians have come to an end. The lightning struck during the dress rehearsal while we were watching a scene involving Stefan, the Bridegroom, veiled Brother Euzebius, the Bride and Lech, the Bridegroom's Friend, rendering a wedding march on his bassoon. Before the scene reached its anticipated climax, Brother Honore stormed into the auditorium, leaped onto the stage, tore the veil off Euzebius's face and slapped the young brother on his cheek, then punched Stefan on his mouth and knocked the bassoon out of Lech's hands. He also belched out that our obscene trickery has been discovered and that he, the guardian of upright behavior, would make sure that our evil treacherousness would be duly punished. I have been in my room for a few hours now, forbidden to leave. I have

not been given food; and I have not seen anybody except Brother Ce-
lestus who brought me a basin of cold water and told me to undress,
wash myself thoroughly and then remain in a kneeling position in
the water for at least an hour. I am writing on the smallest sheet I can
procure, in my special shorthand, and am terribly worried that my
room will be searched and my secret stash and writing discovered. I
am also extremely hungry.

Despite his wife's opinion of him as the most ordinary of men, Adam always found Boleslaw to be a rather remarkable individual; and he liked the man a good deal too. Yet, he has never been able to infuse Nusia with any such sentiments, try as he has. For one, it has always been difficult for him to put into sentences for her a precise depiction of her father's activities in life; certain words were simply inadequate for the task. And then there is the verity of Boleslaw's own testimonies about which Adam is frequently at a loss. For instance, he often recalls a night back in Wielow in the early part of the war, when he went into hiding with Boleslaw. Those were the days in Wielow of persistent rumors of people disappearing nightly from their homes, never to be found again. The People's Tribunal had just dropped charges against him and let him go free, but Boleslaw would spend his nights - out of fear, Adam was guessing - away from home. And that particular night he made Adam go with him; and when they reached his hideout in the basement of an old building, he told Adam to make himself comfortable and try to go to sleep. But since Adam could not sleep, he said he would teach him to play poker (he always carried a pack of cards in the back pocket of his trousers). And when Adam failed to understand the principles of that game, Boleslaw started playing solitaire. In the light of the candles that they had brought with them Adam watched him play his games, spread the cards on the basement floor, arrange them and rearrange them in neat rows and piles; and he watched him repeatedly wipe sweat from his face, neck and palms, even though the air in the basement was cool. In the morning when they were back on their street, he suddenly said that he would have never made it through that night alone; but to Adam's question about what it was that was threatening him, he replied that he would teach him to play poker one day after all. But before they entered their quarters he said quickly, "Don't tell the girls at home where we were last night. Let them think that we were doing something really wicked." And he laughed out loud.

As far as Boleslaw's activities at the Firmament are concerned, Adam knows rather little; only that he has gotten the job not through Konstancya's powerful protector General Jozef M., but on his own, after he ran one day into Emil, a man he knew some years earlier in Wielow. He knows that on the job he always wears his brown uniform with golden epaulets, and is exceedingly polite to everybody; and that at home he is regularly reminded by his wife, Adam's sister, that wearing that hideous uniform and living off gratuities from hotel guests are a disgrace. Adam also knows that Boleslaw regularly brings home sizable amounts of money he nets for his miscellaneous services to the guests of the Firmament; neat, thick stacks he places in front of his wife on her breakfast table.

Even Adam, so ignorant about all matters monetary, realizes that what Boleslaw places in front of Kocia next to her cup of morning coffee exceeds greatly what most citizens of the country would consider their regular incomes; yet, she accepts his gifts cheerlessly, almost unseeingly, often with an air of sad resignation, but with no inquiries about the particulars of his job. She only occasionally reminds them all that Boleslaw's present earnings are negligible compared with what he had had before the War and also that if she only wanted to, she could leave him and go off into the world with somebody like Jozef M. who could give her incomparably more.

How things would have turned out for her had she officially joined her life with Joseph's, no one would ever know, since she declined to live with him or marry him (even after the lengthy proceedings of his divorce had been most successfully finalized); explaining her decision by her total inability to fight her ordained lot of being married to Nusia's father. Not that the general Jozef M. ever losses interest in her or that she is ever ready to do without his powerful patronage or to renounce being his companion at public gatherings, private suppers in his villa or vacations in mountain resorts. It is, of course, Josef M. who has made her an opera singer, as he had promised. Incredible as it still seems to Adam, his sister Mieczyslawa Konstancya has been indeed employed by the State Opera of Broscin as one of its performers, with her name listed in the official records of that institution under the heading of *Soloists*.

Let it be explained here, though, that despite Joseph's promise to Kocia, no new opera house is erected in Broscin; at any rate not during the years Adam and the rest lived there. Her influential patron does try to use his powers among the central authorities in the Capital with regard to that matter so close to his heart, but trying to raise a new opera house turns out to be a process much too involved even for him. It is decided in the Capital that as far as any operatic singing is concerned any existing theater building is big enough and respectably located. And so the place that is chosen is in fact the only theater that survived the War intact, which, luckily, has several hundred crimson-covered seats still in fair condition, a sizeable orchestra pit, an impressive colonnade on the outside and a very prestigious location, only one street from the Firmament. That it has been used for popular musical reviews in the old days rather than serious repertory, does not matter one bit. It is there that Kocia is given a private dressing room; small, but with an extra-large mirror and an antique chaise.

Yes, Konstancja, indeed, is employed by a very respectable opera company. But let it also be mentioned here that – all those famous, tragic, consumed by passion Mimis, Butterflies, Gildas or Violettas – are destined to be performed by her only in front of patrons of provincial houses of entertainment during her yearly tours of the provinces. The more refined audiences of the Broscin Opera are doomed to see Kocia only in roles of companions, friends or servants to leading ladies; all despite her efforts and Jozef M's numerous interventions on her behalf. She does appear to be accepting her lot with a good amount of stoicism, Adam thinks, following each casting decision by the Opera directors with a comment that her voice has not yet reached its full maturity.

Nusia's tenth birthday stays in Adam's memory as a day of events disagreeable and surprising. Besides the horrible encounter with Emil's wife, Nusia's unhappiness and her open confession about disliking her father, there is another unpleasant incident, this time involving a bouquet of roses that Nusia's father gives her on the morning of her birthday. There are two dozen of them, canary-colored, fresh, unopened, with a shiny ribbon tied around them. But Nusia frowns, because she thinks that pink ones, like the ones her mother sometimes brings home, would be much prettier. And so Boleslaw winks at her confidentially and tells her that he did not buy the roses in a flower shop, but found them on a bench in the Grand Lobby, as they were deposited there by somebody who forgot to deliver them to a certain important person, a film star, he thinks, the one who has been staying at the Firmament and whose picture Nusia saw recently in the paper. And Nusia brightens up, thanks him for the bouquet and asks her grandmother to help her put the flowers in her favorite vase. Grandmother says that the roses are truly exquisite, and the two of them place them in the center of a mahogany table in the salon. (Yes, Nusia now lives in a place whose main room is called the salon.) But in the evening of that day when Konstancya returns home from the Opera she upbraids Boleslaw for bestowing upon Nusia another one of his gifts "totally unsuitable for a ten-year old who is already spoiled beyond redemption". And when she hears the story of the bouquet being intended for a film star, she says that she is sick of Boleslaw's lies he comes up with every time he wants to endear himself to

Nusia. Anyway, she is going to take the flowers to the Opera, she says, as she needs something fresh for her dressing room.

Indeed, the following day she removes the roses from the mahogany table and takes them with her to the Opera. And Nusia is heartbroken, as she believes that her mother is angry at her again for some recent transgression; for Nusia knows well (despite what Adam, Adela and others often tell her) that she is the cause of her mother's many pains, even though she never means to hurt her.

The Home of the Divine Providence

As I have indicated, our guardians learned of the secret language code we were using and, hurt and ireful, decided to restrict our activities as a punitive measure. I was confined to my room for six days, and during that time subjected to twice-daily knee-soaking in cold water in the presence of Celestus; and my only daily meal consisted always of gluey semolina, two stale rolls with dollops of red-beet butter and a glass of unsweetened sage tea. And, as far as I know, my fellow wards did not fare better than I did. But for the last few days we have been eating again in the dining hall, we have progressed from one meal to two a day, with semolina having been replaced by boiled potatoes; we have been allowed to watch the fifteen minutes of the evening news on TV after supper, and we have been let outdoors daily (but only for obligatory early-morning knee-bending exercises in front of the Home chapel). We are still not allowed to talk to one another, receive mail or visitors, or amuse ourselves in any way. But I overheard some of the wards whispering today that the brothers could not persist in their anger much longer for their own sake, that is, without jeopardizing the image of themselves that they want to uphold in front of the governors and the benefactors.

9.

Before relating any further events that took place after Nusia's tenth birthday, it is necessary to point out some antecedent circumstances of same, both public and personal. First of all, let it be reiterated and emphasized, for the sake of those whose grasp of history is rather slight, that after the ghoulish War had been at last decreed to have come to an end, the Continent becomes officially divided into two parts: the West, consigned to the care of the libertine and abundant Great Far Western Allied Sovranties, and the East, deeded to the rule of the orthodox and ill-provided Great Eastern United People's Power; this bipartition having been agreed upon by the two concerned powers, with no advice or consent of any other party involved. The dividing line between the two domains takes on the form of a colossal rampart of hard rock and steel, almost impenetrable, erected fast and single-handedly by the indomitable workers of the GEU People's Power. After the War the lands where Adam and his family were assigned to settle lay east of the Rampart.

The City of Broscin, where they were told to live now, is situated in the heart of what was until the end of the War the Realm's eastern region. It is a city shattered by the War, wrecked and blighted more than any place on all of the Continent. When this region became a part of Adam's country it has been been officially totally emptied of those of Realm roots, and thus becomes a promised land for all those of his countrymen who on the ashes of the defeated Realm, are ready to start their lives anew. The territories get the official name of Recovered Western Territories. As Konstancya's prospects for her future in those new Recovered Western Territories are beyond excellent, she makes them all go with her. Even cousin Adela is not able to resist the temptation after she has been offered by Jozef M. the position of an editor for *The Worker*, the main newspaper of the region. Cousin Radomir goes with them too, as he is assured a place at the University of Broscin, with no previous academic credentials and entrance examinations necessary. Of course, Adam well knows, that Radomir would go after Kocia to the ends of the earth anyway, even if no personal gains were at stake.

Actually, they do not go with Kocia, they only follow her, for she travels to Broscin alone, on a train – Adam who has seen her to the station remembers clearly – in a private compartment with a curtained window, with valet service and a dining car at her disposal. The rest of them go a few weeks later, transported in a military motor truck driven by the general's man. But their journey is comfortable and the general's man courteous towards them.

All pre-War history books known to Adam have agreed that Broscin for the first few centuries of its existence belonged rightfully to his country. However, why it started slipping out of the hands of its original rulers does not seem to be settled. The cause of the final loss of Broscin and all the rest of the western territories to the western neighbor, the Realm, is attributed, as far as Adam remembers, usually either to the avarice and military might of the Realm or to the unparalleled goodness and decency of his country of which the devil took advantage.

Most of Adam's knowledge of what Broscin might look like came from an album of photographs of some of its sights, a book he saw once in Wielow. When they enter Broscin for that first time, in the military motor truck driven by the general's man, Adam still has in his memory a few images from that book: frilly railings of gates and bridges, an armed colossus on a lion and a row of neat facades sharply tapered at their tops. But those are not what they see when they now drive into the city.

The street they enter, a desolate and dusty gorge, is lined on both sides with hollowed-out structures, houses that used to be. And only in those buildings which are sliced open from top to bottom one can see remnants of human habitats; painted interiors with bits of furniture, suspended in space. As they drive further, the cliffs of the gorge lowered and flattened into vast tablelands, only to be changed a little further into the precipitous walls of a canyon, and then again into a desert of craters and low-lying rubble. And there is no movement visible, no signs of life whatsoever. Many years later Adam learns that this was what space travelers will say the moon looks like.

It is only after several kilometers into the city that they reach a well-cleaned flatland with a few partially preserved buildings, some vehicles and a bunch of people carrying shovels and buckets. They stop next to an overturned lamppost and a vendor who is selling beet soup from a vat and rolls heated in a fire built in a crater in the pavement. They buy some rolls from the man and he talks to them about how fortunate they are to be coming to the city just then, before anybody else, when the pickings are still fresh; early-comers' good luck, he calls it. Over ten percent of the city's homes have been spared, he says, with everything in them right in place, furniture, rugs, dishes, bedding, what have you; and another ten percent only partially wrecked. All living quarters are vacated by those who were of the Realm, but everything that was in them has stayed, as the fleeing or translocated Realm swine did not have time or were not allowed to take any goods with them. "And everything now is ours, rightfully ours, all the wealth that the Realm's sons-of-bitches hoarded for centuries." And he also whispers to them confidentially that though the new authorities are officially in charge of giving all good living quarters to the people for homesteading, one can just go and examine on one's own any place that is unassigned and empty it out right away, that is, if one has any brains.

When they get back to their truck, mother says something about avarice being the greatest of human afflictions, and Adela states that human attachment to objects is simply ridiculous. But when she expresses the hope that Nusia in years to come will not be finding dishes and bedding the most valuable commodities in life, mother gets upset and says that she wishes Nusia is lucky enough to always have plenty of dishes and good furniture, to which Adela comments that mother is pitifully stupid. Boleslaw then wonders how many corpses are still lying under the rubble and what it will take to do a proper clean-up job on the city. Radomir yells at him to stop calling human burials a clean-up job, to which Adela says that Radomir should stop being so idiotically sentimental. He then directs his raised voice to her and asks her to explain to everybody her relationship with Burak and her cozy existence on his farm during the time when patriots were giving lives for the Cause. And Adela replies that he is nothing but a whimpering hero and a phony. Mother then bursts into tears and calls Adela cruel. And Nusia bawls too, demanding to know why they are not on a train, like her mother, with soft cushions and gentlemen bringing you fizzy drinks on a tray.

They all stop when their motor truck comes to a halt and the driver announces that they are on the Boulevard at the door of Madame Rytwianska's house. They notice that the street is wide and almost clear of rubble, with a strip intended for greenery running along its center, almost grassless now but still with a few trees left. And the house they see has four stories, ostentatious or-namentation all over and two caryatids upholding a large balcony. It is one of a row of similar houses, of which none seems to have been scarred by the War, not at first glance anyway. And their driver comments in a tone that seems to announce to the world that he really knows what he is talking about, "My dear people, the truth is that some things, like some people, just crumble away, while some others survive any calamity."

At the door they are greeted by a sergeant who tells them that the second and the third floors are theirs, that is, Madame Rytwians-ka's, and that they should make themselves at home. He apologizes for the condition of the place, but there has not been time yet to do much except to replace broken window panes and remove some of the fallen plaster, he says. He promises that within days his men will clean the stairs (genuine marble), re-plaster and paint the walls (all the ornamental moldings included) and then sand and wax the floors (the finest parquet the sergeant has ever seen). Then he tells his men to hoist mother's piano on ropes from the street onto the balcony and then push it through the double door inside the house into the room Madame Rytwianska calls a salon. Then the soldiers drive away, leaving them all speechless, incredulous, as if in the midst of an occult happening which could not have been more astonishing if it included spirit rapping or the levitation of bodies.

First they just stare, and then they slowly rove about the place, taking stock of things, which, they have been told, are theirs from then on, restored to their ownership after hundreds of years of misuse along the deviate course of history: tasseled draperies, over-stuffed divans and armchairs, armoires with carved doors, lamps, flower stands, porcelain figurines, coats on hangers, books marked for reading, doilies under crystal bowls. They search, dig and sniff in drawers, trunks, on shelves, in recesses; and they do not quite comprehend. And mother says that she is overwhelmed with happiness, and also that it is not right that it all should belong to Kocia now.

Adam does not recollect what each of them did exactly in their first few hours in the house on the Boulevard, except that at some point Boleslaw emptied the cinders out of the stove in search of hidden money or other treasure, that mother was counting cups, saucers and such and claimed that they were almost identical to the ones they had had before the War in Wielow, and that he and Nusia examined all the wearable apparel left in the place, finding several armoires, chests and trunks almost full, plus the miscellaneous in drawers and on racks. Colorful sweaters, evening togas, tailored suits, full skirts, high-laced shoes, boas, fedoras, rain caps, even black domino masks and little paper hats with sequins. But what Adam recollects clearly is that Nusia suggested that they pile everything on one giant heap, then undress, dive into the pile and search for garments with eyes closed, and then try on whatever they find, and then do it over and over again. And so they did. And shortly, to their delight, they were joined by all the others; mother and Adela stripped to their bloomers, shoeless Boleslaw and completely denuded Radomir who at last managed to completely tear Burak's pinstripe suit off his body.

Before sundown of that day, their first day in Broscin, they go out for a stroll. They put the sign "occupied" in every window, and padlock and bar the front and the back doors the way the sergeant showed them, and they march on, in full dress; mother and Adela in evening gowns, Adela's way too short for her; Nusia in a man's dinner jacket and a sequin hat; Radomir in a summer linen suit; Boleslaw in a homburg and a very long muffler; and Adam donning white tie and tails, black cape, white silk scarf and a top hat over his frolicking he-goat mask. They breathe deeply, move with grace, chat, laugh a lot, and do not mind when those whom they encounter during their walk, newcomers like they, do not respond to their friendly greetings.

When they return home, Adam's sister, Madame Rytwianska, is waiting for them; and so are several crates of provisions straight from a military food reserve. She is in such high spirits that night that she even kisses Boleslaw on his cheek, allows Nusia to drink a whole mug of condensed milk, and says to Adam that his newly discovered domino-masks are beautiful. (Of course, Adam feels that this remark once again shows how pathetically unsophisticated she is; the masks in question, probably left over from some Shrovetide masquerade, are low quality, common, the kind one was able to buy by the dozen in any toy shop in pre-War Wielow.) Well, she also says that night that they are enjoying their good fortune only because of her special friend, the general. And she reminds them that the place (two floors plus some of the attic) has been turned over officially to her, that is, they were entered in the city records under her name as the main occupant. But as she wants to share her lucky lot with others, she says, she is hoping that her cousins Adela and Radomir will take for themselves, in perpetuity, some of the space that is assigned to her, and thus continue living with them as one family under the same roof.

When recalling these early days on the Boulevard, there also has to be mentioned Doktor A.M. Tulpe, a person none of them ever met, but to whose presence they were constantly exposed. Whether Doktor A.M. Tulpe lived among them as a ghost, Adam was never sure, but there would hardly pass a day, or even an hour, without them being aware of him in some way. He manifests himself to them for the first time on their second day in their home, in the library, after Radomir pushes some books off the shelf onto the floor and one of the books opens and on the inside of its cover appears an ornamental bookplate with a handwritten name: *A.M. Tulpe.* Soon they see that name (as they surmise it to be the name of a person) on the inside of the cover of every book at which they happen to glance. And within a short period of time, *A.M. Tulpe* (often with *Doktor* appended to him) will regularly show up before their eyes; on papers of all sorts, silverware, tools, linen, at the base of furniture or inside garments; handwritten, printed, engraved or even embroidered. Actually the whole building, not just their place, turns out to be replete with signs of the Doktor's substantiality, as their new neighbors from the other floors become aware of him in no time as well. Everyone agrees there must have lived a number of other people in the house, most of them of the name Tulpe, but they were probably not nearly as important as the Doktor.

Yet, despite his continual presence amongst them, the Doktor does not seem to affect their lives in the least. Adam often wonders why Doktor Tulpe is passed over with indifferent shrugs, and why his character as well as his past or his present are speculated upon

in the most unemotional way. Maybe if there had been any photographs or personal documents of his around, things would have
been different; but all such traces of him had been removed. Oh,
yes, they are often playing the game of guessing; that the man was
stocky, bald, with protruding eyes, the husband of a dull-looking
wife and a number of equally dull-looking protruding-eyed children; that he probably did not make it safely beyond the western borders to the Realm proper, but either committed suicide
somewhere on the way or was caught by the People's Army and
most likely was executed by a firing squad (with the reasons for his
punishments not being discussed as simply too self-evident). But,
mind you, all the conjecturing is always done in a totally unaffected
way.

Only once, Adam recollects, was the Doktor mentioned with a
certain amount of passion. It was mother who, after having discovered some sheet music with the initials *A.M.T.* on it, said that the
Doktor probably played an instrument, possibly piano, and since
no instrument was in the house, he must have taken it with him.
"Do you think he might be playing it right now and thinking of
this house he had to abandon?" she asked. "And if he does, then he
is... sort of like us... maybe not bad at all..."

Of the early memories of Broscin there is also the image of
the Central (short for the Broscin Central Railroad Station) that
has always stayed in Adam's mind. You see, in those early days
before all the streets had been de-mined and all spaces officially
appropriated, before a cover of green had yet had time to soften
the edges of the stony carcasses of pre-War structures, or a single

public building had opened for the crowd, or military vehicles had given way to tramways – there had been but one place in Broscin for any significant social concourse and communion: the Central, the only functioning station in the city at the time.

That the Central becomes the most important gathering spot in the city is not surprising, for as soon as the last train west, carrying Realm nationals beyond the western borders, leaves the city, the first train from the east, with a cargo of Adam's own countrymen, pulls into the station. From the day the very first clangoring and whistling transport made itself audible in the distance, there are people there on the platform who want to watch the train arrive and greet it. And every day the throng at the station grows larger, and so does the number of people in the city.

They are all heavy freight cars, each with a square panel in the middle and an iron bar across it, like a trap door to a cellar, each full to bursting with people to be implanted on soil on which they never before set foot. The soldiers lift the bar, pull the trap door to the side, and then let the people pour out, one by one; each checked, given stamped papers, and let go. And the undulating crowd on the platform slowly absorb them, and then expand and overflow, spilling into every corner and recess of the station.

There is always a crowd at the Central keeping vigil, for the hours of the trains' arrivals are not known ahead of time; and the anxiousness among those in the crowd is high, for the names of those arriving are nowhere posted. Some wait for their spouses, children or other kin, some for acquaintances, and some just for anybody they can recognize from life past; and there are those who await no one, but just relish being a part of the crowd, agitated, expectant. Some come to the Central only for a short visit and others bivouac there for days on end next to fires, vats with soup and signboards displaying their names and erstwhile addresses. There is also, as Nusia discovers, a great deal of merrymaking going on: singing around the fires, music from accordions, violins and a crank organ, card games, magic tricks, fizzy orangeade, salty pretzels and pink ice cream sold in dollops squeezed between pieces of waffles.

As weeks go by and the freight trains from the east keep coming and new trainloads of dislodged citizens pour in, the swarm at the Central becomes inordinately thick, emotions grow tenser and all the goings-on more frenzied. Bartering and bidding go on uninterrupted, with tinned goods, cash, bimber, clothing and heirlooms being converted one into another at a frenetic pace. Inquiries become louder, and more news-brokers and information-sellers offer their services. There appear also a frightful number of one-legged veterans, maimed civilians, crying women in black, spectral figures with marks tattooed on their arms, and very thin children with badges designating them as wards of public care. And when an increasing number of military personnel and militiamen begin making themselves visible at the station, the family forbid Adam and Nusia to visit the Central on their own again.

Let it also be mentioned that at the Central Adam's family recognizes among the new arrivals some of their own kins people and acquaintances. There arrives on freight trains from Wielow three of mother's second cousins and one of mother's brothers with his two widowed daughters. There also comes Adela's sister Anna, the widow of silversmith Gruber, and with her Canon Banasz, their old confessor, changed so greatly that they would never know him were it not for assurances from Anna Gruber as to his identity. It is also at the Central that Boleslaw runs into Emil, his future employer at the Firmament. And it is also there that Kocia meets one day a woman named Renata, a stranger, whom she brings home with her and offers room as well as a position as her maid and confidante. She intends to do everything she can for the creature, she tells them, as she finds her to be genuinely good, of artistic temperament, terribly deprived and helpless.

At the time of Nusia's tenth birthday they have all been in Broscin for more than four years; Nusia's father and mother pursuing their professional careers at two of the most exclusive establishments in the city, the Firmament and the Opera, respectively. The blighted and rubble-covered city that they first see had only slightly recovered from its War-borne traumas during those four years, and most of the people there have only barely risen from the depth of their wartime miseries; but they, on the Boulevard in the house with two caryatids amidst the spirits from the Tulpe household, live lives of privilege and plenty all along.

They do not occupy two full floors for long, though. As Broscin begins receiving its daily transport of translocated citizens – a legion in every freight car – living space within the city becomes a commodity without price, and so, even Kocia, secure as she is under the auspices of one of the most powerful men in the region, has to give up what is deemed excess room for the avail of others.

Nonetheless, with even one full floor (the one with the balconied salon), she still remains one of the best-situated citizens around; especially that she has time enough to have transferred large quantities of furnishings from the sequestered floor to the one now allowed her, and then secured separate quarters in the garret for her protege Radomir. After the move to the one floor Nusia, Adam and mother no longer have rooms of their own; Nusia and mother are placed together in what used to be the dining room, and Adam is assigned to the rather tight servants' quarters off the kitchen. Still, even with those limitations they are enjoying spaciousness which most others were only picturing in their dreams. As a matter of fact, even in their own building while the second floor is theirs exclusively, the other floors house two families and a couple of unrelated single persons each; and all those other residents, let it be stressed, are individuals with considerable connections, for those without proper contacts could never have been placed in a location as prestigious as the Boulevard. (Well, the only possible exception is Renata, a woman of no connections and no papers, who is – as has been mentioned – discovered at the Central by Kocia. It is only through Kocia's efforts on her behalf that Renata is eventually awarded the necessary documents and status of an official resident of the Tulpe building.)

Now, the general, Jozef M. lives all alone (not counting his dogs, other bodyguards and household help) in a huge villa right outside the city, a place restored to its pre-War grandeur by the hands of miscellaneous military personnel and official funding. But Jozef, a dignitary of great stature, needs extra space as no one else in the city,

Kocia tells them a number of times, since in his salons (he had more than one) he has to hold frequent conferences with various men of power and to entertain them. The family knows what the villa looks like inside only from Kocia's descriptions. (Nusia, who has visited the place a few times with her mother, mentions only a pair of the strongest dogs in the world, a man at the door who has a belt with two pistols, and ham sandwiches that are only so-so.) Kocia is always full of admiration for the place, particularly the green salon with a life-size marble statue of a Hussar, furnished with some of the better pieces from the collections of various national museums; and accordingly, she spends at the general's villa a great deal of her time, actually most of the nights, mornings and holidays when she is not busy singing at the Opera or elsewhere.

That she stays away so much from her home on the Boulevard she explains by her strong dislike towards her neighbors, people she is bound to bump into periodically on the stairway or hear through the walls or open windows. She views the presence of all of them in the same building with her as some horrible error in the normally logical design of things. She claims, for instance that the Kowalskis from the third floor were dung beetles in their former lives, and that Piotr Kurski from the first, a man with a number tattooed on his forearm, is surrounded by an aura of foulness which makes her feel faint in his presence. She refers to the Goralski boys from the fourth as blockheads and the Paluk family from the first as yokels. And she routinely impersonates Maria Lipko, a widow from the garret - her wobbly stride, wheezing voice, wide-spaced teeth and all - a person she is doomed to encounter every time she pays a visit to Radomir, the widow's next door neighbor.

But it is Klusa, the one-eyed veteran from the third, that she loathes; for it was this man who has the effrontery to object to her singing. He not only is in the habit of slipping under her door small notes with requests for smaller doses of vocalization in the building, but also, on warmer days - when all the windows stand open and every louder sound from every quarter in the neighborhood could be heard - leans from his window, stares down and waits for the first notes to reach his ears, and then booms in the direction of the open door of Kocia's balcony beneath him, his voice rolling through all of the Boulevard: "Citizeness Rytwianska, Citizeness Rytwianska, silence, for the sake of the common good! Silence, Citizeness Rytwianska!" Klusa's attempts at intervening in what Konstancya considers her private affairs are quite unsuccessful, but so are her attempts at removing the Klusa family from the building. He, like Kocia, it turns out, has some powerful protectors; and moreover, as he sires a new child every year, obviously can not be moved anywhere, unless to some larger quarters, which, alas, can not be found in Broscin at this time.

Kocia goes on enduring her lot, never failing to let the world know that the burden she has to carry is frightfully heavy. Though, in general, Adam has to admit, she complains of very little in life; actually she tends to refer to her life's experiences in glorified hyperboles, even when what befalls her is not deserving commendation. But, analogously, those few circumstances of her life which she chooses to consider burdensome, she is determined to elevate

to the level of martyrdom. The most onerous load she has to carry
with her through life is naturally her family, she often lets the
family and some others know: her mother and brother incapable of
independent living; her husband who wears a brown uniform with
golden epaulet and cares nothing about the loftier things in life; her
child, thoughtless, uneducable, overweight and tone-deaf; and her
cousin Adela, loud-mouthed, insulting, determined to humiliate
her at every opportunity.

Let it be mentioned that as far as Adela is concerned, she was
ready to pack and leave more than once, but it was Kocia who
asked her to stay to keep mother company and to help raise Nusia,
difficult child that she was. And as for Nusia's being difficult, let it
be emphasized most strongly, that she certainly was not. In an exemplary manner she always tried to please and to comply with the
wishes of those around her; she was also good-natured and totally
sincere. That she was not able to carry a tune and found her singing
lessons, as well as her piano lessons, terribly arduous and unre-
warding was not her fault; neither should she have been blamed for
not enjoying her ballet classes after Kowalska from the third floor
referred to her legs as two extra-fattened pieces of headcheese. And
that she was easily distracted from her school duties, well, that was
the most natural state to be in for anybody of her age who had any
imagination, passion for adventure and general enthusiasm for life.
She religiously listened to Adela, though; and tried to take in all her
advice on life; provided that she understood what Adela meant.
Adela would, for example, disapprove of Nusia's hours of idleness
at the Firmament, especially her culinary ventures there, but at the

same time she would say, in front of Nusia, that there was no place like that particular establishment to get a good education about life; and she claimed that she personally was extremely partial to the hotel's downstairs bar Rigolo and did not visit it more often only because of the steep prices of liquor there. She would also say that the sight of that rather sinister-looking Emil, the head manager, always activated within her strong erotic sensations. You see, those were the type of comments that made Nusia feel confused quite a bit.

The Home of the Divine Providence

Today right after the services at the chapel Brother Simplicius, the head guardian, announced the reestablishing of a state of normalcy in our retreat. Simplicius talked to us for about twenty minutes, with Brother Innocent, the guardian of public exposure and outside affairs, on his one side, and two governors in blue business suits on his other side. Simplicius introduced the two men as our most caring patrons to whose thoughts we owed no less than our very existence and flourishing as an exemplary institution. He also said that it was on the urging of these distinguished men that we, the wards, will be forgiven our wrongdoings, with all punitive measures against us being rescinded. Also, he stressed a few times that both our governors and guardians realized that a great deal of our offenses stemmed not from inherent evil within our hearts, but simply from overstimulation of our minds by too large a flow of information coming into our lives from the world outside of the Home. When after that ceremony in the chapel we all rushed to the Green Veranda to the table piled, just like in the old days, with newspapers, magazines and books, we noticed that some of the familiar items were missing. And from the wall there had disappeared our favorite map entitled Our Country – Guide to Tourist Attractions.

Nusia's tenth birthday has nothing to do with what Adam now thinks of as The Great Turnabout in their lives, but it just happens that it was right after that event that things started manifesting themselves. And Nusia, when reflecting on that period in later life, would also say that the time of her becoming ten marked the very beginning of a new phase in her life, the first painful steps on the new territory of adulthood.

As you probably remember, the day after Nusia's birthday, Nusia's mother removes from the salon's table a beautiful bouquet of yellow roses (which was one of Nusia's birthday gifts from her father), and takes them with her to the Opera as an adornment for her dressing room; explaining her action as a counter-action to her husband's "irresponsible handling of the already spoiled child". It is then, when Adam realizes what she has done and sees the crying Nusia, that he decides to pay his sister a visit at the Opera and retrieve the flowers from her. And if she tries to prevent him, he tells himself, he will have it out with her and tell her, once and for all, everything he thinks of her; and if necessary he will follow her all the way onto the stage in his horned goat mask and create real havoc right in front of the audience.

He gets to the theater while the first act is in progress, and so he hopes that he will find Konstancya still in her dressing room, as she appears on the stage in the second act only. He heads straight for the belly of the place; on the way tripping on ropes and wires, hitting his skull against pulleys hanging from above, colliding with performers walking in the opposite direction and bumping into flats to be used in the next production; and finally he crashes into Renata, the guardswoman, who refuses to let him into Kocia's dressing room, as Renata believes that the most important duty she has to perform in life, at the Opera and elsewhere, is to protect Kocia. Adam struggles with her and almost loses, but then remembers his he-goat mask he is carrying with him, and so he threatens her with impalement on the horns of the mask, and she gives in.

Kocia is in front of the mirror, but obviously ready; her makeup and costume all in place. She turns to Adam with a vacant gaze; and he speaks with passion, letting out all the angry words rehearsed on his way to the Opera. He feels that he is clear and properly emphatic, but when he finishes, her look is still vacant. She says very quietly and indifferently, with a voice he almost does not recognize, "So, what is it, Adam, that you want of me today?"

"Nusia's roses!" he yells and stamps his foot.

And she does not say a word to that, just reaches for the flowers, pulls the bouquet out of the water and quietly hands it to him.

He does not know quite what to say to her now; and then he is completely taken aback, startled almost; he notices tears running down her face. She is trying to arrest their flow with her handkerchief and to prevent her makeup from smearing, but more and more tears are coming and she has difficulty stopping them. She rarely cries, and when she does, Adam never quite believes in the sincerity of her emotions. But not this time. And so he just stands there in one spot, confused and silent, and she does not say a word to him. On his way to the door he tells her that he hopes that she will be alright; and she, all calm again, turns towards her lit-up mirror and starts retouching her makeup.

He knows that she did not weep because of his presence in her dressing room, and certainly not because of guilt she felt after having heard his words. And it is not likely that she cried at the thought of having to come out onto the stage to again sing a part she considers far beneath her talent. It is then that Adam knows for the first time that something is seriously wrong, but he has no clue what it might be.

A few days after he sees her crying in her dressing room at the Opera, mother expresses her personal concerns regarding her daughter's well-being.

"I think she has some great worries, Adam," she says. "She is unhappy in a way I have never seen her before, well more than just unhappy... I think she is either grieving over something or has to make some incredibly important decision and feels... confused."

Adam tells her that Konstancya has never grieved over anything, neither has she felt confused in her whole life; yet, he himself thinks that something might be wrong.

"If there were ways to make her confide in me, maybe..." mother interrupts herself when she sees Renata entering the room.

It is late Saturday afternoon; they are sitting in the salon and awaiting Adela's and Nusia's return from their regular Saturday food shopping trip. When they notice Renata and a dusting rag in her hand they look at each other joylessly. Dusting is not a part of Renata's official obligations in life; and when she decides to do it, she makes sure that there are witnesses to her efforts. And mother and Adam do not quite know how to tell her that she should not bother.

She walks into the salon with a loud, "Well, I might as well do it now," and starts making her way around the room, giving some of the furniture quick whacks with her dusting rag. She shuffles along, almost runs, her feet all the time wide apart, toes turned to the outside. She deals the final loud swat to the back of the Bechstein, and then throws herself on the sofa, a boulder of a woman, disregarding the presence of Adam's body resting on that particular piece of furniture. He does not let her have her way, but the weight of her person is so formidable - much too big for a ballet dancer she claims to have once been - that, in order not to become damaged by her, he squirms out from under her onto the floor, promising himself to always wear in her presence one of his wild-animal masks, or at least always have one handy. (She feels that she has all rights to the sofa, as she has been using it as her bed at night; of course, only since the time when Kocia was forced to move everybody onto the one floor.) Anyway, Renata, the ballet dancer, reposes for a few minutes and then enunciates, "Persons who are superior to others, like our Madame Kocia, always have to bear more than the common herd."

The significance of her words is obvious to mother and Adam. She wants them to know that she is aware of their conversation concerning Kocia and that she, unlike they, knows all that there is to be known about the problems, and also that she is not going to share any of her information with them; which all does not necessarily mean that she really knows anything, except that there is something not quite right.

As neither mother nor Adam answer her in any way, she continues talking more to herself than to them, enumerating some of her usual grievances; not being able to enjoy her Sunday soaking bath properly since Miss Adela is always after her in line, or not being able to listen to her favorite radio program since Madame Karolina (mother) always has to have her music. "In this world high-quality persons sometimes do not even possess a bathtub, a radio or a sofa to call their own while worthless ones grab everything," she says. "But Renata is not talking about you, Madame Karolina, it is some others in this building that Renata means, that take the space of more worthy ones, like Professor Paluk's wife from the first, a low-class Hebrite, if I ever saw one, or that Lipko woman who lives in the garret next to Mister Radomir and has whole two rooms to herself, a true reptile she," says Renata.

She is still nodding her head meaningfully over the unworthiness of Mrs. Paluk and widow Lipko when Nusia and Adela walk in. Nusia announces ecstatically that they have been able to buy some really exciting things. "Even dried apricots!" she screams with delight. (Since the Law of Supply and Demand has been officially abrogated, predicting what is going to be available on any given day, either in state-owned stores or at privately-owned stands is now virtually impossible.) Nusia asks for permission to help her grandmother and Adela in preparing the feast for everybody and to bring Radomir down.

Some half-an-hour later they are all in the salon with Nusia playing the hostess: pouring the steaming cocoa into cups and offering everybody miniature cheese sandwiches, honey crackers and dried apricots. She is ready to wait on Renata, but the woman just gets off the sofa, grabs a handful of the apricots, says that she loathes cocoa and huffs on her way out of the room, "Renata had better go to the kitchen to check in what condition it is now. You can expect anything after some persons have made cocoa in there."

And then comes Konstancya. She does not look well, but Adam cannot tell whether what he is perceiving are signs of some bodily ailment or mental trouble. Since this is her free Saturday, they ask her what she has been doing with herself all day, but she does not reply. She moves among them without a word, jerkily and irresolutely, as if looking for something that cannot be possibly found anyway. She takes a canape from the plate, holds it for a minute or so in her fingers, and then places it untouched on the edge of the table, and then takes another canape, holds it for a while and sets it on the keyboard of the piano. And all the time, Adam notices, she seems to be totally unconcerned about what impression she might be making. Then she stands still for a few seconds, suspended, as if ready to beg or call for help, her knees bent, her arms hanging limp alongside her body; but before they have time to try to help her or press for answers, she turns away from them and leaves the room. Radomir rushes after her, begging her to allow him to help her in some way. And after a little while they hear the door from their quarters to the stairway open and shut, which most probably means that both Kocia and Radomir went to Radomir's room upstairs.

Mother and Nusia sob, and mother asks Adela whether she too has noticed a terrible change in Kocia and whether she knows what might be wrong. Adela has no idea what is going on, but she tells weeping Nusia that whatever it is, it is not her fault.

Suddenly when Adam and Nusia are cleaning up after the feast, Adam notices that Renata is nowhere in sight; and so it comes immediately to him that she has followed Kocia and Radomir to the attic, as on some occasions in the past he had actually seen her glued to Radomir's door trying to peer through a crack in the wood. This time Adam decides to teach her a lesson. He grabs his spotted-hyena mask, the fiercest looking mask he has, and rushes upstairs.

In order to get to Radomir's place Adam has to pass by the communal laundry room. He looks quickly inside and finds there widow Lipko involved in soaking something in a tub, Piotr Kurski with an armload of long johns staring into space, and the wife of veteran Klusa and her neighbor Kowalska exchanging insults. Adam then walks straight on towards Radomir's door, but does not see Renata anywhere. He is ready to turn back, but then hears a faint noise coming from the widow Lipko's place, next to Radomir's; and he is puzzled, knowing that Maria Lipko is presently in the laundry room. As her door is slightly ajar, he peeks in, and then, to his horror, notices Renata squatting on the floor, with her back towards him, quickly rummaging through the open drawers of the night table. At that moment Adam gets on all fours, leaps forward, and with a butt of his hyena head knocks Renata flat on the floor.

Sadly, his triumph over Renata is extremely brief, for as soon as she grasps the situation, she screams out for help; and her voice is so powerful that all of the garret starts shaking and within seconds the whole of the Lipko room is filled with a mob dashing to Renata's rescue. Before Adam can think of any counter-action, it is he who is lying stretched out on the floor, held down by Piotr Kurski and veteran Klusa, whammed on the head by Kowalska with her washboard, his hyena mask kicked out of his hand; while Renata, the victim, free and superior, is discharging vile accusations against him. She followed him to the garret, she rails, suspecting, and how rightly, that he was up to something wicked again; and she found him here in Maria Lipko's room rummaging through her personal things and so she, naturally, told him to stop his wickedness, but he did not, and so she said that she would tell his sister about his wickedness, but then he got really raving mad and hit her, and knocked her to the floor and violated her person all over with his fists and his mask, and was probably meaning to kill her; and how terribly heartsick the gentle Madame Kocia will feel when she hears about her brother's abominable conduct.

Adam is released after mother, Adela, Nusia, Kocia and Radomir enter the room and swear to all those gathered that Adam will not slash or stab anybody, and will not bash up the property either. Adela and mother also tell the crowd that they should listen to his side of the story; but when given a chance to do so at last,

Adam is not able to make the mob believe that Renata was in the Lipko room before him, since nobody remembers seeing her at all in the garret that evening. And Kowalska cuts short any further discussion with, "Jesus Christ, don't you remember how he barged into the laundry room, holding this mask of his in such an odd way? We were all scared. A child would've known that he was up to no good!"

Konstancya tells Adam to apologize to Renata, and after he refuses, she promptly, on his behalf, says that she is sorry and gives Renata a hug.

Adam lies awake through most of that night, sore, discomposed; and when asleep, his dreams are troubled too. When he wakes up the following day, he finds out that Nusia, with whom he has planned to spend that Sunday morning, is gone. They have planned to go for an outing to the neighborhood park, in costume, taking sandwiches and orangeade, together with two of the Goralski boys from upstairs. He asks Konstancya about Nusia's whereabouts and she answers him calmly that Nusia is with Renata who has offered to take care of her for the day; and she, Nusia's mother, feels that keeping Nusia away from Adam and all the rest of them is an excellent idea. Adam is beside himself.

"It has never occurred to you that that... foul bitch could harm Nusia!? She has never taken her anywhere before! So why now?! How could you let her... you blind, stupid.."

Both mother and Adela come to his aid, both quite agitated, telling him that they tried to stop Renata from taking Nusia, but that Kocia was horribly stubborn. "So typical of your goddamn narcissistic narrow-minded ways!" Adela shouts at Kocia.

And Kocia says that she is fed up with Adela's butting into her personal affairs and with Adam's lunacy and that she is not going to rescue him again when he decides to go haywire in front of everybody in the building, and that she has some serious problems of her own to take care of, and that neither of them has ever known what real problems in life are like, and that she is not going to explain it to them, as they in their disgusting egoticism would never understand it anyway. She slams the door behind her on her way out. She has an afternoon performance at the Opera that day.

And they stand there speechless, astounded, not at her words, for she has said similar things many a time before, but at her tone, at never-heard-before desperation and a plea for help that they are sure they have heard now in everything she said.

Adam goes to the park alone. He sits there on the ground next to a large boulder in the shape of pagoda (a never removed relic of the War), and he tries to go over in his head through everything that has happened since he saw Kocia crying in her dressing room. There is a good crowd of people moving around, but he is paying little attention to anybody. A man sits next to him, greets him, smiles, offers him some sweets, then asks him questions of all kinds. Adam looks at him, smiles back, answers him, but the words that pass between them leave no imprint on his memory.

Nusia and Renata return home in the evening. Renata does not feel obligated to say a word about what they have been doing. She informs them only that since one of her radio programs will start in a minute, she does not have time for conversation. Nusia tells them, though, that everything was terribly dull and dumb; an outdoor puppet show appropriate only for children much younger than she; dinner, not at the Firmament, but some really odd place, all fat meat and no proper dessert, only cotton candy in the park afterwards; sitting for ages on benches doing nothing while Renata talked to all kinds of people, and Renata refusing to take her to the Opera to visit her mother. The worst was the Zoo; Renata insisted that they go there. Nusia does not visit zoos, as she knows, from Adela and from a book she read once, that animals are brought there against their will; also she herself once saw there a baboon crying.

Later that night she suddenly recollects something of greater interest. "Oh, I forgot, Adam, there was this really funny man sitting next to us on a bench in the Zoo, well maybe not that funny, but he could do lots of tricks. He had this crystal ball and he would ask it questions about me and he would stare into it, and then he would know everything. And he knew all about me, and also you, and Mommy, grandma, Adela, everybody, and about Mommy's beautiful singing. I don't know how, but it was all showing up in his crystal ball. Actually, there was something he didn't know; you see, he knew about my piano lessons and singing and ballet, but he said that after all those lessons I must sing beautifully and dance like a real ballerina. Well, you know it's not true."

That night Kocia returns home from the Opera, for the first time in anybody's memory, together with her husband Boleslaw. Apparently after the performance she walked over to the Firmament and asked him to escort her home. As soon as they came in, Renata begins evacuating gaggling noises of concern, "You look so pale and worried, my precious. Will you let Renata rub your shoulders for you or maybe wash your hair? Tell Renata your troubles and you will feel better." But Kocia is not interested. She goes straight to her room and closes the door behind her. After she is gone Boleslaw tells them that when she showed up at the Firmament and told him to take her home, she seemed to be completely out of sorts, in a panic, plain scared out of her mind, if you ask him. Not that she explained anything to him.

The Home of the Divine Providence

It has been five days since the normalization of the Home's affairs was announced, which does not mean that things are exactly the way they used to be. Our weekly supply of newspapers and magazines has diminished, our outdoor recreation periods have been shortened, and our menus have been further revised, with the total disappearance of such old standbys as smoked sausage, sour cream or pears. But what happened tonight plainly shocked us and filled us with apprehension about the future. We were waiting for Brother Boniface to turn on the TV so that we could enjoy again – after all those weeks of forced abstinence – the Golden Cobra Mystery Hour, our favorite. We had read in the newspaper that tonight's show was deliciously entitled Murder in the Chapel, and so we were looking forward to the event with the highest hopes. But to our horror, we realized that we were already past the time of the beginning of the presentation and Boniface was not there. We ran towards the TV set in an attempt to switch it on as speedily as possible, but we discovered not only that the set was unplugged, but also that the outlet into which the TV cord should have been inserted was filled with some kind of molding clay which we were not able to remove. We looked for another outlet, but found none; then we tried to move the set to another room, but found it bolted down to its pedestal. We then yelled for help, but no one came to our rescue. It was only much later explained to us by Boniface and Innocent that the cobras had been so detrimental to our physical and mental health that their viewing has been suspended for time indefinite.

10.

It should also be briefly noted here that Adela is not the only person who tries to teach Nusia about the world. There is also Radomir, tormented artist, disillusioned lover, once and future soldier, who sets out to teach her about Life-The-Way-It-Really-Is. He tries to turn her into an adult well before her time, but, quite honestly, his efforts amount to nought. It has to be understood that Nusia is in love with him (for years, since as far back as she could remember); her love is deep and unreserved; and it is for that love that she yearns to reach womanhood as fast as possible; but she does not have the slightest clue how to go about it. She is always eager to accept the Truth from him, the adult truth; and yet, he does not succeed in making her see things the way he paints them for her. He, a young man of weakened lungs, frost-bitten toes and graying hair, an inspired raconteur, relates to her the story of his pain and shattered hopes, of his burnt military uniform and his country's degradation, of human misery, death, betrayal and his people's exile from their native soil; and he tries to infuse into her, with all the passion at his command, distrust and scorn. But she just looks straight at him, nods, and feels joyful and at peace with the world. Being able to be near him, to keep her eyes on him and breathe in the sounds coming from him is already sufficient reward; decoding the meaning of his sentences would have been superfluous.

Yet, all of a sudden she starts growing up. It is not too long after that Sunday when she goes for her outing with Renata that Nusia finds herself not just lightly trotting about the foreland of adulthood; she actually enters on its main expanse. But let it be said right now that it is not Radomir, her dedicated teacher and the man she adores, who makes her suddenly grow up. It is Jozef M., the general – like Radomir, in love with Nusia's mother – who, more than anybody else, becomes responsible for her entry into the real world; even though he has nary a story to tell, emotes little and is considered by Nusia to be profoundly dull.

To explain what actually befalls Nusia and all the rest of them in the weeks following her tenth birthday, another digression is in order. It is one afternoon in early April, some five months before Nusia's birthday, that Jozef M. appears unexpectedly in his chauffeured limousine in front of her school. He opens the door for her, tells her to hop in, and orders his driver to proceed to the Youth Cultural House where Nusia's ballet classes are held. Nusia had been driven in his limousine to classes before, as a matter of fact, quite often; but this is one of very few occasions that the general himself is inside the car, mind you. He tells her that the Youth Cultural House happens to be on his way; he shuts the partition that separates them from the chauffeur and says that it is high time they become better acquainted, and then asks her whether she likes her ballet classes. In the course of the following few weeks he rides with her at least half a dozen times to her lessons, and once he even leaves the car together with her and watches her class for the full hour of its duration.

In June, after the school year is over, they all go on vacation (mother, Adela, Nusia and Adam to a place in the mountains reserved for higher military personnel; and Kocia and Jozef to a government resort in parts unknown), but as soon as they are back Kocia told Nusia that she will continue her ballet lessons without further interruption through the rest of the summer. Nusia protests, but is told that Jozef who saw her in her class, was very much impressed and urged her mother not to let Nusia stop her study, not even for a month or so. And so, she obeys her mother, and soon the general starts riding with her to her lessons again.

In early August she tells Adam that the general is actually fun, at least at times, and that she and he have become, sort of, chums. And then she say, in a whisper, straight into Adam's ear, that the two of them are planning a terrific caper. Well, upon hearing that revelation, Adam tells her plainly that he is jealous and hurt, but she assures him quickly that as far as the caper goes, he most naturally is going to be a part of it; of course on condition that he swears to keep absolutely quiet about it. Nusia says you must keep anything secret that the general wants kept secret since the general's wrath towards anybody who betrays him could be great indeed. She is interested in keeping things under wraps also for another reason; she can, under any circumstances, ever, allow her mother to find out about the affair, the projected caper being nothing less than playing hooky from her ballet class.

When Adam asks how exactly the plan for such a caper came about, she explains that it started when she told Jozef how much she'd like to skip ballet class now and then. He replied that he sometimes feels tired too and wishes he could get away from his chores. Somehow, the conversation turned to the Youth Cultural House and how easy it might be to slip away unnoticed—at least in the summer, when the place is in greater disarray than usual due to the crowds of visitors and children from all over.

Operation Hooky takes place on a Thursday in mid-August. It works out smoothly and, except for its one phase, it goes precisely as planned. Adam is a participant in the action, as Nusia promised. Whether, however, they really enjoyed the whole affair is debatable.

Adam feels displeased with himself realizing that were it not for his natural indecisiveness, he could have suggested a caper of that kind himself long before, as thoughts of similar actions have often crossed his mind. The presence of Jozef greatly dampened Nusia's and his spontaneity, no question about it; on the other hand, Adam admits without reservations, the general's planning of the affair was meticulous and his ingenuity quite remarkable.

The scheme of action and its execution were really very simple. Adam leaves home alone, carrying with him a bag containing the necessary costumes, masks and accessories; he directs himself straight to the Youth Cultural House, enters the House through the rarely used back door, then rushs through the back corridor and the back stairway all the way down to the basement boiler room. He hides himself behind the furnace (not used at this time of year) and waits. In the meantime Nusia is picked up by Jozef in his chauffeured limousine. They stop in front of the House, both Nusia and Jozef get out of the limousine and Jozef tells his chauffeur to wait for him as he intends to watch Nusia rehearsing for an important show; then they both go into the House, through the main entrance, of course. But once they are inside, they turn into the back corridor, rather than the main hallway, and shortly join Adam in the boiler room. There behind the furnace, all three of them change into their costumes – three full sets of chimney sweep's outfits, black, baggy, long tails, top hats, wire brushes to swing over the arm. They also put on masks, which, because of their natural body-color and great amount of soot Adam has sprinkled on them, are hardly recognizable as masks at all. They leave the House through the back door, passing on their way some hurried people who all smile to them in a friendly manner; as in those days, mind you, chimney cleaners were not only a common sight and considered most useful, but also, according to age-old belief, a lucky sight to behold.

In a small courtyard behind a building adjacent to the House there is waiting for them a vehicle called a rickshaw, left there for them by some acquaintance of Jozef. A rickshaw, a conveyance popular in those days, was really a bicycle which in place of its front wheel had a large square wooden crate on two small wheels to hold wares or a passenger; it is Jozef who mounts the bicycle seat to take the responsibility for their ride, while Nusia and Adam place themselves in the box among brushes and other tools used for cleaning chimneys. They leave the courtyard through an alleyway, squeezing with difficulty through a space which definitely is too narrow for anything larger than a rickshaw.

Their ride through the city, though not unpleasant, never comes up to their expectations. Jozef, who even without his uniform and covered with soot, looks imposing, is very fast and accurate, pedals with great skill and energy, and manages to maneuver among buildings, cars, carts, tramways, pedestrians and patrolling militiamen without a slip; yet, he does not seem to derive much pleasure from the ride. His eyes, even as seen through the mask's slits, look much too solemn, and his mouth, quite clearly, does not crack a smile. And every time Nusia or Adam tries to express their enthusiasm aloud, he tells them to restrain themselves, even getting angry at Nusia when she calls out to a passer-by, "Hey, good sir, would you want us to clean your chimney?!"

The original plan had called for them to go as far as the city limits, but as Jozef suddenly starts running out of breath, he stops before reaching their destination. He choses as a place of his repose a curbside in front of a small fenced house on a quiet side street; and the moment he stops, two friendly-looking women come out of the house and invite them to rest in their garden behind the house. Jozef agrees, and the women suggest that they join them in a little picnic; and Adam wonders at their hospitality and their not asking them a single word about chimney sweeping or any other related business.

No sooner do they sit down on a wooden bench among some gooseberry bushes than a plateful of sandwiches and a jug of clabber appear before them. Nusia and Adam start eating, but Jozef asks whether he could first use the convenience and wash his hands, and then immediately goes into the house followed by one of the women.

A few minutes later, when he is still inside the house and they have not quite finished eating, most unexpectedly, a chimney sweep whom they had never seen before (it certainly was not Jozef) walks into the garden and tells them that it is time for them to go. They start asking questions, but his tone is so authoritative that they get up, say goodbye and, reluctantly, go back to the rickshaw. And then they realize that it is this chimney sweep, rather than Jozef, who is going to ride with them back to the House. He impatiently explains that something extremely important has come up and the general must attend to that matter personally. There are a few points Adam wants to have explained to him further, but the man takes off with a speed so high that Adam's head begins to spin and his sight becomes blurry, and he is not able to talk at all.

All the way back they are bouncing inside the rickshaw box, hitting each other and the objects among which they are placed, their ribs receiving painful jabs from the edges of a chimney sweep's ladder. Their man is stopped twice by militiamen for exceeding speed limits, but both times the patrolmen let him go without punishment, after they see an official badge he has under his black coat and hears his statement that an important cleaning job was awaiting him at the Ministry of Privileged Communications.

Their journey ends in the same back courtyard from which they had left on their escapade with Jozef a little less than an hour earlier. The chimney sweep who brings them back bids them goodbye and sternly reminds them how they should conduct themselves and what could happen to them if they do not; and he sounds, without doubt, like a confidant of a very important person. They rush back to the House's basement, wash themselves at a tap in the boiler room and change (their regular clothes having been neatly hidden behind the furnace), and they leave the building. Nusia exits through the front door, and Adam through the rear with the bag containing the costumes and masks hanging over his shoulder. A few streets further he disposes of the bag, as instructed, dumping it into one of the large municipal refuse bins.

When Nusia reaches the street in front of the Youth House, she tells Adam later, Jozef's limousine with the chauffeur inside is still waiting. She, as directed, asks the chauffeur whether he is supposed to take her home, but he wants to know where the general is; and then Nusia, most surprised, answers that she had no idea, as he left her ballet class some half-an-hour earlier, just waved to her from the doorway as she was doing her arabesque, and disappeared behind the door of the dance room, and that was the last she saw of him. The chauffeur tells Nusia to wait, jumps out of the limousine and runs into the building, evidently trying to locate the general; then after a few minutes he comes back in a great hurry and asks Nusia again what happened. She again answers that Jozef watched her class only for a short time through the doorway and then left. The chauffeur asks her then who else was watching her class besides the general, and she says that there was a crowd of people at the door (which was true), but that she did not know any one of them and that the general did not seem to know any of them either; and he definitely left unaccompanied by anybody. The chauffeur, who appears to be quite a bit agitated and troubled, tells her then to go home by tramway.

Nusia, as a rule, is not prone to give false testimonies. She lies rarely, and when she does, her insincerity is usually quite transparent. That she succeeded so well in misrepresenting the truth in this case is probably because she has been rehearsing for that moment of confrontation with the chauffeur for a long while, and also because she is singularly resolved that her mother will never find out about her missing a ballet class. She is also quite confident that their adventure will not come to light, as her ballet teacher, a summer substitute with no knowledge of the students, could not say whether Nusia was absent or not; and the crowd watching the class through the open door was indeed large, so nobody would be sure who exactly was among the observers.

She is a little bit apprehensive for a while, and even regrets her deed, but when a week passes and nothing happens and no questions are asked, she losses her fears and feels quite pleased with herself. She is, naturally, curious about what happened to the general after he went to the washroom in the house where they had a picnic; but Jozef M. does not pick her up again. She does not see his chauffeur or his limousine again either. She does not give it much thought, though, and certainly is not going to ask her mother about the matter. The summer session ends a few days later anyway, and then comes the new school year. By the time of her tenth birthday, she has almost stopped thinking of the event. It is only a few weeks after that, more than a month after that day when she and Jozef played hooky together, that Nusia's sin catches up with her.

A few days after that Sunday when she goes with Renata for an outing and meets the crystal-ball gazer in the Zoo, Nusia is staying home from school. It is Renata who early in the morning that day wakes up Nusia's mother and insists that Nusia not venture outside.

"The child is not herself, my precious; eyes so glary, harsh breath coming out of her, Renata can tell. Nothing really serious, but you never know. You'd better tell her not to go outside today, or Renata will worry to death," says Renata.

Her grandmother says that Nusia looks normal, Adela calls Renata's notions "hogwash" and Nusia herself insists that there is nothing wrong with her, but her mother decides that she should stay home. Nusia sulks, but after she finds herself alone with Adam and her grandmother, the others having gone to pursue their daily activities on the outside, she decides to make the best of the situation. But no sooner does she begin planning her day, when they hear a loud knock at the entrance door. Adam follows mother to the door, and sees her let in three unknown men, and he wonders how they got into the building which is always locked.

"The gentlemen here want to see Nusia about something most important," mother turns to Adam with a timid introduction.

Adam decidedly dislikes the look of the three gentlemen, and so he says that Nusia is too busy to see anybody. However, the three move in closer and in unison – after having quickly dunked their hands in the folds of their jackets – flash three badges identifying them as functionaries of the Special Office of the Ministry of Privileged Communications, regarded as the highest authority of the land.

Nusia is impressed. She is comprehending that she has suddenly grown to be important within the adult scheme of things, which means really important. She is addressed as a dutiful citizeness; she is led by the hand to the sofa in the salon, asked to be seated and advised not to hide anything during the official hearing which is to follow. She has heard of people going through official hearings, but she never thought that one day she would be one of those chosen. She is excited and wishes that she will be able to say things that will please the gentlemen.

At the request of their visitors, mother and Adam leave the salon, but one of the men stays with them making sure that they are a proper distance from the salon door which stays shut. Still, from the overheard fragments they can surmise that the Special Office of the M.O.P.C. is interested in Konstancya, though not necessarily only in her, and that Nusia is doing her best to let the men know that her mother is one of the most important people around and she, her daughter, one of the most dutiful children.

An hour passes before mother and Adam are called back to the salon, as it is time, the gentlemen have decided, to ask them some questions. They want to know about their personal, even intimate affairs, but they obviously aim at obtaining knowledge of things outside the realm of their lives and personal habits. Mother is getting more uncertain in her replies.

"Oh, how can I answer that... I do not really know, and how can this all be helpful to you, sirs?" she pleads humbly.

"So your mommy receives a lot of presents, you say?" one of the men turns again to Nusia.

"Oh yes, she does, all the time, beautiful boxes tied with ribbon, chocolates, pink roses, red carnations, cyclamens in baskets."

"Any of these gifts around, that we could see?" The three gentlemen stare at Nusia.

She blushes and turns her head away from them. "Well not so many right now, but normally there are a lot... it is just now..." she is losing her good humor.

"Well, what if we look for some of those special things around, maybe they are hidden," says one of the gentlemen. None of the three budges. Their eyes are glued to Nusia, making her feel more and more uncomfortable. "When was the last time that your mother received a present, flowers, a package, a letter maybe? When was it? How many weeks ago? What day was it? Who sent it to her?"

They demand now a date, dates, a time, the exact hour, a place, a name, names; and Nusia cannot answer their questions any more.

"And what about your memories?" They turn their attention back to Adam and mother.

Their replies are hesitant, and the men start moving around, casting their eyes on walls, ceilings, pictures. "Mind if we look around the place?" says one of them casually while entering the library which doubles as Adela's bedroom.

"No, of course not, but, sir, what do you want to find?" mother is almost in tears.

They open doors and drawers, and look behind furniture. They praise the high quality of some of the Tulpe furnishings, and express curiosity as to who in the household uses what objects and for what purpose. They do not appear to be looking for anything in particular, though, Adam notices; and they almost lack verve in their performance, that is, until they open a drawer with Kocia's undergarments and a box containing her photographs and letters.

After spending a good deal of time on examining Kocia's private items, they again turn to Nusia. One of the men, his arms and fingers in a series of rapid motions, with the skill of an accomplished prestidigitator displays an object in front of her. "Look what we found! Must be yours... the name is yours! He is showing her a canvas bag with NUSIA embroidered upon its bottom, the bag her grandmother has made for her to hold her ballet slippers. "Where do you think we found it? Well, where?"

Nusia drops her eyes to the floor. "I don't know, maybe under my table, or in the hall somewhere, or... in the kitchen." She is losing ground.

"I am so glad your ballet slippers turned up at last," exclaims Nusia's grandmother, forgetting the presence of the three men. "You told me you lost them at school."

"School, was it?!" The man's voice sounds menacing. "The bag was found not in your school, citizeness Nusia, but in the boiler room of the Youth Cultural House. Want to tell us how it got there?"

"I don't know... I must have left it in the dance room upsta irs... I don't know," Nusia trembles all over.

"Any idea how your bag with your ballet slippers got from upstairs to the basement and into the boiler room?"

"I don't know," Nusia shakes her head with desperation.

All of a sudden another gentleman walks in. He does not show them his badge, but Adam guesses his affiliation with the others from the manner in which he handles himself. He inquires of the men, his lads, as he calls them, whether they have made any progress; and he asks Nusia whether she remembers him. She nods, since she recognizes him as the man with a crystal ball whom she met in the Zoo a few days earlier. Then he turns to Adam and asks him whether he recollects having seen him before. Adam hesitates, and the man reminds him that he was sitting next to him near the pagoda-shaped boulder in the neighborhood park last Sunday, talked to him and even shared some sweets with him. Adam is amazed at the man's ubiquity, since their encounter in the park took place during the same afternoon when he approached Nusia in the Zoo.

"I hear that you lied, and that makes me very displeased," he says to Nusia. But there will be no lying from now on!" he honks straight in her ear. "And if we are all to be friends, we will have to be extra-honest with one another in the future," he addresses mother and Adam. "And we won't tell anybody about today's visit, eh?"

Despite the warning of the man, mother relates the events of that morning to Kocia immediately upon her return home. Mother has no idea what these morning visitors wanted of them, but she is terror-smitten nevertheless; the Special Office has a reputation for disagreeableness of the highest order. But she is confident that if Kocia lets Jozef know that she is in trouble, whatever its nature might be, he will come to her rescue immediately. After all, it is Jozef who runs the Special Office in Broscin and, as everybody knows, his word can become law if he so desires; and if, through some terrible error, his own ministry started investigating Kocia and her family, who but Jozef can rectify the situation? Mother's logic is impeccable, especially that she knows that Kocia, of all women, is the one that this powerful man loves, and also that it is out of his adoration for her that he has made the lives of all of them so comfortable and free of so much of life's unpleasantness.

"Let him know right away, dear. Tell him what happened to us, of all people. Call him immediately!"

"But I cannot possibly do it, mother. That's the whole trouble." Konstancya looks downcast.

"Oh my!" exclaims mother. "I think I understand now. You had a quarrel with him, and that's why you have been so upset recently, and now you are too proud to go back to him. But you cannot be proud anymore! Please go to him, and apologize if necessary, for your sake and for all of us, for our poor little bird. You can't imagine what they were doing to her today..."

"But mother, you don't understand. I can't go to him because... he cannot be reached in any way. I have not seen him in more than a month."

"You mean... he does not want to know you anymore?"

"Mother, he seems to have disappeared."

The Home of the Divine Providence

*Yesterday was Saturday, another Saturday without the Golden Cobra Mystery Hour. Instead of watching our favorite program we played dominoes with Euzebius and Eutropius. The wards beat the brothers in the game, but our enjoyment was not great. Today is Sunday. As in the old days, Szymon and I were allowed to spend one hour on our own in the Green Veranda reading while the others were at the chapel; except that the only reading material available to us was copies of **People's Tribune** and **Work and Culture**, both several months old. And tonight after supper while we were discussing the problem of parental blindness and conceit in imposing on children activities inconsistent with their natural inclinations (a topic I initiated a few days ago), we were interrupted by Brother Klementior who suddenly wanted to know whether we all had liked his new watered-down turnip and parsley casserole. To my surprise Szymon, who detests Klementior's vegetarian casseroles, said that the dish was delicious and that we all felt that way. Then several other wards praised the dish, and even shook Klementior's hands. And Jan gave a whole laudatory speech not just on turnips, but our present life at the Home in general, saying, for instance that playing dominoes is a far more stimulating pastime than watching some cheap Cobra* *thrillers on TV. I was shocked by that hypocrisy, but then came to the conclusion that it was all too blatant to be taken literally by anybody but the somewhat dim-witted brothers. There must be a hidden purpose behind all this, I believe, a covert action of some kind. Perhaps a new language code?*

To questions concerning the reasons for his becoming an agnostic, Adam answers that a thinking and enterprising human being cannot accept Him any more than an artist can acquiesce to create according to a ready-made unalterable blueprint endowed with all the minute details. Simple as his explanation is, it is not always understood, and he is ridiculed, being called the least enterprising creature on earth. Adam rarely bothers to explain then that the activities of his mind, if not those of his body, often happen to be quite venturesome; however, he does state repeatedly that since God is inherently Somebody-Who-Cannot-Be-Challenged-Changed-Or Got-Rid Off, he does not desire to have anything to do with him.

It is the post-War epoch in general and the predicament of ten-year old Nusia in particular that have become permanently associated in Adam's mind with God and His rigid unchangeability. After they were relieved from the agony of the War, and then truncated, expanded westward and fitted into new borders, the course for the future of Adam's country, as in Divine designs, is settled. The people are provided with a blueprint for living, which is a code so sacred, unalterable and detailed that no facet of their existence is omitted from it; be it work they are to do, games they are to play, poems they are to memorize, or thoughts they are to contemplate. The new code that they are to follow is derived from the Principles which had been bestowed upon them by their liberator, the GEU People's Power.

The People's Power, as the supreme arbiter of their part of the Continent, also chooses the custodians for Adam's country, men of authority, whose mission is to insure that the words of the Principles are believed without questioning and that the directives of the blueprint are followed to the letter. It is right after the War, during their very first decade in power, that those overseers of the new order display their dedication to their tasks most strongly. And it is in their commitment to combat enemies of the new order that they, the high custodians of the Principles, particularly distinguish themselves. Their zeal, nay, pure exalted passion to stay vigilant, to fight any dissidence and to destroy the foe are never matched in later times.

The enemies in those days are divided into two categories, the external and internal; internal ones with their origin within the boundaries of the country; and external ones coming either from bygone eras or from beyond the Rampart, that is, from the territories over which the People's Power have no authority. The number of enemies within is very high in those early days, but the number of enemies without is practically limitless. It has to be understood, though, that since the People's part of the Continent had been securely bulwarked from the past and from the rest of the world, moving in time and space is enormously cumbersome, and so very few of the external enemies could ever manifest themselves in the flesh within the country's borders. But since both groups of the enemies had the same aim, abolishing the unchangeable Principles, it is taken for granted that the two worked closely together. And so, it is understood that the collaboration between these two groups must often be indirect, through elaborate twines of go-betweens and chains of commands, with the transferring of people, objects or information from inside the country to the side of the enemy and back becoming feats of monstrous cunning and deceit. The go-betweens, those evil-bearing agents, were of all sorts, but some of the most often cited ones by the leaders of Adam's country were books and newspapers printed by the enemies, pre-War books and any other pre-War printed matter, and short-wave radios carrying news from behind the Ramparts to the Eastern part of the Continent.

For the sake of those who do not know or remember, let it be also mentioned that in those days the side of the enemy was usually referred to as "the other side", and the enemies ranged from "revisionists", "instigators", "saboteurs" all the way to "foreign agents", "murderers" and "traitors to the nation"; and people, objects and deeds involved were described as "malign", "vile", "gangrened", "putrid" or "pestiferous". And nobody was above suspicion, be they young or old, scholar or illiterate, man or woman, artist, churchman, clerk or street sweeper. And those accused were usually found guilty, and the punishment for their deeds was the severest.

Of course, in their luxury quarters on the second floor of the erstwhile Tulpe-building Adam and the others let themselves be only remotely aware of all that. They felt comfortable and untouched by the troubles of the times, that is, for as long as they knew that the powers of the omnipotent Jozef M., like a magic shield, were protecting them.

They remained in a state of ignorance as to the true nature of their condition for at least two weeks after the visit from the functionaries of the Special Office.

Neither Kocia nor anybody else asked Nusia, or Adam, why her canvas bag with her ballet slippers was of interest to the gentlemen from the Special Office, since nobody suspected that Nusia or Adam knew something beyond what was said out loud. Not that the two really knew anything. As days were passing and no other visits were paid to them, Nusia's anxiety about her mother learning the truth about her canvas bag abated. And the grown-ups also managed to convince themselves that the situation was not really serious; that Jozef's absence was just temporary, a top secret mission, possibly; that all the unpleasantness that befell them was just a monumental error, some foul-up which was being rectified at that moment; or that if Jozef had enemies who had schemed to hurt him, he had already caught up with them and had things well under control.

They learned the sobering truth from cousin Radomir, right after it had come to him from some distant corner of the world on the short waves intercepted by his clandestine radio. It was on a quiet Saturday evening that he unexpectedly descended upon them from his garret quarters with an explosive communique, "That goddamn bastard has gone to the other side!" And they knew immediately that the "bastard" was none other than their General Jozef M., and that "the other side" was the side of the enemy, the West that lay behind the Rampart, the territory controlled by the rich, horribly libertine and corruptive Great Far Western Allied Sovranties. They also knew that very instant that their days of tranquility, unconcerned innocence, and clear conscience were over.

It must have been some time during their third year in Broscin that Jozef M. became elevated to the rank of lieutenant-general, acquired a new row of medals to embellish his already impressive-looking chest and was provided with a new navy-blue limousine equipped with a movable writing table and a liquor chest. (They learned about the medals from Kocia and from studying Jozef's portrait that appeared in various papers, for on those occasions when they saw him in the flesh, during his rare visits to them, he wore civilian garb. About the limousine and the liquor they heard from Nusia.) It was commonly acknowledged that the bracket of lieutenant-generals was as high as anybody could ever hope to get, unless of course one was destined to lead all of the nation's armies, which was not what the highest custodians of the country wanted him for. Of his special role in the security branch the family knew from Kocia, of course; but, as the man's importance in world affairs grew, that knowledge became commonplace among the regular citizenry as well as on the clandestine short waves. That he was indeed a man of power was also easily guessed from the number of requests for his benevolent intervention that were regularly coming to Adam's sister, and from his always being able to grant her wishes (of course, when she chose to play the part of a charitable agent). He was able to move mountains, it seemed; make a prison term shorter or commuted altogether, make a space be found for a civilian in a military sanatorium, make quantities of meat and liquor find their way from a governmental reserve to a private party, or even make back taxes owed by a private entrepreneur be stricken off the official records.

Jozef's likeness was often shown in the national press, and his name was deferentially mentioned on the national radio, but the amount of knowledge about him divulged to the public was sparing. It was considered indecorous to discuss the private affairs or particulars of any kind regarding people of national importance; also, the knowledge of details, the custodians of the Principles believed, was likely to dim the understanding of the essence of any great man. And so, the essence of Jozef, as given to the people, was that he was of native roots, a great War hero, a prime leader and strategist of the country's army who had risen from the ranks of the GEU People's Army, a humanitarian and a great man all around in peacetime as well.

Of course, they, unlike others, knew a few more details about him; about his limousine, his dogs, his beautiful villa, all its art treasures, his passion for military subjects in the arts and the life-size statue of a mounted Hussar standing in the most prominent spot in the salon in which the general most often discussed the affairs of the world with men from the Capital and even from the GEU People's Power itself.

That such a man could have become a traitor to his country, to the Principles and to his country's greatest ally The People's Power was, of course, incomprehensible.

"Despicable bastard," says Radomir.

"Listen to him!" shouts Adela. "He who himself always says how nice and free it must be on the other side, and who always listens to their blasted news!"

"I may listen to their news, but I would not sell myself to them! What he did is a treason! And my instincts were right, I always hated him." Radomir is wrought up beyond his usual state of arousal.

"Well, maybe he did not sell himself, my dear," says Adela. "Maybe he worked for the right cause all along, you know, in secret, and we did not know about it. And maybe he was even a decent human being, who never, absolutely never, tortured or shot anybody personally," Adela starts laughing hysterically.

"You are all wrong!" exclaims mother. "He did not do it out of decency or for gain. He did it to spite Kocia, to spite us all, to punish Kocia for not marrying him!"

"I think that it was rather clever of her not to marry him," says Boleslaw. "Imagine what they would do now to her as Mrs. Jozef M.! It was clever of her not to even move in with him. She always had brains, I tell you."

"You don't have to be sarcastic, Boleslaw," says Kocia with dignity. "I always do what's right and moral. And, yes, that decision of mine may still save me, and all of you, from the firing squad or hanging, or whatever it is that is done to traitors. But none of us is a traitor. I certainly am not! Thinking of it, I hardly knew the man."

"Of course, you did not know him well at all, my sweetest," Renata assures her. "The scoundrel just tried to use you, that's all. Well, he was smooth, alright, cheated his own government, probably spying for the enemy all the time, and lying to you. But you never really liked him, Madame Kocia, Renata remembers. And the best thing for you would be now to go straight to the authorities and make a clean breast of things to let them know how it really was between you and him and what you really think about that son-of-a bitch, my dearest."

After a day's reflection on her present predicament, Kocia decides that Renata is right. That she does not run straight to the Special Office is only because she cannot think of an appropriate answer for the authorities if by any chance they ask how she has come to know about Jozef's treason, for his disappearance was at no time announced by the press or radio. And admitting to the possession of information from a clandestine source was under the circumstances about as dangerous as confessing to being an agent of a hostile foreign power.

Actually, the existence of Radomir's shortwave radio becomes an issue of some concern. They all advise him to reduce it to its elements as quickly as possible, and Kocia commands him to take its parts to the city canal, one at a time, and sink them near the city dump where the water is at its blackest and filthiest. And Renata says that anybody less devoted to the family than she would have reported him to the authorities long ago. But he is determined not to part with his set, as they will need the news now more than ever, he says, and brags that he has a perfect hiding place for his radio that no one will ever unearth. And so, at intervals of some few hours, Radomir shows up in their place with the latest news from the other side that he manages to catch on his short-waves.

During Radomir's disclosures and any discussion of their present situation, Nusia, on her mother's orders, stays locked in the bathroom from where she cannot hear what is said in other parts of the premises. This is just precaution on Kocia's part, not a punishment, as she and the others still do not have any idea of Nusia's secret involvement with Jozef that past summer. So Nusia is in total darkness about what is transpiring in the adult world.

As for Adam, he too remains in the dark for a little while, that is, in his slow-wittedness, at first he does not think of himself as involved in the general's escape in any way. He only looks at Jozef's apostasy from the logistical side and sees it as a phenomenal achievement; for one of the most guarded men on earth to elude those surrounding him and to manage the crossing of the world's most strongly fortified frontiers was an act of uncommon boldness and cunning, Adam thinks with envy. Then he starts realizing that the act was far too daring and clever to have been accomplished by the general on his own. And only some hours later, when wondering who Jozef's accomplices were – as the man must have had a number of them on both the sides of the Rampart – the light begins penetrating the cells of his brain. And he feels pain and anger knowing that he was used. During the periods of Radomir's subsequent news releases, Adam is wearing one of his grinning-face masks with the word *Patsy* scribbled across it. Not that anybody notices this new garb.

About forty-eight hours after the original broadcast, the enemy's radio – which regards Jozef now as a solid political ally and an intimate associate – announces that the man is planning to expose himself to the world, that is, is going to reveal the story of his life, with all details, in installments to be carried from his side to the side of his former country exclusively over the short wave. The very first installment, which is to be broadcast the following day, the radio announcer promises, is to describe the general's dramatic escape from Broscin with the aid of a heroic ten-year old child.   ·

It is Renata who is the first to figure things out. "Of course it is she, the little brat... I should have known right away that there was a good reason for the authorities to take an interest in her... Oh, I am so sorry, Madame Kocia, my poor Madame Kocia, but, as Renata always says, some of the most decent people in this world have children that go astray."

Nusia is dragged out from the bathroom and placed in front of the chastising tribunal presided over by her mother. She is too disoriented to answer any questions satisfactorily; and only after she hears Adam demanding that the blame be put on him, the purveyor of masks and costumes, does she comprehend that her mother knows about her playing hooky from her ballet lesson. She cries and promises that she will never, never miss another class; for, as of that evening, she does not know what "going to the other side" means.

Mieczyslawa Konstancya, pale and pain-ridden, gives her daughter a mortified look, saying that she has no strength to go on; drained, she is ready to collapse. In a wink Renata is next to her, holding her tight and telling her that there is hope, in fact a good possibility that things will work out all right, provided that she disassociates herself from certain members of her family as soon as possible. She suggests that Nusia be placed in some solid reform school and Adam be locked in a mental home. It is very likely that Konstancya would have taken that advice, but for the fact that time ran out on her.

The news of Jozef M. – of the Affair of M., as it became later known – even though not announced by the national radio and press, rapidly spread throughout the country nevertheless.

The day after learning about Nusia's and Adam's part in the affair, Konstancya does not want to leave the house alone. She is now being constantly followed by men from the Special Office for weeks, but being subjected to that procedure again on this particular day, all on her own, would be too much for her, she says. As there is no one else around, and mother is too fearful, Kocia asks Adam to accompany her to a rehearsal at the Opera. As the two of them are walking, on the corner of their street they run into Professor Paluk's wife from the first floor and Kowalska from the third. At the sight of them the two ladies shriek in perfect unison, and then turn about and run away from them. And inside the Opera building, the porter gives them another startled look and then scuddles away too. And at the door of Konstancya's dressing room they meet the personnel manager of the Opera who blocks their entry and informs Konstancya that her dressing table, the chaise and all her personal effects have been officially impounded, and all the parts in her repertory have been assigned to a new soprano due to arrive shortly from the Capital.

Within minutes after they return home they hear knocking at their door. Three unknown men, all in grey trench coats, no identifying badges or calling cards, tell Konstancya that she is under arrest. Mother screams, they lock her in the salon; Adam asks for an explanation, they push him to the farthest corner of the hallway. He can see Konstancya from a distance; she stands there and smirks, with superiority, but pleasantly enough, while the men are saying something to her, of which he can understand only her official name pronounced in its entirety: Mieczyslawa Maria Rytwianska nee Czulartian. And then he sees them all move towards the open door leading to the stairway, and he ceases seeing her face, and begins rapidly losing sight of the rest of her too; at the fastest pace her height lessens miserably and the breadth of her form also dwindles to an insignificant sliver of anatomy wedged between the trench coats of the three men who are escorting her away.

An hour or so later, shortly after she returns from school, Nusia is taken away too by her old acquaintance, the crystal-ball gazer, and another man whom they recognize from the previous visit. She is curtly notified that, as already several weeks passed since her canvas bag was found under the furnace in the House's boiler room together with the general's neatly folded uniform, and no satisfactory explanation of that circumstance has been provided by anybody, she, the owner of the bag, will be asked to elucidate the matter before some higher authority. At first the two men are all business, even quite gruff, but after Nusia repeats for the third or fourth time that she does not want to go with them, her old friend gently pats her plump arm and asks her with a sweet-flowing voice what her favorite foods are. She answers matter-of-factly that they are whipped cream, milk chocolate, well-buttered green beans and lots of herring salad, the creamy kind; and then the man says very confidently that he knows for sure that all those things will be available in the place where she is going.

"And even some ice-cream for dessert," he says.

"But no coffee flavor, please."

"Oh, by no means no coffee!" he promises cheerfully

"How long am I going to be there?" Nusia sounds suddenly terribly uncertain of herself.

"Long enough for a couple of nice meals. Do you think I could join you for a little party there?" The crystal-ball gazer is beaming.

Thus it comes to pass that Mieczyslawa, Adam's sister, and Franciszka, his niece, are both gone, interned in a locale unknown and for a duration, likewise, never specified. Since no official statement is ever presented to the family, whether oral or written, concerning the circumstances in which they so unexpectedly found themselves, nobody really knows how things stood with them. Yet, no one ever doubts that the men who took the two of them away were instruments of a superior authority and that both Konstancya and Nusia are now in the custody of the State.

Adam is arrested two days later. Probably it is Renata, though it could have been either Kocia or Nusia, that told the authorities about his role in the affair of M. He presumes that one of them was the source of that information, since the enemy's radio in its daily installments of the adventures of the defected general never mentions Adam at all. The omission of his person, Adam firmly believes, is not an attempt on anybody's part to either slight him or protect him; it is meant to create a more dramatic story for the consumption of the short-wave listeners; for the story of M. has become dramatic indeed. In the episode transmitted just before Adam's arrest, Jozef M. is fleeing the city of Broscin hidden inside a rickshaw box under the bulk of half a ton of anthracite, with a ten-year old girl on the rickshaw's seat, pretending to be a coal de-liverer, gallantly driving out of the city – armored patrols notwith-standing – straight to the general's hideout in the surrounding woodlands.

The Home of the Divine Providence

Our recent dining-table discussions have not been terribly ani-mated; the wards' minds, quite possibly, being preoccupied again with thoughts of some new subversive plots. However, when last night I initiated a discourse on spies, moles (human, not animal), and undercover operations, most wards received my remarks with true enthusiasm. We continued our topic today after breakfast, but when Szymon started relating to us what what was promising to be a truly fascinating cloak-and-dagger adventure, Brother Honore stopped him, forbidding him to talk any further, explaining that he could not allow us to indulge in a conversation that was obviously making us unwell. It was enough to look at our glary eyes and listen to our tremulous voices to know that our brains had been dangerously stirred, he said. After that Szymon humbly apologized in the name of all the wards for the choice of such an unhealthy topic. But later today, after he quietly sneaked into my room, Szymon told me about the new action, Operation S, he called it, that the wards had been preparing for the last few weeks, an event that was going to take place in three days. He explained what my specific part in the operation was going to be and gave me a dozen or so new shibboleths to memorize (which he called 'passwords'), to which I am to respond during the planned action.

11.

The place of Adam's confinement is a minuscule window-less cell lit blue by a swinging ceiling lamp, the light of which never goes out. The room of brown-smudged walls and unclean floor has, for his use only, a cot with a blanket, a toilet, a table and a stool; also a notebook and a pencil in case he feels like jotting down his thoughts rather than imparting them orally to his keepers. Compared with the basement of the Dobce school house (his prison in War time) the present quarters are luxury itself. Also, his main keeper, the man who introduces himself to him as Edek, a bulky specimen with protruding biceps and jingling metal implements attached to his belt, says to him right at their first meeting, "Want to become friends?"

The weeks of his confinement, full of gnawing bodily pain and enfeebling terror, are also, Adam recollects, strangely devoid of physicality; a journey through a dream, long and terribly strenuous. The sense of immateriality is, quite possibly, the result of a huge amount of dust continually swirling in the atmosphere lit by the blue light which is never turned off.

During the weeks of his imprisonment Adam is frequently visited by various men of authority, among whom the only familiar one is the crystal-ball gazer. They are all interested in Konstancya, in Jozef, in anybody that Adam ever knew, and also in Adam himself, particularly in his memory of the day when the three of them played chimney sweeps and Jozef got away. His visitors often suggest that he write down what he remembers and draws the faces of those he saw on that day of their escapade. The crystal-ball gazer, locally known as The Chef, is the only one who smiles to him, pats him on his shoulder and even shows him tricks with his crystal ball and cards. But the man Adam sees most often is Edek the Biceps, always in a tight-fitted short-sleeved shirt of faded blue and with metal instruments attached to his belt. Edek does not smile, but every morning he tells Adam that, no matter what all the others think of him, he finds him personable and sweet, and regular. And every evening, when collecting the pages Adam has filled during the day, he admiringly looks at Adam's sketches of faces and says that he will show those creations to his superiors who are more knowledgeable than he in matters of art. And every few days he takes Adam for an excursion in a chauffeured jeep to give him some fresh air, he says, and helps him locate the house where Nusia and he saw Jozef M. for the last time. Edek, unlike his other custodians, rarely wants to know anything about him; instead he prefers to tell him about himself. He is modest in describing his personal qualities and achievement, but always makes sure that his biceps as well as his implements – knives, knuckles, spikes, chains, cuffs, the lot – are given proper credit.

He talks to Adam a few times each day and says things deliberately and clearly; and towards the end of each heroic yarn of his he gets close to him, his fingers reaching for the sinews of Adam's neck, shoulders and arms suggesting great intimacy; and then he swats both of Adam's ears with the tips of his fingers – one swift, deafening swat – and he asks, staring deep in Adam's eyes, "You ready to become friends soon?" And then he moves half-a-step away from him, stoops a little and rapidly plunges his raised knee into Adam's belly; and when Adam lies on the floor, he kicks Adam's groin, crotch and sides with the metal front of his boot, and he stares at Adam again and repeats his question about becoming friends.

One day in Adam's fourth or fifth week, Edek suddenly says that they have made really nice progress, and that they are almost friends. He is glad to tell him that the house which Adam pointed out to him the day before happens to be the same one that his niece Nusia also remembered, a place the authorities had their eyes on for a long time. "Good job!" he praises Adam.

"No, no, Edek, you should not have paid attention to me... I was just rambling, it was only a tentative identification. I did not say it for sure!" Adam is caught in panic.

"You don't worry. It is the house all right."

"I did not say it for sure! It was not a positive identification! I have been telling you I don't remember anything!" Adam wants to let him know that there could have been an error, and he screams, even though he knows that he will be punished for it.

But Edek does not hit him. His voice sounds friendly and reassuring, "You my friend now, so you don't worry. You don't bother your brain about anything; you just work on the faces now and tell me tomorrow what they all looked like."

But on that day Adam does not work on the faces his keepers want him to recall. He sits in a corner of his cell, covers his face with his hands to keep the glare of the blue dust away from his eyes, and he thinks of the War and other things from years past. He sees the expanse of the land, the endless sky above, the blooming meadow, Nusia gathering cones for the fire, Kocia bringing in heather for the wounded; and he hears the discharge of guns and the partisans running. Then he sees them among the birch trees stalking the enemy, all young, their hearts afire; and he, Adam, is one of them, a warrior, in a khaki-colored uniform with a rifle and an ammunition belt across his chest, like the others, running across the field together with all of them, shooting and shouting in triumph. That day in his windowless cell with the blinding light that can not go out, he wants to be like those others, the only time in his life that he wants to be a fighting man; and he bawls out loud, for he knows that it is too late for him. There are no more fields and forests through which to run, nor farms or country cemeteries that are haven, no rifles to carry, and no enemy who speaks a foreign tongue at whom to aim. They themselves are the enemy now, the traitors to their country and to one another; maybe not all, but one can not tell which of them are betrayers. Adam is one after he identifies the house in which Jozef disappeared, but he was called a traitor before by his keepers when he failed to recognize the same house. And who were the two women that he betrayed, the two in whose house Jozef disappeared? And the man who took Jozef's place on the rickshaw? And why did they all betray little Nusia? How many others did they deceive and waste? He suddenly sees them all meeting him and Nusia on a road near Burak's farm, years past, kind and warm, exchanging secret passwords with Adam and giving Nusia a blessing; and he knows that they are not enemies, not then, as nobody was then. They were all one, as Radomir would say. And so Adam cries for those roads and mountains, and for those times when they were whole; and since he knows again and again that all of that is so far in the past that nothing, neither the holiest wish nor the most powerful magic, can bring it back now, he bawls harder and harder. Then he thinks of the occupied city of Wielow, of Povolians and their hatred for the others, even though they were always told that they and the rest were one. And then he also sees a man on the road to Dobce encountering a Hebrite woman who asks him to hide her in his wagon – just the way the locals told him it had happened, but Adam never wanted to remember – and the man telling the Hebrite woman to pay him for the favor and the woman saying she has no money, and the man telling her to give him her coat and the woman refusing, saying she is cold, and the man then refusing to help the Hebrite woman, and she eventually giving the man her coat and the man taking her to safety, and then coming home and ripping the coat to pieces and finding a packet of money under the lining. And Adam remembers people saying that the man who took the coat from the woman, clever that he was, knew what he was doing, knew that Hebrites, rich and cunning that they are, are likely to have money or other wealth hidden on them, even when on the run. And then Adam also recollects back in the early days of the War freight trains with herded Hebrite prisoners going to their death, and Povolians standing guard over them and all the others pretending not to see. And then he sees mother and himself in their kitchen in Wielow and the thin little Hebrite boy whom they give food, but whom neither mother nor he tries to save from death. And Adam wails and howls in misery.

He must have created a lot of noise because Edek appears in his cell again. But he is not angry. He takes Adam in his arms, like a baby, lays him on the cot, covers his legs with the blanket, and gently strokes his back. "Now you sleep. You worry too much," he says.

When Adam wakes up, Edek is with him again, setting his breakfast on the table. Adam feels hungry, refreshed, calm; tormenting thoughts of fields, khaki uniforms and trains full of people going to their doom are all gone from his mind. That morning he knows that after having achieved the status of Edek's friend he begins to count; he can make things happen the way he wants, at least a few things. He tells his new friend, Edek the Biceps, how pleased he is that he has identified the right house and been of service. Then he asks Edek to make it possible for him to see Nusia.

After a few days Adam is taken to see Nusia at last. The place of her confinement is not unfamiliar to him; that is, its exterior view.

It is an elegant city mansion of classical lines and the parentage of previous centuries, not far from the Firmament. It has a bed of blooming asters in front and an ornamental iron fence separating it from the street; and the sign on a plaque affixed to this fence says that the building is the seat of the International Friendship Society. Edek and Adam are let inside the iron gate by an armed guard in a military uniform, then escorted across the courtyard by another uniformed and armed guard, and then admitted to the building by yet another man in a uniform and with a pistol. But inside they are taken care of by officials in civilian clothing only. In a small office off the vestibule they are received by a young woman in a festive purple dress and pearl earrings who tells them that the Chef has been informed of their visit and will see them shortly.

When the Chef (the erstwhile crystal-ball owner) walks in, the woman smiles to him and walks out of the room leaving the three of them alone. The Chef seems not just content, but joyful, telling them that things have gone so well with Nusia that he will not need her around anymore, not for a while anyway. He explains that for a long time, Nusia was a little resistant, holding out on him, not quite comprehending how important it was for her to remember everything. But all of a sudden she seemed to have understood what this was all about. "I was worried a little bit, you know, my friend," the Chef confesses, "almost a month passed, and still quite a few loose ends, question marks, you know. So that's why I sent Zyta to see your little her girl... didn't have that much hope though, but, luckily for all of us..."

"But for goodness sake, Chef, Zyta..." Edek interrupts him.

"Don't concern yourself, Edek," the Chef sounds superior. "Zyta was all right. I told her personally not to be too rough on the little one... and as I was saying," he turns to Adam again, "things went very well; so well, that if certain information checks out, you both will be able to go home today. How is that for service, eh?!" He seems elated.

"Could you tell me what it was that she was holding out on you? And who is Zyta?" Adam feels he needs to know.

"Your little girl has been very good all along, so this was relatively minor, still, it was of some importance to us. Well, among other things it was a matter of identifying a few photographs for us, the last of the whole batch. She did some earlier, so there were only a few left, but, she seemed to be a little uneasy about those, squeamish, I would say; you know how children are..."

"What kind of pictures were they? And who is Zyta, please?" Adam asks again.

"I have to fly off now, but will be back soon," the Chef waves to Adam on his way to the door.

"What kind of photographs does he mean? And who is Zyta, please, Edek?" Adam begs.

"They get Zyta when there is trouble with some women. But, as the Chef said, you just don't worry yourself no more." Edek makes the last statement very loud and clear, probably for the sake of the woman in purple with pearl earrings who is coming back into the room. She asks them to sit and wait for the Chef.

He comes back an hour or so later, grinning again. He tells Adam that he and Nusia will be able to leave very shortly, but that he would like him to look at something before they go. Adam and Edek follow him then upstairs into a large room full of rugs, puffed armchairs and drapes covering all the walls.

"It will be instructive for you to find out how your little girl lived while under our care," says the Chef. "So many of our citizens believe in stories of our rat-infested prisons and torture chambers, even for the very young. By the way, your place wasn't too bad, was it my friend?" He smiles and pulls some strings attached to the plush drapes on one of the walls, exposing thus a large, square window.

Behind the solid glass pane of the window Adam sees an almost bare room, and inside it there is Nusia squatting on the floor, her eyes downcast, scrutinizing something at her feet. She looks small, almost scrawny, pale and very untidy. Adam calls her name and taps on the window pane to get her attention, and when she does not react, he taps again, and again, and yells out her name as loud as he can.

"She can't hear or see you, my dear chap. This is a magic window; we see and hear through it one way only. Ingenious, eh?"

"I want to talk to her," says Adam.

"Look how well she is provided for... a bed with a pillow and a blanket, a nice little table with a basin on it, clean water... paper and a pencil on the floor, even playing cards... and look who is coming..." he winks to Adam. "Good old Zyta... smock as neat as usual. Well, your girl should know by now that there is no reason for alarm."

The woman is slowly coming towards Nusia while Nusia is moving away from her, backwards, half-crouching, in irregular jerks and hops. Then she scrambles to her feet, runs and jumps on the bed into the farthest corner of it, bunching up her blanket and pillow into a protective pile in front of her. The woman reaches the foot of the bed and they both freeze; the woman is stooped over the bed, and Adam can now see her elephantine posterior raised up on the legs spread wide apart; and Nusia squeezed into the corner of the bed, shrunk under the blanket, peers from behind a pillow, her eyes terror-haunted. Adam screams to the Chef to rescue Nusia immediately, but realizes that he is no longer in the room with him; he rushes then to the door, but finds it locked; he runs back to the glass pane and seeing Zyta climbing up on Nusia's bed, he pounds on the glass with both his fists; but he is immobilized by Edek. His arms painfully twisted behind his back, he still screams demanding rescue for Nusia; and Edek quietly tells him that everything is going to be alright. But when Adam does not quiet down, Edek hits him on the side of his head, and Adam slips into a state of unawareness.

Some hours later he and Nusia are on the street, outside the gate of the International Friendship Society, free. Adam remembers the Chef's words before they left, "Stay on the straight-and-narrow from now on," but he has no other recollections of things that happened after Edek rendered the blow to his head. Neither does he know whether they walked or ran from the Friendship Society, and whether they said anything to each other; and he has no idea how long it was before he became aware of their surroundings, a narrow littered street, and of Nusia's squeezing his hand and talking about being cold.

She has on a school skirt and a school blouse, and a short thin sweater, the same ones she wore on that day when the Chef took her away with promises of revelry and feasting. Her clothes are heavily rumpled, torn in spots and stained all over; her braids are undone with long strands of hair almost completely covering her face. Adam becomes aware of his soiled clothes too, and he feels now the cold November air reaching his skin through the thin layer of his garment.

They ask a passer-by for the directions to the nearest tramway stop, and then they run; but when they get on a tramway, they realize they have no money to pay the fare. Adam asks the conductor whether he could let them take this one ride at no charge as they are both a little under the weather, but before the man has time to consider this request, a woman passenger shouts in his direction, "No, citizen conductor, absolutely not, we are all honest working-class people here and do not want to have anything to do with no-good drunken beggars! Throw them off the car, right now!"

And so they proceed on foot. After a few minutes, quite unexpectedly, they find themselves just steps from the ornate glass-panelled doors to the Firmament. For a second they think of going in, but then remember their unbecoming appearances and the woman on the tramway, and they know that they would not be wanted inside; and Nusia keeps repeating, "Who would want to go in there anyway." Then they see Boleslaw coming out of the door, a hotel guest's suitcase in his hand. He puts the suitcase down and runs to Nusia, "What have they done to you, babee?" he cries.

The time which they spent at the Firmament on that day of their release from internment was as weary and dreamlike as anything Adam had already experienced since the moment of his arrest; and yet all the images of that evening that he retained in his memory are to this day clear and precise.

Here is Nusia acknowledging her father, his brown uniform and all; Nusia hesitantly approaching him, tears streaking down her dirty cheeks, embracing him, hiding her face in the folds of his coat with the golden buttons and wiping her eyes with his gold-trimmed sleeve. Here is Boleslaw in the staff's washroom, scrubbing Nusia's face and hands and braiding her hair. And here they are in the Porphyry Room, Boleslaw putting a white serviette around Nusia's neck, bringing them food on a tray, piling the food for them on the plates and grinning at Nusia. "You eat, babee, eat everything. You're so skinny now. Look what's become of her, Adam!" And there is Porphyry Room, monumental, glary, over-filled with fanciful mirrors and Aaron plants, and Nusia in the middle of it, among all that gaudiness, tired and befuddled, not being able to swallow a morsel. Then there is the bar Rigolo where they have to wait; murky, fumy, disorienting, and Nusia at a drink-splotched table, sleeping, her head on her forearm, her elbow suspended from the edge of the table.

And here is Adela entering Rigolo coming to take them home, since Boleslaw has to work till late; Adela towering over everybody at the bar and laughing at the bartender's jokes harder than anyone else, Adela ordering double cognacs for herself and Adam, giving him a pat on his cheek and asking how he was treated by the big bad wolves.

"And how did they treat the little fat one?"

"Not so fat anymore, according to her father,"

"Let's drink to that," Adela finishes her cognac.

She does not feel like leaving yet, and so they stay. They sit in silence staring at the sleeping and snoring Nusia and at the drunk guests at the bar. "Gay place, isn't it, Adam?" she says without expecting an answer.

And there is Emil, the manager of the Firmament who un-expectedly comes to join them – Emil the beautiful, Emil the fiery-eyed heartthrob of very many females of all ages. "Good evening, Miss Adela," he says. "It is not often that I see you."

Adam does not recognize his voice, gentle and shy almost. All of him is different from what Adam remembers: his smile, eyes, profile, shoulders. He is holding Adela's hands in his and stares hard into her face, with affection that hotel managers do not nor-mally display towards their guests. And she is smiling at him with fondness and motherly tenderness that the Adela they know, the cynic and the wisecrack, does not normally possess. Adam cannot believe his eyes, but then this is a day of altered states all around.

Emil brings to their table a bottle of cognac and a glass for himself. He pours drinks for all three of them, but he does not look at Adam; he is there for Adela only. The two of them drink, ogle each other, laugh and exchange thoughts the meaning of which escapes Adam. He is trying to guess exactly what kind of bond there is between them, and he has no doubt that what links them is big, lies deep inside them and goes far back into their past. They had known each other well, years, years earlier in Wielow before the War, he is certain of it; and he also knows that whatever it is that exists between them has nothing to do with romance, the erotic desire that Adela has been claiming to feel for him.

Adela strokes the smooth hair on the side of his head. "I always thought that you were so special... that one day you, of all of them, would become... well, a great politician, a judge perhaps or an inspired reformer... or at least a literatus extrao rdinary..." she laughs, but there is sadness in her voice.

"I never meant to disappoint you, Miss Adela," Emil too sounds joyless. "But I have had some success in life, haven't I?" He changes his voice again, this time back to the well-familiar voice of Emil, the manager of the Firmament. She is talking again to him, but he leaves their table and the bar Rigolo without as much as a single look back at her.

Adam did not have the least notion, premonition if you will, on that night that in some months hence he would learn more about the mystery linkage between their cousin Adela and Emil the handsome and that he would wish then that the details of that liaison would have never come to light.

They stayed at Rigolo that night for another hour or so, until Adela and Adam finished all the liquor which was in the bottle that Emil brought. They went home in a taxi that Boleslaw hailed for them; and Nusia slept all the way.

On the second day after their return, Nusia's grandmother, greatly worried about various scars and dark and large maculations on Nusia's body (particularly her thighs), takes her to see a doctor. Nusia screams at the sight of the man and his female assistant, and only lets herself be examined with her grandmother present at her side all the time. The doctor says that Nusia will be all right, but he would like to know how the bruises and other injuries were incurred; and Nusia's grandmother tells him that Nusia has been in a terrible fight with some other children at school.

Mother indeed did not know how exactly Nusia had acquired her bruises, since Nusia refused, then and ever at any time later, to talk about them. Once only did she mumble, "I guess I was just punished." And Adam got angry at her, telling her that she had not done anything bad to be punished for. But as she did not want to listen or talk about the matter, he let her be, especially that he himself decided to keep mum about what precisely befell him. To try to put the experience into coherent sentences was not only inconceivably difficult; but also to relive everything was too hurtful and of too little merit, he felt. He did not even tell Nusia about the magic window through which he saw her; neither did he tell her that he knew about the photographs and Zyta; not that he really knew about any details concerning photographs or Zyta, thinking of it.

A week or so after seeing the doctor, Nusia goes back to school with a letter signed by her father stating that she will triple her efforts to make up for the time so regrettably lost during her illness (measles, as far as Adam recollects). It is the only way to explain and comment on the situation, since Nusia's school was already informed some time earlier by the Chef about the disease that she had contracted.

When Nusia gets back to her classroom, she finds the seat next to her empty and her classmates, all aware of the shame that fell on her family, especially her mother, unwilling to talk to her. The class teacher asks the children to show Nusia the magnanimity of their hearts, but nobody budges. Nusia is despondent; her grandmother goes to the teacher and asks for intervention, but the teacher says that she cannot do a thing more in the matter. It takes Jurek Goralski, Nusia's neighbor from the fourth floor, two months before he decides to sit next to Nusia again and to resume talking to her. Adam feels that two months was much, much too long, but Nusia is overjoyed that she has got her friend back at last.

At the time when Nusia and Adam were given back their freedom, Konstancya was still gone. Where she was and what was happening to her was not known to anybody. But, as mother said to Adam, everybody concerned about Kocia was searching for a contact, a line, to a person of influence who would have the power to effect a turn-about in her fortunes.

As soon as she knows that Renata is nowhere around to overhear them, mother confides in Adam that she is hopeful that the same people who made their (that is Nusia's and his) release possible would help Kocia as well. And the way mother aspirates her syllables indicates that she is not supposed to mention those wonderful individuals by name. Adam tells her that their release had nothing to do with any influential individuals, but she repeats in the most assured whisper that they are free only because of the intervention on their behalf of some extremely influential personages that the family was able to contact.

"Believe me, mother," says Adam, "Nusia and I owe our freedom only to our willingness to..." and he is almost ready to tell her about the Chef, Edek the Biceps, Zyta the Vampire, and about all the valuable information with which he and Nusia provided the authorities. But mother knows better.

"Oh, no, no," she insists stubbornly, her voice full of a worldly wisdom she usually lacks. "No matter what it may seem, important things never happen without the intervention of a person of power; that's what I have learned, my dear. You cannot move ahead in this world, if you do not have a protector, a patron somewhere in high places."

What she is saying annoys Adam so greatly that he just tells her in an appropriately rude manner that he does not wish to talk any further about anybody's protectors in high places. He shrouds his face with his frolicking he-goat mask and leaves the room. He is furious and greatly distressed. Not that he has any idea what precisely is the cause of his anguish. It might be the thought of the Chef's incredible duplicity and deviousness that is so bothersome to him. But since he never considered the man trustworthy, why should any additional lies of his bother him so much? It could be the feeling of his total incapability of ever being in control of his own destiny that he dislikes so much; but then he has lived with that through most of his life. The roots of his anger may, of course, lie simply in his realization that the act of his turning informer was probably gratuitous, not at all instrumental in saving his skin. But he is asking himself again whether he has really committed an act of betrayal.

The following day, despite his protests and his goat-mask, mother manages to tell him everything she knows or conjectures. She knows personally, of course, only the people she calls their direct friends and non-friends; all those who either have served as initial links in those lifesaving lines of contact or have refused to do so. And only through hunches and theories can she guess names and positions of all the others, those forming ascending lines of contacts leading to the very top.

She carries on at length first about the bad, the timid, the false-hearted, the God-have-mercy-over-their-miserable-souls bunch; all those important guests of the Firmament, all regulars and so indebted to Boleslaw, but not willing to even listen to his plea; and Emil himself, on a first-name basis with so many of them, refusing to talk to anybody on Boleslaw's behalf; and Adela's boss, the editor-in-chief of *The Worker*, telling Adela off most rudely and threatening her with dismissal from her job at any further mention of the traitor Jozef M.; and Professor Pal... from the first floor shutting his door in her face; mother in her pain and aversion to the man, cannot even pronounce his full name anymore. But her dejection disappears as soon as she mentions the other group – the brave, the willing, not great in number, but, oh, so well-intentioned.

"Things always work in the most unexpected way; I opened the door and here he was, his glass eye staring in my face," the remembrance of veteran Klusa from the third floor brightens mother's countenance. "Obviously it was all *à couvert* ; I was alone that afternoon and he talked very low. But how kind and tactful he was, didn't even mention Kocia's singing and how it would keep his babies awake; he just implied that she was a little vain and you and Nusia a trifle spoiled, though he didn't mind her playing with his children. He definitely did not believe that Kocia or you, or any of us, were enemies of the State or opponents of the Principles... we had just fallen victim to the schemes of a bad man, he said, and that's why he wanted to help. He did not call her "Kocia", by the way, only "Citizeness K.R.", and he said that she was exploited by an unprincipled man, a beast, who preyed on her innocence and natural womanly vanity." Mother quotes Klusa with fire in her eyes, but admits that, quite possibly, she is not being literal; he might have said "villain" instead of "beast" and called Kocia "naive" rather than "innocent".

Mother has great trust in Klusa's connections. She reasons that his man in the Capital, in a ministry that Klusa does not want to disclose, must have always been far more potent than Jozef M., since, had such not been the case, Kocia would have had her way long, long ago, and Klusa and his family would have been transferred to a different building, far away from the Boulevard. Also, the power of his connections is quite evident, she says, from the fact that the day before Adam's and Nusia's release he told her (in passing her on the stairs) that their case is progressing very smoothly.

The one-eyed veteran Klusa from the third floor, who so miraculously turns out to be a friend of theirs, is by no means the only one from whose lips comes a pronouncement of Konstancya being a victim of the machinations of an unscrupulous man. Shortly after Klusa's visit mother is again hearing such an opinion, though from a man who represents a liaison with the pinnacles of law and power of a very different kind from Klusa.

The man in question, a Father Reszka, a prelate residing in the prestigious parish of Saint Andrew's, imparts his evaluation of the matter in a muffled breath straight into mother's ear (the right ear, to be exact) through the ornamental grating of a confessional. It is an extraordinary occasion for her; she has never known Prelate Reszka before, except by reputation; and she hears that he is on the most intimate terms with the highest personages in the Capital, both ecclesiastical and secular. Also, as a prelate, no common servant of God, he listens to confessions rarely, usually of a selected few of his parish, but mother does not even belong to Saint Andrew's; and besides, she has not been to confession in almost six years, not since a day before that Easter bombardment of Wielow after which Konstancya decided to flee west. Anyway, mother has quite forgotten how to go about confessing properly, that is, how to coordinate the shifts of weight from one knee to the other with the two-way motion of the head so that the lips and the ear could properly alternate their respective positions against the confessional's grating. Consequently, even though this confession has been quite carefully prearranged, mother finds it horribly trying. Still, she somehow succeeds in telling the presence behind the grating (she assumes it is the Prelate himself) about her sorrows, and she is in turn assured by the voice coming from the other side that the Lord has never yet left any of his flock unattended and that she should have faith. And she is also told that they all, and especially Kocia, have been victims of the handiwork of an exceptionally evil man.

Let it be explained that the family's contact to the venerable Prelate was mother's first cousin Anna Gruber, Adela's sister, the widow of silversmith Gruber who, you may recollect, before marrying Anna, had offered his love, name and silver to the service of Adela. It might also be worth mentioning here that Anna Gruber, like other translocated citizens from Wielow, had arrived at the Broscin Central Station on a freight train some four years earlier with merely two suitcases (which was the maximal load permitted to be carried by any single translocated citizen), but that her suitcases, unlike luggage of others on those freight trains, were filled with rather precious silver objects; so at least the popular lore of post-War Broscin had it. Well, it could have been an empty rumor, since the extensive properties of silversmith Gruber were known to have been confiscated by the People's authorities; still, within weeks after her arrival at the Central, Anna opened a small shop specializing in selling devotional objects made of silver; medallions, neck chains with crosses, miniature crucifixes, sacred hearts enveloped in flames. Anna's place, which was really more of a booth than a shop, was situated in Saint Andrew's Close, a few steps from the parish church, and was given the name of The Holy Bedrock.

Now, it has never been determined what the contents of Anna's suitcases were, since what was for sale at the Bedrock was not considered evidence enough as to what Anna brought with her from Wielow, her present ware being often described as far from genuine. Even Boleslaw, a discreet man, would refer to Anna's flaming hearts as "all plain plated", and Goralski's mother-in-law from the fourth floor, also a native of Wielow, would say that Mrs. Gruber had desecrated her husband's noble trade and the memory of one of the finest establishments in pre-War Wielow. Still, Anna's booth of modest brick and plywood, thrived, from the very first day it started selling its devotionalia, plated as they might have been; and it prospered for years, even at times when mercantile enterprises of other private citizens crumbled. Since Anna and her shop were serving primarily Saint Andrew's parish, they were receiving from that holy establishment guidance and protection. And, as popular lore had it, Anna Gruber not only became rich again, but also experienced neither the meddling into her affairs of the secular authorities nor hardship brought about by governmental decrees against private commerce.

How intimately Anna knew Prelate Reszka mother did not know. Actually, mother was not even sure whether it was Anna herself who set up the meeting at the confessional or whether it was somebody of a higher stature. At any rate, mother felt enormously grateful to Anna for her willingness to serve as a liaison.

After her rendezvous at the confessional mother places a packet of money in a collection box, and then at Anna's shop buys a new rosary for herself (the first one since her desperate renunciation of God in the Hidden Vale some five years earlier). That night at home she also discusses with Boleslaw the exact amount of a donation for St. Andrew's to be sent to Prelate Reszka directly, as she is most hopeful about the Prelate's powers. The voice that comes to her from behind the confessional grating, which promises her Saint Andrew's mediation in Kocia's affairs, is authoritative, though tender and trustworthy.

By the way, mother is also thinking of rewarding their new friend veteran Klusa with an appropriate gift, but anxious not to offend this man, she can not decide on the manner of presentation.

And so, as mother explains to him, more than one power has been summoned to rescue Konstancya and more than one hidden hand is now pulling the invisible strings to bring about her release. Adam realizes that his attempt at describing some of the inner workings of those forces called to Kocia's rescue might appear incongruous, in particular the case of the dual nature of those forces. Some readers may feel confused when trying to picture in their heads a world in which ruthless secular rulers, who claim the infallibility of the order over which they preside, work hand in hand with ancient religious institutions and the faith of the people whom they are trying to subdue. For the sake of those, then, who are unfamiliar with the actualities of the life in Adam's country, let it be explained that though the people have indeed been living in accordance with the new Principles, they have been disregardant of the very first tenet of same, namely, the demand that this new set of laws be the sole faith of the land. And what is more, the post-war rulers of the country allow the people to keep their old creed; as long as they do not loudly deny the supremacy of the Principles. In particular, they allow them to keep all the markings of the religion, all those distinguishing trademarks that the nation hold most dear: the smiling Virgin, the bleeding Christ, genuflecting pilgrims, benevolent saints, excoriating priests, gilded altars, candles, thick vapors of incense.

How they have become a nation adherent to two faiths simultaneously is often debated (even on the other side, Adam understands), with no agreement on the subject; with some ascribing the phenomenon to the benevolence of the country's leaders, some to their laziness, and still others to an oversight. But Adam is certain that it is due to the great cunning of those men in power that the people have been allowed to follow the way of two divergent codes. He reasons that the two, both rigid systems of laws decreed infallible, are at heart very close to each other, being at odds with each other on the surface only; and the country's rulers have always been aware of it. It is because of this inherent kinship of the two, that the people have been able, without sacrificing their sanity, to replicate every people's parade of red banners and military drums with a procession to the glory of the Virgin; every icon of a People's hero with a shiny image of the crucifixion; every address from a public rostrum with a homily from the pulpit; and then match every pious whisper at the confessional with the reverent words of an ode to the People's Cause or every acceptance of the wafer of the Holy Communion with a solemn vow of loyalty to the People's Power. Adam professes here, then, that those in charge of his country's affairs have allowed the people to believe in two codes, knowing that the two, being the same by nature – even when vying with each other – would only reinforce each other and ultimately mold people's minds in such a fashion that thoughts of life not ruled by unchangeable sacred precepts would be inconceivable.

The Home of the Divine Providence

First I heard the loud sound of a detonation of some kind coming from the downstairs of our villa, and then another one coming from somewhere above me; and soon the odor of some burnt material began to filter into my room. Then I heard a great commotion; lots of scurrying around, bumping and thumping of all kinds, bleating, howling. And then I was summoned to perform my part, which was to take a position at the closed door of the Home's kitchen, and then scream as loudly as possible that the Home's food provisions were on fire; then, if any brother was to approach the door to the kitchen, to shove the brother inside the smoke-filled interior of the kitchen and shut the door behind him, myself remaining on the outside. Amazingly, I did everything that was required of me. The operation came to a successful end at dawn. In the middle of the kitchen, with heavy smoke lingering in it, there were seven befuddled brothers inside a large fishnet. The remaining five brothers were caught in a similar net in the attic. Then the wards gathered in the Green Veranda, and Lech, after he had played for us some gleeful fanfare-style piece on his bassoon, said, "We have taken over!" All the details of Operation Sniff have been already explained to me, but even though I myself was part of the action, I still remain in a state of shock and disbelief. How was it possible, I cannot stop wondering, that Tytus managed to construct in secret two bombs and then so perfectly synchronize their detonation with the setting ablaze of the rubber? And how was such a quantity of rubber collected, and when did it get into the kitchen oven and into a tub in the attic? How did Stefan make his two gigantic fishnets in secret and how he acquired all the twine? And how did the wards manage to disconnect the phone, lock all the doors and windows and then so successfully lure the brothers to either the kitchen or the attic? Well, maybe the only explanation is that "enough is enough, and we have had it", as Jan put it. And I do believe that the straw that broke the camel's back was the brothers' decision to deprive the wards of their Saturday Cobra Mystery Hour.

Konstancya is returned to her family a month or so after Adam's and Nusia's homecoming. Of course, no one has a clue as to who, or what, has been really responsible for her release; and she, like Nusia and Adam before her, refuses to discuss any particulars of her imprisonment with anybody. She is now definitely skinnier, paler, softer-sounding and a little bit twittery, but otherwise rec-ognizable.

Since the day of her return home Kocia is readying herself for the role of a witness in the coming trial of Jozef M.; for he, traitor to his country, is going to be tried shortly, in absentia, obviously; and she, one of the principal victims of his machinations, is going to be a witness for the prosecution.

12.

Jozef M. is tried in February, in an overheated, airless room with darkened windows and walls covered with portraits of the country's leading heroes. Facing several rows of long wooden benches is a stage, a massive two-level structure, with the official accusers of Jozef M. aligned on its lower level, and the judges on the upper one. All the others present at the trial are placed in the audience section facing the stage.

Konstancya is assigned a front-row seat between two men from the Special Office. Nusia and Adam, sandwiched between two other officials and separated from each other by another man, are placed a few rows behind her. Mother and Renata are seated next to each other on a small side bench with a standing guard watching them. The other members of their group, despite their efforts to be present in this courtroom, are not admitted.

At the outset of the proceedings, during his opening statement, the head judge tells those gathered in the room that Jozef M. is going to be condemned and that punishment by death is the only possible, nay, conceivable measure of justice that the highest court of the land could prescribe for a man who has betrayed his country. He also says that in the very near future, the people of the country will be hearing about the horrible crimes of Jozef M. and experiencing shock and dismay, thus learning a lesson for the future.

The trial lasts two weeks, with close to a hundred witnesses passing before the accusers and the judges, every day of the proceedings recorded in the nation's papers; which is not to say that all who are called to testify will actually talk and that all that is said is reported. Nusia and Adam, for instance, are placed in that class of witnesses who are called to the stage more than once, but are only asked, for reasons of expediency, merely to confirm the accusers' statements by certain quick bodily motions (bobs, nods, blinks, etc.).

"...you were well acquainted with the accused."

A bob of the head.

"You were intimidated by him."

A nod and a flourish of the arm.

"You were used by him."

A multiple nod.

"You began suspecting treason!"

A deep bow towards the judges' platform.

And so on.

Both Nusia and Adam do very well, they are told by the man sitting between them, a commendation they accept with some indifference. Since nothing that has been said refers to matters familiar to them, they are actually slipping during that trial into a state of inattention and dispassionateness. Of course, if they were asked, say, about their rickshaw ride through the city or Jozef's discarded uniform, or whether they recognize among the accusers somebody like Chef or Zyta, they would be more alert, but would not perform as well. Anyway, their testimonies turn out to be not the most significant of the trial.

To Adam's surprise, one of the most evidential testimonies comes from mother.

"...you, the mother, gentle, loving and blind, because a parent's love is often blind, trying not to see what was happening to your beloved daughter..." The accuser's chiding voice is also soothingly mellow. "...you, the mother, declining your duty as a citizen of your country, your duty to report to the authorities..." The voice is louder and loftier.

"But I had no idea, sir..." mother bursts into tears.

"Citizeness, we know well that you had no knowledge of his actual treason, but you saw warning signs, and so you should have acted. You had serious misgivings about the man, didn't you? And you knew how much your daughter feared him and felt powerless in his clutches. And so you knew that he was evil. Can you deny it?" The voice is more powerful than before.

"No, I can't deny that. I knew that he was evil." Mother's voice also gains strength, and so does her bawling.

"And you referred to him as a fiend. Don't deny that!"

"I will not deny it, sir... I referred to him by many bad names." The tears are gushing down her face.

"And you hated him! Hated him with all your heart! A mother's heart! Don't deny it!" The accuser's voice reaches the apex of its possible power.

"Yes, I hated him. Always hated him!" Mother's voice soars to the very height of the judges' platform. And the judges look at her kindly and nod approvingly.

The following day mother's close-up photograph appears in newspapers all over the country; pained face, teary eyes, wrenched mouth, a handkerchief pressed to her nostrils. But the caption under the picture identifies her only as one of the numerous witnesses recalling humiliation they suffered in the manipulative hands of the traitor.

Renata's disclosures turns out to be even more shattering, to the reputation of Jozef M., that is. Oh, yes, she can recall everything that citizeness Rytwianska confided in her. Yes, she has always considered Renata her best friend. Yes, she would tell her everything, maybe except those few times when she was so eaten up by shame that she could not talk and only let Renata guess her trouble. Oh, yes, citizeness Renata knows that ugly and shameful things were going on in his villa and in his limousine where he would use citizeness Rytwianska's body and her voice for his low purposes. But he could not carry on for long, not with Renata around. "Just once I looked him straight in the eye and I knew; he was like that basilisk..."

"Then he abused her physically and mentally?" The accuser wants to know.

"Oh, yes, he did." Renata does not hesitate. "And not just her, some others too, from citizeness Rytwianska's family, and that includes children and the weak-minded..."

"Then you say he indulged in perversity?!"

"He certainly did! There was plenty of that, and drunkenness and all kinds of orgies..."

"Please describe those events known to you, citizeness!"

"As I said, he used her body, and forced her to do things."

"What things? Explain, please."

"He forced her to, what he called, perform in front of all those people he would be with. You know, the enemies, or some that he tried to make join the enemy's side."

"Explain how she was to perform in front of those people."

"I can't, no, I can't say that in public. I have been a decent woman all my life. Please don't make me say those things! It was unspeakably evil!"

The accuser looks at Renata with understanding, and then turns towards the judges' platform and resonantly echoes, "So unspeakably evil!" And the judges nod approvingly.

Kocia's turn as a witness comes a few days later and, disappointingly, for the most part it lacks the quality of high drama that mother's or Renata's testimonies has had. She is allotted a little more time than other witnesses, but is not asked to divulge more than was deemed essential; and also the tone of her voice and her overall appearance is less effective than one could have expected. She is clear in what she says, and she looks appropriately frail and dolored, but somehow lacks a bit in passion. But the very end of her appearance is quite impressive; on what sounds like the last syllable of her statement she suddenly sinks down to her knees and then collapses at the foot of the judges' platform. The following day her picture appears in the papers; a swooning figure being held by a doctor and a nurse; the caption identifying her as yet another victim of Jozef M.

On the last day of the trial the head accuser makes his final presentation in the case against Jozef M., erstwhile lieutenant general of the people's army, betrayer, fugitive from justice, evildoer. He asks not for any specific form of death to be meted out to the man, but only for the most humiliating and physically painful way of dying. And after his plea is heard by the judges, out comes the defender in the case. He is a man of small stature and high-pitched voice, who until this moment has been occupying a seat on the lower level of the platform and thus is taken by most of those gathered in the room to be one of the accusers. He stands erect and punctuates his clauses with slight forward movements of his arms. He thanks the accusers for their thorough presentation of the case, he thanks the judges for their patience in listening, and then he calls upon all those gathered to remember the diabolical forces that inspired Jozef M. in his life of depravity and treason; forces without which crimes like his could not have been committed: the country's pre-War past and its deviant ideology, the corruptive Great Far Western Allied Sovranties and all of their agents, their thoughts, books, radio programs and money, all seeping through the walls of the country's frontiers trying to cause despoilment of people's achievements. Then the man raises his arms and his voice, and recites an incantation popular in those days:

We shall tear them asunder –
we'll feel no remorse!
We shall trample them down –
we'll not hold back!
We shall kill them all – we'll
cheer out loud!

And this promise of death to the enemy resounds through the room still for a while after he gets back to his seat.

The trial ends with a short statement of the head judge who says that the severest manner of punishment by death has been chosen for the traitor and that this punishment will be dispensed most promptly.

Before closing here the story of Jozef M. let it be mentioned that a few years after his trial Adam and the others heard (from a person of extensive contacts) that justice was eventually meted out to the man, not on his native soil, but in one of the Far Western capitals, by a secret agent who, after having collided with Jozef in a busy intersection, pricked him with the pointed tip of an umbrella, injecting him thus with a powerful toxin coming from a minuscule poisonous dart. However, about a year or so after the news of his fatal encounter with the toxic stinger, they suddenly heard (from a different source) that Jozef M. did not meet with his demise after all, but was well and alive - albeit somewhat changed after plastic surgery he had undergone - spending his days among herdsmen somewhere in a remote mountainous region on the antipodes.

And as far as Jozef's accomplices in treason are concerned, they are, to Adam's best knowledge, not brought to trial, not at that time; and the very existence of such individuals is never reported. Yet, the short-wave communiques from the other side insists that most of those who have been found to be connected with the affair of M. are disposed of or interned in places unknown.

The Home of the Divine Providence

The brothers are still inside the nets, being released only in case of emergency, individually, of course, for short visits to the downstairs lavatory. Tonight's supper prepared by a ward named Bartosz, a culinary expert – cold ham with home-made mayonnaise, green pea salad, crispy rolls, fresh-strawberry compote – was truly outstanding. We also consumed generous quantities of well-aged Tokay wine from Simplicius's private reserve, which, by the way, we discovered only yesterday hidden from anybody's eyes in a closet behind Simplicius' desk. Also, during the supper tonight we were discussing the possibility that the brothers, for the abuses of their powers, be put on trial, with us, the general assembly of the wards, serving as the court. The idea was dropped, however, and instead it was decided that our ex-guardians should simply be prevailed to sign appropriate documents guaranteeing the wards all rights and privileges due them.

After it is all over, the voices of outrage over Jozef M.'s crime not heard anymore, and his name no longer mentioned in public,

Adam and the rest return to their routine existence. Not that things are exactly the same as before.

The day after the trial Adam has to cede his private room to Renata. As far as he recollects it is not mentioned by anybody that he should move from his little room off the kitchen onto the sofa in the salon; yet, on the morning after the trial Renata starts transferring her personal things from the salon into his place. He protests, of course; he hisses and laughs from behind his spotted-hyena mask, calls Renata an ugly name and even manages to flush some of her hairpins and hairnets down the toilet; but to no avail. He gives up when he realizes that all the others want her to have her way, are even helping her move and are telling him that he will be better off in the salon on the sofa.

It should be stressed that Renata had already before the trial moved quite a bit up in life. She was officially promoted by the personnel office of the State Opera of Broscin; from a part-time sub-assistant to the supervisor of the ladies' dressing rooms to a full-time assistant to the supervisor of costumes for the Opera. On the day when it happened she said that they should all be proud of her and that some others, like Fela Paluk the dirty Hebrite or the detestable widow Lipko, will soon find out who their betters are.

Adam often thinks now of the day when he found Renata snooping in the Lipko room and he got blamed for her deed. And sometimes at night when he is still awake, he actually thinks that he could hear her stealthy steps all around the rooms, and he could almost see her prying body flattened against Kocia's or Adela's door; and so he gets up and rushes to apprehend her. But only hears her snorting coming from his old room. During one such night he goes to see Maria Lipko in her garret quarters. She is not angry at him for waking her up; and when he tells her that he is not the one who disturbed her things on that day, she smiles to him with her wide-spaced teeth and says that she knows very well that he is not the one. And when he tells her to watch out for Renata, she whispers that she is trying, and even got herself a new key made. And then she tells him to leave quietly as it would not be good for either of them to be seen together at night talking.

A few days after the trial Konstancya is officially notified that their quarters, of which she is the principal resident, housed presently only seven people, and thus possesses a large excess space, ample enough to easily accommodate one or two extra persons. Shortly their premises are looked over by inspectors from the Office of Urban Housing Allocations, and Kocia is told to cede The Tulpe library (Adela's bedroom) to the Office. She is also informed that the room is large enough to be partitioned to create a kitchen inside it. Adela's books and her desk are then transferred to the salon; all her other things, including her bed, go into mother's and Nusia's room; and all the rest of the things from the library go to Kocia's and Boleslaw's bedroom. Adela is calm, if not to say nonchalant, about the whole affair; she only tells them all never to try to touch her desk (which stands now next to the piano within easy reach of everybody).

The person who moves into Adela's room is called Sabina Wolska. She is probably over forty; she has red-dyed hair, an oversized bosom and a dog named Maximilian; and as they discover shortly, she also has a passion for fried foods.

Another noted difference in their life at home is the amount of time that each person is now spending indoors. Konstancya, with whom the Opera seemed to have severed all ties for good, stays in all the time, sitting and staring through the window in her room, dusting and tidying up on occasion, and once in a while lecturing Nusia or providing inspiration for Radomir. Mother also finds it very difficult to face the world on the outside, particularly what she calls the consequences of their economic degradation and the contemptuous gaze of everybody around. Nusia does not go out much either, as she is not required to take ballet classes anymore and is forbidden by her mother to roam around the building or the Boulevard for fear that her activities might bring about another disaster. And Adela takes fewer walks too, explaining that she is not so energetic as in her younger days.

Boleslaw also stays more at home, appearing among them at hours when they would normally expect him to be at the Firmament. Kocia calls this to his attention, that is, the fact that his absences from work are causing his family undeserved financial hardships; though she does not harp on the issue, as Adam would expect her to do. And Adela says to Boleslaw whether it is possible that his business is slacking by any chance, as she does not believe that his kind of business would ever slow down, no matter what political figures toppled; and she laughs, as is her custom. And he just mumbles, "No extra money and no headaches." And then once Adam hears him say to Adela that some others, like her boy Emil, should follow his example and start taking it easy, and that Emil should learn that the times are hard and mighty dangerous.

It is then for the first time that it comes to Adam that they don't really know what Boleslaw - alone or together with Emil - does at the Firmament; who pays him, and exactly for what services; his earnings always seem to exceed so greatly anybody else's; those neat piles of banknotes of many colors and denominations, from various parts of the world; money he regularly puts on Kocia's breakfast table. Is it all lucre from a well-run brothel? Or is Boleslaw a spy for the other side? Or an informer for his? Or an ideologist ready to take money from anybody or any side as long as it is to advance the Cause he is fighting for. And Adam remembers Edek the Biceps who had beaten out of him the secret of the house where Jozef M. disappeared; and he wonders whether Edek could beat out of him the secret of Boleslaw bringing home money that comes from the other side; and he recoils in fear. But then Boleslaw's breakfast gifts to Kocia have stopped already, shortly after the affair of M. became public knowledge; and so Adam breathes with some relief.

It is Renata who, unlike the rest, is spending considerably more of her time away from home these days. She does not dust or do dishes anymore; but she is keeping her room (Adam's old space) spotless so that they could be proud of her, she would say, and she is willing to do Madame Kocia's hair, wash and curl it beautifully, and how saddened she is that Madame Kocia is not as interested in her hair as she used to be. But despite her prolonged hours away from them, there seems to be more of her around than before. As she works full time now, she needs her daily late afternoon rest on the salon sofa (Adam's present bed), and she needs her daily, rather than weekly, soaking bath, and she can never forgo her favorite radio programs in the evening. And in order to stay in good physical condition she has resumed ballet practice, using for that purpose mother's Bechstein piano as a barre and mother's person at the keyboard as her accompanist. And Adam wonders why nobody ever appears to be bothered by her presence among them; at least nobody is saying anything.

Actually, there is one instance, which Adam remembers very clearly, that Renata gets reprimanded. She sits one day at Adela's desk (the one Adela forbade them all to touch) and she pushes Adela's papers to the side and spreads her own stationary in front of her. At that time mother and Adela are in the kitchen involved in dyeing some of their old garments to be altered for Nusia. (Dying garments at home by means of the old method of first soaking and then boiling them in a dye-bath was a popular undertaking in those days.) Nusia runs to the kitchen to inform Adela about what happened and Adela comes into the salon immediately and tells Renata to leave her desk; but Renata does not even move. She tells her again, but Renata only grins.

"Some people think that everything belongs to them, and not to others. Lucky that times have changed, Miss Adela, and the poor like Renata don't have to mind the well-to-do anymore," she says.

Adela does not say a word more. She goes back into the kitchen, straight to a vat containing a solution of blue dye with garments soaking in it; she lifts up the vat, heaves under its great weight, struggles with it into the salon and quietly walks in. She stalks behind Renata, and pours the entire contents of the vat over Renata's head.

A few weeks after the blue-dye incident Adela gets demoted at *The Worker* from the position of an associate editor to a road reporter. The family does not discuss the possibility that there might be a connection between the two events, except that mother tells Adam that she is convinced that there is, because she overheard once Renata on the stairs boasting to Fela Paluk that she, Renata, knows people who work for newspapers and that does not include somebody like Miss Adela. Anyway, the way Adela related the story to them, she is simply informed by her superior editor that she has been found lacking in deeper understanding of the Principles and thus should educate herself in the matter by directly observing and interviewing working-class citizens in factories, warehouses, farms and such.

Of other new elements that enter their lives after the trial there has to be mentioned Maximilian. Sabina, his owner, the woman who, you may recollect, moved into the Tulpe library and started thus sharing their quarters with them, claims that he is a dog; though Adam suspects that he really is a cross between a bear and a very large sheep. Maximilian falls in love with all of them, from the first sight; he rolls on their beds and rugs, eats off their plates, asks to be scratched on his belly, and they do not mind at all; with the exception of Renata, and mother who always feels a little uneasy in the presence of Nature the Primitive. On the day when mother sees Nusia and Boleslaw on the floor next to Maximilian, all three rubbing their backs on the salon's rug, their legs up, wildly punting the air, she goes into shock. Though it is not so much Maximilian's size, exuberance and the openness of his nature that overwhelms her, as his hairiness. Not only is his impenetrable fur giving him an unearthly appearance, mother feels, it also throws into the atmosphere around him hairy particles which acquire a life of their own; fuzzy little balls which swirl in the air, meander around the floors, then fasten themselves to objects and stare at her. They are everywhere – on garments, bedding, the keyboard of her piano and among the edibles; and mother has no idea what to do about them, as inside her vacuum cleaner they often cause stoppage in the functioning of that machine. She goes one day to Sabina to talk about the matter, and politely starts with saying that Maximilian's hair is amazing, and then asks whether it ever gets cut, sheared, actually. And Sabina smiles brightly and says that his hair, indeed, is of superior quality and it gets sheared once a year in May, when it is at its thickest and softest, so that it can get spun into the silkiest and yet most durable yarn; and that she herself does all the spinning and then knitting; both most relaxing and useful exercises. Mother then forgets about all the pain and frustration caused by Maximilian the Wild, and just listens to Sabina, spellbound. And Sabina, a woman most communicative and sociable, talks to her at length about the ancient art of spinning and shows her her own spinning wheel, spools of yarn, and a number of beautiful wooly objects she has knitted out of Maximilian's treasured fleece. And, hard to believe, within a few days of this conversation, both mother and Kocia are taking lessons from Sabina in spinning and knitting.

It has to be explained right away that mother's and Kocia's new interest in crafts stem very much from certain practical considerations. It is an exceptionally cold and long winter; and they all feel its severity in a particularly acute manner, since it is for the very first time during their residence at the Tulpe house that they have become their own purveyors of warmth-giving coal. Until that winter no vigil in a line in front of a state warehouse was required of them, as coal then had been sent to their door, cost-free, in quantities unrestricted, the best anthracite with the glow of diamond; dispatched to them either by Jozef M. (man of power) or Emil (man of contacts), persons with easy access to the output of the state-owned mines. In those untroubled days their coal would arrive in front of their building in a military motorcade or on a well-appointed civilian van, greeted by the Boulevard, like some winged, festooned chariot of a regal pageant, with sighs of awe, envy and respect; and they would accept that grant of warmth and comfort as a given, but graciously; and they would occasionally even share it with others. But now Jozef M. is gone from their lives for good; and Emil, after having learned of Jozef's treason, has cooled to them considerably, and then, after Boleslaw's withdrawal from special activities at the Firmament, lost interest in their welfare altogether. Anyway, that winter they are terribly cold, and so mother and Kocia feel that they should learn to make things which could help to alleviate the condition. Well, unfortunately, they turn out to be both not particularly capable at handicrafts. They jointly produce only one object, a woolen toga-like outfit, as far as Adam remembers, made from the yarn of old undone sweaters, which they present to Radomir whose garret room is particularly chilly that winter and who, in general, is horribly prone to chest colds of all kinds.

But Radomir does not fall ill that winter. As a matter of fact, of all the new things that are occurring in their life after the trial it is the metamorphosis of their cousin Radomir that is most striking. Here he is, suddenly growing younger and healthier by the hour, developing a content, almost cheerful, appearance, becoming handsome and well-groomed once again.

Without a word of prompting from anybody he reduces his short-wave set to fragments and consigns them one by one to the city canal; and then announces that he does not need help from any foreign news purveyors to fight his war against forces oppressing his country. Shortly, he even starts questioning the verity and sincerity of the information that the foreign sources are providing; and all of a sudden he becomes even appreciative of the activities of the national organs of power. And then he says one day that he is very pleased with the way things went at the trial, that is has been good that people are able to learn some truth about Jozef M.; though he is disappointed with the security apparatus being so sluggish in its efforts to apprehend Jozef M. "Imagine, letting the bastard slip away like this!" he exclaims.

Within a couple of weeks after the trial Radomir resolves: one, to rework in his mind (and on paper, if possible) his view of history, primarily of the past decade; two, to bring out to daylight one of his Tulpe suits, have it chemically cleaned and properly altered; three, to go to Adela's boss, the editor-in-chief of *The Worker* and to put his writing skills at that newspaper's disposal, in particular to ask for a chance to work on the column *The Right and the Wrong.*

That it is always the sensitive and the gifted that are hit the hardest by the adversities of life, Kocia never doubted; and that her cousin Radomir was one of the most ill-fated of men was simply proof of her contention. Circumstances of his life have always plotted against him, she says; an orphan in early childhood, raised by his grandfather, a hatter, with the prospect of becoming one day a hatter himself; being notified of the acceptance of his first story for publication, at the age of fifteen, on the day which turned out to be the first day of the War; an invalid at the War's end, at twenty-one, the victim of a dreaded lung disease and permanent frailty of body. That through the War he had fought heroically for his country was proof of his superior character, but that he had chosen the wrong side showed how young he was; and that after the War he could not understand that the past had been just foolishness and the future still all his, showed how little living and learning he had done. Though nobody should expect that any living or learning could have been done by somebody who spent the first half of his life in trenches and cellars and the second half in hospital wards, Kocia would say.

Radomir has been down on his luck a few times, Adam never denies; yet, Kocia's view of his life is, quite predictably, wide of the mark. His encounters with wartime trenches and post-War hospitals both occurred in the second half of his life; and also, his total hospital stay did not exceed a period of but a few months. And as far as his fighting on the wrong side is concerned, well,

Radomir's side during the War was the same as everybody else's, Kocia's included; since, some may still remember, the occupied people of their country had then only one Resistance and one Underground Army and nobody told them, not until after the War, that they should have all been on a different side, on the side of one of their occupiers, the People's Power.

How much of formal scholarship Radomir has had nobody knows. Clandestine classes which he had attended in the occupied city of Wielow never yielded any document attesting to the level of his achievement; and the studying he undertook in post-War Broscin, likewise, did not produce any substantial certifications; though he always tended to assume an appearance of someone with profound knowledge in just about every field. He was enrolled at the University of Broscin on three separate occasions; each incident of his sudden leave-taking followed by denunciation of the school's political mendacity, and then by yet another lapse into ill health.

He tried to work for pay too – a voice in a children's radio program, a librarian at a hospital, an assistant to a property master at the Opera, a bellhop at the Firmament, a salesman of devotional objects at the Holy Bedrock – finding each occupation debasing and each establishment employing him ridden with corruption. Shortly before his twenty-fifth birthday he retired with a small governmental pension for the disabled; granted to him through the intervention of the office of Jozef M. (At first he did not want to accept this charity as coming from Jozef whom he detested as his arch-rival for Kocia's favors; but he eventually took it, with a snicker that he would now have enough time to devote his entire life to activities aiming at destroying his country's present rulers.)

But he writes; on history, freedom, soldiership, metaphysics; essays, poems, allegorical stage pieces, chapters of novels never to be finished. He writes on pages torn from note books, in pencil, in large tilting script; he pains when he is writing; and he writes when the hurt is at its worst. And sometimes he cries, lying on the floor, face down, for hours, and then rising abruptly and erasing line after line until the page in front of him becomes blank again; and then he shreds the blank page into hundreds of little pieces. His brain is always filled with words and phrases perfectly orchestrated, ready to burst out into the open in full testimony to his innermost thoughts; every neuron in his body resonating with sounds for a perfect story, he claims. So when he does not write at all, for days or weeks sometimes, it is not because he is dry inside, he says, but because he lacks the power to transmit onto the outside what is inside him, or because he fears that the cadences of his thoughts would not be intelligible to others. He writes mainly for Kocia, dedicating to her most of what he creates; even though she so often accepts his efforts with indifference or irritation; frequently refusing to serve as a muse to somebody who is wasting his talents on writing things that are not only too obscure for any normal reader, but which also, if known to the general public, could offend and anger the authorities.

Whatever it is that suddenly begins to free his tormented body and soul from pain and to rein in his rebelliousness must be quite powerful. It could simply be his having Kocia all to himself now, like years before, has made the whole difference, as he always thought of Jozef M. as a dark evil force that had taken Kocia away from him. (In contrast, her husband, Boleslaw has always been, in his view, just an invisible man of no consequence.) But it could have also been his reaching the age at which one sometimes has to make a big turnabout in order to go on further at all.

At any rate, as far as his family is concerned, his metamorphosis is defying logic and challenging them with its brash arrogance. Since in those days, according to mother, they are once again pushed into the dark pit of deprivation and joylessness, his becoming younger, comelier and happier is plainly indecorous, indecent even, inconsiderate of the feelings of others, if not to say cold-hearted and even cruel. And Konstancya says that his spending a whole month's worth of his disability pension on a tie, a haircut, manicure and the alteration of a suit – without inquiring about the needs of the family – is plainly selfish.

Yet, when he appears before her in his transformed Tulpe suit, shoulders broadened, lapels newly tapered, cuffs perfectly pressed, a clean new shirt, Kocia sighs with approbation, "Oh, darling, you look so... perfect". And the day he brings her a freshly-printed copy of *The Worker* with his own piece in *The Right and the Wrong* column, she says that it is the happiest moment of her life. She reads it carefully, then rereads it, and, obviously understands every word of it, despite all the complicated symbolism that Radomir is using. She beams.

"Oh, Radomir, this is so moving... and it is all about me... about my... sins, but also about my love for our country... and about that horrible person we won't mention by name... and about the horror of treason. It is so beautiful, darling."

And he tells her with pride that his little piece made quite an impression on a lot of people, even on a certain important person from the Ministry of Culture from the Capital, and he, Radomir Milewski, a young unknown, has actually been asked to work further on that little piece of his and possibly try to expand it and broaden its message. "And if I do well, if it is really good, they may publish it as a regular book!"

And she tells him that she always knew that he could do anything, and also that she would love to work on the book with him. And so it comes to pass that a literary collaboration between Radomir and Kocia (with her as his muse, of course) indeed starts on that very day when he brings her his first printed piece.

The first fruit of that joint labor, it might as well be revealed here, appears in print less than a year after the original article, as a sizable book with beige covers entitled *The Affairs of M., Consequential and Puny* put out by the Progressive State Press. Adam has no idea how many copies it sold, but it was widely distributed to bookstores, libraries and newspaper kiosks, as its publishers wanted its message to reach the broadest public possible.

The Home of the Divine Providence

As of today only Honore and Benedictus remain in the nets; all the others were released two days ago after they had agreed to the terms presented to them by the wards; the obduracy of the two being purely symbolic, as Brother Simplicius and the others have already signed all the documents in the name of all the brothers. The signing ceremony took place in Simplicius's office with everybody in attendance. The documents, in triplicate, were written in stylized hand on aged parchment and signed with an old-fashioned grouse quill, and the main portion of the papers – the granting to the wards of the right to rule-making – was richly illuminated in crimson and gold. After the ceremony we made a call to Stationmaster Jaworski to inform him about these most recent developments and ask him, the operator of the sole telegraphic machine in the area, to spread the word afar, so that the governors and the benefactors of our retreat could learn the news. Yesterday we held a rally at the chapel to hail our newly-formed Bill of Rights and Liberties, and then we all went mushroom hunting, and then we built a pyre on the exercise field next to the chapel, in which we first cooked some delicious mushroom stew and then burned some outdated documents from Simplicius's office. Then late at night we had a dancing party in the dining hall, tangoing and slowfoxing till dawn.

Sometime in May or early June suddenly died widow Lipko (Radomir's next door neighbor in the garret); poisoned herself, they say in the Tulpe building, drank a whole bottle of some horrible chemical and was gone for good, just like that; got bloated and black in the face, they all say. Adam and Nusia see her, just for a few seconds on the stairway as she is being carried down on some kind of a stretcher, face uncovered; the two of them returning from a walk with Maximilian. Adam would not have let Nusia see the sight, had he had time to do anything about it.

It is also said in the building, mostly whispered in the communal laundry room in the attic (where Adam and mother would now often do the family's laundry together) that before she took her own life, Maria Lipko had been visited a couple of times by men from the Special Office. "Must have had a lot on her conscience and known she could not get out of it," concluded Kowalska.

Anyway, after she died, her place is officially searched and then sealed for a while, and then some of her relatives or such came to collect whatever there was in her place. Then in another week or so, the quarters are legally assigned to the usage of Renata, who, by the way, does not move to this new place of hers right away, as she has to restore it to sound condition, alter it and pretty it up, she says.

Before she moves out from their floor, she not only has the whole contents of her room off the kitchen transferred upstairs, but also she has appropriated two armchairs and an oil painting from their salon. And when she settles in her new place, she invites them to take a look at what she managed to do with something that was once just a hole. And when they decline her invitation, she says with tears in her voice that some people just do not have manners and treat others like dirt, and too easily forget who their friends are; particularly somebody like Madame Kocia who would have been rotting in prison for the rest of her life, had it not been for Renata's devotion and loyalty and even Renata's perjuring herself at the trial. They never see her new garret apartment, but hear that she made it quite pleasing, almost elegant. She even gets herself a real bathtub there, and a radio, and makes the windows really pretty with fine white-laced curtains and red geraniums in pots.

Shortly after Renata's move to the garret they acquire a new resident in their quarters, a man assigned by the Office of Urban Housing Allocation to what used to be Renata's room. He introduces himself to them as Master Ociszek (the "master" referring to his academic degree, recently conferred upon him by the University of Broscin); but despite his obvious pride in his intellectual achievements, he is rather unobtrusive. He is rarely at home, never enters their salon, hardly uses the kitchen, never uses their favorite marble bathtub (as far as they are able to tell), and if not for the smell of the fumes coming from his cigarettes and occasional shouts at Maximilian, "Please get out of my way!", they would not even know that he lives with them.

They are quite aware of Sabina's presence though; not that she is inquisitive or loud. She is in fact one of the most tactful, nay, civilized, people on earth; but most of the time when at home she has to keep the doors of her quarters wide open to keep a free running passage for Maximilian, who, if confined to one area without free access to all of them, will wail in the most heartbreaking way. She also cooks quite a bit (mostly on Sundays and late at night); the aroma of her creations – calves' liver with onions, sizzling pork patties, potato pancakes - which is suffusing the air and their body cells with the potency of an intoxicating opiate, makes them by turns terribly hungry and queasy. She also one day starts taking piano lessons from mother.

First, Sabina, a believer in the restorative power of work, suggests that mother start taking paying students; but mother has no clue how to go about it and doubts her skills. But then when Sabina presents her with the detailed schedule of lessons she herself wants to follow and with advance payment for the first lesson, mother accepts her proposition without resistance. Mother enjoys her role as a teacher, and can not quite get over Sabina's determination and no small musicality, wondering whether it is not true that one's brain is indeed capable of absorbing new knowledge at any age.

That Sabina in general is a woman of talents not often encountered is obvious to all of them. She works for the Office of Native and Foreign Archives in Broscin where it is her familiarity with foreign tongues that is utilized. She seems to be able to understand every language and script in existence and to know who has been using it, when and for what purpose; yet, how she acquired her extensive knowledge is not clear to them. She talks little about herself, never brags, has unbounded enthusiasm for life in all its forms, but refers to the past, hers or anybody else's, as something of intellectual interest only and of no emotional relevance whatsoever. Her greatest talent, though, Adam believes, lies in her uncanny ability to disassociate her passions (and those of her interlocutors as well) not only from the past, but also from the knowledge that she possesses and shares with the world. She talks, for example, with great authority about the customs and the peoples of the West, the official enemy lurking on the other side of the Rampart, but there is no warning of danger in her words, and no anger or hatred either; but neither do her words carry admiration, praise or even a trace of envy for the lot of those on the other side. She is able to expound her topic with such calm and detachment as if she is relating stories from a different planet or presenting the solution to a jigsaw puzzle.

One day Sabina enters upon the plan of familiarizing Nusia with the mysteries of foreign tongues. After observing miserable-looking, sulking Nusia during one of her piano lessons, she simply says to mother and Kocia that Nusia, incapable as she may be of practicing with the metronome or memorizing even the simplest measures of music, might have some other abilities and talents hidden in her, worth exploring. Nusia receives the news of the termination of her music education with cheers, and the prospect of language lessons with a willing heart and mind. And after a period of a few weeks of instruction she is pronounced by Sabina to be intellectually curious, linguistically gifted and a hard-working young person all around; and Sabina promises to continue teaching Nusia for as long as she can, and at no charge. And since this is the end of June and Nusia brings home, first time in anybody's memory, an end-of-the-school-year certificate with grades a little higher than satisfactory and no derogatory comments about her conduct, Nusia's mother says, for the first time also, that she has some hope for her daughter.

But it is at the same time that Nusia herself, suddenly suffering from terrible melancholia and heartache, does not feel joyous in the least, not for prolonged periods of time. It does not affect her study, but feelings of guilt and personal worthlessness, as well as thoughts of death and damnation come over her again and again, making contentment difficult. It started, Adam is certain, on the afternoon she caught a glimpse of the dead body of Maria Lipko being carried down the stairway. She tells him the following day that she now understands what being dead means, and that it makes her feel queer, almost faintish, kind of sad, and really scared. And a few days later she tells him that she caused the death of the man in the chimney-sweep outfit who took them back to the Youth Cultural House on the rickshaw after Jozef M. disappeared in the house where they were having a picnic; she heard some children in her class whispering that they had heard from those who got news from the other side that the man who helped Jozef cross the border was found out and shot to death; and she heard it already some time ago, but it is only now that she understands that she is the one that was the cause of it. And then she says that being the cause of anybody's death is the worst of all mortal sins that one can commit. Adam tells her first that nobody was executed after Jozef had fled; but she knows better. Then he tells her that even if somebody died, it was not her fault, and besides the man who helped Jozef cross the border was definitely not the same one who rode their rickshaw; but he can not convince her of anything. She has already figured it all out; if she had not played hooky from her ballet class, then Jozef would not have had a chance to flee and nothing bad would have happened; or even if she had done what she had done, but had been more thoughtful and careful, she would not have left the bag with her ballet slippers in the boiler room and no one would have ever found out what had happened and no one would have suffered or died. And then she says that she has also been thinking about all the other bad things that she did earlier in life, all the trouble she caused, and the people who died because of her during the War.

"What I did can never be forgiven. I cannot be absolved from it by any priest ever. You know, I cannot, Adam."

Her oppressive thoughts and bouts of fright are only periodic, inconstant, leaving her some space for gladness and non-remembering the painful, yet they worry Adam terribly; especially that she really believes that her having been a prisoner of the Chef was punishment from God for the bad she had done; except that now she realizes that that punishment was not an absolution, as her sins were simply too grave. And so, she would tremble and crouch next to Adam and tell him how dreadfully scared she is of fire and brimstone and tortures that will last forever.

Of course, he can easily recognize in her words an echo of what she has been hearing around for years. But though Adam knows that her words are not really her own – just facsimiles of those of her perpetually-guilt ridden grandmother, of sermonizing priests, of the Chef, or any of the profane rulers of the country with their threatful and scorching pronouncements – Nusia's pain is real, deep and uniquely hers.

Then towards the end of summer she falls ill with whooping cough (contracted from one of the young Klusas whom she watches over on occasion). They are told that there is no danger of any kind, not at her age, and yet she suffers greatly for several days, cough and spasms making her days and nights miserable. On her worst night, dizzy and very weak after a sudden attack of severe choking and vomiting, she asks Adam whether there could still be hope for her, could she be absolved and not punished by the fire of hell; could God forgive her if she prays really hard and do only good in case she is going to live. And he wants to tell her that there is no God, no eternity and no hell, certainly not after death; but he only says that he knows for sure that she will be forgiven.

13.

On her eleventh birthday they give Nusia a little party at home; Sabina presents them with a fried chicken and Boleslaw brings some delicacies from the Firmament's kitchen (all discreetly concealed in miscellaneous pockets of his garments). It is sometime right after this party that mother says to Adam that she suddenly realizes that after a lifetime of alternating ascents and downfalls, they have all reached a state of averageness and normalcy. It is probably not what one aspires to, especially in one's youth, she says, and it is not the same as having peace of mind and contentment, but it is not a bad state to be in nevertheless.

"It simply means being like everybody else," she states, "nobody notices us or minds us anymore, and we are as deprived of things as anyone. But we do not feel totally trampled upon by life anymore, I mean, harshly, ruthlessly, do we? Only a little bit, in a kind of moderate way. I for one have always felt, all my life, either excessively privileged or beaten down really hard, trampled upon... but now I am just one of many; the first time in my life I work for pay." Mother is almost proud of her two-afternoons-a-week job at the Youth Cultural House teaching music. "It is not that easy, and the tramway is always so full and they push you... but then everybody uses tramways. And Adela now uses trains, well, has to, sometimes twice a week, to go to all those little places and talk to all those farmers and others, but she does not complain. (Mother is referring to Adela's demotion to a road reporter.) She knows that one cannot do anything about local trains which are horribly inconvenient. Adela always understood about being just average, one of many...

"And Radomir is progressing so well, obviously pleasing his new boss... my goodness, he is almost famous, but... do you notice, Adam, even he is kind of like everybody else... he does not really write much differently from others. Well, he could, he is so talented, but he does not want to... stand out, I suppose. He does not suffer anymore, though, like he used to; his health seems to be fine now. I am really glad of that. And Nusia is so good suddenly. Oh, she has always been very good-hearted, but now she is also trying to please everyone. And you and Kocia working together... That is really wonderful!" Mother is almost incredulous that even Adam has achieved the rank of working man.

It was a few months earlier that Sabina sent Konstancya and Adam to the director of the Young Theatregoers' Playhouse with a personal letter recommending their unusual talents. For the audition Kocia sang a folk ballad that Sabina suggested, rendering the piece in one of the rural dialects that Sabina taught her; and Adam presented a pantomime *The Firebird, Defender of People* – Sabina's idea – with his costume, mask and choreography. They did very well, and were used right away in a children's pageant. And shortly they were both hired as full-time performers at the Playhouse, with formally drawn agreements stamped by the Broscin Office of the Ministry of Arts; Kocia's position being described as "a secondary player" and Adam's as "a non-essential player", which meant that hers was a rung above his, with a salary commensurately higher.

And as for Boleslaw, he works now at the Firmament only two days a week, since he got (through Sabina's influence, of course) a part-time clerical job at the warehouse for the Office of Archives, with the promise of becoming a full-time employee there by the end of the year.

It has to be understood, though, that their success in achieving this highly desirable status, described by mother as averageness, was due principally to the almost flawless biographies with which they were able to provide the authorities. Let it be quickly explained that at that time it became required of all citizens to be in possession of detailed written accounts of their lives to be carried on their persons and presented upon request to anybody in authority; and required of every institution in the land to make sure that life-accounts of its employees were always available for evaluation. It was particularly important to have one's familial background described most truthfully as well as one's activities during the pre-War and Wartime periods dutifully portrayed. Fashioning their biographies seemed to them at first to be a task most onerous, if not to say, impossible, since so little in their past, they felt, was commendable and so much objectionable to the authorities;

yet, under the guidance of Sabina, a woman extraordinary, they were able to produce documents which turned out to be wholly satisfactory. Sabina, first of all, made clear to them that choice of words was of vital importance; and so, for instance, the phrase "manual workers" as a description of most of their forebears was far superior to "hatters", or the phrase "self-educated" more pointed than "not in the possession of a diploma". She also explained to them, that in personal statements factual accuracy (especially with reference to the past) was much less important than the proper presentation of the spirit and motivations of acts described; and she pointed out that most of material evidence of their past had been destroyed by the ravages of War, that is, was not obtainable for verification. It was due to Sabina's keen mind that both Kocia and Adam, for example, wrote in their biographies that one of their main activities during the Realm occupation was running a clandestine theater for children of the underprivileged. And at Sabina's suggestion Boleslaw wrote in his statement that already at an early age he broke off with his rich and tyrannical father, lived for years among working class men, was disinherited, and came into some money later only through a legal mix-up, but gave that money away anyway; an assertion like that being necessary as Boleslaw's coming from a noble and very rich family was a circumstance considered most compromising in the eyes of the people's authorities.

Anyway, they all more or less agree with mother that they are now living an existence which could be described as normal and not unlike that of anybody else's in their part of the world, and that it has some advantages. The main advantage that they suddenly start perceiving is that their present mode of living is actually tantamount to some kind of stability and even security. Being indistinguishable from others, not bothersome to anybody and possessed of a moderate load of troubles looks like a good way of preventing true cataclysm.

And yet, even though all the divinations, insights or reasonings are saying that nothing extraordinary (particularly of a highly unpleasant nature), should happen to them, it is not to be the case at all. One quiet September day, some couple of weeks after they had openly proclaimed their averageness, falls the Firmament; and they know that instant that some horrible personal tumble is about to follow.

Even though the press describes the events under the heading of *The Fall of the Firmament*, not all of the Firmament fell by any means. As a matter of fact it was only the walls of Emil's private office that went to wrack, and then a couple of less important interior walls on the first floor, a column in the Porphyry Room, some mirrors, a door or two, and some glass got shattered. Of course, there was heard a strong blast, gun shots, yelling, sirens, and a great deal of smoke and dust was hanging in the air for a long time. They learned most of that from Boleslaw who happened to be inside The Firmament during that whole time.

Nobody had had any premonition, it seemed. Even Boleslaw, who was there so often and knew how to keep his eyes and ears open, had not suspected a thing. Actually, only a few days before the events he had said that when he would eventually start his full-time job at the Office of the Archives he might miss the old hotel quite a bit. Anyway, it was only one day before it all happened that Boleslaw came home from the Firmament visibly disturbed. He walked into the kitchen when Adam was making tea for Adela and himself; she had just returned from one of her reporting trips to the country, and was soaking her feet and breathing hard. Boleslaw asked for tea too, but never sat down. He paced the kitchen in all directions, stopping in front of Adela now and then and throwing his arms up in the air. And she said that if something was bothering him he should try to soak his feet too – always helped her. Then he muttered that the Firmament was for hours crawling with fellows from the Special Office.

"You've seen them there before, many times, so why are you so excited now?"

"It was not routine today. They knew something they had not known before. And I have never seen so many at once... and they will be back shortly. They spent an awfully long time trying to get to his private office, much too long."

"You mean to Emil's office?"

"Yes, and they knew what they were after."

"You mean Emil did not want them to see his office? Do you think he has reason to be worried?" There is a touch of concern in Adela's voice.

"They did not get to his office; it was locked, always is. Emil wasn't in today. Decided to spend a day out in the country with his new girlfriend... I will be damned! It just came to me that it could have been Lala, his previous one, who... made a call or something... yea... she has always been too much interested in everything, and jealous like hell. Not that he would have told her much of anything, but things slip... Anyway, I am sure that they will be back when he is in."

"Then you don't think they have found anything yet? And if they have, what could happen to him... and to you? Is it really bad? And what is it? As if you were going to tell me!" Adela sounds almost anxious.

And he tells her that he has not seen most of the stuff that's in Emil's office. The man keeps things well hidden, out of everybody's sight. He used to be less careful with Boleslaw than with others, still... he, Boleslaw, has never had anything to do with Emil's affairs, the really bad ones, that is. So he doesn't know what is in the office, but he thinks that whatever it is, it will be awfully bad for Emil if they find it.

Boleslaw drinks his tea in one long gulp and says that he will be going shortly to his evening job at the warehouse of the Archives.

"Then he doesn't even know that they have been there today?" Adela is wiping her feet dry.

"Probably not. How would he?"

"Then do you think you could warn him somehow? If he could go to his office before they come again, at night maybe, and remove the stuff, whatever it is, destroy it, hide it somewhere else. You probably could get in touch with him somehow... or even with that wife of his. Stupid and crude, she may still want to save him from real trouble... Did I ever tell you that he was the most beautiful child I have ever known, also the most sensitive and intelligent..." Adela's voice is unusually soft. She is pleading with Boleslaw.

"I guess you said something like that before. But he is not a child now; he stopped playing children's games long, long ago. Can't do a thing for him."

"Please, Boleslaw..."

"Sorry, Adela, can't get involved. And let's just stop talking about it. Not a word more! Already too much has been said!" Boleslaw shouts the last two sentences, then looks hard into Adam's face and leaves the kitchen.

Some two hours later, Boleslaw gone to his evening job and the others ready to sit to supper, Adela suddenly says that she is going for a walk and may stop to see somebody from her office on the way, so they should not wait for her. Adam thinks he knows what she is up to, and so when she returns later that night, he asks her confidentially whether she has delivered a certain message to a certain person, and she answers that she has no idea what he is talking about.

Emil did not sleep at home that night, at least it looked that way, Boleslaw tells them. He came to the Firmament around ten in the morning, Boleslaw saw him; washed himself, shaved and changed in his office, and went on with his day as usual. Around noon somebody must have said something to him, warned him perhaps, because he locked himself in his office and started burning things in this big tiled stove he had there; that's what everybody was saying, but Boleslaw did not know for sure. The men came a little after one and headed straight for the office; but Emil did not open the door for them when they knocked. Then after they hit the door with an iron bar several times, he came out, smiling, shutting the door behind him; when they tried to press on and get inside, he twisted his way out of their midst and ran; and when they were bearing down upon the door, a violent explosion from inside blustered through it and knocked them to the ground. And as they were chasing him through the corridors, he hurled a grenade in their faces; and as he was running through the Porphyry Room, he threw another explosive in their direction. They eventually got him, shot him dead, in the back stairway right at the door to the alley behind the hotel.

When the family asks Boleslaw what it was that they wanted of Emil, he says that he has no personal knowledge of things; can only guess this and that from what was said during the questioning that followed the blast and the shooting. Emil really was somebody else, it seems, different name and all, one of the leaders of the Povolian renegades in the Eastern Provinces before the War and during, also involved in some really bad business against the People's Power during the War and after; had some big contacts now with the other side too, that's what it seems. "But it may all be just a mistake; maybe they were really after somebody else. How can I know?" says Boleslaw.

"You mean all that terrible bloodshed, death, destruction, and you say that it could have been a mistake?" Mother is horrified. "You knew him in Wielow, then you should know who he really was!"

"Never knew him in Wielow, **never**," Boleslaw is emphatic." Saw the man for the first time at the Broscin Central about five years ago," he stresses every syllable.

"Of course, Boleslaw had never known him before, mother!" Kocia is shocked at mother's ignorance.

"But there must have been others, I mean there are so many people in this city who came from the Eastern Provinces... How is it possible that nobody knew who he is... was?" Mother's consternation is great.

"I am sure there have been people who knew him before, but as Emil; he apparently started using that name long before the War. And a few who maybe knew him under some old name had no reason to be suspicious of anything. People do change names, you know... And if he was the leader of some underground group he probably used an alias, and certainly did not advertise it." Boleslaw states things firmly. "But as I said, **he had not been known to me under any name,** until I met him here in Broscin," he is even more emphatic than before.

Boleslaw also tells them that he was released to go home due to the confusion at the Firmament, but that he will probably be called back for further questioning.

When Boleslaw is telling them what has happened, Adela sobs; first very quietly, almost unnoticeably, and then gradually harder and harder, until real tears, great big tears, start pouring down her face and pained cough and wheeze escape from her lungs. It is the very first time ever that they see her weep. But when after a little while she blows her nose and wipes her face, it is all over. They never see her cry again; not when she is taken away a few days later, and not even when she is read her verdict at the trial.

The press acknowledged the events for the first time about a week after they had occurred. They are described, most briefly, as an act of high treason perpetrated by a ring of murderers paid by a Western power; terrible conspiracy against the country and its ruling Principles; this most frightful plot having been discovered and thwarted by the security forces and the heroic militiamen. It is only several months later – after the investigation, the trial and the condemnation of the guilty had taken place – that *The Fall of the Firmament* articles start to appear. Unlike the trial of Jozef M., which was presented to the public during its progression, the trial of those involved in the Firmament Conspiracy is related as a story in retrospect, anecdotal and symbolic. The Firmament, occupied by treason and perversity – its ornate walls breathing out putrid air, its gilded-framed mirrors reflecting wry faces – has been the temple of evil which turned to rubble under the weight of its crimes; so the story went. And Jarek Huczko a.k.a. Jan Kazimierz Emil a.k.a. the Daimyo a.k.a. the Killer, a depraved, murderous narcissist, presiding over all that evil, who was envisioning himself to be the sovereign of a powerful kingdom and believed to be above any law, met his death at the bottom of the kitchen stairs next to a dirty refuse bin. Emil's exploits throughout his depraved life and the fiendish conspiratorial goings-on at the Firmament are given to the public in florid, lurid, terror-breathing Gothic details, whose ultimate meaning, however, is clear and simple.

The Home of the Divine Providence

The nets were all folded days ago, arranged in a compact pile and supplied with a sign proclaiming their uselessness in the newly acquired harmony at the Home. In general, time has been passing quickly and quite enjoyably, with lots of sitting and talking around the fire, great meals, refreshments throughout the day, dancing (even with some invited guests from the village) and visits to the village market; a good deal of these activities being performed jointly by the brothers and the wards. There has also been a lot of TV watching, far too much in my opinion. (The reasons for this latest fad is that we are now in possession of two TV sets, the second one, large-screened, with color reception, installed only a year or so ago in the closet behind Simplicius's desk for his eyes only, has been recently transferred to the dining hall and made available to everybody.) However, yesterday Tytus and Stefan, addressed us during supper with some urgency reminding all of us that it was time we faced certain unpleasant facts, started seriously thinking about them and initiated appropriate action immediately. As examples of serious concern they mentioned our extremely low cash reserve and food supply and our persistent inability to reach by phone or mail our governors or benefactors. That something is indeed amiss here is not to be denied. When yesterday I mentioned to Brother Benedictus, guardian of finances, that, with the new rules in place, I would expect some of the money from my generous niece Nusia to reach me directly rather than through the brothers, he answered that all the money from our benefactors goes first through the governors' hands, and the governors cannot be reached at present.

The trial, which lasts several weeks, is taking place, like that of Jozef M., in an airless room with a raised podium for those representing the law and low-positioned benches for the rest. They are all there; Boleslaw and Adela among the accused, and the rest of them as witnesses. It is a high-level conspiracy case, but the trial is not run as efficiently as Adam would have expected. Not only are there fewer accusers, judges and witnesses than during the proceedings against Jozef (despite a great number of defendants), but also the questioning prosecutors are not always quite sure of their facts and demanded more detailed information from the witnesses. Also, there are as many as two public defenders who at least on one occasion disagree with the prosecution. And death is not the only penalty conferred upon those who are tried. The differences between the two trials, Adam eventually decides, are due not to the nature of the crimes involved, but to the social position that Jarek Huczko alias Emil and his associates once had held, so notably lower than that of somebody like Jozef.

Boleslaw's luck holds again. As he is found guilty of failing in his duty as a citizen to inform the authorities about Emil's activities as a sex procurer, a definitely minor charge, his sentence is only an eighteen-month prison term. That he is found not to be an associate of Emil in those activities, or any other proscriptive actions, is because Boleslaw firmly disclaims any possibility of such association, because his family and acquaintances firmly seconds this disclaimer and because one of the judges in the trial, who has known Boleslaw back in Wielow, firmly believes it to be the case. That particular judge (who as a young lawyer was in some way,

Adam vaguely remembers, involved in running Boleslaw's estate which he had just inherited) made a revelational pronouncement, which is never questioned. He says that Boleslaw, born to the upper-class rich, has proved through his life-long activities that he rose well above the usual vices and warps of his class. On the other hand, the man says, Boleslaw, the son of a rich, but nevertheless patriotic, family native to what used to be the Eastern Provinces, could have never gotten rid of his aversion towards anybody of Povolian roots; disdain and scorn bred into him deeply through generations. Somebody of the name of Jastrzab-Rytwianski could not have, under any circumstances, been an associate of a man called Jarek Huczko, the judge states categorically.

Whether the court's lenient treatment of Boleslaw has anything to do with the family's efforts to find appropriate lines of contact to people of power will never be known. Mother claims that it didn't as – in their present financial situation – they are not able to procure even the meagerest donation to anybody or any place. However, Kocia is convinced that it is her personal interview with Prelate Reszka (over the confessional's grating, naturally) that has made all the difference.

Adela does not fare nearly as well as Boleslaw. In fact, she does extremely poorly; and mother, Kocia, Radomir and Adela's sister Anna, upon hearing her testimonies say that she sounds like a person of no brains whatsoever, at times like a raving maniac who wants to be found guilty and sentenced to life behind bars. When she is asked whether she went to Emil's place on the night before the events in order to warn him about a visit of men from the Special Office, she admits her guilt without a trace of compunction, almost bragging.

"Of course, I wanted to warn him. I only wish I had been able to warn him. He was not home. I don't think his wife even tried to give him my message."

"You knew that he was involved in criminal activities."

"I did not have the slightest notion in what kind of activities he was involved. I only wanted to tell him that the Special Office seemed to be interested in him."

"Well, if you were not aware of any criminal activities on his part, why did you want **to warn** him? Why would you be worried about something if he was innocent of any wrongdoing?"

"There is always something to worry about when the Special Office takes an interest in you. The Office has a terrible reputation! Everybody knows that!"

"You are out of line, citizeness! You are contemptuous towards our organs of authority! There is a penalty for behavior like that!" The prosecutor roars at her.

"You can penalize me as much as you please, but it won't change the facts!"

"Will you tell this court what it was that he was hiding in his office, what it was that he did not want the authorities to know about!"

"I told you already I haven't the slightest notion what he had there. I have never even been inside that goddamn room! I only heard that some men from the Special Office were sniffing at the door of his office through most of the day, so I went to his place to tell him about it."

"Our security officers do not sniff, citizeness! And explain to this court how it was possible that you did not know anything and yet you went to tell him to destroy the contents of his office. Here is a statement from his wife: 'And that woman Adela said to me to get in touch with him as quickly as possible and tell him to remove everything from his office before morning, all the documents and other things, or better to destroy them, so that there was no trace of anything that could incriminate him and the others...'"

"I don't care about any statement from that stupid cow!"

And that's how Adela is throughout the trial; contemptuous, defiant, loud, making her accusers and judges angry and vengeful, leaving them no room for leniency of any kind.

"How did you know that representatives of our organs of security visited the hotel earlier that day and that they wanted to see the manager's office? Who told you?" asks the accuser.

"Nobody in particular. I was at the hotel bar Rigolo, drinking, I like to drink sometimes, and I overheard people there saying that the hotel was crawling with men from the Special Office who were interested in Emil, but Emil was not there."

"'Crawl', like 'sniff', is a derisive phrase, citizeness, inappropriate for describing the activities of our organs of security."

"It was not my phrase, but I do not think that it is inappropriate!"

"I am warning you! Who were the people you talked to at the bar Rigolo?"

"I did not talk to anybody. I just heard people around me talk about it; actually, I should say that the whole bar was buzzing about it. Or is 'buzz' an inappropriate word too?"

"Are you going to give us the names of all those that you knew at the Firmament, that you normally talked to when you were there, your associates? Was Boleslaw Rytwianski one of them?"

"I did not know anybody, hardly ever talked to people there. When I was there in the bar, I would just listen to all those drunks and others, found it interesting. And I never talk to Bolelsaw Rytwianski. He is not only totally uneducated, but also dense and boring as hell."

"You obviously had a higher opinion of your other acquaintances at the Firmament, and especially the man who was known as Emil. Well, are we going to hear any names from you?"

"No, I don't have any names. Emil was the only person I knew."

"You refuse to give us names. All right, let's hear more about Jarek Huczko then. Or didn't you know that this was his name?"

"When I knew him as a little boy and a young man that is what he was called."

"Well, let's hear about it!"

"There is not much to hear. It is... personal," Adela sounds a little softer.

But after some probing she does tell the court about Jarek Huczko, that is, only what she claims she knows about him, which is much less than the court believes she knows. And since the court believes that the two were part of the same conspiracy, it cannot accept the notion that there was a special bond of affection between the two.

"You claim then that you went to warn Jarek Huczko, forty years old, criminal and traitor, because some thirty years earlier you knew him as a little boy who had irresistible eyes. It's laughable! Contemptuous towards the authority of the people's court!"

"I have just explained. He was a little boy who was begging on the street. I had never thought before of children who did not have proper homes and beg on streets... somehow meeting him that day changed my life. I went with him to where he lived; the place was horrible, as I have just told you. And after that I could not live anymore the way I had been... eventually I moved to the Puddles myself, that's what our slums in Wielow were called in those days, and that's where children like Jarek lived. I taught there, and I made sure that he went to school and learned. He was so intelligent... his progress was amazing, and some years later he went to the university. I was actually proud... that he, and a few others, got education and became... better because of me. Can't you understand this?" Adela turns to the judges.

"Let me remind you, citizeness, that you are here not to ask questions, but answer them!" the judge sounds angry. "And it is most disturbing to hear you say in this people's court that you felt proud of a man like Huczko!"

"I did. Back then in Wielow before the War, I did."

"Shame, citizeness, shame!" roars the judge.

"Actually, instead of screaming at me, you, judge of the people's court should be praising me for my activities, my work for the poor, the underprivileged. Isn't that what our citizens normally get praised for? Why can't you understand that I was trying to do something good for those children, and that even years later I still felt something for those that I knew personally? When I heard that he was in some kind of trouble, I just wanted to help him. I did it, well, for the sake of... my memories. Is it that difficult to understand?!" Adela sounds challenging.

"There are still many comrades around who remember well who was involved in what activity in the old days. Odd that they all remember you only as an activist in reactionary nationalist Povolian groups, and not from any revolutionary group working for the poor."

"I never belonged to any official group. I was never a member of any party! I was an Independent!"

"Our sources tell us that you were always part of nationalist Povolian organizations, before and during the War, and also after the People's Power liberated our country! And you wrote articles for *The Spirit* , the most reactionary and immoral magazine that there was in pre-War times, the paper which supported libertine causes and praised Povolian renegades. You cannot deny it!"

"I **will** deny it! I was never part of any group! And *The Spirit* was the most progressive of publications; and the word to describe the causes it supported should have been 'liberal' and not 'libertine'. Your honors, I want it to be a matter of record that the wrong word was used to describe what *The Spirit* and I stood for."

"This is an outrage! You are not here to teach the people's court its job. One more contemptuous remark from you and you will be removed from here... permanently, as not worthy to be even on trial!" The judge's face acquires a tinge of apoplectic red.

Adela stays conformable to the court's rules for the next round of questions. She admits that she knew that Emil was involved in the nationalist Povolian movement before the War, but denies again that she had any knowledge of what he did during and after the War. But when the accuser's curiosity shifts to Adela's own activities during the War, she starts losing her composure.

"I was not involved in any activities aimed against the people's power! Can't this court understand that? I lived on a farm all the time, worked there, taught village children and occasionally took care of wounded soldiers."

"Exactly! Our sources tell us that you were in charge of a place which was called a hospital, but in fact harbored soldiers of the Underground Army who were involved in hostile activities against the People's Army!"

"Bloody lies!"

"Watch your language, citizeness! And that is not all that our sources tell us. We also heard about one curious incident that took place there. Just before the final victory of the People's Army over the Realm, on Christmas Eve, to be exact, a murderous Povolian mob attacked several villages in that area, your village included. It was one of those bloody attacks on our population inspired by Povolian leaders like your protege Emil, in those days known as Daimyo the Killer. Anyway, curious fact is that on that night every single house in the area was burned to the ground, that is, every one except the one where you lived. When the Povolians approached your place, you just came out and talked to them and they withdrew. Amazing, isn't it?" The accuser's tone is highly sarcastic.

"It was a miracle, or haven't your sources told you that?!" Adela starts laughing.

"You are out of line again. This is the last warning! Stop that contemptuous laughter and explain yourself!"

"Your honors, miracles cannot be explained! But it was not I who did it, but this saintly man, the farmer. And your sources were wrong again; this farmer did not talk to any Povolians, but directly to God; and God listened to him and created that big wind and then made this burning thatch move and drop on the heads of the attacking mob. Wham! You see, God disliked those Povolians the same way you all do!" Adela is laughing herself silly, shaking, choking, wheezing; seemingly not able to control her merriment.

The judge's face turns deep purple. He is not able to say a word, just moves his eyes in the direction of the guards and his pointed fingers towards Adela. And within a minute or so Adela is removed from the courtroom; her laughter still coming to them from behind the door that was shut after her and the guards.

She is brought back one more time, on the very last day of the trial, to hear the judgement. She is found guilty of some two dozen felonies and misdemeanors of which the gravest ones are her decades-long association with a traitor to his country and her decades-long activities in disseminating ideas hostile to the People's Power and to people's rule. She is sentenced to imprisonment for a period of twenty years.

"What disgrace! What agonizing disgrace and humiliation!" cries Kocia after the trial. "Our lives ruined once again... after having been involved in something like that, not that we really were, but it will look like that to everybody, Adam and I may be removed from the next show, you know, mother, the one with me doing the Good-Magic Sorceress and Adam one of the Bad Demons of the Past... Well, with the Sorceress's husband in prison for a crime against the State... But, no, his is not a political case, not by any stretch of imagination. He is a victim, really, like I was before..." Konstancya cries harder.

"But, you know, mother, he handled himself very, very well at the trial, much better than I would have expected, unlike some other people... Oh, what treachery that was! What abominable treachery!" Konstancya starts screaming. "Ugly duplicity! Perversity!" Konstancya is referring now to Adela's crimes; however, not to those against the Principles and people's rule, but to those against her family and her benefactors.

Kocia is outraged; at Adela's harboring of dark secrets for years, allying herself with a Povolian murderer, willfully making herself an outcast from society, with full knowledge that such an action would throw a deep shadow on the lives of her family, particularly her nephew Radomir whose job at *The Worker* is so sensitive; the same Adela whom she, Kocia, took under their roof, made one with them and upon whom she once bestowed all the privileges that she herself was enjoying; the same Adela whom she had forgiven all the insults of the early years in Wielow, and to whose guidance she would so often entrust her only child. What ingratitude! What perfidy! Kocia is never going to forgive her any of that.

Anna Gruber, Adela's sister, the owner of the booth with devotionalia at St. Andrew's parish, will not forgive Adela either. Not after she had gone to all the trouble and put herself and her booth in jeopardy in order to reach the venerable Prelate Reszka and some influential parishioners, all for the sake of Adela, and Adela repaying her with all those obscene, revolting scenes at the trial. And if The Holy Bedrock will now be closed by the authorities, Anna will know who to blame. "She has always been getting other people in trouble, then mocking them and enjoying the misery that she caused and the spectacle that she created," says Anna Gruber.

Kocia too has convinced herself that it is Adela who is at the root of all of Boleslaw's misfortunes. It is she who had introduced Boleslaw to Emil at the Broscin Central five years ago, and then over years just watched Boleslaw sink into the muck of that diabolical place that her protege Emil was running, and then just laughed. That Adela always laughed is most unforgivable. "Oh, I hate that woman!" cries Kocia.

"Don't say such things! Not now when she is not going to see the world ever again," says mother. "She does say strange things, but she is good, really. And she did not want to condemn herself or us, though I guess it sort of worked out that way, though she definitely helped Boleslaw by saying that she disliked him and that he is so stupid. But whatever she said was what she had to say. I mean, she could not help it; it was inside her, even when she knew that she should be quiet. I am the same way, only in reverse; I cannot help being silent when I know that I should talk, or saying stupid, polite things when I know that I should be saying just the opposite. Twenty years is so long I cannot even think about it without feeling all queasy. And another thing, I know that you don't want me to say this, but I do remember that Boleslaw had known Emil back in Wielow during the War, called him then a big cheese or something like that... you remember that very well too, I am sure."

"Well, if you choose to be against us, mother... I am very much disappointed in you, that's all," Konstancya ends the conversation and walks away.

But mother still has to talk, especially about longevity behind bars. "Sabina, please tell me whether twenty years is really too long for anybody. Is she going to be... alive?" mother follows Maximilian into Sabina's room.

"Oh, my dear, no doubt about it; she has so much vitality and mental reserve. I would not worry," says Sabina. "Also, she will be pardoned in a few years, I am sure. Everybody gets pardoned sooner or later; it's been like that since time immemorial, in all societies... rather comforting. I do hope, though, that they provide good occupational programs for the inmates. Weaving, of course, would be ideal, also plain sewing or woodworking. I understand some places do bookbinding. When you see her, advise her strongly to take up something as soon as possible, but no writing, that would not be wise."

The Home of the Divine Providence

As I have mentioned, in the last few weeks we have acquired a host of hedonistic and purposeless habits and have become terribly profligate; nor have we agreed on what the future organization of the Home is to be. It has not been resolved what schedule of activities we should adopt or whether we even need such a schedule at all, who is to perform what duties, whether brothers should be included in any functions, etc., etc. Besides, we have not as yet received any formal acknowledgement of the new situation at the Home by the governors, no cash from the State Bank and no food from food suppliers (except for a tub of frozen tripe and ten liters of mineral water). And we are continuing to have great difficulties in reaching anybody from the outside by phone or mail. Still, the general mood is upbeat, if not to say jubilant. Everybody seems to be optimistic about the future, especially after a successful money raising event called Evening of Poetry and Music, which we presented last Saturday at the village of Kobyl-ka. And tonight, after – still delicious though quite modest – supper, we decided to proceed most vigorously with further fund raising efforts, to formulate the Carta (the Home's new omnibus of laws, rules and guidelines), and to start working on a new production of a play. The discussion on the choice of our new play was progressing very smoothly, when suddenly at the mention by me of the possible usage of masks and makeup, I was booed by everybody present and called an imbecile by Jan, who said that in this new era of freedom and openness at the Home no goddamned phony, nauseating masks and illusions were necessary.

Kocia is certainly feeling low, uncheerful, close to desperate, and yet not quite despondent and helpless. Well, in the face of those new terrible adversities that became her lot, she just had to muster all her courage and cleverness, she told them, so that she – husbandless again – could support and steer through life the four of them, her charges, so feckless and helpless without her guidance. And so, first, she makes Radomir rush to the editor-in-chief of *The Worker* and explain to the man what his personal position on things is, and then write something really politically uplifting to prove how he feels. Then she makes Radomir officially give up his garret quarters and move to theirs on the second floor, explaining the move to the Office of Urban Allocation as necessary since Radomir – now the main breadwinner of his family, she writes for him in his application – has to live with them. And then she gets control of all Radomir's earnings. She also goes together with mother to the Youth Cultural House to see the head of the House to explain mother's position on political issues; and then she secures for mother two extra hours a week of teaching music; and then she gets control of her salary too. Since she knows that Adam would object to her collecting his salary and since she can not count on Adam's saying the right things to anybody, she just commands him not to, ever, but ever again, show himself in his Bad Demon makeup on the street before a performance (unprofessional behavior that drove the director of their theater up the wall!). Then she advises him to rework his Bad-Demon-of-the-Past act in such a way so that the Past (obviously their country's past) looks even more repellent than before.

Also, as their financial situation is still not quite as it used to be (after all, they lost not only Boleslaw's, but also most of Adela's income), Kocia simply converts into cash, sells, that is, to the State Antique Shop, a good portion of the Tulpe furnishings and sundries; a dining set, a few oil paintings, a few Persian rugs, a carved armoire, a Meissen dinner set, glasses, forks, napkins, etc., also Adela's desk and the chair that went with it.

When some two months after the trial they are still in possession of their jobs and income and do not get into trouble in any way, and Radomir brings even a bonus home, Konstancya, quite predictably, becomes all self-congratulatory. But even when smiling and bursting with self-admiration she can not find it in herself to become more charitable towards Adela. When mother receives from the prison authorities a permit for a visit to see her cousin and suggests that they all go, Kocia refuses to join mother in the expedition and forbids Nusia, Adam and Radomir to do the same.

On the day designated for the visit, when mother is waiting at the guards' station at the gate to be admitted inside the prison, she is informed by a messenger from the warden's office that Adela Milewska has just been transferred to another facility. She is then given the name and location of that institution and told that it is situated about four hundred fifty kilometers east of Broscin, and that it has very liberal visiting policies. Straight from the prison mother walks to the railroad station to inquire about a possible train connection to that distant place and is informed that indeed there is one, a twelve-hour ride with two train changes on the way. She also receives information about the fare, and then calculates that the return ticket plus a sleepover at a hotel will amount to three-month's worth of her piano lessons at the Youth Cultural House. At night she tells them about what she has learned that day, ending her story with a plea to Kocia, "Do you think that one day... I know we could not possibly afford it now, but one day, do you think I could somehow go there?"

Boleslaw is lucky again; that's what he tells Nusia and her mother when they go to see him for the first time. Not only is he placed in a fine old fortress situated right outside Broscin, but he is also given a cell with a window from which he can see some of the river with boats on it, that is, if he stands on his cot and stretches a bit. He is treated decently, he says, and his two roommates seem to be well-disposed, friendly, in fact.

After Nusia and her mother returns from their visit to the fortress with the view of the river, Kocia announces that it was the first and final time that she will go to see Boleslaw; not because she is not concerned about his fortunes, God forbid, but because too much is at stake.

"There is Radomir's career to be considered, and Nusia's future one of these days, and of course our jobs... we cannot possibly appear as a cozy married couple; I explained it to him, and he seemed to understand."

"Well, if you feel that you shouldn't... but certainly Nusia and I can visit him from time to time... no harm will be done. He must be so miserable."

"He sounded cheerful enough when we were there. And I definitely feel that neither Nusia nor you should pay him any visits in the future." Konstancya does not wish to discuss the subject any further.

In the evening that day Nusia goes to Sabina. She tells her what her mother said, but that she, Nusia, would like to go again, though she would not know what to say to her father.

"You can tell him all kinds of funny stories, you know, about Maximilian, about Adam practicing demon dances, about Master Ociszek falling asleep in the bathroom, about Jurek Goralski trying to kiss you at a dance..."

"I couldn't tell him that."

"Of course you could. He will be laughing, you will see. Both of you will enjoy your visits, I am certain of it."

"What about Mommy?"

"You can arrange it all on your own; you are next of kin, so it will be very simple. And when everything is set, just tell your mother that you are going, you know, in a grown-up way; and explain to her why you want to go; and just go. Alone or with Adam and Maximilian who can both wait for you outside. Well, if I were you, I would not miss that experience for anything. Of course, before you go, you will have to bake him a cake or something of that kind, really, really good. Obviously at the Fortress all those silly guards will cut up your cake into little pieces, searching for secret documents or a weapon; but it won't matter, your cake will taste great either way, cut up or in one big chunk."

"But I have never baked."

'It's time then that you start learning."

"But what about Radomir? Mommy says that if we go to the Fortress again, it will ruin Radomir's chances in life."

"I would say on the contrary, it would be a great opportunity for him. One day he will write a book about the Fortress, your trips there, cut up cakes and all, you will see."

It is not long after mother's attempt to visit Adela that Radomir brings them a copy of his first book *The Affairs of M., Consequential and Puny*. Mother is sitting at the piano, her hands idly on the closed keyboard, her eyes red and swollen from tears, and Kocia rushes to her and kisses her on both her cheeks, "Mother, it happened at last!"

Mother is incredulous that it is Radomir's name that she can see on the cover, and that there will be several thousand copies of that opus printed and distributed to bookstores and libraries all over the country, and that Radomir is going to be famous and extremely respected, and that she is going to be bought a new spring coat and a hat. She does not know what to say except that she is happy and that she hopes that Radomir will not be angry at her if she does not read his book now, her mind being so terribly preoccupied with other things. Later that day she says that she would forgo the coat and the hat if she could visit Adela instead. She also says that, no matter what anybody will think, she is going to send Adela a food parcel; mainly apples and onions, the best source of vitamins one does not get in prison, that's what she has heard from Sabina.

When the book is finally at the bookstores and kiosks, Radomir brings home two bottles of wine and a walnut torte, and sheepishly asks Kocia whether they can celebrate the event. And she calls him extravagant and kisses him on his forehead. And mother says that it is nice to celebrate something from time to time and asks whether they could invite some of the family and friends they have not had over for so long. And then Kocia gets angry; no family have had them over since the affair of M. became known, and has mother forgotten that her own brother calls her a mooing pushover and always refers to Nusia as a blimp, or does she intend to talk to cousin Julian who got so senile that he thinks that he is still in Wielow making hats, or does mother remember how rude Anna Gruber was to them when they last saw her at St. Andrew's and Kocia refused to buy from her a new holy medallion for Nusia. Mother admits that they indeed are not blessed with many good friends and relations; and so they celebrate on their own.

After the party, when there is still some half of the walnut torte left, Nusia says that she would like to take whatever is left to the Fortress for her father. She is next of kin and so it will not be hard for her to deliver anything to him; of course, the guards will look for things inside the torte, maybe for a hidden weapon, and so they will cut it up into small pieces, but it will not change the taste of the cake at all, she says. She will go tomorrow right after school and she only needs money for the bus outside the city, she has just enough for the tramway to get her to the city limits. Nusia's grandmother asks her how she knows about cakes being searched by prison guards, and Nusia answers that she is grown up enough to talk to people.

The following day, despite Kocia's protests, Nusia and her grandmother deliver the walnut torte to the Fortress together.

They do not see the cake being actually cut up, but they are informed by the guard that it will be checked before it is given to the prisoner. Nusia is also told that she cannot be permitted to see her father on that day, but is supplied with information on future dates and times of visits, also on the rules governing delivery of letters and packages, contents of packages, and so on. At home she makes a chart for herself on which she marks two days in every month on which she will write her father and one special day on which she will visit him and deliver a parcel for him. She also asks Sabina to teach her baking and some cooking.

On the evening before the scheduled visit to her father Nusia works with Sabina on a chocolate-flavored sponge cake; and that is how Konstancya and Adam find her when they come home from the Playhouse: in an apron, greasing a pan for the batter.

"You are not going there again!" shouts Kocia.

"I am, Mommy. It's all arranged. I cannot disappoint Daddy and the Warden who is counting on me. And you don't have to worry... I wrote down that you and Daddy had been at odds for a long time and that you will be divorced as soon as he is out."

"What kind of nonsense is this?" Kocia is aroused.

"Well, I had to write an application and a letter to explain things, so I did. And I said that I wanted to see him regularly because I wanted to help him... rehabilitate himself, which means that I wanted to make sure that he understands what went wrong and that he becomes a useful and regular person when he comes out. Anyway, it was a long letter, but it must have been good because the Warden of the Fortress wrote me back saying that he was proud of me and that our country should be proud of me, and he asked me not to disappoint him and come and see father regularly and that if I want, he can give me extra time with Daddy. And, so that nobody else could get in trouble, like you or Radomir, I wrote on the application that I am the only one who is interested in seeing Daddy and that you will be divorcing him anyway. So, of course, I have to go, and you and Radomir should not worry." Nusia explains the situation clearly and matter-of-factly.

"Was it your idea?" Kocia turns to Sabina.

"Only some of it. Nusia is so grown-up now and has developed quite a good grasp of things."

"Well, I wish she had shared some of it with me, her own mother, but... yes, when put this way, it does sound rather good, puts things in a different perspective... Nusia helping to rehabilitate her father, a convict; yes, it does sound impressive. I should have thought of that myself, I probably would have eventually. And this thing about the divorce, that is not too bad either. You are very clever, Sabina." Kocia seems a little diffident. Sabina is the first person Kocia has ever met whose judgement she has to openly admit is on occasion superior to her own. Not that this makes her feel comfortable.

The following day Nusia goes to the Fortress accompanied by Adam and Maximilian. They wait for her a few steps away from the guards' booth. She walks confidently to the booth where she shows the guards a piece of paper and the contents of the net she is carrying: the chocolate sponge cake, hard-boiled eggs, apples, onions. The guard lets Nusia go inside without her parcel; the provisions are sent in separately to be further examined.

After she returns she reports that her father enjoyed all her stories, she says, especially the one about Maximilian pushing Master Ociszek into the bathtub. But he did not get much of the walnut torte she sent him last time; most of it kind of crumbled away, the guard told him.

It comes to pass that sometime after his book appears on the shelves of bookstores and libraries around the country their cousin Radomir is officially noticed by the Ministry of Culture. Whether it is his insights into the affairs of Jozef M., or whether it is his contribution to *The Right and the Wrong* column or whether it is he himself, incredibly handsome and eager, that is the main cause of this new ascent in his life, Adam is not sure. But whatever it is, he is summoned to the Capital; and there in the Ministry of Culture he is praised for his work, advised on the further course of his life and given the position of an editor of *The Standard* . For anybody from the provinces to be given a high level job in the Capital is a distinction of almost no equal; and that *The Standard* is merely one rung below *People's Tribune* (the organ of the Party of the Principles) is common knowledge; and so their cousin suddenly finds himself being launched into a zone of the blindingly bedazzling limelight of importance.

He tells them the news at the Central after having descended off the train that had brought him back from the Capital. Kocia swoons and is stricken dumb, and then cries, with lavish, un-tamed streams of tears (in the manner of mother).

"Oh, darling... it's so wonderful, so unbelievable... I am so happy for you, and so proud. And I will miss you terribly..." She is not able to contain her sorrow.

"But Kocia, listen, I am not going anywhere without you. I have already talked to people there, and it will not be a problem for you to go too and get a job. You are so immensely qualified for so many things!"

"You mean, I could go to the Capital, with you?! Oh! But I could not leave mother, Adam and Nusia all alone here!"

"Oh, Kocia, we will all be going! I told them at the Ministry that I have family I am responsible for. Now, listen to this: I am going to get brand new quarters in a building they are just finishing on the Central Avenue, and a certain person at the Ministry hinted that there is a good chance that they could give you a place in the same building!"

"Oh, my dearest!" is all that Kocia is able to produce at that moment.

Of the directives that Radomir received during his visit at the Ministry of Culture the most important ones were to join the Party of People's Principles and to start working on a book dealing with social-class bias and education in pre-War epochs. It was indicated to him that he should fulfill both wishes of the Ministry before he assumes his new post with *The Standard* and receives the keys to his new quarters on the Central Avenue.

Radomir does not feel much put upon. Joining the Party of the Principles, the ruling and only party of the land, is a formality he is not anxious to go through, but which is nevertheless only a formality, as the hardest part of that initiation is already behind him; his biography polished to perfection, filled-out application forms and recommendation from the editor-in-chief of *The Worker*, all sent in and accepted months earlier. All he has to think of now is to prepare himself for the oral querying of the District Committee and then the swearing-in ceremony, which meant primarily memorizing some lines and various verbal and body responses; the worst of which is probably remembering whom to address as "comrade" and when.

Starting work on his new book on education and the underprivileged is the easier, and certainly more pleasant, of the two tasks, since it is he himself who had suggested the topic, first to his publisher and then to the people in the Ministry of Culture. The idea had come to him during the trial while listening to Adela's testimonies on Jarek Huczko a.k.a. Emil when he, Radomir, was awaiting his turn to be called as a witness. There in the courtroom he suddenly closed his eyes and saw a little barefoot boy begging in front of a luxury shop with ladies' fashion; "Nice lady, please!" the boy's big pleading eyes and his thin extended arm reaching towards a lady in furs entering the shop. Adela, who never wore furs, was not part of the vision; it was the boy who was important, a youngster with expressive dark eyes who instead of going to school had to beg for his living. And then the picture expanded; Radomir saw a pre-War street with underage vendors and shoeshines hustling their services, a liveried page being whipped by a sadistic master, a little parlor maid scrubbing floors in a mansion of the rich, a whole factory swarming with tubercular child-laborers, and himself, a very young apprentice in a hatter's workshop being denied his supper as punishment for ruining a small piece of felt; and Radomir's eyes moistened. Anyway, he suggested to his publisher and then to the people at the Ministry of Culture that he was going to make it all colorful and anecdotal, and very moving, and obviously historically accurate and politically sound. And they all liked the idea very much.

Though Kocia is the one taking credit for everything Radomir does or for whatever befalls him in those days, some good demons must be aiding him as well, since his energies, enthusiasm and accomplishments go beyond what any self-subsistent mortal would have hoped to attain. Within a period of some three months he becomes a full-fledged member of the Party, participates in several high-level literary discussions sponsored by same, is introduced to most of the literary and cultural elite of the country, is interviewed on the radio a number of times, writes most of his book on education and the underprivileged, writes drafts for a novel and a play, composes a poem for Kocia, and secures for her a full-time job in the Capital, at no less than the Ministry of Arts!

It is probably the most triumphant period in all of Konstancya's life. The position she is shortly to assume in the Ministry of Arts is in the Division of Opera and Operetta of the Department of Music, and it is that of assistant to a director of Repertory and Personnel Decisions. It is the first time in her life that she is given a chance to show her true worth, the whole breadth of her intellectual capabilities as well as her artistic intuition, she tells mother.

Kocia is not particularly concerned about what persons inferior to her, those unworthy of regard, think of her; yet, it gives her high satisfaction to let them all know of the latest developments in her life. First she transmits the news to Goralski's mother-in-law, briefly, when passing her on the stairs, knowing, of course, that within an hour or so the woman will manage to pass the word to the Kowalskis, the Paluks and others in their building and all along the Boulevard. Then she delicately whispers the information to a couple of ladies with whom she shares her dressing room at the Young Theatregoers' Playhouse, knowing that they will tell the news to the lead players of the Playhouse immediately and then spread it throughout the rest of the world of theatre in Broscin. She even feeds a lie to them, saying that Adam also has been offered a position in the Capital, nothing less than chief makeup artist for the State Ballet Theater. She also makes Radomir call his aunt Anna Gruber and, as if in passing, mention her latest elevation in life; and once St. Andrew's parish is in possession of the information, Kocia is certain, most of the city of Broscin in no time will know too what transpired.

She is not a vindictive person, she often says, yet she now relishes the prospect of being able one day to even the score with the director of the Broscin Opera, the man who locked her out of her dressing room when the Affair of M. became known and who for years had humiliated her by assigning to her only lesser parts of his Opera's repertory. She does not doubt for a moment that working in the division of Opera in a ministry in the Capital will indeed empower her to do almost anything to anybody, especially to those who are employed in the provinces.

That night after she goes public, Adam and Kocia walk home from the Playhouse a roundabout way, slowly, taking their time. She is ecstatic, feels like walking and walking forever, she says, and daydreaming a little, and she does not mind at all that Adam has not taken off the ugly-demon makeup he wore for the last act of that night's show. They pass the Firmament; its ornate glass-pan-elled doors gone, replaced by simple wooden ones; its new name: The Hotel of Workers' Unity faintly showing on the surface of a freshly made signboard. Kocia wrings her mouth in disgust. They pass the Opera; the glass in one corner of the marquee broken. Kocia makes another face and comments on the ugliness of the building. "Shortly it will all be behind us; that horrible, ugly world. We will be free of it at last!" Through the rest of the way she talks only about the Capital; having accompanied Radomir on one of his trips, she knows what to expect. Big, wide spaces everywhere; buildings reaching to the sky; the bustle; the enthusiasm; the con-struction of the new; and they in their new place in a freshly erected building covered with limestone blocks, simple, yet so powerful and real, still smelling of mortar and paint, airy, clean, devoid of all the bad demons of the Past!

The Home of the Divine Providence
Today is the first time in three weeks that I have been able to write again. Three weeks ago this Friday, just hours after we had finished

celebrating the completion of the Carta (which, by the way, awarded the brothers rights and privileges equal to those of the wards), we, the wards, while asleep, were attacked by the joined forces of the brothers, governors, militiamen and some local hoodlums. We were tied up, gagged, placed inside fishnets (the same ones which the wards had used earlier for restraining the brothers) and informed that we had been placed under Penal Law. Within two days there was also built around the premises a cordon made of felled pine trunks and a moat with a drawbridge across it. The raiders, as we found out later, had arrived that night on jeeps and motorcycles, and then stealthily on foot entered the chapel, where they were met by the brothers and from where they were led by same through a secret passage into the Home itself. We also found out that the brothers – from the very first day of their release from the nets – while sabotaging our Home telephone system and intercepting mail from the outside – were communicating with the governors by means of a pay phone in the village. We are back to normal now, that is, back to three meals a day, reading, talking and watching TV (even the cobras); however, we are not allowed to cross the moat, receive uncensored mail and visitors, and all our movements are monitored by various new-age devices that the governors have supplied the brothers with (e.g., 'inter-buzz' by means of which a person talking into a special microphone in one area can be heard throughout the rest of the Home, or 'talk as you walk', a private telephone-like gadget given to each brother to facilitate their contacts with one another.) Regarding other changes, Brother Simplicius, found to be incompetent, has been removed from his position of head guardian and replaced by the energetic Brother

Innocent, whose position as guardian of public exposure and outside affairs was in turn assumed by Brother Hyacinth; and in turn his job as guardian of the dining hall was taken over by a new brother named Reparatus. All the others are still performing their old functions, except that Euzebius was suspended for a few weeks as punishment for his fraternizing with the wards during the period which is referred to now as the Mutiny.

They move to the Capital in early November. They travel by train, and their effects are transported by a truck hired by Kocia through some of Radomir's new contacts at *The Standard*. The move goes smoothly, and their new place on the Central Avenue – still smelling of mortar and paint, just as Kocia had said – meets Kocia's expectations. Yet, there are two circumstances that dampen somewhat the general agreeability of the events: on Konstancya's insistence, mother's Bechstein concert grand piano is not traveling with them; nor is Konstancya's daughter Nusia, who despite her mother's urging, refuses to leave Broscin, at least for as long as her father remains in prison.

The case of mother's Bechstein concert piano is not just a matter of space, Kocia is explaining to them, but also of good taste and overall political and social appropriateness. Well, it is a matter of space, of course, it would be silly to say that it is not when the main room in their new place in the Capital measures only about twenty square meters and the other two rooms have fourteen and six meters respectively and the kitchen and the hallway are on the small side as well; still, there is more to the issue than physical dimensions; Kocia tries to be as clear on that as possible. All living quarters that are being created in the buildings presently constructed in the Capital are not only of moderate, very moderate size, but have been designed expressly to serve working-class households; and so they are simple and unpretentious. Anything oversize, ornamented, overwrought would be so terribly out of place there, clashing... plainly wrong; and especially something as grandiose and fanciful as mother's Bechstein, so non-working class, so totally from the past!

"There is nothing fanciful about my Bechstein and certainly nothing from the past! Its sound is as perfect now as it was seventeen years ago when I got it... oh, I am sorry, my dear, I quite forgot that it was you who bought it for me, so, of course, it is yours to take away... Oh, yes, dispose of it, make money on it! Why should I have a piano in my old age? A grandiose piano at that?!"

Kocia then assures mother that the piano will not be sold for profit (like most of the Tulpe items that Kocia is getting rid of); it will be donated to the Youth Cultural House in Broscin. And, once they are in their new place in the Capital, mother will get a brand new piano, a small upright one, which Radomir has already ordered for her right at the place where it is being made.

"Well, it may take a few months before we get it, Kocia. This is the only piano factory in the country, and they have something of a backlog there. But, we are on their waiting list!" Radomir sounds quite optimistic.

The Bechstein is removed from the Tulpe building the same way it entered it, through the salon's balcony. It is loaded on a flat lorry and taken to the Youth Cultural House; and there it is hoisted on heavy ropes from the street to the second floor window of that building. And then, just then, the movers realize that it is too bulky to get in through the window; any window in the House. But as the movers have no instructions in the matter and they need their lorry right away, they just push inside the building the parts of the piano that will go in without resistance, leaving the rest on the outside, suspended in the air. The director of the House, when reached, decides that as soon as there are workmen available to do the job, the Bechstein will definitely be moved inside the House, possibly by having the window frame and some of the bricks removed. However, for the time being, as the country is just on the eve of the official two-day long All Hallows Day (the most holy time of the year devoted to the dead, ghosts and memories), the piano will have to stay where it is.

And so it does, for two days and almost two nights; hanging precariously from a window sill, its beautiful body suddenly sagging, swaying ever so lightly in the chilly autumn wind, cemetery-bound crowds stopping and ogling it with bewilderment. And during the second night, right before dawn, it disappeared. There is a lot of noise heard that night around the Youth Cultural House; clattering, slamming, rumbling, ringing of all kinds, but because of the darkness, nobody sees exactly what happened. Because of its exceptionally large dimensions (so rightly pointed out by Kocia) and hence obvious difficulties in concealing it from anybody's eyes, it is hard to imagine that their Bechstein had actually been stolen; but since it is never found again (despite the efforts of militiamen and security forces), they have to assume that it was what really happened. They hear rumors, never confirmed, that the thieves were simply one of numerous rings specializing in heisting goods to be disassembled and sold as hard-to-find parts to either private persons or to State-owned shops. Mother is heart-broken, more than Adam has ever seen her before, appearing even more dejected than she was in the Hidden Vale during the War when she threw her rosary down the foul pit and proclaimed that she did not want to live any longer.

During the first few visits to her father at the Fortress Nusia sits in front of a small window-like opening fitted with horizontal and vertical bars; and her father, a few feet away in a different room, is looking at her through another window-like opening also fitted with a grating. Between them, that is, between the two grilled barriers through which they are peeking, there runs a passageway in which the figure of a walking guard periodically appears. Nusia suggests that she and father put their arms through the grill and try to shake hands somewhere over the floor of the passageway. And so, they press their bodies to the grills and then stretch their arms as far out as possible; but when Nusia's fingers are just about an inch away from her father's, the guard appears and tells them that touching is not permitted.

But things change some time after the Warden of the Fortress receives Nusia's letter asking for permission to see her father regularly. The man is so impressed with Nusia's wording of her intentions to help Boleslaw in rehabilitating himself, that he allows her to see her father in a room next to his office where the two of them can sit next to each other at a table, and he gives them an hour together at each visit.

Part of Nusia's rehabilitation design (the one she thought of all on her own, without Sabina) has been to teach her father how to cook; for becoming a cook (preferably in a first-class restaurant) is what she thinks would be the most appropriate profession for him once he is on the outside again. And so, during her visits she tells him about her own progress in cooking and presents him with descriptions of the foods, techniques and recipes that she is studying. And as she says to the Warden that she wishes she could demonstrate some of the things, he gives her a one-burner electric cooker and a pan; which is all that he is able to provide. She makes an omelette once and fried cubed potatoes a couple of times. On the occasions when she cooks, she is allowed to stay longer, and the Warden stays with the two of them and is treated to Nusia's food; and then the three of them play poker for a little while, with pretend money of course. Nusia is not very good at the game, but her father is, though the Warden must be even better, as he wins every single time, even when it seems at first that father will take the hand.

During her visits Nusia also gives Boleslaw news about things she thinks are either curious or funny; Jurek Goralski making a pest of himself; Mrs. Kowalska throwing poor Master Ociszek out of the communal laundry room for smoking those smelly cigarettes of his; Maximilian chasing Master Ociszek all along the Boulevard; militiamen chasing a man who was holding a cage with some birds and screaming that he was Saint Francis; somebody stealing a bronze statue from the neighborhood park which weighs more than a hundred kilo; Professor's Paluk's wife getting a fur coat which Nusia thinks is very elegant, but Mrs. Goralska claims is made of dyed squirrels.

She also talks to her father about Adam's work, shows him some of his latest masks, demonstrates the makeup he uses at the Playhouse, and does some pantomime for him. And one day she even makes up Boleslaw into one of Adam's Bad Demons. The Warden at first is a little taken aback and asks why she has made her father look so ugly; but when she explains that he is supposed to look ugly because his makeup was that of a Bad Demon of the Past and the Past is something father should be embarrassed about. The Warden is awed by her intelligence. It is after this event that the Warden contacts *The Worker* and asks that a piece be written on Nusia, a most exceptional young person. And *The Worker* obliges by printing – for the edification of the young people of Broscin – the story of a girl who of her own volition has embarked upon the project of educating and reconditioning the mind and character of her father, a hardened criminal and a political deviant. The article states that the girl in question spends every free moment of her time not on play with young people her own age, but behind bars with her father, working on his improvement. The piece extolls Nusia's hard work and the remarkable results she is achieving, but, as is the custom of the day, neither Nusia's name nor any specific details of her efforts are mentioned.

Anyway, Nusia explains to her mother very clearly why under the circumstances it is impossible for her to go to the Capital and leave her father behind. Konstancya gets furious and says that Nusia is coming, even if she has to be bound with ropes and carried on the train like a package. Kocia changes her mind only after Sabina explains, one, that after the article in *The Worker* Nusia has become a public figure and hence acquired official obligations to stay at the side of her father until he is released, and two, that while remaining in Broscin Nusia could live with her and be supervised by her.

Of course Nusia's stubbornness about not leaving has several roots, Adam knows well. As much as she thinks it impossible that she could leave her father, it is equally unimaginable for her to be divorcing herself from her present life in the shadow of Sabina and her wisdom, not mentioning Maximilian. Is Adam jealous? Oh, yes, and how; though he is also pleased that her old desire to be always near her mother and Radomir has been giving way to other sentiments. There is also another thing – Nusia's new passion for reading forbidden literature could not be fulfilled in the Capital.

Let it be explained that at the beginning of that summer Sabina arranges a job for Nusia at the warehouse of the Archives, where Nusia's task is to help move the contents of an old stock room into a newer room; and that's how she comes upon a stack of books published in old days somewhere in the West in the language of the Far Western Sovranties (the most important tongue of the other side). The books have glossy covers that look like photos from glamorous Western films. By the way, Western art and entertainment of any kind are banned, and so is the viewing of stills from Western films, naturally; but in the old days of the Firmament some customers of Rigolo would bring such photos to the bar sometimes and show them around, and so Nusia is familiar with the genre. Her heart starts palpitating from excitement when she sees them now at the warehouse. With her meager knowledge of the language she is able to translate only two titles, as far as Adam remembers, *Desire in the Jungle* and *Death Lights a Blue Candle*, but that is enough. Unnoticed, she puts the Jungle book inside her undergarments and then moves all the others into a remote corner under a pile of things which are not going to be removed from the room for a few days. Within the next week she brings home with her (either inside her undergarment or in the pockets of an apron she wears under her dress) about a dozen more books, most discreetly, not mentioning the affair to anybody but Adam, remembering to immediately put heavy brown paper over the cover of each of the books that she thus acquires, so that it can not be distinguished from her school textbooks. She is a little nervous when showing the loot eventually to Sabina, but her mentor neither praises nor scolds her. She says that she assumes that all the pilfering is done properly, that is, without arousing anybody's suspicion.

Sabina also explains to Nusia that these kinds of books, often referred to as cheap romances and melodramas, are usually not considered literature; and also that they are not allowed to be printed or even read in Nusia's country, especially in the language of the Western Sovranties; and also that if they are discovered by anybody from the Office of Archives, they would be burned. On the other hand, Sabina says, it would be a pity if they got destroyed as, their silly contents notwithstanding, they can provide excellent material for studying the language they are written in; and she urges Nusia to start using the books as means for more intensive study of the language of the Sovranties. She also tells her that as far as her new literary pursuits are concerned, she will have to be totally mum about them, in a grown-up way. And so, before they are ready to go to the Capital Nusia is already in the middle of the second book from the lot, and can not wait for all the rest of them as she is becoming quite expert in the language.

On the train mother cries all the way to the Capital, dividing her tears equally between the loss of the Bechstein and poor Nusia's predicament of having to become at such an early age her father's keeper. And Konstancya keeps saying that she is terribly worried about Nusia, mainly because of certain flaws in her personality, her lack of any intellectual curiosity, for instance. "She is probably the only child in this country who, having an opportunity to go to the Capital, would not get excited about it! She did not show any interest in it at all, did not ask us a single question about it, and actually said that she would not mind living in Broscin for the rest of her life. I am afraid that she has what I understand is described by psychiatrists as flat affect."

In late June of the following year Nusia is officially informed that her father's release will take place a full week before the prescribed time, in honor of the eighth anniversary of the birth of the country as people's republic.

When she is getting on the bus from the city limits to the Fortress on the scheduled day, the bus driver she has befriended asks her whether she forgot her bag with provisions, and she answers that she does not need it anymore as her father is going to be released. When the driver asks what her father is going to do now, she says that he will get a job as a cook.

She feels horribly downhearted that this is not the truth; her mother had already found a job for him, a job so wrong that Nusia cried when she heard her mother announce it to her over the phone. He is to become a janitor in the building where her mother and Radomir live. He is to get his own quarters on the ground floor and he is supposed to say, if asked, that Madame Rytwianska who lives upstairs is his cousin. He certainly is welcome to stay upstairs with the family for periods of time, her mother says, but never for so long as to arouse suspicion. Nusia is not too familiar with the profession of janitors, but she knows that it is similar to bellmen in hotels, only much, much worse. After she hears the dreadful news, she bawls for hours and asked Sabina whether she and her father really have to go to the Capital. Can't they stay in Broscin, just the two of them? Sabina tells her that they certainly can, but that under the circumstances they both will have better opportunities for the future in the Capital; and she assures Nusia that Boleslaw will not have to be a janitor for the rest of his life.

"He is extremely resourceful, my girl. But, of course, you will have to continue working on his rehabilitation. Don't move in with him, though, just visit him regularly and have a plan for him. Also, he will have one great advantage now – he will be free, I mean, living on his own without the burden of marriage. You cannot imagine how wonderful it feels sometimes to be suddenly unmarried! I have gone through this twice myself."

Nusia meets her father outside the guards' booth. He stands there for a few moments staring at her and then says that he didn't realize before, when seeing her in the Warden's room, how incredibly tall she has grown. And she is almost ready to tell him then that she never realized how horribly short he is and how much weight he has lost recently; but she only says that they should hurry so that they can catch an early bus to the city. But as the bus Nusia wants to take has already left, Boleslaw suggests that they walk to the city limits; and Nusia likes the idea. But she all of a sudden does not know what to talk to him about; the latest news on Kowalska, Master Ociszek or Maximilian seems not that interesting and funny anymore; and Nusia suddenly also feels embarrassed about all those things that she told him before, as he had probably thought her to be really silly, quite immature.

"Still, it was a very good walk," she tells Adam later. "We made it on foot into the city, the two of us just about the same height, buying ice cream from a vendor, and father telling me some funny stories that I had never heard, like about the dog he had when he was my age or how he once locked one of his teachers in an empty classroom."

The day after Boleslaw is released, he and Nusia take a tramway to the center of the city and Nusia invites him to dinner at a new restaurant that Sabina recommended. Nusia has been saving money for this occasion for a while, from the monthly allowance her mother is sending her. It is only during the dessert that she decides to face up to telling him what is awaiting him in the Capital.

"I just heard from Mommy about this job that she thinks you should have, but well, I don't know, maybe you could try something else..."

"Oh, don't worry, babee. Worse things happen. I will have my own place, I understand, and it is a big building, so I will be quite important."

"So you know about it already?"

"Oh, yes, got a letter from the old girl a few days ago."

"You don't mind?!"

"I mind a little, but it will be a move up in life from the Fortress."

"But I am not going to pretend that you are not my father!"

"Oh, I will not be angry at you if you call me something else; but you do whatever you feel like."

"What does a janitor do actually?"

"I am not sure what it is like now in the Capital, but it used to be that such fellows would watch after the whole building, maybe call a plumber if necessary, help somebody if they get locked out, keep the place clean, you know, sweep stairs and so on."

"I will help you with sweeping stairs; I am really good at such things now, Sabina taught me. I even learned to do windows the other day."

EPILOGUE

*H*aving had the experience of the last twenty-five years at the Home of Divine Providence and the life-long experience of the cyclical nature of things, I am reporting here without the slightest surprise that last night, when I suggested, for our after-supper discourse, the subject of prisons and their repressive role in a society, I was not hushed down, but praised by the smiling Brother Honore, "Bravo, Adam, bravo, excellent topic!" I may also report that as of the past few weeks we have been allowed to cross the drawbridge on the moat almost at any time of the day and without a personal search; that we have been receiving uncensored mail; that Sundays have been declared days of either leisure or work, depending on one's inclinations, with worship and meditation optional; that the Green Veranda has a new map of the World and plenty of colored glossy-paper foreign-language magazines, some even with pictures of voluptuous nudes inside; that my personal allowance has been increased; and also that I am back to one or even two cups of cocoa a day.

It was a few nights ago while my old friend from outside Station-master Jaworski and I were having a little libation in my room (con-sisting of cocoa, fruit and biscuits) that he approached the subject of my account of Nusia's formative years. After having read my story, he insisted that it was not finished; and I said that if I had failed to make my story complete, so be it, no ending will ameliorate that. Since he continued nudging me, and I was determined not to write a word more, we eventually decided on a compromise. I agreed to answer orally some of his questions concerning my protagonists and to have both his questions and my answers tape-recorded, treating this exchange of ours as an optional appendage to my original work. Here it is:

Stationmaster: I have heard from somebody who recently met your sister that she was describing you as a great dramatic actor who unfortunately did not always realize the magnitude of his talent.

Adam: Good Heavens! What will this woman say next?! She was telling people not long ago that several of my masks are in the permanent collections of the world's major museums!

S: Did you return to the stage after you settled in the Capital?

A: Yes, I did. I worked at the Contemporary for two years. I was doing a variety of things there; helped the wig maker, sewed some costumes, painted flats, occasionally acted, usually silently.

S: And so, you left, dissatisfied.

A: No, I was dismissed.

S: For insubordination, by any chance?

A: No, for indecent exposure.

S: Is this a metaphor of some kind?

A: Not at all. It was in the middle of the hottest summer I remember and I had to wear through a whole act a heavy padded coat, and I was not wearing anything under the coat, obviously; I was sweating enough as it was, and the audience could not tell what I had under the coat anyway. Immediately after I exited, I started unbuttoning my coat just to get some relief from the heat, but this actress I did not notice was standing right there. She was not supposed to be there; in the theater during a performance everybody has his precise position, and there was not supposed to be a soul in that passageway. The actress screamed, which broke the mood of whatever was happening on the stage. I was labeled a pervert...

S: Was that the end of your theatre career?

A: The absolute end.

S: Was it shortly afterwards that you moved to the Home?

A: No, I still lived with Konstancya for a few years. But she was getting more and more difficult. One could say it differently, of course, that she was finding me more and more burdensome.

S: Was your niece married at the time?

A: No, she just got engaged. It took them about three years to fight red tape and other hurdles before they were allowed to get married and live together, but they prevailed.

S: That's true love for you. Did you once tell me that they met in jail?

A: Not exactly. It was on the street in some not very attractive part of the city. He had left a tour and went on his own, wanted to see some local color, I guess, but got lost, did not know the language; and she was on a tramway, saw him and knew right away that he was somebody from the other side and in trouble, so, she jumped off the tramway and offered to help him. He was, of course very grateful to her and certainly impressed with her knowledge of his language. Well, I suppose they became impressed with each other after a while and decided to do some sightseeing together, instead of going to his hotel. Nightfall caught them in a town just outside the city. It was there that they were stopped by a militiaman and, naturally, arrested; they spoke a foreign language and neither of them had their personal papers on them – you know how it was in those days. But this was, of all nights, Holy Saturday, and this militiaman was anxious to go home for his Easter celebrations, and couldn't get in touch with the appropriate authorities in the city anyway, so he just locked them up in some upstairs room at the station and left. He wasn't back until Tuesday.

S: How horrible! No food, nothing, for two days!

A: Actually it turned out to be the best two days that either of them had ever spent, Nusia told me. They were locked in all right, but she managed to get somebody's attention through the window, and then in exchange for cash – his foreign money, and you know what that was worth in those days – they had some local people deliver to them, through the window, things like pillows, blankets, food, even wine. Yes, they had a marvelous time, and decided to get married as soon as possible. But they couldn't, as it turned out; he was deported and she was put in some place of detention in the Capital. (Not for long, though; Radomir got her out.) But the two never gave up the idea of getting married; though, as I said, it took them three years. They were very lucky that they met at the time when they did. Imagine, if all this had happened a few years earlier, when all contacts with the other side were considered a heavy crime! Well, a few years earlier they most probably would have never met, as we did not have any foreign tourists from the other side then.

S: I presume her infatuation with her cousin Radomir did not last beyond her childhood.

A: Not infatuation. Love! And it lasted until she was almost twenty. By that time she had known some other men, but I always felt that she considered those... affairs as if preparation for that moment one day when Radomir would be ready to acknowledge her as a woman. She never tried to take him away from her mother either, lure him in any way; she just waited for him. Then one day it all ended; he took her with him to some kind of reception (the kind to which he would usually go with Kocia), drank quite a bit there and then afterwards all of a sudden told her that he was lusting for her, or something to that effect. In a taxi on the way home he made some lewd comments about her yummy thighs, etc., tried to kiss her and was even forcing himself upon her; and she was mortified. She told me the following day that she suddenly had found him not only shallow-witted and pathetic in general, but also physically revolting.

S: A fallen-idol condition, I suppose.

A: Something like that. She met her future husband a year later.

S: How did your sister fare in matters of the heart? She divorced her husband shortly after you moved into the Capital, didn't she?

A: Oh, no, no. She did not divorce him; had never intended to. **He divorced her.** *You misread her character. If she had wanted to be rid of him, she would have never found him a job in the* *same building where she was. She thought that she was being really clever, having Boleslaw right there, ready to do her bidding at a move of her finger, groveling at her feet all the time, and yet living separately. And she did not really mind people finding out that he was her husband, as long as she looked like an angel, a martyr, an intellectual who so bravely endured the condition of being married to a janitor. That was the state of affairs for about four years, until one day he decided to marry somebody else.*

S: *Who was it? How did he meet her?*

A: *She lived in our building. A midwife by profession, a widow, about Kocia's age, rather personable and sweet-tempered. It was Nusia who got them together; she felt they were meant for each other. But what a blow it was for Konstancya! Believe me, she has never quite recovered from it. Even now, after more than thirty years the very remembrance of his betrayal (that's how she describes it) touches a raw nerve in her, for regardless how she treated him and what she felt for him, she considered Boleslaw to be an integral part of her life, and he had the effrontery to step out of it. And when she found out what role Nusia played in it, she went berserk; she locked the poor dear out of our place, threw her personal things through the windows and out of the door and told her that she was through with her for the rest of her life. What anguish and confusion it caused Nusia! She really believed that by playing matchmaker for her father, she was acting in her mother's best interest too.*

S: *But your sister forgave her eventually?*

A: *Yes, about a year later she magnanimously accepted Nusia's apology.*

S: Did Boleslaw stay a janitor for a long time?

A: No, he eventually got a job as a postal clerk.

S: And the marriage?

A: Has worked out very well, as far as I can tell. They are still together; kept in their old age in reasonable prosperity by Nusia's gifts.

S: Did Konstancya ever marry Radomir?

A: Oh, no! Though Radomir's part in her life was that of another bondman who would do anything at her bidding, he was also a lover and an artist that she had created and nurtured; and the position of husband was not compatible with that. Of course, just as with Boleslaw, she had believed that things would go on forever unchanged.

S: But something changed?

A: Oh, yes, considerably. A few years after Boleslaw's desertion, Radomir told her that he was going to marry a girl who was pregnant with his child.

S: And did he?

A: Yes, he did; and Kocia could not do a thing about it; not that she did not try. He married the girl, moved away, had a child, and then another, and then two more, twins in fact...

S: You don't say...

A: But then, I suppose, he got a little overwhelmed by all that; he came back to Konstancya begging for forgiveness and help with his work.

S: And she took him back?

A: Naturally.

S: So, he left his wife and four children for Konstancya.

A: No, no, he just divided his life between Konstancya and his family. He moved all his books and writing stuff to Kocia's place, kept his better clothes and a small art collection at Kocia's too, but had most of his meals with his family, and slept in both places.

S: And the two ladies involved agreed on that arrangement?

A: Kocia did not like it and fought it constantly, but his wife did not mind it, I think. She had more time to devote to the children when she did not have to pander to all his whims.

S: Would you say he was a good writer?

A: I never read any of his books, but one or two were quite popular, I understand. Well, if he had lived just a few years longer, he would have had the opportunity to write about what he used to call the truth about the War and the Uprising, that is, about his heroic days as a young fighter of the Resistance, but, as it happened he was already gone when it became suddenly acceptable, well, even fashionable, to talk about our Past and the Underground Army of the Wartime period with praise...

S: How did he die? He seemed still so young.

A: The old War thing caught up with him. His lungs. He was in his early fifties. Kocia has never stopped wearing black; and she has never stopped trying to run the lives of his wife and children, even though the woman remarried and the children have grown up. Konstancya believes she has obligations to his memory.

S: What happened to your mother? Did she like her new upright piano that was waiting for her in your new place?

*A: You obviously forgot; it was not waiting for her, she had to wait
for it. It had been ordered at the piano factory, the only piano factory
in the country, and they had a terrible backlog. Mother was on their
waiting list for **more than three years**! But it came eventually.
Obviously, she would not have liked any piano after her Bechstein;
besides, this one was rather unattractive and also defective in some
way.*

*S: How typical of the products of our industries! But did she use
the piano at all?*

*A: No, not really. She had lost interest in playing after the
Bechstein was taken away from her. She died a few months after the
new piano had arrived. Rather unobtrusively, in her sleep.*

*S: You don't mean that the new piano had anything to do with
her departure?*

*A: No, of course not; but then, who knows, maybe it was the very
last blow, in a long series of horrible adversities, that she had no more
strength to withstand.*

S: Did she ever visit her cousin Adela?

*A: Yes, she did. Yearly, as a matter of fact; she turned those visits
into a ritual and a vacation. Radomir paid for them. I went once
with her; it was a labor camp of a kind surrounded by the most
picturesque woods, lakes, wild nature; mother would rent a cottage
on a lake and see Adela every evening after she was through for the
day. She worked in a lumber yard.*

S: Good God! A woman, at her age, in a lumber yard!

A: She seemed to be the right height.

S: What happened to her eventually?

A: She got pardoned, just like our wise friend Sabina had pre-dicted, after less than seven years. You probably remember how at that time everybody was pardoned or even apologized to, you know, after all those students' riots that we had and the major shakedown within the ranks of the Party. Anyway, after a hiatus of a year or so Adela returned to journalism; she got a job with The Daily, where she stayed for the next twenty years. You must have read her column Written in a Bathtub, which she always signed 'The Old Maid'?

S: My word! I had no idea it was she. What wit! But I would say she stuck to only a limited number of topics; learned to be cautious, I suppose. I presume that she is gone by now?

A: Oh, no, not Adela. She has been living in this old people's home for the last few years, generously subsidized, as you may guess, by Nusia. She is about ninety-three or four now, her eyesight is failing and her hearing is not too good, but otherwise she is fit and fine. As a matter of fact I got a call from her yesterday. She wanted to tell me a joke she just remembered. She could not hear my reaction, but I heard her on the other side roaring with laughter.

S: Is Nusia really that rich? What does her husband do?

A: Well, almost everybody from the other side seems rich to us here; but I have no idea about Nusia's financial status. All I know is that her husband is a dentist, the son of a dentist, and that he also inherited some money and other properties.

S: How did Nusia's mother react to that marriage?

A: She was devastated, she claimed. I think that the worst for her was finding out that he was a dentist. She had always had this low opinion of some professions as horribly mundane, unimaginative,

*almost vulgar. Dentistry was one of them. Anyway, she has been
telling people that her daughter is married to a surgeon.*

S: You mentioned once that she went to visit Nusia?

*A: Oh, yes, she has been there twice in the last few years. As you
know, our citizens are now allowed to travel to the other side, as long
as they do not take a cent out of our country. But Nusia and her
husband are most generous.*

S: What does your sister tell you about Nusia's life there?

*A: She disapproves of it. She calls the town where they live
maudlinly provincial and their house monstrously large, with no
style and in disarray to the point of chaos. She feels that their wan-
tonness in spending money is vulgar, that their children, her own
grandchildren, are mannerless, the dogs undisciplined, Nusia's taste
for trashy novels, easy music and gaudy colors deplorable, and loud
parties to which they invite guests without regard to their social
position shocking. I have not heard yet what she thinks of Nusia's
latest venture of opening a cooking school! Anyway, I am sure that
she tells her other audiences (that is, not me) all kinds of splendid
stories, possibly about her daughter being a patroness of the most
important opera company in the Sovranties. By the way, as you know,
nowadays to talk about life on the other side of the Rampart with
praise is not only permitted, but politically appropriate. And Kocia,
in her seventies now, is still very much aware what is ideologically
appropriate.*

S: How did Konstancya do at the Ministry of Arts?

*A: Not badly. She advanced to the position of a vice-director of
something or other in the department of Music, retired, and even*

got a medal of some sort. And she has even acquired the status of a grande dame of the arts on a national scale, having managed to convince everybody that she indeed was once a great opera star.

S: Does she ever visit you?

A: She stopped a few years ago. I was getting too obnoxious in face to face encounters, she was claiming. But she calls occasionally.

S: Have you ever tried to visit Nusia?

A: Once, a few years ago, but it got too complicated – all the permissions and passes. Brothers' recommendation could have helped, but they did not want to exert themselves on my behalf; possibly were afraid that I would not return and they would lose Nusia's checks. Well, she managed to come here for a visit; though this was quite a while ago. But I just got a letter from her, and she says she is planning to come this summer!

S: That's good news! What does she usually write about?

A: About everything, her husband, children, dogs, neighbors, places they go, things they do; and if she has time, she reports on books and films. And she always stresses what a wonderful life she has been having; not just since her marriage, but her whole life, since the day she was born.

S: Really?! Doesn't she have memories of things that she has seen and gone through?

A: She does, indeed. But it is because she remembers everything, all that happened through her life, that she considers herself uncommonly lucky. No matter how terribly wretched the world around her has been, no matter how lost she has felt, she says, she has always been

*rescued somehow, led out of chaos and ugliness, given another chance,
allowed to be happy.*

   S: That's remarkable!

   *A: She does worry sometimes, though, she tells me, that she has not
been putting enough back into life from which she has taken so much.*